REWRITE

loops in the timescape

Also by Gregory Benford
The Berlin Project

REWRITE

Loops in the Timescape

GREGORY BENFORD

SAGA PRESS

LONDON SYDNEY **NEW YORK** TORONTO NEW DELHI

SAGA PRESS

AN IMPRINT OF SIMON & SCHUSTER, INC.

1230 AVENUE OF THE AMERICAS, NEW YORK, NEW YORK 10020

Text copyright © 2018 by Gregory Benford & Michael Rose | Jacket photographs copyright © 2018 by Thinkstock |
For information address Saga Press Subsidiary Rights Department, 1230 Avenue of the Americas, New York, NY 10020. | SAGA PRESS and colophon are trademarks of Simon & Schuster, Inc. | For information about special discounts for bulk purchases, please contact Simon & Schuster Special Sales at 1-866-506-1949 or business@simonandschuster.com. | The Simon & Schuster Speakers Bureau can bring authors to your live event. For more information or to book an event, contact the Simon & Schuster Speakers Bureau at 1-866-248-3049 or visit our website at www.simonspeakers.com. | Jacket design by Dan Potash | Interior design by Mike Rosamilia | The text for this book was set in Perpetua | Manufactured in the United States of America | First Edition | 10 9 8 7 6 5 4 3 2 1 | CIP data for this book is available from the Library of Congress. | ISBN 978-1-4814-8769-6 | ISBN 978-1-4814-8771-9 (eBook)

*To David Hartwell and Jerry Pournelle,
two giants who made history themselves*

Absolute, true, and mathematical time, in and of itself and of its own nature, without reference to anything external, flows uniformly . . . It may be that there is no such thing as an equable motion, whereby time may be accurately measured. All motions may be accelerated and retarded, but the flowing of absolute time is not liable to any change.

—Sir Isaac Newton

The Beginning

People living deeply have no fear of death.
—Anaïs Nin

The old blue Volvo pulls slowly out of George Washington University, turns right, and creeps down the dark, snowy street. The late-evening traffic is light.

Charlie Moment ignores the dashboard light and buzz telling him he hasn't fastened his seat belt. He sits back and listens to Eliot Karpinsky's new audiobook on his Volvo's bashed-up cassette player. The voice blurs and slurs because the car stereo is nearly gone, but he can make it out: "The corporations don't even want to compete anymore. They stand in line for government handouts, less in need than our poorest poor." Karpinsky's tenor voice rings with sour conviction. "Greed is their only mission."

Charlie expels a long, sad "ahhhh." He thinks of his green years, demonstrating in Chicago as a high school student, the McCarthy campaign. *Hell, no! We won't go!* In the days when his back was strong, his hair dark brown and long. *Not like today. Not like goddamn gray middle age.*

His glasses are grimy, so he rubs them with his free hand. The defrost isn't working well and the car windows keep fogging. Headlights ahead wear halos of red and white. He clicks on his seat belt. A woman's voice interrupts Karpinsky: "Please insert cassette five for the remainder of chapter twenty-four." The cassette pops out automatically and the radio comes on.

". . . today's hearing on the Whitewater scandal revealed new inconsistencies in the testimony . . ."

"Damn," says Charlie out loud, turning down the volume. He hates the way they break up audiobook cassettes in the middle of chapters. *Couldn't they use forty-five minutes per side, instead of thirty?* He flips to a rock station. It's playing a Fleetwood Mac song, "The Chain," with Stevie Nicks growling "Damn your love, damn your lies" over a grinding electric guitar. The light ahead turns red and Charlie stops. He undoes his seat belt and leans over to rummage through the cassettes on the floor in front of the passenger seat. Some ungraded exam papers fall off the car seat and slap onto the pile of cassettes.

A car horn honks behind him. Charlie looks up and sees that the light has turned green. He steps on the gas, looking down at the jumble of cassettes and exam papers. He dreads the night's grading, alone in his apartment. It's his birthday, but he has made a point of not mentioning it to his friends. He doesn't want to celebrate anything so soon after the final divorce decree. It's easier to suffer alone, without people trying to cheer him up.

He sits back and realizes he should in some abstract sense be satisfied. Still alive, at least. Maybe a bottle of a good Cabernet can rub those cares away. . . .

A blare of horns. A big black semi looms on his right. *My God, I forgot the damn seat belt.* . . .

With a shrill scream of tearing metal, it plows through his right door. Light explodes in his head. Pain cuts sharp across him. The truck rolls over his Volvo, crushing the passenger compartment.

Charlie sees a bright-red color. Feels an overwhelming pressure. *Ahhh* . . . A hard, dark nothing swallows him.

Part I

Tangent to the
Circle of Life

Bliss was it in that dawn to be alive,
But to be young was very heaven!
—William Wordsworth, *The Prelude*

1 Charlie's body jerks backward against a mattress. His arms and legs snap inward to clasp his gut. Panic squeezes the air from his lungs with a grunt, and he can hear his heart pounding raggedly. His skin is clammy with sweat. A tight fear clamps his chest.

Reason returns in slow pulses. *The car. The truck. Where am I? Hospital room? No. My apartment. A nightmare.*

Dark silence all around him. The fear eases, loses its grip, and his legs relax, so his feet can touch the bottom sheet of the bed. He makes his fists unclench.

But something isn't right. His body feels *wrong*. His hands look for his gut—and find it gone. Where his comfortable paunch and frizzy mat of hair were, he finds smooth skin and taut muscle.

Faster than thought he grabs for his genitals. Still there, limp. He is still a man and himself. He starts to relax again, his breathing slower. He slowly runs his hands over his body, discovering hard, smooth surfaces that are strange yet oddly familiar.

He reaches for his jaw with both hands. The beard is gone. *Am I dreaming?* Charlie wonders. He chuckles. *What a joke—first I die, and then I have my teenage body. Still dreaming.* Charlie swings his legs out of the bed and sits up quickly. *I'm moving so fast in this dream,* he thinks. He rubs the side of his head and finds long, wavy hair, slightly greasy.

He sniffs his hand. The hair smells of smoke. No, not cigarette smoke. Dope.

He laughs to himself, a dry chuckle, then reaches for the dim outline of a lamp. He finds its switch with fingers that seem to know where it is. The room bursts with light, and he flinches. A multi-colored blur greets him.

Ah. Right, I'm still myopic in my dream. His hands explore the bedside table and find wire-rimmed glasses. He puts them on and his vision is perfect.

There is a poster of Jimi Hendrix in a surrealistic painted silk jacket, flanked by Mitch Mitchell and Noel Redding, all three sporting Afros and wild looks. Beside it is a poster of Cream, Eric Clapton in a dated bomber jacket. Just like the poster he had on his bedroom wall in high school . . .

This bedroom wall. And this bedroom. He feels a cool prickling at the back of his neck.

Then Charlie notices a Garrard record player stacked on top of a Marantz receiver. His Marantz receiver. He reaches out and touches the large volume button on the Marantz. The feeling of the cool metal terrifies him. *I've never had such detailed sensation in a dream before.*

He turns to look around and sees the full-length mirror on the door. He sees himself at sixteen, long hair, smooth face, large dark eyes behind his wire-rimmed glasses, hairless chest with its swelling pectoral muscles.

Charlie sits down on the bed and begins to cry.

I've lost it. My second divorce and my dead-end career at GWU and I've lost it. I'm insane. They probably have me on drugs up to my gills, and I'm wearing a straitjacket in the loony bin.

This is how insanity feels. Not like those movies with special effects. Sharp and clear and still crazy.

He flops back onto the bed. It is just too confusing, too much—
dying, and then *this*. His young body finishes its sobbing; the tears
ebb away. *Who needs self-pity? I'm forty-eight years old and I will survive
this, too. They'll keep me on the staff in Social Studies. I have tenure—
that must cover even psychotic breakdown. Who else will teach those first-
years American Government 101? Nobody else is willing.*

He sits up again and looks down at his naked body. He notices a
thick leather band around his right wrist. It has a peace sign embla-
zoned on it. Charlie snorts. What a detailed hallucination!

He looks at himself in the mirror again, hesitantly at first, and
then with a smile. Long brown hair, dead white skin, pug nose, and
large eyes. *Dude, you're in the sixties!* No HIV, no Moral Majority, the
best music, no heartburn—and . . . Charlie looks down. Energy flows
through his muscles as his heart speeds up, a sensation he has not
felt for decades. *Maybe I can get something out of this hallucination.*

He looks around the room again. A stack of textbooks on a chair,
with two three-ring binders below them, stuffed with paper. His
chest of drawers has a red T-shirt hanging on a handle, with another
peace symbol silk-screened on it in black. A pair of blue jeans crumpled on the floor by the door.

His alarm clock says 4:32, and the dark hallway outside is leaden,
scented with a faint flower aroma. *Something Mom used to spray . . .*
A fresh calendar shows that it's January 1968, the days blocked out
beneath a naked girl draped over a motorcycle. *1968.* Every day is
crossed out before January 14, and that day is outlined in black, with
Birthday! written inside.

This is, this was, *my birthday*, Charlie thinks. *Thirty-two years ago.
I'm sixteen. Hah! Sixteen, ready to go, no back taxes, no alimony, no
backache.* He looks in the mirror again and puts his hand on his
stomach. He looks at his strong, young chest and sighs.

The sharp, lancing shriek of the truck crushing the life out of him
briefly comes back, but he pushes it away with a shudder. *Maybe I'm*

in heavy sedation during surgery, he thinks. The image of an operating room, bright lights, green-coated surgeons, and white-clad nurses hovering over his illuminated body comes to him. But it doesn't stay. This world does.

Screw it! Let's see how long I last in 1968. My parents are still alive, probably down the hall. My little sister, Catherine, had, has, *the bedroom next to them, thirteen-year-old terror that she is, baiting me about girls, Trudy especially, every chance she gets. But I know she dreamed about Paul McCartney, like every other pubescent girl on the block.* Dreams, he corrects himself. *Let's do this right.*

His young body is fully energized, so Charlie goes over the contents of the room, his hands carelessly moving over his youthful diversions. *There are my albums; those were—are—my paperbacks: Hesse, Castaneda, Marx, Huxley, Orwell, Chandler, Hemingway, crisp Heinlein, obtuse Marcuse, wild Lafferty, Greenway. Greenway? I don't remember Greenway. Is there a glitch in my hallucination?*

He opens each drawer in his chest of drawers, inspecting the clothing, carefully cleaned and folded by his mother. Even his underwear, uniformly white. Did they have colored underwear in 1968? No memory of that.

Charlie lies back on his bed, letting the outer world slip away, breathing easy, and . . . recalls. He can remember all his academic history, his doctoral thesis, troubles with women along the way. But below that lies a whole plane of teenage Charlie, sharp and clear and somehow more immediate. A layer of life led. That time he was afraid he'd drown in Lake Alice, the late-summer water dragging at him like syrup. His F in ninth-grade science. The heavy, damp smell of the boys' locker room. For a long while he lies there, mind spinning.

2 When dawn comes, Charlie is dressed in his red T-shirt and jeans, staring out the window. A thin layer of snow covers the brown grass of his suburban Chicagoland home. The large houses, bare trees standing silent black vigil, waiting for the spring. *The sky the color of a curate's egg*, he thinks. *Curate's egg?* Charlie reproves himself—not a phrase that a teenager would use.

The question of hallucination or insanity or surgical coma has faded. *This is real. Or real enough, anyway.* He thinks about how to get through this experience, however long it is going to last, and whatever it is.

A knock at the door. "Charles, can I come in?" It's his father's voice, all baritone certainty, thanks to lungs already starting to hollow from smoking.

"Uh, sure, Dad." Charlie's voice is a bit higher than he remembers.

His father comes in, wearing his dressing gown over pajamas. He holds out his hand, the sour smell of his first cigarette starting up Charlie's nose. "Congratulations on sixteen years, son."

Charlie faces his father, who died in 1992 at the age of sixty-six, an agonized victim of lung cancer and the inability to imagine his own death. Now his father is just forty-two, still with some hair on the top of his head and a firm handshake.

Charlie looks away, swallows hard, and looks back into his father's eyes. Charlie tries to hide the compassion welling up in him, but he fears that his face is betraying him anyway.

"A big day, I know, Charlie." His father's smile creases his smoker's face. The wrinkles are all kind. "I wanted to get you up before everybody else, but I see you're already awake."

Charlie nods and looks down. He is grateful that his long hair hides his face. His throat is tight and he cannot speak.

"Come on, son. Something to show you." A wink.

They go down to the garage, padding lightly on their feet to avoid waking up Charlie's mother and sister. Charlie's father opens the door from the kitchen to the garage.

There stands the Dodge Dart that he got for his sixteenth birthday, his father's old car, before his father got the Cadillac.

"It's yours, son. I signed the papers on a Cadillac yesterday. Pass your driver's test, and you're a grown man."

Memories of the car descend on Charlie—hanging out in the bright neon drive-ins with James, the sparkling beers in their brown bottles, caressing Trudy's body when they parked in the dark. His eyes fill with tears.

His father puts his arm on Charlie's shoulders. "I know it's a shock, son, but you've been a good boy—mostly. It's time you get a little freedom."

Charlie looks straight ahead at the Dodge Dart, tears making his vision watery, and says in a voice that shakes only slightly, "Thank you, Dad."

He sits in the car after Dad goes back in to get coffee started. The vinyl scent startles him. Indeed, everything in this refreshed world seems sharp, clear, vital.

He snaps on the car radio, a plastic knob. "All You Need Is Love" soars from the grille, the Beatles at the end of their middle period. He turns the dial and "Brown Eyed Girl" eases into the air, Van Morrison waxing nostalgic in rich tones. He twirls again, finds "Ruby Tuesday," by the Stones, swarming into the close, sultry space, sad and wry. Another turn gets some country stuff, and then another brings him the roar of "I Can See for Miles," by the Who. He leans back and lets it wash over him.

That day Charlie and his family had gone to the tennis club for lunch, so they are going to do it all over again. He can't remember this part as well.

Riding in his mother's crisp two-tone Ford Galaxie 500, his father driving, Charlie contemplates his sister, Catherine, with the interest of an entomologist looking at a brightly colored caterpillar. She wears a powder-blue parka with a trim of fake white fur, her blond hair pulled back, eyes darting. Her breath condenses on the window as she stares dreamily at the Sunday-morning streets passing by.

"Mom, Charlie is getting weird again." Her voice is a whine in the key of C minor.

"Now, Cath, you know it's Charlie's birthday. He has a lot to think about."

If they but knew . . .

"Tell him to think about it without looking at me."

His mother expels a voluminous sigh. "Let's have a nice day, okay?"

Catherine pointedly crosses her arms and stares out the window again, in full sulk.

Charlie looks down at his young hands sticking out of the sleeves of his dark-green parka. They feel slightly cool because the car's heater can't quite warm up the backseat without toasting the driver. Charlie still can't get over how good his body feels.

They sit down for lunch at the club, his father already changed into his tennis whites. He will only drink a Pepsi. Charlie can see the veins in his father's neck clearly, the blood pressure already creeping up. It will cause the postoperative stroke when they extract the cancerous lobe from his left lung. *Or it did.* Charlie shakes his head from the confusion.

"Trouble, honey?" his mother says. Her face crinkles warmly, though it still has its customary shadows. She will commit suicide in the early stages of Alzheimer's in 1998, at seventy. *Or she did,* Charlie thinks. He looks at his mother, then looks away and tries to hide his emotion. His mouth wobbles, eyes go blurred.

"Charlie's getting weird again," says Catherine. "It's drugs!"

Ned Moment cuffs the back of his daughter's head, quickly but gently. "Leave your brother alone."

Catherine crosses her arms and looks away, kicking a table leg with quick feet. Some soda spills from Charlie's untouched Pepsi.

His mother looks at Catherine steadily. "I think you need to get changed for your tennis lesson, young lady. You obviously aren't interested in lunch."

There is a quiet pause while Catherine's brow furrows, and then she stomps off to the ladies' locker room.

Charlie had forgotten how irritating she could be. Ned laughs, reaches for his squash racket, kisses his wife, and is gone.

Charlie is left alone with his mother. Will she see through him?

His mother slumps a little and pulls a strand of hair back from her forehead. That loving but weary smile that will later grow so thin embraces Charlie, and his chest almost melts in the love that he thought he had lost forever. How did he find his way back to this day? In delirium, under the knife? Or perhaps this is an afterlife?

"I called Trudy yesterday," his mother says. "She will be here after she comes back from church."

Charlie nods awkwardly. He feels a sudden note of embarrassment. To have a seventeen-year-old girlfriend? At his age? But his loins stir from the distant memory of making out with her in her parents' car. Just thirty-two years ago, he calculates, and eight days earlier than this now.

"I know you like her, Charlie. Don't act cool with me." She reaches out with both hands and takes his hand between hers, inspecting his fingers. He never knew why she did that, but he always liked it. Her face has a pleading loneliness that will grow horrible after his father's death. Charlie looks at his mother with sympathy, disquiet, and love—then realizes these feelings could get him into trouble. No sixteen-year-old boy is going to pity his mother with such depth of understanding. He pulls his arm back and sits on his hands, looking down at his untouched hamburger.

"It's a hard time for you, Charlie. You are becoming a man, but you're still mostly boy." His mother's empathy is battering at his defenses, and the weight of coming back to her is pushing him hard. What *is* all of this? He has adult thoughts but the surging emotional tides of a kid. Maybe his racing hormones? Or can this be hallucinations after surgery, or a coma with—

"Charlie!" Trudy kisses the side of his head and plops down onto his sister's chair. She is wearing her tennis whites, her light-brown hair swinging in a short bob, all dimples and bright-blue irises. His zingy girlfriend, yes. Impossibly young.

"I thought we might get a squash game in, Charlie!" Trudy's good spirits are indomitable. Charlie feels his old affection for her burst out into a smile and a lingering look. Trudy reads this as a declaration of interest, and her sense of triumph and ownership makes her chest flush pink. Charlie's mother notices, smiles ironically to herself.

Charlie recalls that his mother and Trudy never entirely settled the terms of escrow for the deed to his soul, which may have played a part in their eventual breakup during his first year of college. He stands, happy to get out from under his mother's searchlight. He kisses her cheek lightly and runs off with Trudy.

As they turn the corner toward the locker rooms, Trudy stops him. "What about your squash racket?"

Charlie turns toward her without a word and presses himself against her, catching her by surprise, his lips soundlessly confessing to her his years of longing for her—for her as she was that day, so full of hope, fresh and yielding. And now here it is again, and it's better than the first time.

"Charlie!" She pushes him away and stares into his eyes with amazement and joy. "Now I know you love me. You can't hide it anymore."

"Of course I love you, Trudy." His voice rings with the depth of emotion and wisdom that he never had at sixteen.

He tries to put his arms around her again, but she keeps him away with a stiff-arm and a mysteriously powerful look in her eyes. She holds him with her hand and her gaze, and then grabs his hand and runs away with him.

In her father's car, deep in the underground parking, she pulls down his pants, kissing him hard on the mouth. With his hands pushing her top up to find her breasts, his erection is instantaneous. Trudy grabs him. His groaning warns her that he is about to come—

It happens incredibly fast, his whole body strumming with pleasure. Middle age had stolen more from him than he knew.

He leans back on the cold leather of the car seat and looks fondly at her in the dim underground light. *This is a dream*, he thinks. *Gotta be.*

I will wake up now, he thinks, *in terrible pain in a hospital bed somewhere in DC, in 2000, and none of this will be here for me. Trudy will be married to a stockbroker, rich and bored in a Connecticut commuter village, and I'll be an associate professor at George Washington.*

That night Charlie helps his mother scrape and rinse the dishes for the dishwasher, not saying much. His father is catching up on the Sunday *New York Times*, while his sister gabs on the phone upstairs.

"Did you enjoy your squash game this afternoon, Charlie?"

"Uh, yes, Mom." His body hummed with joy at the exercise, his shots coming without effort. Part of it might have been Trudy beforehand, the simmering zest of it singing in memory. Youth relived is still better than his memories.

"She's a nice girl."

Charlie blushes and looks down at the stray pieces of lettuce in the salad bowl.

He hopes this dream will last forever. Could forever be possible? He dredges up the memory. Once, spending hours in the library, avoiding a social studies term paper in college, he happened on a book about the Hindu doctrine of reincarnation. Though the details have always been fuzzy to Charlie, they envisioned a past and future that stretched on endlessly. Humanity dwelled in a timeless universe, no beginning and no end, never mind what modern cosmology said. The whole scheme was based on returning again and again as you moved up or down a karmic ladder. The returns were described in multiples of grandfathers, and by rough calculation Charlie found that the time span implied was longer than anybody thought human beings had even been here. So maybe they'd all started as frogs or something?

Back again in 1968, he has no frog memories, no memories of being a bird or a cat or another person, except himself as the first Charlie, Charlie One, who died the night of his birthday in 2000. He has come back somehow, on a fresh tangent to the circle of life. That has to mean something profound. But what?

Can he change his life? He knows the history of this time pretty well. Not enough to predict stock prices or who will win the World Series, but Charlie recalls the big events that he can't change and the small ones from his own life that maybe he can. Okay, he can't stop the Cold War or pioneer the computer revolution—he doesn't have the skills—but maybe he can yank himself out of the trajectory that led to a life he knows he doesn't want to relive.

Unless this is all some kind of hallucination, a posttraumatic freak-out. Maybe he is in some other reality, or else out of his head and actually chewing the straps on a straitjacket in some damp, shadowy concrete cell.

As his mother speaks, he nods. A sudden shudder runs through him and he nearly falls. He realizes that he has just made a major decision.

"Charlie?" A warm smile. "Do you love her?" His mother's face swims in a shining kitchen glow. Warm, soft, far back in time and right here, now.

"Um—yeah."

He recalls a phrase, *A fool's paradise is better than none.*

3 The walk to school on Monday is eight blocks of winter memories. Charlie's feet bring the world toward him slowly, so he can savor flavors long lost: earthy aromas, sharp slanting sunlight, crisp dry breezes, murmurs of Fords trailing their lead-rich blue exhaust.

He dreamed of the car crash, but now it seems to be just a dream. This world is real. It echoes, too—he is living this and remembering it at the same time. He has a curious double sensation of immersion in a recalled memory, while feeling that memory like a layer on the running present.

Back in the Charlie One life, after his father died they had to sell the house. Alone, his mother became depressed, sleeping all day, watching infomercials all night, unable to cope. Charlie and Catherine hoped that their mother's girlfriends would stand by her once she was widowed, but they all faded away, clinging to their surviving husbands, perhaps fearful of Jane Moment's lingering beauty and poignant vulnerability. Such a woman might easily tempt the heart of a man a few years older. They tried an apartment in the area for a while, then a small house near Catherine in Madison, Wisconsin. Nothing really worked for Jane.

Woodrow Wilson High played a large part in Charlie's development—teaching him how to write essays, at least. That exposed him to stories of injustice rarely seen in the leafy enclave where his father's car-parts business provided his family with a good home. *The Grapes of Wrath* was Charlie's favorite book. For him the ending was especially wrenching, the woman nursing the sick man and the dead baby being sent down the river. Part of Charlie stayed with the starving Okies, making their way across the country to the false promise of California. When Mr. Owen preached liberalism and reform from the blackboard in grade eleven, Charlie paid close attention.

He walks up the steps to the redbrick building the sunny day after his sixteenth birthday, his second sixteenth birthday, trembling inside. Charlie's nostrils wrinkle at the commingled smells of hormones and cheap perfume filling the hallway to his locker—and feels the memory of it layer the experience. The banging metal doors, clicking heels, and cacophony of young voices dizzy him. *My body is my guide now. Gut knowledge.*

"Hey, Charlie, you ol' fuckhead." A handsome jock punches Charlie right in the middle of his chest. Charlie lets go of his books but squats quickly enough to grab them before they hit the floor. It's Robert Woodson, his fake-tough buddy—who died, he recalls as he looks at Robert's smooth face, in a terrible 1971 car crash fueled by fraternity-party alcohol. Here he is, back in the flesh—thick brown hair, quick smile, on top of the local pecking order.

"Sixteen and still a virgin, you loser." Robert grins broadly and shoves Charlie down the hallway, turning away to bound off to class, his powerful legs springing along the polished hall floor, a superhero off to fight crime in the metropolis.

Charlie shakes his head. "Not so," he says to nobody. But he's still reacting inside, with clashing responses from Charlies One and Two. *Robert! The jock!* Charlie feels dizzy from his interior time swings. The Charlies fight for control. He breathes deeply.

Robert is dead in that other now, dead in 2000—*Like me*. Perhaps this *is* a crazy afterlife?

Steadying, he recalls his locker number: 555. He's already past it, doubles back and sees James standing at 557. Charlie glances sideways, has to stop. The sight of the pale James is almost supernatural in itself. Bony, big Adam's apple, thick wrists and hands like dots at the ends of his thin arms making exclamation points, shirttail untucked, long stringy hair with dandruff like melting snow. Charlie takes a breath and walks up to James, who turns with a downcast, embarrassed gaze.

"Sorry, but I didn't get you anything for your birthday."

Charlie speaks softly to his friend from a perspective of decades, easy and low. The living speaking to the dead. "Hey, that's all right, James." James insisted on the dignity of his full name. He was institutionalized for progressive schizophrenia with catatonia. Or will be. His blond hair and pallor make him a ghost in Charlie's eyes. Charlie wonders if he can make it through the day.

"Just kidding." James grins and reaches into his locker and pulls out a plastic-wrapped LP of Cream's *Disraeli Gears*, the huge cover a jumble of orange and red psychedelic images.

"Wow, with 'White Room,'" Charlie comments.

"That song isn't on this album, Charlie." James looks confused. "'Sunshine of Your Love,' that's the big song on the album. 'White Room'?"

"I think I heard that's the new single." Charlie Moment is panicking, afraid of being caught out.

James frowns.

A lanky boy with thick glasses yells at them as he walks by, "Ready for the test?" Charlie tries to remember who he is, but fails. Then he's gone.

"What test?"

"The big history test, Charlie! You're the brain! Hey, did you score some dope for your birthday, Charlie? Don't tell me you gave it to Trudy, to get her to put out." His slack-jawed shock seems genuine.

"Trudy isn't anything like that."

"Okay, okay. Lay off me, man." Rolling eyes. "Like, I'm your best friend since sixth grade, you *jerk*." James gathers his books together and locks up.

"Sorry, James. I didn't sleep well this weekend."

"I know, man. I'm getting a lot of headaches—can't sleep worth shit myself." He looks pointedly at Charlie's open locker. "Don't you think you should go to the test too?"

The history exam covers the American Revolution and the Constitutional Convention. Charlie breezes through the five short-answer questions but sits stumped by the assigned essay. Mr. Owen wants five hundred words on the question of states' rights in the framing of Congress? Maybe one hundred thousand would scratch the surface.

He buckles down to work, his loopy handwriting filling up line after line with fluid ease. Maybe education is wasted on the young. He looks up with a smile. He is a bit surprised to see Mr. Owen gazing wanly at him with soft eyes. *I wonder if he's gay*, Charlie thinks. His teacher is wearing his usual black suit, threadbare and shiny, with a white shirt and thin black tie. Lincoln Owen was a major influence on Charlie, turning him from a soft-focus liberal to a radical just in time for the Chicago riots during the Democratic National Convention.

Weird, looking down the long periscope of time at this, he thinks, drifting forward to that summer of 1968, still to come. The riots. His arrest.

He brings himself back to the room by studying Owen, the thin neck and thinning hair. *He looked so ancient to me*, Charlie thinks, realizing that Owen must be no older than his late thirties, a decade younger than Charlie One was, is, would be. Charlie sighs out loud. The cute blonde next to him gives him a scowl. What was her name?

He returns to his essay with a surge of libidinal energy and within the allotted time period has an essay that he can live with. He hands it in to Mr. Owen with a conspiratorial smile, but the teacher looks startled. Charlie realizes that he isn't acting like a high school student, and proceeds to slouch out of the class with the appropriate degree of insolent apathy—shoulders hunched, mouth twisted scornfully. Years of college teaching have given him many role models for the ritual indifference of the young.

Charlie wakes up in the night and wonders where his paunch is, why his body feels strange, vibrant. Then he remembers what has happened, and feels an odd wash of nostalgia for his older self. Charlie One made his way in the world, struggled over the hurdles. There was some achievement in that.

The feeling passes. He realizes that he has to get on with his new life.
Has anyone else ever had to do this? he wonders.

James and Charlie are watching basketball on the television in the basement of James's house. The image is so low grade it is like watching the game through a kaleidoscopic snowstorm. James's parents are much older. They always seemed surprised to have James living with them, and the fact that he had even one friend was obviously a miracle to their eyes. They generally left him alone downstairs. It makes Charlie think that perhaps James was adopted, but he never learned anything about it the last time. The last time, Charlie wonders, *was* there a last time?

"Man, were you adopted?"

James starts coughing and quickly hands Charlie the tiny roach that he was toking off. "What?"

"You know, your parents. They're hardly aware that you exist."

"We can't all have dads who're Fred MacMurray." James seems hurt, pushing some of his blond hair behind his left ear.

"Okay, man. I'm sorry."

"Yeah . . . uh, well . . . I was. My birth mother was a teenager, they tell me. No way to raise me, so she gave me to an agency." Now James is like a deflated balloon, air rushing out from his admission.

Charlie takes a toke off the clipped roach, feeling a need for some self-medication in his new life. "That's tough, man. Real tough."

He makes no move toward comforting James. He remembers that James doesn't like to be touched.

Their evening basketball broadcast is interrupted by a newsman with hollow eyes and what looks like bright-orange makeup. "This just in from the Pentagon. The USS *Pueblo* has been taken by the naval forces of North Korea. President Johnson has ordered the aircraft carrier *Enterprise* to proceed toward the area. More news at eleven. We now return you to your regularly scheduled programming."

James says, "Fuck, man! Those commies are doing it again."

Charlie laughs. "Commies?"

"Yeah, like first in Vietnam—well, maybe first in Korea. But now they're acting up again in Korea, too. Johnson has to get tough."

"What are you talking about, James? Vietnam is a lost cause. It's a civil war between the communists and the corrupt South Vietnamese regime."

James rises up from his ancient sofa, his posture quite rigid, the rims of his eyes red. "Stop with that shit! I am so sick of your attitude. Don't you care about your country?"

With a sense of shock echoing through the paradox of time, Charlie snaps into the present, a 1968 rife with intense polarization. Vietnam is a bleeding wound in the American psyche, and the pain of it will touch everyone. James will soon be drafted and go to Nam. There his mind will fray beyond recovery from the killing and the lies, starting his long slide toward psychiatric oblivion.

"It's all right, man. I'm on your side."

Late the following Sunday afternoon, Charlie takes a long shower after spending the afternoon on driver's training. He has a driver's exam scheduled soon. To his surprise, he still has to pick up some of the wary road skills. Muscle memory, he guesses. It isn't all in the brain. The warmth, moisture, and relaxation of the shower let him reflect with some peace of mind.

This can't be a dream. Dreams don't last so long, with so much consistent detail.

He wonders if he has died and gone on to the next life. But going back to live your life again doesn't fit with any biblical conception of heaven, hell, or purgatory. It seems more like Hinduism. But you are supposed to go up or down the karmic ladder, not repeat.

A thumping on the bathroom door. He hears his father's muffled voice but can't make out the words. He turns off the comforting water and steps out of the bathtub.

Now he can hear what his father is saying. ". . . overrunning American positions all through South Vietnam. We're taking a lot of casualties. You should see it, Charlie."

"Okay, Dad. I'll be right down." January 30, the 1968 Tet Offensive. The final nail in the coffin of the Johnson administration. Charlie thinks briefly about all the good things that LBJ managed to accomplish before Vietnam sucked him into rigid anticommunism. Then he gets dressed in jeans and a T-shirt to join his father in front of the TV.

The rest of the week brings the war in Vietnam back to Charlie with a ferocity he had forgotten by 2000, even though he worked for Eugene McCarthy's 1968 campaign as a volunteer. He spends a week wondering if he should do it again.

And then a day or so into the Tet Offensive, he sees the defining footage. Again. February 1: A South Vietnamese officer drags a Vietcong prisoner in front of the American cameras and executes him with his pistol. Right there, in front of millions of people. The networks play the scene over and over again, until it becomes part of Charlie's dream-life, the instant when the victim crumples to the ground, his face locked in a grimace, dead. The man had set off bombs, killing many in an apartment building. There would be no peace in Southeast Asia. The war would go on and on. So many American lives would be lost. We would never give up. All the millions who would die, who *did* die . . .

Charlie grows tired of thinking about time in two directions and resolves to think about his past in Washington, DC, as the future. Perhaps even a future that will never happen. Whatever brought him here, catatonic insanity or a cyclic afterlife, he accepts that 1968 is his present.

4 Charlie goes to a nearby university library to work on how he found himself with a new life. The librarian at the desk is a portly lady in a frilly blue dress who frowns, wondering why a kid is interested in the philosophy of quantum mechanics.

Charlie shrugs. "I hear kinda odd things about it, want to know." This seems to do the job. The librarian sniffs skeptically.

To work. Sitting and plowing through abstruse books, even physics journals, is better than another afternoon with prattling teens at a malt shop.

He soon discovers that an odd variant to quantum theory envisions other universes created by quantum effects, and so he vectors in on that, reading intently.

There is even a name for the idea, the Many-Worlds Interpretation—physicists like to capitalize their notions. It seems the core idea is to interpret what the equations of quantum mechanics say about the real world by having the mathematics of the theory itself show the way—rather than tacking on some extra ideas to the math.

Charlie learns that a guy named Hugh Everett started to do this in 1956, starting from what was called the measurement problem. This riddle had apparently bedeviled physicists since the 1920s. Their question was, how do we get from our theory to the smooth, sure world we live in—what they called the classical world—to the tiny quantum world? Elementary particles like electrons existed in two or more possible states of being. Something called a wave function told physicists how probable a measurement of an electron would be, if they made it. The quantum view was that an electron was a "superposition" of different locations, velocities, and ways its spin pointed.

Charlie wonders why anybody worries which way a particle points. Who cares? But he plows on.

It seems that whenever physicists really measured a particle's properties precisely, down in the microscopic realm, they saw a definite result—just one of the elements of the superposition (that is, of guesses, Charlie supposes). A clean, sharp number, not some vague combination of them. In big objects, say a car, it was either parked or moving, not both. Nothing wishy-washy. No weird superpositions.

The measurement problem boiled down to a question that Charlie can understand personally: Why does the unique world of solid answers that we see emerge from the alternatives on offer in the superposed quantum world? Physicists use wave functions to represent quantum states—a list of all possible outcomes. Each outcome is equally real, though not equally probable.

Charlie gets up and walks around the library, wishing he had paid more attention to math in high school. Even the philosophical stuff, which he hoped would be clearer, talks about some Schrödinger equation that shows how a quantum system's wave function changes through time. No randomness—the wave function evolves smoothly.

But! When anybody measured the system with a scientific instrument, the wave function collapsed into one choice of the superposition—a sudden jerk into the world we big beings lived in. *Jerk—here we are!*

That jerk-collapse had to be added as a postulate, to make quantum mechanics make sense. Messy. Ugly.

Smart guys had scratched their heads over this for decades—guys named Bohr, Heisenberg (head of the German A-bomb project, Charlie learns), Schrödinger (and his equation, which Charlie couldn't fathom at all), and even Einstein. They agreed on a way of thinking about quantum mechanics known as the Copenhagen interpretation—named for where Bohr lived. They had to—quantum mechanics predicted experiments perfectly, including the probability that an experiment would yield a result, like a particle pointing *this* way, not *that*. The *jerk* was real but was not in the equation. *Don't look at the guy behind the curtain.* . . .

Then . . . along came a guy named Everett. In stark contrast, he said the micro- and macroscopic worlds *merged*. No real difference! No jerk to get the right result, either. But . . .

Everett made the observing scientists and their instruments part of the system observed. He said there was a universal wave function for a single quantum system—everything! No jerk to go into the classical world where we live.

Everett asked, What if that wave function continuously evolves, which is not interrupted by measurement? So the Schrödinger equation always applies to everything—objects and observers alike. No elements of superpositions are ever exiled from reality.

Charlie sits back from reading a description of the paper the guy, Hugh Everett, wrote in the 1950s. Charlie was about five years old then.

He shakes his head, trying to think. The warm air seems to buzz around his head; the ideas are making him dizzy. There is a flicker. A fluorescent light? No. A flicker again.

Charlie shakes it off, forcing his mind to reason. So: What would Everett's world look like to us?

Everett said that the universal wave function, as he called it *split*. All possibilities peeled off a whole, goddamn new *universe* every split second anything happened.

Charlie rocks back. In all of this he, being a big thing, is an observer, as Everett called it. For Everett, each branch of the ever-spawning universe had its own copy of the observer, who saw just one of the outcomes that quantum mechanics said could happen.

So . . . Charlie is sitting in one of an infinite number of universes? No wonder he is dizzy.

Plus—he goes on reading, feeling as though he is in some fantasy abstraction—from a fundamental mathematical property of the Schrödinger equation, the branches, once formed, did not influence one another. Each branch that peeled off embarked on some different future, free of the others.

He can't follow the math at all. So he takes it on faith.

Just how the ever-peeling branches became independent and looked like the classical reality was called decoherence theory, he notices. Meaning that each copy of a person feels he or she is one of a kind? But in the full universal wave function reality, every alternative on the quantum menu happens. Peeling off universes willy-nilly is independent of humans; it is the way the metauniverse is built. (By God, maybe? Or is he the final observer?)

Anyway, aside from the temptations of theology, this stuff seems to be an accepted part of modern quantum theory. Amazing. Not everyone agreed with Everett's view that all the branches represent realities that exist.

Okay, fine. Charlie sighs. Everett broke new ground by making a multiplicity of universes straight out of the equations of quantum mechanics itself. The existence of multiple universes came as a *consequence* of his theory, not an assumption.

In a big book on this, an essay mentioned that Everett's thesis had a footnote: "From the viewpoint of the theory, all elements of a superposition (all 'branches') are 'actual,' none any more 'real' than the rest."

Charlie stands, stretches his supple spine, feels joints pop easily. "A beginning, maybe," he whispers to himself. At least some high-powered types thought some kind of other peeled-off universe could exist. But none of them ever talked about moving into the *past* of another track. Why?

Time is flexible, maybe—and yes, isn't there something about space-time? That they are wedded together somehow? Einstein said something like that, right?

"Plenty more to learn, that's for damn sure," he mutters as he leaves, a bit unsteady on his feet. The librarian in the blue dress eyes him skeptically.

After the second history test of the term, in early March, Mr. Owen asks Charlie to stay after class. The test was a cinch, of course; he didn't even study. Algebra is another matter; it has vanished. Equations are entirely opaque. Charlie wonders if he has revealed too much knowledge in his just-wing-it class essays, but it is one of his few intellectual pleasures now, so he is loath to give it up.

Lincoln Owen closes the classroom door and turns to face Charlie with his hand still on the handle. It almost looks as if Owen wants to be able to escape quickly.

"Young man, you have really blossomed in this class." Owen pauses, the canted mouth uneasy, perhaps to give Charlie a chance to reply to this compliment.

But Charlie is uncertain about the appropriate response of a teenager, so he just glances at the teacher awkwardly, then ducks his head and hides behind his long hair. He didn't know Owen that well, last time around. Owen was the distant inspiration for Charlie's sixties-style radicalism, not a personal mentor.

Somewhat embarrassed by Charlie's silence, Owen blurts, "That essay was the best I've ever seen from a student. Truly."

An awkward pause.

"Well, I was thinking that a young person of your obvious intellectual depth might appreciate the company of people who think as deeply as you do."

Charlie scoops up his books to go.

"I mean . . . I mean . . . ," Owen stutters. "There is a group, an organization, that you might be interested in joining. Someone there— our cell leader, actually—she wants to meet you."

Charlie realizes that he has to speak up or this exchange will be interminable. "Some kind of youth thing?"

"Exactly." Owen pauses with evident relief, eyebrows rising, to pat his forehead, which has sweat beading on it. "There is a Chicago-area student rights organization. I know the organizers quite well—very well, in fact. They are very interested in meeting you. Very."

Owen's voice trails off into silence. Charlie realizes that this time his chance to get involved in politics will come a few months earlier, well before the summer of 1968. In a flash he decides to embrace this alteration in his path. Maybe it will bring him greater happiness, just as Trudy did.

"I would like that very much, Mr. Owen."

Without thinking it through, he has decided to change Charlie Two's life. Somehow.

One of the teachers that Charlie forgot about is Mr. Montini, who coached the baseball team and taught English the last time around. Now Charlie Two finds him stimulating. Montini is the most enthusiastic of Charlie's teachers, a broad-chested shorter man with an oily face. Charlie hardly noticed him before. Charlie makes the mistake of sitting in the front row of Montini's class when the teacher is discussing Shakespeare's Italian plays. By the end of the class, Charlie has been hit by the spittle of the man's animated hyperbole several times. When Montini is at the blackboard with his back to the class, Charlie puts on a show of wiping the spit off his face, making his classmates laugh. Without hesitating, Montini spins around and melodramatically winks at Charlie, then returns to writing with the chalk.

One sign of Montini's impractical joy in teaching is that he gives his students the choice of writing essays on novels and plays, or doing some creative writing of their own. The first time through, Charlie had little interest in creative writing. In that fevered Charlie One youth, he had no time for things that weren't serious, political, or analytical. But now his youth isn't being wasted on a young mind. He has lived, fought, loved, failed, and somehow survived it all, even his own death. Now he has plenty of things to write about, burdens to drop on the page, where they might do him less harm.

Charlie decides to write about his marriage to Gwen, the girl who was everything to him but nothing to herself. He describes the ardent romance in their late twenties. Passion is hard to describe, so he just skips it, working the edges with dialogue. He was frustrated by her lack of arousal. Gwen never had an orgasm, not in the years that Charlie knew her. Charlie could yearn for her all he liked, kiss her over and over, cover her in flower petals, work hard with all his antennae out—but in the end her vagina would still be dry and her physical desire only simulated. Charlie would take what pleasure he could, but their life as husband and wife was hollow.

Each day she went off to her job at the bank, and he went to the University of Minnesota library to write his thesis. In the evening when she came home, he would cook for her while she read magazines and listened intently to Carly Simon's melancholy lyrics. He now realizes that maybe he should have taken a hint from "You're So Vain," Simon's sardonic big hit. Certainly a later Simon hit Charlie recalls, "Nobody Does It Better," didn't fit their marriage.

Her strange anger at him was a puzzle he never figured out. The marriage was a death-in-life happiness for him, and it slowly wore down during the years it took him to get his doctorate. They divorced over his first job, a temporary position teaching at Amherst College, in Massachusetts—too far from her family in Saint Paul, she said firmly with down-turned lips. Gwen was too dependent on her parents to go off with him, and he knew too well that he had only been a resting stage before she found somebody who could stir passion in her. She married a successful attorney three years later. Charlie received a wedding announcement, safely after the ceremony had taken place. He had already taken up his tenure-track job at George Washington.

Charlie types his story out on his little electric typewriter, a thousand words of *tap-tap-tap* each night. It is a form of therapy for him, replaying his past life. It takes him only two weeks. He corrects the manuscript using Wite-Out, so it looks fairly messy by the standards of the word-processor age. He has moments of wishing for the easy speed of a computer, but the sound of slamming keys has a manual feel he likes, a taste from his college years. Charlie is more comfortable now with his anachronistic life, so he isn't too bothered that he can't print out a flawless manuscript. It ends up a novella, about twenty thousand words.

Charlie hands his novella in with two brads holding it together, just like a screenplay. He used to read screenplays as part of a screenwriting course he took for fun in 1996. He even wrote a genuinely lousy action-hero screenplay as part of the course work. Now the brads are just an amusing affectation.

He expects Montini to wonder how a teenager would know about thirtysomething disappointment. Charlie realizes he has grown sloppy in his renewed life. No one has found him out yet, and he is remembering more about his teenage existence every day. His lack of caring about that doesn't bother him. Maybe a symptom of even more sloppy thinking? As he settles into this bright world, striding through it in his effortlessly springy body, he sees that nobody is going to catch on to him. His truth is secure because it is quite beyond belief.

5 After class on Monday, Mr. Owen invites Charlie to a meeting of the Youth Progressives. It will be held the night of the New Hampshire primary, Tuesday, March 12. Charlie knows what is going to happen— Johnson repudiated, McCarthy damn nearly beating a sitting president in the first primary—and the unleashing of forces that will ricochet through all of 1968 and so into the awful political swamp that will follow.

At the address he finds an older brick warehouse off a side road, the parking lot wet with muddy puddles. At first he feels some dismay at the grungy industrial site, but then he reminds himself that this is his second life, and he can be brave now. *You've already died once.* Sixties radicals aren't going to intimidate him now. After all, he was one once himself.

The door into the warehouse is slightly ajar and leads directly to a stairway. The steps smell of damp sawdust. Fine particles float in the air, lit by a naked lightbulb at the top of the stairwell. As he rises, loud voices come from above.

A battered green door lets him into the room. A large table fills most of it, with papers and books scattered in messy piles. On the wall are large Soviet posters of Marx, Engels, and Lenin, and of course Che—all drawn in profile, each face a study in cartoon courage.

He feels dizzy, suppresses a laugh. Don't these clowns realize they're feeling advanced and radical about a crushing tyranny? The Soviet monster was dead by the early 1990s, and Charlie forgot how gullible people were as recently as the 1960s. Never has he felt the warp of time so severely. *This* he took seriously?

There are six or seven people there—a few earnestly nodding hippies with sweat-stained headbands, a bald man with a mustache in a dark suit keeping to the shadows, Mr. Owen improbably wearing a black leather jacket and beret, and the only woman in the room:

Elspeth.

Right there in 1968, looking so fresh and sultry, her pert little breasts pushing aggressively through her clothing, the sleek curves of her hips, her dirty-blond hair, the wire-rimmed glasses riding on her peculiarly sharp, prominent nose. *Not the hard, lined visage from the first divorce trial in 1998.* Now Elspeth's face has a round softness even as she barks out dogma to the passive hippies.

Charlie stands in the doorway, unable to move. *But we don't meet until I come to George Washington in 1982,* he thinks. When she already had tenure, a rising female star in political studies, the flame that his mothy wings beat toward, the woman who dominated him completely, owning his body and soul for years. Until she discarded him and moved to Harvard, divorcing him as a minor afterthought to her years climbing up the academic and media ladders in DC. He knows that she was an undergraduate at the University of Chicago when he was still in high school. But their paths never crossed in Illinois.

Yet here she is, he thinks, bewildered. *She was nearby me all the time and we didn't know.* So young, like something he can bite into, taste the sweet syrup. His breath surges, his mind races with anger, love, hate, amazement—and abject confusion. He sways slightly, then catches himself.

Elspeth quickly notices Charlie and turns to Owen. "Is this the kid you told us about?" There is something unusual about the way she turns to Owen and then back to Charlie.

Owen nods nervously, plainly embarrassed. His beret wobbles. Something behind Owen's eyes knows that he is a clown fish among sharks.

Elspeth strides forward, her eyes evaluating Charlie. "What's your name, kid?" She asks the question, but Charlie senses that she already knows the answer.

"Uh, Charlie." He blushes and hates himself for it. Still, it helps him stay in character until he gets the feel of these people.

Elspeth smiles slightly, the haughty curl of her lip telling him that she already is quite sure that she holds Charlie's entire being in her hands. "Welcome! The revolution needs recruits. We can use another comrade."

The other revolutionaries support this declamation with effusive nods and indistinct mumbles. "We're basically a student rights organization," Owen says. "Rights" was a big Leninist-front word, Charlie recalls, and loses all respect for Owen at that moment.

Clearly, Elspeth leads this desultory group, which would be nothing without her. She radiates energy and confidence, a commanding aura. He found it a heady lure in his first life, and it is just as powerful now. But he wonders why she is so interested in him, a kid from a local high school.

Elspeth takes her magnetic gaze off Charlie, gestures toward a frayed Queen Anne chair, and resumes chairing the meeting. "Owen, what have we pulled together for our anti-Johnson rally tomorrow?"

Owen looks around the table nervously, his eyes briefly lighting upon Charlie, who looks away pointedly. "We have arranged for two cadres to march in front of city hall, uh, Comrade. They have already made placards and banners. They only await our word."

Light seems to radiate outward from Elspeth, illuminating the transfixed faces of her drones. Charlie sees, finally and clearly, that he was her drone too, convenient, pliant, and adoring, a mere dog to her wolf bitch. Now he is faced with his past, or his future, in a way that he didn't expect. This is truly a new world, a world with marvels that he barely tasted last time.

At the end of the boring meeting, Elspeth gathers up her keys and a camouflaged ammunition bag. Charlie realizes that it must be her purse. The bag hangs heavily on her small shoulder, a striking contrast to her light-yellow minidress. The weight shows off the tight muscles beneath Elspeth's soft skin. Charlie longs to touch it again. But loathes the feeling too.

"Kid, come with me. I want to learn some more about you." She points the way with her sharp nose.

Charlie follows Elspeth down the stairs, his head full of questions. Outside in the cold of the parking lot, in their parkas, one of the men calls out to Elspeth in a slightly Spanish-tinged accent. "Comrade, do you need a ride?"

"That's okay, Tocayo. Charlie will take me home. We need to talk."

The shadowy figure gets into his Buick and drives off. Charlie watches the car purr off into the night. There was something odd about the Latino.

"Which car is yours?" Elspeth asks abruptly, derailing Charlie's rumination.

"Uh, over here." Charlie walks over to the Dodge Dart, unlocks the passenger door, holds it open for her. She gets in without a word.

Charlie's car reaches the street and he stops. "Turn right," she says.

Charlie nods slowly and drives on. He feels the reins and the bridle back on him. They feel good and they feel bad, and he isn't sure what he wants. He thinks of Trudy momentarily, but it is like he is forty-eight again, and Trudy is only a distant memory. He is with Elspeth once more, and she has never been more attractive to him than now, sleek and young and powerful, a goddess to be followed into battle, her bare breasts swinging with her sword as she hacks her enemies apart.

"What do you take in high school?" she asks.

Charlie laughs to himself. *Like I give a damn right now?* But he decides to treat Elspeth like anyone else in 1968. At the edge of his consciousness is the intuition that he may now have an advantage over Elspeth, that her mastery might not be quite so complete this time.

"The usual stuff. History, English, you know the drill."

Something about the way he answers the question sparks her interest. "Have you visited the society yet?"

"What society?"

She blinks. "Nothing. Forget about it."

When they get to Elspeth's brownstone, she tells him to park his car. He obeys without question, suspecting what her next step is going to be.

Inside the apartment Elspeth makes them tea. *Jasmine, her usual,* thinks Charlie. He smiles ruefully while her back is turned. But his body is sending him strong instructions. Somehow Elspeth's familiar-but-fresh anatomy is still a favorite back in 1968, even without makeup or contact lenses. She will be much more glamorous in the 1980s, but now she obviously doesn't need glamour, or want it. A familiar reek rises from her as she opens a bottle of red wine, a cheap Spanish. The wine bespeaks seduction.

She sits down and pulls her chair close to him.

"Do you like girls, Charlie?"

He hesitates.

"Of course you do. You probably have a cute little suburban girlfriend who goes down on you on Saturday nights but is saving her virginity for that big wedding night. Am I right?" She downs a glass of wine and pours him one as well. Jasmine aroma on soft air, mixed with sharp rotgut red. Charlie doesn't dare contradict her but doesn't feel any need to either. She sniffs. "Of course I am." She reaches out and feels his burgeoning bicep with her strong fingers. "You look good to me, Charlie." A pause. "I want to fuck you."

He marvels at the brazen power play. She thinks he's a kid, so she can skip the stylish stuff.

She fills the gap. "Can I fuck you, Charlie?"

6 Grit rasps in Charlie's shoes. He trudges through the desert alone, throat dry, condors circling high above. His friend has already died, lips swollen and tongue leathery. No more water. He can see a highway far ahead and to the right, but he knows he can't go to it. Not for another ten miles at least, maybe more.

Then, in a jagged lurch, he is shuffling into the old adobe house, home. Hunger gnaws at him. Muscles ache from his day's work at the shoe factory. The door creaks behind him and he hears a rustle just before he sees his mother sitting at a little wooden table between the grimy stove and their small living area. There is something covering her plate.

"Beans, *chiquito*, we only have beans tonight," she croaks in Spanish, yet he can understand. But he can smell the meat that she has been eating. His mother swallows guiltily and gets up quickly.

The scene jumps, flickers, wrenches—

And now he is only a little boy, but his father is beating a cane hard against his bare feet and thighs. He cries, but his father just laughs.

Another jump, the scene spiraling away, the terror of falling—

Charlie rises from the bed, opening his gummy eyes. His bladder hurts. He stumbles around the bare room. Elspeth watches him but says nothing.

He smacks into the doorframe and finds the bathroom, snaps on the light. His head pounds. He lets fly into the toilet but something isn't right. The bathroom flickers. His face in the mirror is distorted, the skin brown, the shadow of a thick mustache playing on his upper lip. He closes his swollen eye.

The desert is closing in on him. He lies facedown on the hot sand, next to a creosote bush. A scorpion hustles past his eyes but is not interested, keeping its claws up, its tail darting slightly, the poison tip glistening in the noon glare. *The scorpion, the scorpion.*

He feels his life sweep away from him, his stomach lurches, he is falling—and he is back being beaten by his father, feet and thighs, feet and thighs, stinging. The laughter.

Charlie's head spins. He holds on to the porcelain.

He is in a room, a cheap hotel room. Hard, ceramic light everywhere. On top of the TV lies a hypodermic syringe and some ampules, one used up. He knows that they mean release, *no pain, no pain.* Bliss . . .

A gun gleams on the bedside table.

He picks up the chrome revolver, flips the chamber open, sees a brass round ready to go, clicks the chamber back into place. His thumb pushes the safety off. He puts the muzzle into his mouth, his full white mustache between the steel and his nose. He doesn't even hear the blast as his brain stem blows apart.

A merciful second of blank nothing washes over him. Then—

Dark pressure sweeps over him and pushes down. Blunt force swarms up in him, *darkness, darkness.* Charlie slips on the cold tile floor, his balls smacking down first, then his thigh crushing them as the rest of his weight hits the hard surface and rolls. The pain is a red sword against the billowing blackness. Charlie rolls onto his chest, hitting his head on the toilet bowl. *Where am I?*

Elspeth turns on the light. "Tocayo?" Charlie wonders what she is talking about. Hasn't he heard her say that before? He turns on her with a fierce frown.

He asks blearily, "What?"

"Oh," says Elspeth. She shrugs. "Not this time." She turns to go back to bed.

Charlie pulls himself up using the toilet seat. Maybe she gave him something? Or it's a side effect of . . . what?

Slowly he composes himself, and an undertow of fatigue starts to seep back into his body. He urinates again and it stings, biting at him suddenly, so that he gasps. He drinks a glass of water and staggers to bed. This time sleep is dreamless and kind.

When Charlie wakes up again, he lies cold and alone in Elspeth's bed. The old brass-frame piece creaks, shining in morning light, surrounded by piles of books and papers. He has to shake off the memory of the night's dark episode. He wonders if he is back in another hallucination, if he will go to some other place or time. Then he realizes why he has woken up. Elspeth is yelling at him from the living room.

"Holy fuck! Charlie, get your little white ass in here right now."

Charlie lurches into the living room naked, his mind churning. Elspeth, naked, doesn't look up. "McCarthy almost beat Johnson! The revolution is coming! That fat old Democrat is going down. The country's going to leave Vietnam."

She bounces up from the sofa, throws her arms around his neck, and kisses him. She runs her hands down his beautifully muscled chest, then grabs his cock with her right hand. But Charlie pulls back.

She glances angrily up at him. "Don't do that, Charlie."

"I have to get back home. My parents will be worried about me."

"Your parents? Your fucking parents! Your old life is over, and you're worried about your *parents*?" The familiar storm cloud gathers on her face.

Your old life is over. . . . What could she mean? Just this political stuff? Or something else?

He shakes his head. Mostly he wants to think about the nightmares.

If they *were* nightmares and not some other reality he was slipping into. Some place that's a brutal desert, and . . . he wants to blow his brains out.

"Okay, you can fuck right off, you stupid little schoolboy. Scoot back to your white-bread suburb."

Charlie searches for his clothes while Elspeth rants. At least he knows how to deal with her caws. He's had years of practice not listening to her. Besides, he is sure that all will be forgiven within a week or two. That was Elspeth's way.

Not this time, Elspeth. He wants to get away from the apartment, away from the night's evil dreams.

Pulling into the driveway of his parents' home, lips pressed white, Charlie knows his mother is waiting for him alone. Not from memories of Charlie One, but from intuition. His father is away at the office. Charlie parks his car and pats it fondly, knowing that he won't be driving it again for a while. His teenage hangover pounds at his temples.

His mother stands in the kitchen smoking, something she did only when she was under stress. She smoked a lot when his father died.

Charlie walks toward her with heaviness in his lungs. His hatred for cigarettes is particularly strong when his mother smokes.

"I'm so disappointed in you, Charles." Her voice trembles with anger and sorrow.

"I know, Mom."

"I know that you were at a political meeting with one of your schoolteachers, what's his name?"

"Mr. Owen."

"I don't care. I don't like people like that. We're Democrats—we support the president. We don't need those troublemakers."

She seems to expect a response, but Charlie has no idea what would be the best thing to say to reassure her. She wouldn't respond well to the idea that smoking was far more important to her future than her political opinions.

"Your father and I have spoken on the phone, and we have agreed that we don't want you to get involved in politics while you're still in high school." A frown, an anxious drag on the Lucky Strike. "I know we talked about you volunteering to work for the McCarthy campaign"—the event that took him to the streets of Chicago in the summer of 1968 and then on to a life of radical pointlessness—"but we can't let you do that now. You could get into trouble, and then where would you go for college?"

"Yes, I—"

"Don't interrupt me, Charlie. You can't use your car for the rest of the month. And if we catch you going off with Mr. Owen again"—her voice betrays bitterness—"we won't let you have it back."

In the silence that follows, Charlie relives his arrest with the other demonstrators outside the Democratic National Convention, the arrival of his parents at the jail, his mother's worry, his father's anger, the fights that he had with them. He isn't going to go that route this time. What would be the point?

He speaks very softly, watching smoke curl up like a funeral pyre. "Okay, Mom. I'll behave myself."

It goes well for the next few days. Charlie relaxes into the era, listening to the music; staying up late with no ill effect; relishing the whoosh of air in young lungs as he runs, the snap of biting an apple, the fat richness of savory cheese on a double burger, wind rushing in his hair with his head stuck out the car window; cackling like a loon at *Laugh-In*. He returns to the warmth of it all and it soothes him like a hot tub. The nightmares don't return.

He thinks up a new aphorism to describe his Charlie Two life: *You are only young twice, but you can stay immature indefinitely.* He feels a deep rush of gratitude that this is actually, incredibly so.

Watching TV with his dad that Thursday, he sits through a Fred Astaire movie. Dad is surprised that Charlie likes it so much, especially the dancing on the ceiling. Charlie blurts out, "Wow! To do that with no FX!"

His father skews his mouth, puzzled. "What?"

"Uh, with no effects. I mean, special effects."

"Looked pretty special to me. They did it by rotating the room."

Maybe this is his destiny. Some Hindu cycle nobody thought of. Or that guy Everett. Or maybe if he doesn't get this right, he'll go back to being a frog. Or worse, an associate professor. Fate.

Trudy picks Charlie up in her father's car on Friday night. She isn't pleased. She goes to a girls' private high school, and 1968's political ferment has yet to touch her oatmeal world. To her, Charlie's Tuesday night with Mr. Owen seems deeply suspicious, possibly—did she dare think it?—homosexual.

Charlie plays it appropriately remorseful, the very model of contrition. "I was all alony by the telephony," she says, which he finds endearing. He promises her nothing like it will happen again. To himself he wonders if he can really fulfill his promises to his parents and to Trudy. Then he abruptly decides—*Sure, easy.* But he wonders what he will do if Elspeth comes looking for him.

They go to see *The Graduate* at the local movie theater. Though he knows that Trudy talks in public as if she is still a Doris Day virgin, he can tell that she is turned on by the sex. It's her rapt stillness, eyes filled with the screen, and the way her flesh seems to breathe. Later, in her father's car, she rides him hard until she comes.

Slumping on him, covered in sweat, she giggles. "You know I can't stay mad at you for long, Charlie." She sighs a long, cool breath of Coke and popcorn. "That was . . . wonderful."

Charlie is walking over to James's place after school when Elspeth pulls up in a noisy red Beetle. She stops next to him, opens the door, and whistles. Charlie stops, wondering what to do.

"Get your ass in here, cutie-pie!"

He gets into the car reluctantly.

Elspeth radiates joyous triumph. "Ah, my little hunk of jailbait. You can call me Mrs. Robinson."

They don't talk much while Elspeth hunts for an obscure place to park. It isn't easy, trucks honk at them as she changes lanes too quickly, but finally she comes upon an alleyway behind a TV repair joint.

She goes down on him briskly, swift and slippery, swallowing his come within seconds. Then she swings her legs up around him and shoves her pussy in his face. She comes in a few minutes, the whole length of her body jerking spasmodically.

Elspeth relaxes for a few seconds and then gets back into the driver's seat. "Where can I drop you off, little boy?" The hardness in her voice repels him.

"I'm scarcely a little boy." He says this sharply, trying to load the tone with implication.

"Oh, aren't we?" She even smiles.

"Not anymore."

"We all have our secrets."

Charlie takes a careful breath while his heart seems to stop. He looks away.

He has to get away from her. He lifts his eyebrows, nods, and gets out of the Volkswagen.

She swallows hard and looks down. Charlie can tell that she is holding herself back.

Then she turns toward him and smiles with an expression sure and powerful. "Next time, Charlie. Next time."

Mr. Montini keeps Charlie after class, during the lunch break. The man has the look of a worried dog, as if he has to do something difficult, or something important.

"Your novella is the finest work I have read in my twenty-two years teaching in this high school." The man's broad face radiates a sincerity that Charlie finds a bit embarrassing.

"Uh, thank you." Charlie knows what it is like to be a teacher who rarely finds a talented student. He tries to give Montini some sense that he is appreciated. Charlie One would have wanted the same consideration himself. "I learned a lot from your classes."

"I want you to think about becoming a writer."

Charlie is amazed. Is this how writers start? No trumpets, nobody notices much, just a few words of encouragement.

"I know that you probably are thinking about law or something practical."

Charlie laughs to himself. "No, not really."

The tension in Montini's face vanishes and a broad smile flowers in its place. Charlie can see a plan growing inside the man's head, just behind his little brown eyes, in a face so beaten down but still warm. "I have a friend who is a published author. I would like you to meet him."

Charlie thinks that this may be the oddest turn his second life has taken. *A writer?*

The friend of Montini's turns out to be a chain-smoking, fidgety man called Bob Greenway, lanky with a worn face that looks like it was made of dried snakeskin. Montini and Charlie meet him in a nearby diner after school, a long, hollow room with a tinny roof, a worn row of plastic booths framing Formica, a miasma of fryer fat. After they exchange pleasantries, Greenway has a coughing fit. Montini glances at Charlie with some embarrassment. Charlie tries to smile in a reassuring manner, but he knows that he just looks like a nervous kid out of his depth.

A chunky blond waitress with uneven red lips comes over to take their order. Charlie asks for a Coke. She looks at Greenway quizzically as she chews her gum. Montini shakes his head at her, a bit pensive himself, orders coffee. The woman leaves with a shrug.

When the hacking stops, Greenway speaks in a voice that has seen too many late nights. "Not bad, for a juvenile work. Amazing, really, the feel for this loser's life, how he never really connects with his wife." Greenway taps Charlie's novella with yellowed scaly fingers, semicircular coffee stains now decorating its cover page.

Charlie winces at this succinct evaluation. But it is becoming another person's story in his mind.

"But look, kid, you don't really have good visuals. It's all conversation scenes. Five senses! You don't get a feeling for the taste, the smell, the touch, of this guy's world. You don't feel his hand on this chick's skin. You aren't thinking like a good novelist. The reader just can't get there."

Reasonable criticisms, Charlie thinks. He knows he is no Thomas Mann or John Updike. The novella was therapy, an exercise in recovery from whatever this whole experience is.

Montini breaks in with some irritation. "Listen here, Bob. Charlie has talent. He could go places. You know this story has narrative authority. It feels genuine. Don't you remember the way you wrote in college?"

"Sure." Greenway smooths the hair combed over his bald spot, looking a bit chagrined. "Earnest, crappy. People said I had 'promise' to avoid telling me what was wrong."

"Right! Bob, he needs a chance. Can't you get him a magazine commission or something?"

Greenway laughs unpleasantly, showing off his dingy teeth and yellowing tongue. "At his age, who will want him? He's a punk."

"So don't tell them his age."

"Listen to me, Nono, you don't understand this business."

Montini's face darkens and his thick chest expands as he jabs a finger at Greenway. "Just give Charlie a damn chance! You owe me, Bob."

"Back off, Nono." His voice is small. "Uh, I'll do what I can."

A considered pause, his mouth twisting. "Do you like the movies, kid?"

Trudy and Charlie end up at that same diner for their usual Saturday-night dinner date. Charlie is starting to like the greasy charm of it as he listens to Trudy go over her rivalries at school, how Jeanette stole Trudy's favorite gold circle pin when she tried it on her blouse, the spate of gossip about the prom queen. He gives her just enough attention to seem to be listening.

Almost brazen, he finally breaks into her monologue. "I think I'm going to become a writer."

She blinks. "Charlie Moment, you'll do no such thing." She frowns severely. "You're going to the University of Chicago and become a lawyer."

Charlie had no idea that Trudy was already mapping out his life. He knows that women think that way, but he didn't realize that it started as early as seventeen. And . . . a lawyer?

His mind whirls and the clinking sounds of the diner recede. The light around him flickers. Maybe this is how schizophrenia feels from the inside? Whirring, dizzy fog in the mind? He thought it would be easy to live life as a teenager with an adult's experience, but it isn't.

The same chunky waitress comes up to them. She gives Charlie an amused look, maybe a touch of a leer in the downward dip of her scarlet lip. "You lovebirds ready to order?"

* * *

Bob Greenway's apartment is a study in gray drab and nicotine. Charlie can hardly breathe, but his excitement overrides any need for oxygen. Greenway leads him into the dark cranny that serves as dining and living space. Greenway has been reading Charlie's second manuscript for a week, and Charlie is eager to hear his comments.

Greenway pushes a plate of ancient egg yolk and cigarette butts to one side, and drops the thick manuscript down on the wood veneer of the stained plastic table. He absently waves at a chair for Charlie and pulls up one for himself.

"It's not bad, kid." A hoarse breath. "The way you sketch this bitch of a woman! I've been there, let me tell you. Plenty of times! But . . ."

Greenway pauses to look for a pack of cigarettes. Finds one, gets out a Camel but doesn't light it, just holding it in his fingers as he gestures with his hands.

"It's really more like a *diary*. You just assume that your reader knows what it's like to live in DC. What I kept wanting was something about the streets, the traffic, the food these people eat. Five senses, y'know."

"But does the dialogue work?"

"Sure—crisp stuff always works. I liked those lines where the gal keeps pressing him and he gives one-word answers. Great!"

Charlie knows enough to just let him run. Greenway's face twists, eyes narrow. "Yeah, I know every fucking thing this broad says. But then the prose, it doesn't go deep. You don't go inside."

Charlie fidgets while Greenway lights up. He loathes the tightening in his lungs from the smoke, the stink of the place. But his need for Greenway's comments is much greater than his discomfort. He tries to breathe better air by turning away from the table and looking around the room. A battered television, probably black-and-white, in the corner with some small photos on top of it. Greenway's family, Charlie guesses. *What happened to them?* he wonders.

"Look, I don't think you have it to write fiction. You have a feel for narrative, dialogue, sure—but their inner life is simply not there, see? You only report events and not people's gut-check times."

Greenway rubs his hands together very slowly, without disturbing the length of ash on the cigarette. Then he puffs and takes a deep drag and seems to be making his mind up. "Look, I have this buddy in Hollywood. He needs people to read scripts for him. People who can do dialogue, know if it feels right."

Charlie flinches. "Hollywood?" He didn't see this coming at all.

"Your strengths are screenwriting ones—dialogue, plot. Maybe you could take on a few of the assignments that I don't have time for? We'll see if you can't learn more about writing from seeing how other people do it." Greenway laughs bitterly, looking at something in the air near his kitchen. "And do it not very well, at that."

Days stream by, their small incidents and dreams poignant. Charlie is seeing through the lens of time, aware that these ripe 1968 days are a pivotal age. Beyond the clashes of 1968 lies the fracturing of the American people into factions. Divisions over what Vietnam proves will echo into wars in the Middle East. Nixon's War on Drugs will send millions to jail and lower drug use not a bit. Charlie decides he will not go to Chicago to fight cops with teenage fervor, at the Democratic National Convention that anointed the loser Hubert Humphrey. Instead he reads books he should've before—*War and Peace, Pride and Prejudice, As I Lay Dying, A Farewell to Arms, A Canticle for Leibowitz, The Moon Is a Harsh Mistress.* A passage from Fitzgerald's essay on his own 1936 crack-up strikes Charlie: "The test of a first-rate intelligence is the ability to hold two opposed ideas in the mind at the same time, and still retain the ability to function." *I'm keeping two times in my head,* Charlie thinks. *But I'm no first-rater.*

He makes himself write steadily, and soon the years he spent writing dry social science drone-prose in front of a screen fade. He loves the *smackety-smack* of keys on a platen, and the *ding!* at the end of the line.

Charlie is lying in Elspeth's bed while Elspeth listens to the chattering radio. It's April 11 and the riots have already started.

". . . and the Reverend Ralph Abernathy said that the marchers were going on to Washington, DC, to present their grievances to the president and Congress."

Charlie yawns. Charlie One was fixated on 1968's cascade of horrors, but now he finds it tedious in its inching detail, like rereading a whodunit.

"Local sheriff's deputies say that they have already taken down eyewitness reports about the shooting. Dr. King was apparently standing on a balcony when—"

Elspeth abruptly snaps the sound off. "They're not going to catch the shooter. The pigs probably shot him themselves—bastards. Now they'll find some redneck loser with a gun and a psychiatric record and pin it on him."

Charlie clears his throat quietly and rolls toward her. She is dead-on about the eventual arrest. "Don't you think King was the perfect target for a middle-aged white schizophrenic, like one with paranoid tendencies?"

"Don't go all psychiatric on me."

"I'll also bet that the guy who shot RFK last week, that Delgado, was a nutcase too," says Charlie. "And not a very good shot, for which I'm grateful."

"What the fuck do *you* know, Charlie? Kennedy is one of the Establishment. You've just been suckered in by his pretty face and the whole Camelot thing. That fat-cat family is a bunch of fascists. You're a middle-class white kid from the suburbs of Chicago. You can't even vote."

Elspeth reaches over his body to get her cigarettes, her right breast pushing against his chin. She keeps talking and he lets the words slide by. He wonders how much longer he can revisit his sexual obsession with Elspeth. He still carries the loathing from his past life with her.

"When are you going to come back to the meetings? McCarthy has a good chance of being the nominee."

"I'm not that interested, Elspeth."

She rolls her eyes and smiles scornfully. "Whoa, the worm turns. Char-lee boy, you're *mad.*" There is a twist to her voice, like an affected accent. Elspeth is delighted, and turns to him with a big smile, her cigarette-wielding arm swinging wide, her breasts peeking out over the sheets.

"It's over, Elspeth."

"We'll see, Char-lee boy."

It's a good time for Charlie and his mother, sitting together in the dining room, his father still at work and his sister off gossiping with her friends. His mother is reading his latest manuscript, a series of scenes about an older woman and a young man who comes to understand the world even as she is dying. Charlie has taken the story of *Harold and Maude* and made something sweeter, less morbid, less sexual. It isn't quite a screenplay, but the scenes are short and effective. Charlie's images reflect the depth of his forty-eight years, together with the perspectives of coming back to life, young and fit and deeply confused.

Near the end of the reading, she starts to cry. Charlie freezes. He doesn't know what to do. Memory thrusts him backward to the crying, helpless woman facing the disintegration of memory and continuity that would be her Alzheimer's days. He feels on the edge of tears himself.

"Charlie, you're so good, so good." She smiles at him and takes his hand in both of hers, the lines around her eyes a latticework of devotion mixed with sadness. "Charlie, you're going to be a great writer. Everybody will know who you are. You are everything a mother could want in a son."

This is too much for him. He looks down with great concentration and tries to control his emotions. She takes this as a gesture of humility.

"I know I'm only your mother, but I've spoken with Mr. Montini. He loves your work. He says you are the best student he has ever had, Charlie. He can help you. He has told me that he has introduced you to his writer friend."

"Bob Greenway."

"Yes, and your father and I have been talking. We want you to enroll in that creative writing program they have at the University of Minnesota. You could write the next great American novel." She takes his chin by her hand and lifts his face up toward her. Her love washes over him with a cleansing wave. No, she isn't dead by her own hand in 1998. *That didn't happen*, Charlie declares to himself. *It won't happen. I'll make her happy. Dad can quit smoking.*

"Bob thinks that I'm not suited to writing novels."

"What does he know?"

Driving the Dodge Dart, Charlie pulls away from a stop sign and glimpses a Ford pickup coming at him. He slams on his brakes and the Ford screeches sideways, then zooms by his hood an inch away, its driver a big blond woman leaning on her blaring horn.

He stops the car and sits, feeling fear and memory flickering. Then the flickering stops.

His death can come back at him, just like that. This is the worst yet. He breathes in long sighs.

James and Charlie are stoned way far out of their minds, watching silent televised images of the riots while listening to "A Day in the

Life" from *Sgt. Pepper's*. As the long final chord fades out in the room, Charlie's mind seems to expand to fill all space and time.

"You know, I'm from the future."

"Fucking right. Like, 'I don't live today, maybe tomorrow.'"

"No, I died on my birthday, January 2000."

The needle clicks in the end groove, once every two seconds. James doesn't say anything.

"Are you okay, James?"

James starts to whimper. Then he stops to speak. "Don't try any more of that weird stuff on me, okay? I have it hard enough, okay? Hard enough."

Charlie's mind expands around him, spinning the long, snaky coils of his two lives out into the timescape. It is like he is being made one with something far greater. Everything around him seems to go still. The room drifts away.

But then he pulls himself back. James comes into focus, facing down on the sofa. Charlie realizes he can't let his first life capsize the people around him. He has to focus on this life, even if it is a rewrite.

8

Charlie is sweating, groaning, tasting the hot breath of her, thrusting into Trudy below him on the back-seat of her father's Cadillac. With the extra room, their sex is less clumsy. Charlie is more comfortable going for longer before coming. This teenage body, he has learned, can be tamed. He takes Trudy's hand and pulls it down. Her soft flesh is a pillow from heaven. Her eyes widen at the idea.

When she starts to gasp, slick and sweating like him, moaning intensely, he speeds up and, with a sweet, jerky drive, comes himself. His shuddering gasps she echoes below. Trudy grabs his buttock hard with her free hand and pulls him harder into her.

Afterward Charlie hears the spring crickets like tiny voices chirrup in the park around them. *Nature's chorus, never ending.*

"That was sooo good, Charlie," she sighs softly. "I . . . I just want to do it with you every night. Sometimes I can't study in my bedroom, just thinking about you . . . you—you inside me like that."

Trudy sits up and pulls her panties up her legs. Charlie wonders how their sex life could have been so narrow the last time, so quick and functional. Hurried, dull. They both were so different, in his first life.

Trudy finishes dressing, moving faster as she recovers from the stupefaction of orgasm. She looks at Charlie with a little impatience.

"Get dressed, silly! The police are sure to come around to check out a big white Cadillac parked here."

"I think they have more important things to do, these days."

"Let's not talk about politics, Charlie. Richard Nixon will save the country."

"If he doesn't turn the United States into an armed camp first."

Trudy shrugs with exasperation. "Charlie, can't you just accept that Republicans might be right sometimes? Even the president and the Kennedys are supporting Mr. Nixon now."

She frowns and he recalls that she hates it when he patronizes her. She likes the way he has become so much more understanding—mature, she said once—but he makes her feel like he doesn't take her opinions seriously.

"You'll cut your hair and grow up. With your brain, you'll have no trouble getting into a good law school."

There it was again. That agenda. Become an attorney like her father and spend all his time in a skyscraper downtown, getting paid for helping corporations screw people.

"This writing thing is okay for now," she allows. "Daddy says that a good writer can be a good attorney. There's a lot of writing in law."

"Yeah, bad writing." Learning about life from someone who has just seen her eighteenth birthday strikes Charlie as the biggest joke of his repeated life. He chuckles.

"Don't laugh at me, Charlie Moment. I know you think you are smarter than me. But there are some things not even you know."

"Like what?"

"Like how much I adore you." She lunges at him, and soon he finds himself rolling around with her again, on the backseat of her father's Coupe DeVille, again and again, time without end. Somehow Charlie knows that he has experienced this night a thousand times, but does not know how he knows.

*   *   *

Charlie spends several hours a day working on a new screenplay, mostly in the morning, when he can look like he is taking notes in class. He free-associates around the basic plot, writing scenes that pop into his head. Later he types up a more orderly, plot-driven set of scenes played for satire. He finds the bare-bones feel of script format a useful slimming down of the apparatus of stories and novels. Movements need little description, background still less—it's all in the dialogue. Greenway was right. The medium does suit him.

It all comes from movies Charlie One saw. Plus, he adds insights that come from the immediacy of the turbulent 1968 unfolding around him.

He gathers momentum, feels it zip through his veins, hammer in his ears. But the return of youth has made him careless. He says to friends at a bowling alley, "Y'know, life is like this—gutters and strikes." The high school crowd picks up and repeats this epigram. He even feels a little guilty, because it's a lift from *The Big Lebowski*.

His parents are surprised that in addition to the University of Chicago and University of Illinois, he also applies to Stanford and two Universities of California, Berkeley and San Diego. He knows that Chicago, Stanford, and Berkeley are long shots, with his spotty grades, but UCSD and Illinois are plausible. When his father casually mentions wondering which one he really wants to go to—obviously hoping it's one of the far cheaper publics—Charlie is struck by how blithely young Charlie assumed that with his B+ average he could get into a UC. By 2000, high schoolers will paper dozens of university admission offices with their xeroxed or online pleas, counting on shotgun statistics. In 1968 it is not really a big deal.

"Why so far away?" his mother asks. He hasn't the courage to say, *That's precisely why*. A plan simmers in the back of his mind and he doesn't want to discuss it yet.

Charlie has come to treasure time spent with his parents and sister—just watching TV shows or going to see narrow-eyed Steve McQueen zoom his Mustang through steep San Francisco streets in *Bullitt*. On a Sunday picnic their transistor radio plays tracks from the new *White Album* by the Beatles. Charlie picks up on the joy that the tunes bring to them. He watches his mother dance around a redwood table under dappled eucalyptus shade, singing the lyrics to a Beatles song all wrong, in her high soprano, nearly in tune. He loves it all anyway, as his first life as a teenager never allowed.

Everything is different this time. On Sundays his mother's lengthy grace doesn't grate on him. This time he savors each one

At high school he recalls who wrote poetry in Klingon, who sold dope, who was really gay and thought nobody knew. Friends, long forgotten by his late forties. As they pass by him again, he has a sad appreciation of how fleeting it all is.

Charlie is back in the diner with Bob Greenway, hamburger sizzle flavoring the air. Their chunky waitress with the sloppily lipsticked mouth waits for Greenway to decide between a cheeseburger and a club sandwich. She smiles at Charlie, eyeing him in a manner that is a little bit more than friendly. She glances back at Greenway and then throws Charlie a slow wink, saucy chin below vibrant red.

"Uh, Charlie?" Greenway says, and Charlie realizes he is staring at the waitress.

"Uh, oh, just had a plot idea . . ." He looks away from her, trying not to be rude as he does.

Greenway announces his carefully considered decision to have a cheeseburger with onions and turns to the typed pages that he has brought to their meeting. "I like what you're saying about those three screenplays. There isn't anything fresh about them, and your idea of a dramatic arc is good. In LA they don't seem to have much of that. Y'know, I thought that the science fiction idea about this future in which scientists use parapsychology to find a killer was kinda interesting."

"Pretty standard, really." Charlie's comment pops out of his mouth without thought, before he realizes that it's an anachronism in 1968. The psychic paired with the detective hasn't yet become hackneyed.

"Okay, well, you go to the new movies—I don't."

Charlie is relying on the many movies that he has seen, will see, in the videocassette era. That, and Heinlein and Asimov and Philip K. Dick. Greenway still lives in a world where new movies can be seen only in cinemas, while television runs ancient movies hacked up to fit commercials. Charlie is beginning to understand that this gives him a substantial advantage in dissecting futuristic screenplays. "I know the ropes and the tropes," he says.

"Tropes?"

No teenager would know that term, so Charlie covers the mistake. "Picked the word up from Mr. Montini."

"To be honest with you, Charlie . . ." Greenway takes a pull at his Camel. "I'm kinda gettin' uncomfortable acting as your middleman with the studio guys. I can't even take fifty percent of your reading fee anymore—you sure don't need me filtering your reader reports."

"Hey, I appreciate that. I've learned a lot from you." Waits a beat, then: "What if we were to do a screenplay ourselves?"

Greenway clears his throat and takes a sip from his Coke, his face a mixture of eagerness and doubt. "Kid, have you got the time? You aren't even out of high school. You must have a lot of history and stuff to learn."

Stuff I've been teaching for years, Charlie says to himself. "Believe me, Bob, you aren't going to be able to prevent me graduating from Woodrow Wilson High."

Adult confidence slips into Charlie's voice, but he can't stop himself. His hunger to do something creative for the first time in his life drives him.

Greenway laughs wistfully.

9 Charlie turns off the ignition of the Dodge Dart, sliding quietly in neutral gear into the dark park that has been their regular Friday-night place for more than a year. Trudy was nestled against him the whole ride here, her muscles tight from her silent anticipation. Her scent had that musky tang already.

The night closes around them. Crickets sing of joy. He thinks of a sudden rhyme, the sort of thing that is coming to him often now as he imagines becoming a writer:

> *Nothing in the cicada cry*
> *Suggests they are about to die.*

Waiting only a beat, Trudy reaches for his belt buckle.

Charlie squirms slightly. Trudy pushes on his stomach and sits up. "What *is* it, Charlie?"

"I have a surprise for you, baby. Something to show you."

"Yes, Charlie?" Her voice rises an octave. *Oh God*, Charlie thinks. *She's hoping for an engagement ring.*

He breathes in the cool night air and decides to go on despite his misgivings. *I know her so well now. . . .* "Let me get it out of my pocket."

Trudy quivers with anticipation, her grin wide. Charlie knows at once how she sees this moment. Charlie waiting for her in front of the altar, his hair trimmed neatly, wearing a beautiful tuxedo, James as best man. Organ music swells around her, Mendelssohn's triumphant wedding march. Her father is holding her tightly around the waist, *so proud* of her as—

But then she sees that it's an envelope, an official-looking one. Her smile drops away and the muscles of her shoulders go slack. No, it isn't a ring.

Charlie takes a piece of paper out of the envelope and hands it to her. "What is this, Charlie? Is it the draft or something?"

Charlie laughs. "I'm just seventeen, sweetheart. They can't draft me for another ten months. I have three more months of high school, too. Not even the Nixon administration would do that."

"There you go about the president! He's not as bad as you think."

No, he's a lot worse, Charlie says to himself.

"Look at the check."

"It's a check? Why are you showing me a check?"

"Read it, baby. Just read it."

"'Pay to the order of Charles B. Moment.' It starts out well."

"Go on." Charlie is starting to tense. Why can't he work this through better?

"The sum of twenty—*twenty thousand dollars.*" Trudy gasps, then falls silent.

Charlie was expecting cries of joy by this point, but none come.

She studies the signature. "It's from some movie studio company, isn't it?"

"Yes, it is. For a script."

She jerks her head, shrugging off this detail. "You're not going to college? What about—"

"I got into UC San Diego." The letter came in days before, but he has told no one but his family.

"And?" She peers at him. He says nothing.

"You're going to go to Hollywood, aren't you?"

"After graduation."

Trudy bursts into tears and rage, fists slamming Charlie on the shoulder. "You *aren't* going to the University of Chicago. You *aren't* going to be a lawyer. Daddy *was* right. You're no good, Charlie Moment. You're *no good*." But she sobs on his shoulder, throwing her arms around him.

Charlie's father bangs into the house with an ebullient "Hey, everybody!" and tosses his hat and coat in the closet. Charlie gets up from the sofa, holding his envelope, hoping it will catch his father's attention.

His father's eyes narrow with worry. "What do you have there, son?"

He tosses it on the table, delaying the issue. "I have to talk with you, Dad."

"Sure, Charlie. Sure." His father pats Charlie's shoulder, easing out of his day.

They go into the dining room, the stuffy citadel of family business, and sit down kitty-corner to each other across the polished maple sheen. Charlie hands over the rumpled envelope without a word. His father opens it, raises his eyebrows, and unfolds the check.

"Twenty thou. They bought the screenplay, didn't they, the one about the president?"

Charlie nods. He has learned to let silence do the talking for him with his father.

Eyebrows arched, lips pursed, his father pushes down on the table with both his hands, fingers splayed. He exhales stale breath, his Adam's apple squeezing up from the knot of his tie. "Charlie, you will be the first person in our family to make a name for themselves."

He puts his hand firmly on Charlie's arm. "I'm proud of you, boy."

"Dad, you know what's going to happen, don't you?" Charlie can see that his father might not see the full implications.

His father just smiles distantly and folds his hands.

"I'm going, I mean after graduation, going to Southern California. They will need me to work on the script during production."

"No problem, Charlie. You can do that this summer, right?"

A beat. "Well, movies aren't filmed to fit college schedules."

His father leans back in his chair, a study in bright enthusiasm.

"I see, Charlie. You're worried about going to college." His father slaps Charlie on the upper arm. "Look, son. This is the real world. I'm lucky if I clear fifteen thousand a year at the gearbox, uh, the transmission factory. They've given you more for a hundred pages of words . . . just pages of words."

Actually, a hundred and twenty pages I wrote in three weeks, he thinks but knows not to say. His father blinks, amazed at the thought. *Mere words.* Then he sucks in a raw breath, coming to terms with a new world. "And I know you've got plenty more in you. Your mother and I have the greatest faith in you, Charlie. You've become a serious person, at least since you gave up on that"—his father's voice drops a few notes for the phrase—"political stuff.

"You're a fine young man, and your mother and—"

"And what, Ned?" Charlie realizes that his mother has been watching them from the hallway, holding a dish towel in her hands. "What is that on the table?"

"Why, it's a check from a studio, honey."

"What is it for, Ned?"

"Twenty thousand, sweetheart." Charlie sees from his father's quick, suppressed frown that things are not going to go as well as he thought they would.

Storm clouds flicker in his mother's face. "What about our son becoming a writer?"

"This *is* writing, honey. Very successful writing."

"So he goes off to Hollywood and becomes a drunk like Scott Fitzgerald." Her tone skates on acidic ice. "Nobody ever hears about him because he never does write that great American novel. What about our son then?"

Charlie did not see this coming. He stands, hands open to her. "Mom, it doesn't have to be like that."

Her face wrinkles. "You're only seventeen! What do you know about failure, about disappointment? You aren't the only one here who has dreams." His mother's wrenching desperation scares Charlie. *Is there something I don't know?* he asks himself. Something going on between his parents?

His father's tone thickens. "This is Charlie's big chance. He can *make* something of himself." A low note sounds in the man's voice, a yearning Charlie has never heard. "Maybe he won't have to sweat it out in some dull white-collar job, be a nobody? Let him take that chance, honey. If it doesn't work out, he can apply to start college a year later. A chance like this may not come again."

His mother doesn't reply, quietly wringing the dish towel in her hands. She turns away from them slowly and her footsteps echo down the hall.

"Charlie, I'm sorry. Your mother and I . . . we haven't been . . . happy lately, okay?"

Bob Greenway and Charlie Moment slide into their usual booth, don't bother to pick up their menus. It's their last meal in the diner where they first met. They both know this is it, and excitement flows through them. Their chunky waitress sways over to them promptly.

"The usual, gentlemen?"

"That's right, Doris," Charlie says, smiling at her.

Doris returns his smile with more of her mouth than usual. "Two cheeseburgers coming up, Charlie."

Greenway takes out a Camel but doesn't light it. "Ever thought about growing a beard?"

"Sure. Why?" He had one most of his adult life, the last time.

"It would help with the studio. I think we could sell you as twenty-eight with a beard."

"Ah."

"Maybe get a tan, too. Looks count in Hollywood."

Charlie can see that Greenway is right. He nods pointedly. "What about my hair?"

Greenway laughs, soon devolving into coughing. Charlie waits for him to finish. "You really are a keen son of a bitch, aren't you?"

Greenway blinks, realizing quickly that Charlie's ambitions are not to be mocked. "Uh, okay. The way I see it is the studios are fucking scared right now. The sixties blew up in their faces. The old formulas stopped working. Once Frank Sinatra doesn't define cool, they got no idea where to go. This guy Lester makes these stupid movies about four mop tops—no offense, Charlie, okay?—and cleans up. He's hip. So question is, how can they make money with *real* pictures?"

They still don't see how big the Beatles thing could be? Charlie wonders. "Yeah, let the hair stay long." Greenway can't fight off his addiction any longer. Lighting the cigarette, he takes a long drag. A slight shudder runs through his body as his nerves settle. Charlie recalls a favorite saying of his father's: *Never miss a good opportunity to shut up.* Clearly, Greenway has never heard of this rule.

"Your long hair, mustache . . . maybe beard, the twenty-eight years we're going to give you, this script"—he picks it up, slaps it down with relish—"they say hip, cool, young. The studios aren't going to be interested in an old hack like me. They will flip for you as, like, that Paul Lennon."

"John Lennon."

"Okay, sure. Point is, they need you. With your insights and my writing ability, we could be huge."

"My writing is getting better."

Greenway leans back and smiles, slapping his belly as Doris slides their cheeseburger plates in front of them. She pats Charlie on the shoulder and gives him her largest crimson smile, teeth radiantly white.

Greenway picks up his juicy burger. "Don't get me wrong, Charlie. I love the screenplay that Action Pictures bought. It's just that the whole plot thing, substituting for the president, is kind of *Twilight Zone*, you know. It was nifty making it a comedy, though."

Charlie just watches. Greenway barely gets the point. Cultural swerves take a while to sink in. Charlie already has a short list of movies that he is going to chisel into screenplays, all carved from rough-stone memories of hit movies that he has already seen. This was the first he tried, and it was even easier than he had hoped.

Greenway puts the cheeseburger down to pick up his cigarette for another puff. *Why does everybody smoke in 1969?* Charlie wonders. *Didn't anybody read that surgeon general's report?*

"But you still need to work on your scenes. I think you write too short. But we'll see when we get notes from the studio." Greenway bites into his burger. Charlie finally picks up his and takes a bite, the taste bursting rich and juicy on his tongue. *Savor it. . . .*

Part II

Long Upward Spiral

Hide not your Talents, they for Use were made.
What's a Sun-Dial in the Shade!
—Benjamin Franklin, *Poor Richard Improved*, 1750

10

Bob Greenway meets Charlie at the gate in Los Angeles. Charlie hasn't been in California since a social science convention in 1996. Of course, in 1969 LAX is nothing like it was in 1996. It's kind of poky, with lots of towering palm trees. Pleasant. There is a band of saffron-robed, shaved-head types with their "Hare Krishna, Hare Krishna, Krishna Krishna, Hare Hare" on the sidewalk coming out of baggage claim. Charlie smiles; he knows more about reincarnation than they ever will.

They walk through the shimmering July heat to Bob's new red Buick. "I'm betting the farm on this," Bob says as he starts it with a throaty growl. "You're my ticket back in." Just as Charlie starts sweating, the cool breeze from the vents in the dashboard rescues him.

Bob leans over and speaks with whiskey-rich, baritone authority. "Can't live in California without air-conditioning." Bob apparently sees himself as Charlie's Virgil, guiding the young man through the Hollywood inferno. *Hey, let this old guy have his fun,* Charlie thinks. He has lived more years than Bob anyway. He turns away to look at Century Boulevard whizzing by. Not quite as bland as it will be in the 1990s. Refreshingly tacky. He chuckles.

"What?" says Bob.

"I expected more steel and glass."

"You'll get 'em—downtown. But first, gotta look cool."

Greenway takes him to a Ford dealership right away. They buy him a dark-green Mustang, the new 1969 model, more powerful looking than the 1966 style, more of a muscle car. "Hip, but American," says Greenway. Bob arranges for the cash transfer.

Charlie's mustache makes him look much older. His long hair hides the trim lines of his smooth face. Under the sheets of sleek hair, behind the mustache, he could be any age, maybe even thirty.

Charlie drives the Mustang with a certain swagger, settling into his new role of hip young moviemaker.

Greenway's Buick leads Charlie to the apartment booked for him. It's absurdly expensive for something in a shabby two-story stucco rectangle on a narrow side street just down from Hollywood Boulevard. The landlord smells of cheap red wine. He tells Charlie that the complex dates to the 1920s. "Raymond Chandler times, y'know." Charlie knows that Chandler was an oil executive in the 1920s who read *Black Mask* magazine and never lived in a dump like this. "Ah." The musty apartment looks onto a shared courtyard with a yawning empty pool and long-dead fountains of concrete, sculpted metaphors. Charlie thinks of hapless William Holden floating facedown in *Sunset Boulevard* but dismisses the comparison. *I've come to take this town*, he thinks, *not end up shot in somebody's swimming pool. Especially not an empty one.*

"I have something special planned for this evening," Greenways says. "Get a shower and put on a jacket. See you at eight."

When Charlie reaches the curb at eight o'clock the night has already cooled, its dry breath stinging with car fumes. *Why didn't I move to California last life?* he asks himself. The answer squirms into his mind like a fat python. *Because I bought into all that tweedy, uptight shit. I wanted to be a "significant thinker."* He laughs at himself. *I'll make up for it this time.*

Charlie feels awkward in a jacket, his long hair rolling over his shoulders, and his mustache a bit prickly still. After Chicago, the streets of Hollywood are a summer flesh festival. A blond girl in a bikini top and jeans strolls by, her hair parted in the middle, a smooth, deep suntan screaming of basal cell carcinoma.

And then she flickers. Charlie starts. His blond vision has become doubled. He looks away, at the buildings and parked cars. No double vision there. Back to the girl. Now there are two of her walking down the street, clearly separated.

Charlie's stomach feels hollow. Both girls turn toward him with a puzzled look. More flickering. There are now multiples of them, overlapping one another. He hears echoing voices, high pitched, but can't make out words.

He closes his eyes, his head hurting. His body shudders. He waits it out.

The throbbing stops. He opens his eyes to look down at his shoes. They are okay.

Bob squeals up and honks, bumping Charlie out of his reverie.

"Come on, kid. Your future awaits!"

The familiar voice helps to bring Charlie back to self-possession. *For a published novelist,* Charlie thinks, *Bob has a taste for clichés.*

Bob pulls up in front of a restaurant and hands off the car to a uniformed attendant. "Valet parking," he explains proudly. Recovered enough to take in more of his surroundings, Charlie notices the name of the restaurant: Chasen's. Despite himself, he's impressed.

Greenway addresses the maître d' as Tommy, an ancient ruin with the gray skin of a vampire victim. His eyes dimly recognize Bob when he palms the twenty-dollar bill, giving him a nod, but it could have been a reflection of the lighting. As they are led to their table, he sees Peter Sellers. Then the young Anthony Hopkins.

"Is that really Anthony Hopkins?" he asks Bob.

"Who the fuck is Anthony Hopkins?"

Charlie reminds himself that in 1969 Anthony Hopkins is still an unknown in Hollywood, despite his turn as Richard the Lionheart in *The Lion in Winter*. Few would have noticed him then, next to Peter O'Toole and Katharine Hepburn.

Their booth is cozy, the menus produced promptly. The light is dim, to flatter elderly actors. Charlie watches Bob's older eyes struggle to make out the items.

"Uh, do they still have that peppercorn steak?"

"Yes, they do, Bob."

"I'll get that. Rare enough to smell Texas." Bob waves for a martini. Though their waiters shuffle about with the spirit and grace of funeral home directors, dinner proceeds efficiently enough. The food, even Chasen's chili, is heavy and fatty to Charlie's palate from 2000. But the visceral comfort of it helps him get over the flickering. George Burns stumbles by at one point, squinting, hunched. Bob sees him too and leans forward, whispering, "All washed up."

Charlie does not predict to Bob that George Burns will know more success in his eighties and nineties than he ever saw before, and will even play God.

"Over there," Bob says, a little louder. "No, farther over. See him— the short, older guy with the thick glasses? Billy Wilder."

Wow, Charlie thinks.

Bob looks around furtively. "Washed up."

Charlie bites his tongue. *Sure, the guy who made* Double Indemnity, Sunset Boulevard, Some Like It Hot. *We'll never be that good.*

The flickering has left Charlie edgy. "How do you know so much about Hollywood, Bob?"

Bob puts his steak knife down and chews thoughtfully. He gulps some water to force the steak down, then displays his yellow incisors with pride. "I was here, you know."

"Here, when?"

"The last days of the studio system. The fifties. Worked at Warner Brothers. Boy, was Jack Warner a bastard. He ran that place like a drill sergeant. I was one of their writers. Slavery."

Charlie knows that Bob has returned just in time for the last convulsions of the moribund studios. *Variety* bannered a portent just last week, BIG PICS DRAIN STUDIOS. As this sunstruck Rome totters, plenty of Huns are waiting to storm the ramparts. But his key to this is Bob, a relic already, so he has to pretend interest. "Really. What screen credits did you get?"

"Nothing you've heard of."

"Try me."

"They don't even show them on the TV, kid. Way before your time."

"Try me, Bob."

"Okay. *Only the Damned*. Kinda film noir, about a guy—wants to kill his wife."

"Saw it! With Dagmar Kruger and Frank Randman."

Bob leans back against the overripe upholstery, his face slack with disbelief. "Wow, kid, you are *good*. No wonder you can spin out all those treatments."

Charlie grins, says nothing. He has made his point, thanks to lonely nights of classic movies in the 1990s. Bob will show him more respect in the future. They chew their mediocre food in meditative silence. The martinis help Charlie fully recover his composure.

A smooth-looking thirtysomething man appears in an off-white jacket and paisley cravat. His hair sprouts at random angles, and Charlie can tell that he has spent some time in front of a mirror trying to make it look longer than it really is.

"Hi, Bob." A hand shoots out of a jacket sleeve and meets Bob's. Bob rises slightly and smiles broadly with heartfelt unctuousness.

"Great to see you, Merrill."

Bob waves his hand in Charlie's general direction, his eyes shifting back and forth between the two younger men. "Merrill, this is Charlie. Your studio's new acquisition"—big hand wave—"and may I say a *very* promising young writer indeed."

Charlie slides out of the booth and stands up to shake hands. He isn't going to let this studio slimeball tower over him, even if the guy does have a clipped Yale accent. Hollywood is full of C students from the Ivy League. Charlie makes a point of inviting Merrill to sit with them, taking some of the wind out of Bob. Merrill accepts, saying he has already eaten at another restaurant, but maybe he can have dessert, fresh fruit perhaps. He turns on the polished kilowatt smile. "How is LA treating you, Charlie?"

"Fine, thank you, Merrill." Charlie makes the further point of being polite. Even though he has a trendy look, he doesn't want to be treated as the flavor du jour. He has come to Hollywood to make a serious career, some serious money. He has his family in Chicago to look after, and his legacy of middle-aged frustration to overcome. And he has his secret knowledge, which sets him apart from this world.

Merrill pointedly ignores Charlie's tone, goes down-market. "Like the pussy here, Charlie?"

"Just got into town, Merrill."

"The girls here say that there's no such thing as an ugly director."

Charlie doesn't crack a smile.

"Or producer. Maybe even screenwriter, Charlie."

"I'll take my chances. You know the one about the blonde from Kansas who was so dumb she slept with the writer."

They nod. It's a classic.

Bob breaks in, "Boys, boys! Let's talk about the movie, okay? You can go out looking for girls later."

"Sure thing, Bob," replies Charlie, looking steadily at Merrill.

"Merrill," says Bob in an insider whisper, "I hear maybe the studio is getting William Holden for the part."

Merrill has become a bit somber. "Not really. He's sort of washed up. Who would want to see him as president, anyway? He's way older than Nixon, even. We were thinking of Jason Robards."

Charlie warms up a bit. "He would be great."

"Yeah, but he was kind of stiff in *The Night They Raided Minsky's*. There wasn't any real box office. He may be kaput."

Charlie bites his tongue again.

"What about using an unknown, making the *concept* the star?" offers Bob.

"I don't know," Merrill says, no life in his eyes.

The man is utterly hollow, decides Charlie. *He must have graduated from Yale and gone to work for his uncle in Hollywood. These guys will fall when the cushy studio system topples.*

Charlie tries to rescue Bob from Merrill's indifference. He realizes that Bob has been hurt by studios and even now is sensitive to their power. "You could take Bob's idea and cast someone who has a Nixon feel to him, the president himself being a kind of Republican, the impostor being a kind of Kennedy Democrat. That way we could highlight two of the stronger presidential figures of the 1960s."

Merrill's cool gray eyes show more light. "Not bad. Wouldn't cost as much. The trailer could make the guy look like a real leader, so that makes Nixon look good. Angled right, we might even get a White House showing. My dad contributed a lot in sixty-eight."

11

"How's my boy doing? Dating any movie stars?"

"Not really, Dad. I was at the dry cleaner's the other day, reading the signed actor photos on the wall. That's about as close as I've come."

A mellow laugh. "Are you sure you can afford the long distance, son?"

"The studio has me on a retainer. And I get paid for every treatment I write."

"What's a treatment?"

"A synopsis of a film. It has to get a green light before they'll spend money on a script. They have me working on two screenplays now—the revisions for *Dick* and a big summer action picture."

"Sounds exciting."

"Not as much as you might think. But I still enjoy the writing."

"Listen, Charlie, you're seventeen years old, you have all this success. Have a little fun, too."

"Thanks, Dad."

"Bye, son."

"Best to Mom. She there?"

"She's off at her sister's."

Charlie hears the tenor strain in his father's voice. More trouble, somehow. He doesn't want to think about that. "Uh, too bad. Bye."

Charlie wonders what is going on in Chicago. His mother doesn't usually speak to him when he calls, unless she answers. Then she is distant, motherly but oddly reserved. Plenty of short sentences, and then she calls his father.

Sunlight and balmy air call to him. Charlie's body cries out for the rich delights of this gaudy world. But Charlie finds himself holding back. The freeways intimidate him, so he walks around his neighborhood in the evenings, finding a menagerie of hair, bangs, bouffants, manes, beehives. These ride above decal eyes, stretch pants, French thrust bras, brush-on eyebrows, elf boots, ballerina slippers, leather jeans, eyelashes like black butterfly wings. Yet he worries about what happened his first evening in Hollywood, the jittering images.

The Sunset Strip has lost its Old Hollywood connections and now pops with rock counterculture. For the price of a few drinks, he hears Led Zeppelin, the Doors, the Byrds, Frank Zappa, and others playing the Whiskey a Go Go, the Troubadour, the Experience.

In the Whiskey he is listening to a shaky rock group rummaging through chords when a lyric penetrates the smoke-layered air: "I'm reincarnated, brother, don't give me no other, / I live again and again, hopin' to find a friend, / Oh, Lord, will this ever end?"

He waits in the side alley afterward for the sad-looking rhythm guitarist who sang. When the lean, stringy-haired kid stumbles out of the stage door, glaring angrily back at someone, Charlie says, "Loved that set! That song about living again, where'd you get that from?"

"Huh, man, what?"

"Living again. Were you in a past life?"

Bleary eyes search the blank sky above the alley. "I maybe was."

"When was it? Are you living through your life again?"

"I was . . . I was a disciple, man."

"Of who? When?"

"Well, *Jesus*, man, that was my life before. I *knew* Judas was going to rat him out."

Charlie steps back. "Uh, so you're in the Bible?"

"I *was*, man. They writ me out, is what happened."

"You woke up on a birthday or something, you were back in your—"

"Hey, you tryin' to work some magic shit on me!" The scrawny figure walks away with jerky strides, guitar case banging the jeans-clad legs.

Charlie doesn't know what to think. Was the guy delusional, or just like himself? Didn't seem like a disciple touched by the holy. He feels a bit of a dolt. He will have to keep that from happening again, he decides.

Dick is not going well in development. Merrill has tried out several directors, some old list, some young Turks. The studio also approached several male leads, but none are interested.

Charlie labors at the script himself, a card from a buddy named Rotsler tacked above the humming typewriter with the mottoes he's trying to follow:

Funny is better than serious.
Short is better than long.
Short and funny is where you stop.

Easier said than done. His fingers want to dance and sing, but that makes for long scenes and slack tension, alas.

Charlie has been summoned to Bob Greenway's office on the lot, just off Santa Monica Boulevard. Bob has used his connections. Action Pictures has converted an old factory complex, equipping it mostly with stuff cannibalized from the Twentieth Century Fox sell-off, after the studio got into trouble earlier in the sixties. An office at the studio is the official sign that Bob is a senior writer, though it isn't much of an office. The cramped window boasts an air conditioner sticking out like a rude humming tongue. The carpet has a sour smell of better days.

Still, Charlie envies Bob his rumbling, wheezing air conditioner. Charlie doesn't like his apartment's stifling heat in the afternoons, especially on the dry "red wind" days. He flees to the beach on hot days, letting his apartment cool down. Sometimes he takes his Mustang up to Mulholland Drive to catch the breeze from the top of the Hollywood Hills, looking down over the dim San Fernando Valley, seeing the choking smog more than the suburban housing. Today he gets to enjoy Bob's frigid air, even though stale cigarettes stink it up. Charlie coughs, watching Bob read his revisions for the act I scenes.

Bob throws the pages at his desk, one typed sheet floating too far, landing on the floor in front of Charlie.

"Damn it, Charlie! Good, but . . . that scene was perfectly good the last rewrite. They're just spinning their wheels waiting for a director."

"Or maybe a decent lead."

"They don't need a name. You were right. A Nixon type would get the box office going. Nobody can figure out the bastard! One day tough with Vietnam, the next day talking about wage and price controls. Where does he come from?"

"And where is he going to end up?"

"Reelected, I'm sure."

"And after that?" Charlie is thinking about Nixon's second term, then Ford, then Bush. Republicans without end. But yes, the domestic side of Richard Nixon's White House, from policy to politics, was kind of malevolent screwball comedy.

"Who gives a flying fuck? We have a movie to get together before this jerk leaves office. It's only funny because he's so weird."

"So what about Merrill? What's he thinking?"

"He's just the errand boy. It's his father I worry about. I don't want him to lose interest in this picture and fire our asses."

"But we're the only writers on the lot who have new ideas."

"Ideas aren't enough, Charlie. Getting a picture made is *way* more than that."

"We're only writers, so we can't do much about this mess, can we, Bob?"

Bob looks at Charlie meaningfully and his irritation turns into something else. "You know, Charlie"—Bob exhales smoke expansively and tilts back in his chair—"I might have an idea about that. I might even get a producer's credit."

Greenway jerks forward, eyes alight. "Let's clean up this script before the end of the day. I have plans for us this evening, at SC."

At dusk Charlie piles into Greenway's Buick and they take Santa Monica Boulevard to the 101, shooting downtown. The traffic flows easily, not like the jams that became famous in the 1980s. The city works these days, for the last time.

Charlie lets the air from the cooling vents stream through his long hair. At times he can scarcely believe he's here, climbing a pyramid Charlie One never dreamed about. Endless fun—the heedless hubba-hubba wongbonga ding-dong rapturama that will ring through decades.

Charlie has now spent a long year of edgy work in LA, his ties to Chicago slipping away. Los Angeles City Hall and the skyscrapers downtown hardly impress Charlie, compared with the soaring pinnacles of Chicago, the city that gave the world the modern skyscraper. But there is news back home. James has signed up for the marines and is in Richmond, Virginia, for his first posting. Charlie went to Virginia Beach once with Elspeth in 1994, a disastrous vacation Elspeth spent deriding the US military as a fountain of war crimes. They had to beat a quick retreat from a biker bar near the beach where she'd had three martinis and let her mouth run off, sloppy drunk. Some Vietnam vets had threatened to cut Elspeth's tongue out and eat it raw. She was monumentally pissed off that he hadn't risen to her defense, but by then he had grown tired of fighting ideological battles with big, smelly men in leather jackets. Political correctness had become very old for him by the 1990s.

Turning onto the 110 Harbor Freeway gets them to the University of Southern California campus in excellent time. Walking through the campus and seeing the smooth white student faces reminds Charlie of the university education he has given up in this second life. He has few regrets. Education is what you have when you've forgotten all the damn details.

He strides through USC but thinks of Illinois. Trudy is studying at the University of Illinois for her bachelor's degree in social science. If Charlie wasn't going to become an attorney, she announced on their last date, then it was up to her to follow in her father's footsteps. She spoke as if law were a high calling. Charlie has complete faith in her future as a lawyer. Elspeth just disappeared. Off in graduate school, he is certain, pursuing her Marxist utopia of command. Why was his first life filled with controlling women?

They stop in front of the USC film school. Bob waves a hand at the fake English architecture. He has always derided film school graduates from USC to Charlie, but now they need one of them. "This Lewis guy we gotta meet, he's done some good small stuff, works out of the film school here. Young flash in the pan. But we can break the studio logjam with him, maybe."

Bob checks his watch, looking out of place with his suit, short hair, narrow black tie. Charlie notices that his own long hair and now full beard are still a bit beyond the groove at USC, where the men's hair is just mid-Beatles longish, their beards tentative. Charlie is now comfortable pretending to be about thirty.

After a few minutes of watching the girls go by, a somewhat older guy looking like a student walks up to them wearing jeans with a blue oxford dress shirt and brown belt, colors mismatched. He's muscular but not tall.

"Mr. Greenway?" he asks uncertainly, eyes shifting.

"You must be Lewis Cantor." The two shake hands. "This is my writing partner, Charlie Moment."

Charlie studies Lewis as they shake—awkward but obviously genuine.

"Know a decent restaurant around here, Lewis, where we could talk?"

"I'm sorry, Mr. Greenway—"

A cracked smile. "Bob."

"Bob, but things haven't been too nice down here for several years."

"I heard. The riots."

"USC has become kind of an oasis."

"Okay. Let's say we meet back at Chasen's in forty minutes."

"Could I ask you to drive me? My VW minivan is up on blocks these days."

The maître d' at Chasen's welcomes Bob and his sawbuck with a well-oiled, papery smile. They have no problem getting a table on a Tuesday night. Charlie has come to understand that this second Hollywood sojourn is a sweet reprise for Greenway. The last time Greenway slinked back to Chicago, and his friend Nono Montini, under a humiliating cloud. Charlie suspects that there was some kind of breakdown.

Lewis seems a bit nervous in Chasen's, but he plunges into his pitch without hesitation. "As I see the script, we need a quick feeling, like a Billy Wilder black-and-white, natural—but funny."

"But not as forced as *Kiss Me, Stupid*," Charlie interjects. He has been doing his homework. To Charlie One it was more like history, so he just needed reminding. Amazing, how the years of details come back, once you've lived them already. Just a hint and you're back there again.

"You saw that picture, Charlie?" Bob smiles expansively, beaming, obviously feeling good, as if he has the power of a real producer.

But Lewis shakes his head. "No, no. I'm thinking of *The Fortune Cookie.*"

Charlie brightens. "What about getting Walter Matthau?"

"Washed up!" pronounces Bob with scorn.

Charlie marvels at the lack of insight that Bob parades like a badge so frequently. *No wonder he's a marginal writer, not much of a novelist, mostly a screenplay mechanics guy,* Charlie thinks.

But Lewis is not be deterred. "No, I think that the studio is right about getting a Nixonian unknown. That way we can play your script right down the middle, between satire and uplift."

Charlie blinks. When did Hollywood start this playing down the middle, having it both ways? He thought it was the 1980s. The films of the 1970s, like *Chinatown,* seemed so serious. Ironic, hip, but serious without being merely solemn. Even *Shampoo,* which would have had a joke every twenty seconds in 1988, hardly had any laughs when it came out in 1975. Will *come out,* Charlie corrects himself.

"Switching an Everyman for the president of the United States— the idea has an unavoidable charm." Lewis is obviously ready to suck up to get this directing job, so fresh and bright out of film school.

Greenway smiles broadly at Lewis, holding an unlit Camel while waving his drink. "We have plenty more, just like that one. Right, Charlie?"

Charlie contents himself with nodding quietly, then fixes Lewis with a cool stare. This guy could be very useful, even if he's short on clout. Lewis *gets* the concept, sees the possibilities.

Lewis's eyes shift uneasily from Greenway to Moment. *Yes*—Lewis is starting to realize where the screenplay's vision came from. *Yes.*

12

Lewis and Charlie are auditioning actors for the Nixon role. Tough work—but it's the big time, Charlie keeps reminding himself. *Gotta pay your dues.* Besides, he doesn't know how much longer this particular life is going to last, so he isn't holding anything back.

Action Pictures has come through with production money and even some help from the casting department. From the expanded list of hopefuls Charlie dimly recognized a few and managed to get them into the first batch of auditions. Bob and Lewis have spent some time fending off attempts from vice presidents trying to insert their girlfriends and drug buddies. Lewis and Charlie are learning the slippery art of seeming to do as the VPs say, yet keeping the movie headed along their own trajectory.

Bob gave up earlier in the day, saying he had to meet with Merrill. Charlie was happy to send him off to beg for more production funds from the East Coast weasel. He would rather learn about the audition process.

The actor before Lewis and Charlie is thirty-six, a nervous, flinty Nixon look-alike with the heavy jowls and receding hairline required for the part, as far as Charlie is concerned. Charlie checks the name from the portfolio Xerox: Frank Stanton. Day job: Chevrolet salesman in Encino. *Good,* thinks Charlie, *this is a man who can lie with ease.* There is also something genuinely grasping about him, a shifty look in his eyes. Hard to fake.

"You've done some theater," says Lewis neutrally.

Stanton replies in a solid Nixon imitation, showing that he's a method-actor type. "*Death of a Salesman, Picnic,* you know. The usual stuff. I have the reviews in my portfolio."

"Your movie experience—"

"Just a few one-line roles."

"—minor, at best."

Charlie marvels at the low-grade sadism that Lewis uses to grill Stanton. He has seen friendlier arrests of vagrants on Hollywood Boulevard.

"Pick up the script and open to page forty-three. Charlie, you lead off with the Tellinger line."

"Now, Mr. President," says Charlie from the script, "we aren't supposed to nuke Ann Arbor just because Michigan has beaten the Trojans."

Stanton shakes his wattles and speaks in a resonant, almost rich, voice. "Damn it, Tellinger! Can't I have a little *fun* as president?"

"Sell me the line, Frank," says Lewis. "Sell it."

Stanton looks up at Lewis nervously, then focuses harder on the script, as if the Courier font is going to reveal more if it is scrutinized with greater care. Charlie notices sweat forming on the man's brow. *Perfect Nixon sweat,* Charlie thinks. *This guy is the best creep all day.* Charlie decides to cast him for the part, whatever Lewis thinks.

"Damn it, Tellinger! Can't I have a little fun as president?" The last syllable hangs in the air for three long beats while Charlie looks at Lewis, his big smile hidden from Stanton by his long hair and beard. Lewis looks back at Charlie, poker faced.

"Thank you, Mr. Stanton. Our secretary has your phone number."

Stanton gets up slowly. "I would like to thank you for this

opportunity, Mr. Cantor." Still in character, he nods awkwardly at Charlie and leaves the office.

"I love this guy!" says Charlie.

"No, we can't use him."

"But he's so real! He has that Nixon realpolitik feeling."

"Realpolitik?"

Charlie feels exposed, showing too much education. "I mean, you know, that feeling that the guy would do anything to keep the world under his control."

"You're right, Charlie, he fits the part. But we still can't use him."

"*Because* . . ." Charlie scowls.

"Because the audience won't like him. They aren't going to spend ninety-two minutes with a guy they don't like. He has to be creepy *and* appealing at the same time."

"Like Matthau."

"Exactly, except Matthau's too expensive and he's washed up."

Charlie wonders how an actor could be expensive, be washed up, have an Academy Award on his mantel . . . and be a future host of the Academy Awards.

"You mean we need a convincing creep that Middle America can love," queries Charlie, "just like Nixon?" The very idea tastes foul to him.

"Exactly. And I think I know where to find one."

Among the many Hollywood Hills parties, the most useful to Charlie have more producers than directors, more directors than actors, and more actors than writers. So he goes to those when invited. He avoids other screenwriters, who always want inside dope on what producer is looking for a hot new script.

Mostly, Charlie just watches. The parties are short on listeners, so he supplies a patient ear and learns more than with his mouth open. He learns to make producers see specific scenes when pitching a project. Assembling a film is really about shooting scenes, some-times months or even years apart, then squeezing them against one another in the final film. Each must frame the other, the transitions in mood accomplished in collaboration between the moment of shooting and the moment of truth in the cutting room.

Lewis got him invited to this particular party and now is working the crowd around the swimming pool. Charlie stands at the edge, silent.

"I think of myself as a writer, really," a director says to him, well into a second bottle of Barolo, a great Tuscan red. He seems unaware that this is a cliché.

"So do I," Charlie says, but the director doesn't pick up on his irony and turns away.

Charlie glances sideways and sees another playing the listener role, nodding at the right places, saying little. The man wears a well-pressed double-breasted suit that makes him look like a shoebox standing on end. To Charlie, there is something midwestern about the suit and face. He works his way around to the guy, introduces himself, and gets back, "I'm Rog Ebert. My claim to infamy is I cowrote the screenplay for the Russ Meyer film *Beyond the Valley of the Dolls.*"

"Somehow missed it," Charlie says, intrigued to be talking to a man who had so much power over the movie business once he started to review films on television. At least in his last life.

Ebert grins. "Our next title is *Beneath the Valley of the Ultravixens,* just to show I can go lower."

Charlie laughs. He recalls this dog of a film will take a decade to do, it stinks so much. He likes the utterly non-Hollywood glee in the confessions. "Something tells me you're not here to build a career."

"Nope, I'm actually a film reviewer for a Chicago paper." He gives a shrug, as though this is nothing. Already a tad too overweight, he probably gets ignored by movie types, Charlie figures. But his eyes are quick and shrewd.

"Ah!" Charlie does the I'm-from-Illinois-too number, trading horror stories about Midwesterners in Hollywood, and works Ebert around to how he reviews movies. Apparently, Ebert is too new on the scene to have producers buzzing around him, hoping for a favorable review. "So . . . what's your reviewing method?"

Ebert says, "Relative, not absolute. I estimate a movie's prospective audience, with at least some consideration of its value as a whole." He stops, seems to realize the phrase is wrong, and adds, "But I want to get away from the term-paper pomposity that I learned at college."

"All that sapheaded objectivity?"

"Right, take *The Sound of Music*. I said it should've been called *The Sound of Money*."

Charlie laughs and Ebert says, deadpan, "It does that crucial thing, right? To play on an abiding human desire to be honestly manipulated and charmingly ripped off."

"You're funny."

"My deep fanzine insight," he says, rolling his eyes. "I come out of science fiction fandom."

"Which means?"

Again deadpan, Ebert says, "It's hard to explain puns to kleptomaniacs because they always take things literally."

Charlie laughs, liking the nonlinear style. "Okay, I won't try to compete. What are your fave films lately?"

Without pause Ebert rattles off, "1967: *Bonnie and Clyde*. 1968: *The Battle of Algiers*. 1969: *Z*. Now: *Five Easy Pieces*—"

"Not *2001*?"

"I'm an SF fan, sure, but—hey, Action Pictures could do some SF films! It's a ripe time for that. *2001* cleared the way."

"Um, maybe. I've read a lot of it, could try something. And I wish I could get the Chicago papers here."

"I'll send you my reviews. People keep asking for them; there must be some kind of national market. But say—do try making SF movies!

Drop me a note about the screening of your next movie," Ebert says, handing him a business card. "Expand minds!"

Charlie realizes Ebert knows much more than he lets on about how things work out here. And that Illinois guys stick together.

The strip club's better days are long gone. Charlie wonders why Lewis has brought him here. Not only is the wallpaper peeling, the stained drinks menu is barely legible in the grimy light. Charlie can only make out that the prices are about five times the going rate at the regular bars and music clubs on Sunset Boulevard. He knows that the place will soon close as the music industry takes over every available nook in this part of town. The band is long haired and semi-hip. A scritch-scratch guitar comes in on the backbeat, along with paired lines of funky melodics sidling in, carrying the bass line, popping up bright in the main driving song. *Bump-de-bump.*

In the meantime, Charlie checks out the action on the small stage. Unfortunately for his young hormones, the stripper seems like an antique with stringy blond hair, sagging breasts and stomach. *Probably a thirtysomething junkie, old beyond her years,* he thinks.

He turns to watch Lewis scan the room. Lewis has no interest in the decaying flesh onstage. Charlie turns back to the stage. The older blonde is gone.

A shapeless middle-aged man has taken the stage. He has a receding hairline and jowls, his smile too eager.

"How did you like that, ladies and gentlemen? The last time I saw action like that, she was my wet nurse." The drummer raps out a snare-drum roll and a rim shot. A bald guy barks out one sharp laugh.

"Anyway, folks. Did you drive here today? Did you check out the traffic? I saw a guy selling used cars parked on the 5 freeway, with their drivers still in them!" A few beats on a bass drum. A few more laughs. Not many.

Charlie leans over to Lewis. "Does he get any better than this?"

"Not really. But look at him. You want him to do better, to be funnier than he actually is. He sucks in your sympathy."

Charlie inspects the comic with greater interest. There is something about the guy's body language that is both greasy and sympathetic. Have him play stiff for the real president and then loose for the impersonator. Yeah, it could work.

"What's his name?"

"Shecky Brown."

"We'll have to change it."

"I don't think it's his real name anyway."

13 Shecky is popping sweat, flustered by the makeup girl adjusting the thickness of powder on his cheekbone. He sits behind an enormous desk in a mock-up of the White House's Oval Office, or at least half of it. The young redhead leans over him, her full chest provocatively close to Shecky's face.

"Listen, babe, can't you just put your lips together and blow it off me?"

The crew laughs, not for the first time. The makeup girl's face shows only a trace of a frown. She's used to actors, especially the ones who think they're funny.

"Okay, Shecky," calls Lewis from his high director's chair, "settle down. This isn't burlesque anymore."

"Sure, Lewis. I gotcha." The man has an eagerness to please that sucks Charlie in. Charlie wonders if this is part of the appeal of Richard Nixon himself, a man that Charlie always instinctively loathed, never more so than when he was the Grand Old Man of the GOP, during the Ford and Bush presidencies.

"Now, Shecky, this is where the Speaker of the House is going to call you about the meeting of the Appropriations Committee. You don't know what appropriations are, right?"

"I sure don't, Lewis." The man's sincerity and comic timing cause another ripple of mirth among the crew. Charlie sees that Shecky indeed has no idea what Lewis is talking about. *Perfect*, he thinks.

"All right, we don't have a voice track for you to follow, so I'll say the lines that we'll edit in from the Speaker's side of the conversation."

"Sure, Lewis. Whatever." Shecky is obviously confused.

"I'll be your prompt, okay?"

"Sure, sure."

"Clapper!"

The man with the clapper lunges toward the camera. "*Dick*, scene forty-seven, take one!" *Crack*—the clapper comes down, audiotape visibly spooling. Charlie marvels at how audiotape and film were separately synchronized in the glory days of film. It strikes him as bizarrely crude.

The sound effects man makes a telephone ring as Shecky looks at five phones on his huge desk, eyes bulging. He picks up one, listens while the ringing continues, picks up another, still more ringing. On his third try the ringing stops.

"Hello, this is the president." His jowls break out into a fatuous, self-satisfied grin. "The president of these United States of America!"

Lewis reads from the script, flat, without finesse. "Dick! Speaker Crumhollow here. We have your bill stuck in Appropriations. Is there any way we could make a deal?"

"My bill, my bill? What does it come to?"

"Thirty-six million," reads Lewis.

"That must have been a lot of steak dinners."

"Well, the lobbyists paid for them."

"So why do we have to pay for them again now?"

"Cut!"

Lewis looks around uneasily. The crew stops filming and relaxes. "Charlie, let's talk."

Lewis stands up on the footrest of his director's chair, the chair unnaturally pyramidal behind the cameraman, and climbs down using the armrest as a grip. Charlie wonders if Lewis has a bit of Napoléon in him, although he knows that Napoléon's height issue was a piece of Austrian propaganda. They talk away from the crew, Shecky looking at them anxiously.

Lewis frowns. "Charlie, do you think that the lobbyist-steak-dinner joke is going to be picked up here?"

"Some people will get it. The rest will have the sense that Shecky doesn't know what he's talking about, even if they are a bit confused about what the Appropriations Committee does."

"So then they will sort of share in Shecky's confusion, right?"

"Exactly."

"Okay, I think we can do this scene on those two levels."

Charlie smiles with as much warmth as he can project through his long hair and beard. "Sure you can."

Charlie and Bob Greenway are munching on sandwiches in Bob's air-conditioned office, bottles of Pepsi on the desk.

Bob talks with his mouth full. "Now's the time to sell the studio on two more projects. That way if they pass on one, we'll still have the other. One will be science fiction."

"Good plan, Bob. There's momentum from Kubrick's 2001 we can ride on. Even after two years."

Charlie is surprised that the studio system just plain doesn't get the technical accuracy and hard-edged grandeur of 2001. Their idea of a near imitation will be *Silent Running*, a maudlin, sentimental, forgettable pic, which hinges upon nobody's realizing that a space-borne greenhouse would get less sunlight as it cruised out to Saturn. Charlie could field that script idea himself, but even thinking about doing it makes him shudder. Ugh.

Certainly, Hollywood isn't ready for the dislocations of Philip K. Dick that will gain momentum in the 1980s and '90s. Charlie found out from Ebert that Dick lives in a small apartment in drab Santa Ana and doesn't wear sunglasses indoors. Not the Hollywood type at all.

"And this time I want a guarantee on my producer's credit. Full-card credit. I still don't know if they're going to stiff me on *Dick*, even after I lined up the director and the lead."

Charlie admits to himself that Bob got the ball rolling by recruiting Lewis, who came over with the studio as a hot new-idea director. Still, he feels slighted that Bob hasn't tried to get him a producer's credit also. Not even associate producer, a standard gimme that means nothing. This leads him to think about other inequities in their relationship.

"You know, I could use some air-conditioning, Bob."

"Your apartment too hot, kid?"

Charlie hates that Bob knows he is still only twenty. He likes to think of himself as "about thirty," especially since he has actually slogged through fifty years. He feels like some odd synthesis of both.

"That's not it. I was thinking of getting an office here on the lot."

"Well, this is our office, isn't it?"

"Then where's my desk?"

"There isn't room for another desk in here." Bob shrugs.

Charlie realizes that there is no arguing with Bob. He will have to wait for his situation to improve. There, Lewis will come in handy. They are headed into a whole new age for movies, the Second Golden Age, as it will be known. Bob doesn't understand that directors aren't going to be studio flunkies in the 1970s.

Bob takes Charlie to lunch at the studio café with a seasoned, swarthy scriptwriter sporting many broken blood vessels in his large nose. This is the one Charlie learns to call the Wise Hack, whose favorite line is "Shit has its own integrity. It has to be true to itself." The Wise

Hack knows that a certain exuberant badness often leads to passing popularity and absolutely cannot be faked. "Great pop stuff has to be written by second- or third-raters who utterly believe in the importance of what they're doing," the weathered man says over a pastrami sandwich.

So certain eternal truths emerge. Children in jeopardy hold audiences, endangered pets, too, and women stalkers—all rivet the eyes. The more gunshots the better, but not much blood—you want the kid audience too. Scenes of men fondling their guns, though good, should be kept to a few—the critics will get what you mean, but not the audience. Fistfights are always good, but write in some acrobatics to make it look original—the actors like those because they get credit for the big, physical hero work done by their stunt doubles. Happy endings? Is there some other kind?

So instead Charlie takes a new trajectory, the flip side of the Wise Hack's. Sure, have a clear plot. Respect and bow to the three-act truth. But use wit with a dash of undercutting irony, mix action with mood scenes, stay hip to new counterculture signals. A touch of bittersweet in the happy ending is better than schmaltz. Most important, do fresh things. Keep audiences guessing. Slip them some satire when they least expect it. Keep the jaded gatekeepers, those lined faces scowling in pitch sessions, guessing how scenes will turn. Show them the arc, then surprise them with jump cuts and reverse twists. That is the coming future of the next Golden Age. His future. Go cool.

Finally the afternoon heat in Charlie's apartment is too much. He zooms over to the studio and storms into Merrill's office suite, past the obligatory, elegant, high-cheekboned secretary, interrupting Lewis talking to Merrill.

"Merrill, I need an office, see—or my agent will petition about contract violations. I'm supposed to have a goddamn office."

Merrill looks delighted to have an opportunity to take Charlie down some. "But you have an office with Bob."

"You know that's bullshit, Merrill. Bob doesn't share it with me."

"That's between the two of you, I'm afraid, Charlie." Merrill's tone is as slippery as beef tallow.

"Merrill, I talk with Charlie every day on the set," Lewis comes in, steel smooth. "It would be a lot more convenient for everybody if he worked here regular hours." Merrill blinks, surprised, but his lips purse, calculating. Charlie watches the ideas shift across his face. Merrill sees that Charlie and Lewis are now allies, a fact lost on him before. He recalculates the balance of power, sees that Charlie's days as Bob's protégé are over.

"Very well, Charlie. You know I like you. You've really brought a young perspective to the studio. I'll get you that office. Would you like a secretary, too?"

Having an office gives Charlie more status. He meets people in the studio café and soon enough is pitching his new idea to a movie producer over lunch. Following Rog Ebert's urging, he's invented a space drama.

"Sharp idea, Charlie," the heavyset studio guy says, sipping coffee. "Everything seems set. That female lead character is particularly right, a match of motivation with the plot."

Charlie looks at the sidekick producer, a woman in her thirties, wanting her reaction. She leans across the table and says, "She's just about right, now. Only . . . how about halfway through, the male lead tears off her face and—she's a robot!"

Charlie looks around the studio eatery. At murals depicting famous scenes from old movies, at the current crop of tanned stars in shades dining on their slimming salads in their casual finery . . . at the sweeping view of little purple dots that dance before his eyes because he has neglected breathing after that last remark. "Robot . . . ?"

"Just to keep them guessing," the woman adds helpfully. "I want to really suck the juice out of this moment."

"But that makes no sense in this movie."

"It's science fiction, though—"

"So it doesn't have to make sense," Charlie finishes for her.

14

The premiere of *Dick* is at one of the old Westwood cinemas. The creaky barn has seen better days and the tatty curtains give off a moldy flavor. But Charlie has never been photographed on a red carpet before—even a scrungy used one. Charlie doesn't merit the multiple shots that the film's stars receive—Sherwood Wrightman, born Shecky Brown, and Sally Kirkland as the president's wife. They preen and strut, courting the press. It strikes Charlie that Hollywood isn't a lot different from high school. There is always a prom queen and a class president, always an audience of geeks and dorks. And the show must go on, good or lousy.

Charlie's parents are goggle eyed by the Hollywood glitz laid out even for such a minor film. Charlie has already seen the film in almost final form, sitting next to a tense Lewis, who would cross his legs more often in scenes that were a bit awkward. Charlie felt too much pride of authorship to be critical of the finished product, at least while watching it alone with Lewis.

Charlie likes how the lack of background music, imposed by a budget crunch in postproduction, gives the film's humor an ironic hue. He decides to use that method on more-solemn work in future, too.

When the movie ends, there is a respectable round of applause, and Lewis takes a bow along with Shecky and Sally. Even Merrill gets a bow and a round of applause. Of course, Charlie will have an edge on them now. It was his idea, and some people know. The right people too.

The review in the Friday *Los Angeles Times* is generally positive. The directing is "fresh," and Shecky is described as "a natural." Sally Kirkland gets great press. Reading the paper in his new office, Charlie is unsurprised that the script is never mentioned in the review, as if the movie grew out of an organic collaboration between actors and director, a mushroom in a basement. The invisible screenwriter.

He walks down the balcony to Bob's office. Bob's secretary gives Charlie one of her warning expressions, but Charlie is not to be stopped on this day.

Bob doesn't look up before starting in on his tirade. "The fuckers! I give them a hit movie—"

"We haven't seen any box office numbers, Bob."

"—director and star, both, and I don't get a full producer's credit."

"Maybe next time?" Hoping for a single-card credit at this stage of either of their careers is like asking for Mars on a plate.

"Goddamn right. And I want a bigger office now too."

Charlie heaves a long sigh, but he can tell that Bob doesn't notice. Clueless. He understands how Bob's last shot at Hollywood failed, and knows that nothing has really changed—except that Charlie's here with him now.

The numbers are indeed good. Though the slow rollout of the picture is frustrating for Charlie, he has come to understand that the days of the massive opening weekend are still mostly in the future. Word of mouth and published reviews are more important in the 1970s—and theirs are good. The satire commingled with respect allows the press to play the film any way it likes. For *New Republic*, the movie "reveals the festering sore that is the Nixon White House." In *National Review*, the only publication that discusses the screenplay thoughtfully, the movie is "a welcome attempt to humanize the much-maligned, too-often-underestimated Nixon administration." The *New York Times* seems puzzled but concludes with a positive recommendation. It will be a while longer before people see that New York isn't the cultural be-all anymore. *Time* equivocates but quotes an unnamed White House source as saying that the president got a laugh out of it. Charlie wonders if Nixon has even seen it. But then Merrill tells him that the White House was sent its own print—and hasn't returned it. Maybe somebody there watched it.

Charlie and Merrill have been getting along better, now that *Dick* is a success, and Merrill wants another high-concept picture out of Charlie and Bob, with Lewis directing again. Lewis is edgy, but Charlie can tell that Lewis wants to work with him again. They have a generational rapport that leaves Bob and Merrill on the outside. They get each other's allusions to dope and Hendrix and sex, and they get the way they make those allusions, not smarmy or lecherous, but slightly ironic, a bit obscure. Just, well, cool. But then, it's easy for Charlie to be cool when he knows what's coming next.

Still, Charlie is surprised by the commercial success of *Dick*. He was ahead of the wave, and it paid. He's eager to take advantage of the momentum, so he decides to continue with a father-son identity-swap screenplay. Rather science fictional, but present time; his attempt to pitch outright SF has soured him. Plus, he has a desire to write about the feeling of finding yourself in a much younger body for no apparent reason. It's terrain that he wants to push out of his head into the external world. He wants to make some sense of what has happened to him. Writing as therapy.

He pitches the identity-switch idea in Bob's new "producer" office. Bob has been mollified by an official memo declaring that he is now a producer-writer. It's all about Bob getting back for his humiliation in the 1950s. Charlie wonders how much longer his career is going to be tied to Bob's sense of entitlement and injury. This day doesn't help.

"Charlie, your idea is just pathetic! Who's interested in this young-old thing? Kids are kids. Adults are adults. Ne'er the twain shall meet, and let's keep it that way."

"I tell you, Bob, there could be a lot of jokes in this picture. And some good uplift."

"Uplift!" Bob's snort goes a little too far and he has to blow his nose. Charlie waits patiently, feeling he has been waiting between Bob's expostulations for too long.

Bob is soon ready to orate again. "What Hollywood needs is a return to the gritty realism it had before television made people all soppy. *The Postman Always Rings Twice. Double Indemnity.*"

"*Chinatown.*"

"What?" Bob looks mystified.

Startled, Charlie covers up. "Uh, I was thinking of going Chinese for lunch."

"Sure, kid." Bob's tone becomes magnanimous. "We can let you and Lewis work on your identity thing, as a side project. You help me with an idea I've been working on—*Bitch on Wheels*. Who knows, maybe both pictures will work."

"The studio will let you use 'bitch' in the title?"

"Times are a-changin', my boy. They never would have let a long-haired kid like you on the lot before either."

"What about Fonda and Hopper?"

"See what I mean? They shot *Easy Rider* on a long road trip away from here. I want to do an updated noir, with the bored young wife of a rich older man, his young nephew, the young couple spending a lot of time together. They decide they have to kill the old guy. But you know what—"

"The old guy tricks the younger man, frames him for murdering his wife, the younger man is fried, while the older man ends up alone and wiser at the end."

Bob's mouth is slack. "Did you look at my treatment?"

He didn't have to. "It's a deal, Bob. I'll cowrite with you if you'll put in a word with Merrill for my own switcher screenplay."

It's going too fast for Bob. "Uh, I'll cowrite your film with you if you like."

Charlie can tell that Bob is just being polite to stall, which suits Charlie fine. "No, you've taken me a long way, but I can't lean on you forever, Bob. If I need any help, I can probably get it from Lewis. He learned a lot at SC."

Confused, Bob starts to search through the piles of paper on his desk. He needs to keep distance from such an obvious loser idea. "Let me give you the treatment for *Bitch*."

But Charlie is already backing out of the office. "Just have Gladys bring a Xerox to me, okay?"

Bob looks up, blinking at this new world. "Sure thing, kid."

A few weeks later Charlie has recovered from his first attempt to push a science-fictional idea, so after lunch he finds himself talking to a story editor. Rog Ebert's enthusiasm may have a point— Hollywood is wide open to fresh ideas now. Charlie has written a five-page approach about discovering life on Mars, portraying how it would really be, hard and gritty and unforgiving. A story editor likes this "a whole lot," a "breakthrough concept"—but she has her own creative input too.

"I want a magic moment right here, at the end of the first hour," she says.

"Magic?" Charlie asks guardedly.

"Something to bring out the wonder of Mars, yeah."

"Like . . ."

"See, when the astronaut is inside this cave—"

"Thermal vent. From an old volcano—"

"Okay, okay, vent it is. In this vent, he's trapped, right?"

"Well, not actually; the vent is where he discovers this lichen—"

"So he's banged up and he thinks he's going to die and he thinks, 'What the hell.'"

"What the hell."

"Right, you get it. He says what the hell, he might as well take his helmet off."

"Helmet. Off."

"Right, you got it. Big moment. Cracks the seal. He smiles and takes a big breath and says, 'Oxygen! There's oxygen here. Let's take off these helmets!' Whaddaya think?"

"I liked the robot with a mask better."

Charlie takes the afternoon off to cool down. He goes west up Sunset to the UCLA bookstore to find something to read, something to make sense of his life. While he tries not to think about his flickering moments, they are always there as a fear around the periphery of his new life. He wants to see some words that will make sense of what happened. Maybe even settle for lies from traditional religions, if only they will work to quell his anxiety.

While he is looking through the textbooks on comparative religion, he notices a leggy blonde eyeing him farther down the stacks of the textbook section. He wanders in her direction, carrying one book on Hinduism and another on Hinayana Buddhism.

As he gets closer, he notices that she has a book on the films of the fifties. "You in film school?" he asks.

She smiles sweetly but not quite shyly. "Uh-huh. Are you taking comparative religion?" Her face is breathtaking, fine features set off with blue eyes.

"No, I'm not a student here."

"Do you teach?"

Charlie realizes that he does in fact look "about thirty." Near this girl's blond youth, it makes him feel awkward. "No, not at all. I'm a screenwriter, actually." Using the word "screenwriter" also makes him feel uneasy, but he has no taste for being a professor again, not even in another person's misapprehension.

"Have any scripts I could look at?"

She probably assumes I'm a waiter or a store clerk writing on spec, Charlie thinks. *Maybe it's the T-shirt and jeans, or all the hair. She has me figured for a loser.* The thought irritates.

"Did you see *Dick?*"

"That piece of Republican propaganda? No way." Her lips curl with disdain.

"I wrote it. Well, with Bob Greenway."

She blushes and looks down, evidently fumbling for words. "Uh . . . I'm sorry. I—I thought you were more of an experimental-movie type."

Charlie laughs gently, his tone forgiving. "We can't all be Fellini. You can apologize for your good taste over a coffee, okay?"

"All right." She shows some relief, and her broad white smile makes his heart beat a bit faster.

After spending the afternoon with Michelle, especially after her lips gently touch his when they say good-bye, Charlie finds himself energized. He gets into his Mustang and pops in a new Stones tape. He now prefers the naked lightbulb swinging by a black cord of the Rolling Stones to the lit-up rotating chandelier of the Beatles. He feels that the Stones will keep the flickering multiverse away. And with Michelle, maybe all of this is all that is real.

Charlie savors the sharp, slanting light rippling over him as he zooms through backstreet traffic, but he is plotting as he drives. He thinks back to the Mars pitch to the story editor. Maybe he should have said, *Sure, we can take the helmet off. When can the studio cut a check?*

Downshifting and popping the clutch to get that lion roar, he heads up the Hollywood Hills to the new home. He bought it outright for cash, paying a tiny fraction of what it will be worth in the 1990s. It's got a Jet Propulsion Lab disregard for mere gravity, all angles and slanting beams hanging the wedge-shaped thing out over dry air. As he makes the jackknife turns with lots of tire howl, he catches glimpses of it hanging above—hiding behind eucalypts, as if waiting to spring out, all elbows, on passers-by.

He parks in the drive and hums "You Can't Always Get What You Want" as he passes beneath the trumpet vine with its sweet, downward-dipping yellow flowers swarming over the roof's lip. Or maybe now he can.

Charlie is working long and hard at the studio and this night has lingered to get some script points nailed solid. The studio grounds lie deserted, which to Charlie makes them echo with the glamorous luster of Old Hollywood. Ghosts of the great seem to whisper in the back alleys, their shadows flickering just at the edge of vision.

He fits his key into his car and suddenly the whispers and shadows condense. An arm yanks him around, pinning his hands. A gloved hand claps over his mouth. Someone behind him ties his wrists.

He can't see who they are in the gloom. They lift his feet off the ground. A man—Charlie can smell the sweat—lifts him by his shoulders. Charlie wriggles. Not a word spoken. Until—

"Hey! Whozzat?"

It's the voice of Ernie, the night guard.

Charlie thumps down hard on asphalt. He watches two figures run away into the dark, followed by a flashlight beam. One short and stocky, the other shorter and small.

A shot cracks the night. Charlie rolls over and sees Ernie sighting along his .38 revolver.

"Nah!" Ernie spits out. He lowers his aim.

Two more shots. Charlie hears two yells, one high pitched.

"Winged 'em!" Ernie yelps, happy.

Charlie gasps, "My hands!"

Ernie bends and unties his bonds. "You hurt?"

His shoulder aches, but Charlie says, "Nah. They didn't have time to do much to me."

"Damn funny. Usually it's the stars they go after."

Charlie gets up, a little wobbly. "Nobody kidnaps writers."

Ernie smiles. "You got it. Get a look at 'em?"

"No. Can't figure why they'd want me."

Ernie marches him around to the guard office, and he alerts the others on watch. One of them has already found an unlocked gate at the back. "They're gone by now, no question. Out the way they came—only a block from your car."

Ernie brushes off Charlie's clothes and walks him back to his car. Charlie has no idea what the hell that was about.

15

Charlie is noticing competition from other upstarts. A lot of them work night-shift jobs as waiters and worse, but they churn out scripts for anyone at Action Pictures who will listen. Merrill has them sit through endless script workshops run by Greenway—who charges for his wisdom and secondhand smoke. Charlie now works alone and delivers his finished scripts to Merrill, Lewis, and Bob. Much better to spend time imagining scenes, dialogue, odd defining moments for the camera's eye, instead of arguing with Bob.

Action Pictures is accepting him as their bankable young writer. Small steps toward the new cinema are adding up into his own style. With a little push from the studio, an *LA Times* puff piece says he has "bold curiosity for the fresh, brash risk-taking, raw ingenuity." He mails a copy of it back home to Chicago. His father's voice booms with pride on the phone. But no word from his mother.

Good start, getting some good ink—but what next? He could work his screenplays, sure, but there might be better ways to play this. Carefully he tries to excavate everything he can from Charlie One's movie memories. It was a great time for film during his first life, as the sixties became the seventies. The Cassavetes guy was making avant-garde movies with handheld cameras, shooting grainy black-and-whites with pocket change. Movies like *The Trip*, he recalls, shot by the low-rent Roger Corman, caught the wave of druggie culture. Charlie remembers—what odd details come up!—that *The Trip* highlighted an actor who wrote his own script, Jack Nicholson, whom he has met in passing. Nicholson is well on his way to building his reputation as Hollywood Hills' party boy.

The major players to be, guys like Spielberg, started back in the 1960s but didn't catch on until the early 1970s. Spielberg's TV movie *Duel* was about an ordinary guy pursued by a crazed driver of an eighteen-wheeler across a rugged western landscape. Charlie remembers it well, with all the hallmarks that Spielberg made a cottage industry—deft cutting, shots of boots as the characters walk into cheap diners, gas stations at night, brooding highway landscapes. In this, Spielberg paralleled Stephen King, with their shared taste for small scenes with character flags that open out the narrative flow. A boy calling his lost dog seconds before a shark attack, a passing glance at the camera, self-involved kids calling one another names while danger approaches.

So where is Spielberg? Charlie decides to look.

He finds the man quick enough, because Hollywood is a self-centered one-industry village. They agree to meet in a Westwood café, a mediocre Greek place. Spielberg is waiting at a small table al fresco—cap, shades, long hair, sharp eyes. Charlie is in shades and long hair himself, with his fuller beard complementing his mustache.

"Nice to meet you, Mr. Moment."

"Charlie, please."

They order drinks. Charlie is never asked for ID. His body language says at least thirty.

"I liked *Dick*," Spielberg offers.

"Thank you. I enjoyed *Amblin'*." Though actually he hadn't.

Spielberg tries to hide his surprise that a mainstream screenwriter, even one with the cool-hippie look of Charlie Moment, has seen his very minor early effort. Charlie of course saw it in his last life, when the smallest item from the Spielberg oeuvre was cherished by film cognoscenti. Charlie hopes to impress Spielberg, but instead his comment has disconcerted the man.

After that the conversation doesn't go very well. They spend some minutes on cagey back-and-forth about possible movie projects, but Charlie realizes that Spielberg has his guard up, as if Charlie is competition for the Crown Prince of Hollywood title that Spielberg will soon win. Or did, last life. Charlie is impressed with Spielberg but knows that this isn't their moment. Not yet.

Only on the drive home does he recall that Richard Matheson wrote the story and screenplay for Spielberg's first hit, *Duel*. They're probably wrapping on that TV movie right now. With Matheson, Spielberg doesn't need a writer. Not yet.

Charlie phones Michelle to go see the Truffaut at UCLA, *Shoot the Piano Player*. She is a little stiff when they meet again, but he plies her with some measured wit about Truffaut and New Wave French cinema, and he soon has her animated again. He barely notices the film, which he saw more than once on both IFC and video. *Who would care about French film if they had such a woman next to them, stroking their arm, squeezing their thigh?* Charlie thinks.

Walking her back to her room is like ascending a staircase for Charlie. He has feelings for Michelle he can't remember from his last life, and the newness of it catches him off guard. When they get to her room, he is surprised by himself. His body isn't ready to go. He seems to want something else.

But Michelle just matter-of-factly takes her clothes off and gets into bed. A bit awkwardly, Charlie does the same.

Between the light-yellow sheets, she slides toward him. He manages to position himself so that only their chests touch.

"I want to get to know you better."

Michelle looks at him quizzically. "Like what?"

"Like what you really want from life."

They talk for some minutes, and then hours, kissing from time to time. It isn't until 1:00 a.m. that Charlie's body demands its tithe. Charlie is gentle with the girl, as if he doesn't want to break off the parts of a china figurine. But near the end she grabs him forcibly, pulling him down on her repeatedly with the vigor required to make both of them come.

Breathing heavily afterward, she says, "At last! I've wanted to do that for days."

He lets the talk of the evening glide over him as he drives home. He does not know how to surf these waves of introspection that snatch him up and plunge him into frothy emotional surf. And then there are his flickering moments, when this world seems to unspool from a hidden film projector. He shudders against the Mustang's bucket seat, remembering those. What would explain them? Could he be epileptic?

Charlie pushes that thought away by wondering how much trouble he has found for himself with Michelle. Dark clouds with purple bellies, boiling beneath the cottony white topping of fresh love, come lumbering over his horizon.

Charlie phones Spielberg, who is shooting a commercial in Laguna Beach. Their conversation goes better this time. Spielberg needs start-up money to go up the ladder from USC. Advertisements shoot fast, pay well. They arrange to meet again.

Charlie goes down to Laguna the next day, and within half an hour the Spielberg gang has him in a pickup basketball game on the half-courts at Main Beach. On the small courts you run less and maneuver more.

Charlie marvels at the energy of his young body; he hasn't pushed it so hard before. Perhaps the freight of middle-aged caution slowed him down, made him forget about the surging joys of athletics.

But not on this vibrant sunlit day in Laguna. He makes dunks— double pumps, spin shots, classic alley-oops. Shouts of glory, high fives, backslapping, grins and glowers. Charlie keeps up but isn't there to shine. It is enough to pour himself into the game. Everybody there has the moves. Trick dribbles, footwork fakes, the collapsing full-court press. The fine art of the slap steal, the squeeze, the trap. And the one-on-one sparring—blocking, getting in the other guy's face, hitting the outlet man on the fast break, maxing your free throws. Charlie's body sings.

They finally break for beers. This time Charlie and Spielberg talk about everything but movies, grinning, getting into the beach groove. Spielberg keeps his baseball cap on, the emblem that will become a cliché for striving comers. They exchange wry comments, Charlie hanging back and letting the guy come to him.

But Spielberg has a tight little entourage around him, and Charlie can't seem to take the right tack with them. They are TV people, caught up in hammering out shows for Rod Serling's *Night Gallery*, *Marcus Welby, M.D.*, and a new series getting started, about a detective named Columbo. Mass production work, not Charlie's kind of thing at all. Spielberg will make it big in movies, but that comes later. Now he's in TV land. Maybe the work on *Duel* is downstream; Charlie doesn't ask.

They walk down the beach a bit and hit the surf in their cutoffs. The brassy, salt-air day is fine, never mind career ambitions. Charlie thinks of *Jaws*, a big hit years away. Perhaps this day will let him acquire Spielberg for the project at Action Pictures, an investment that could lead somewhere. Among them Charlie's a movie guy, higher in the pecking order, and he understands their hungry looks.

A guy named Lucas comes by and downs a few beers, and it takes a while before Charlie realizes the quiet guy is the *Star Wars* creator.

Lucas is stiff, phlegmatic, and seems interested only in Spielberg. Not really one of the boys.

Late in the afternoon Spielberg talks with Charlie in a California-casual way, vacillating between politics and movies and gossip. Does he really know Lew Wasserman? Charlie knows enough now to downplay his associations, since everybody his age is doing the opposite. It works. Nothing said, but Spielberg's look conveys respect.

"Hey, maybe we can work sometime," Spielberg says in farewell.

Charlie shrugs. "Sure, let's." But he knows he has Spielberg on his hook.

On the drive back he takes it slow, windows down, following Laguna Canyon Road up through the Irvine Ranch. There are still plenty of orange groves in Orange County, and he drives slowly through the biggest, savoring the thick citrus aroma that swarms through the windows and up into his head.

Charlie knows that he is a decent scriptwriter but no genius. Reading a few dozen great scripts from the 1940s onward proves that. He has learned about camera angles and moving shots, but he will never be a brilliant director like Spielberg. Instead he has perspective—maturity, sure, but far more; he knows how future tastes will run. He can keep ahead, sense the coming anxieties in need of release in the dark tunnels of movie theaters, where the human tribe gathers and watches the flickering screen, like early humans hearing stories by firelight.

Charlie's plans solidify. He will go with the flow, look for fresh angles, and stay ahead of the wave.

Lewis is full of ideas for *Switching*, so they go to Merrill and make a deal. Lewis will get cowriting credit, and Charlie will get an associate producer credit, each on a shared card. The three of them are starting to get comfortable working together, sharing tasks according to ability. Charlie is the idea man, Lewis the canny worker between dialogue and scene setup, and Merrill . . . is Merrill. Charlie wonders why he took such a dislike to Merrill in the first place.

Bob's *Bitch on Wheels* is a harder task. Their screenwriting meetings start out tense, coffee fueled, protracted. But then Charlie hits on a strategy of letting Bob's instincts rule, just helping him with the mechanics of scene construction and the dialogue of the younger characters. Bob can't write for characters born after 1940, so he appreciates Charlie's dialogue, while still feeling that he has control. This in turn lets Charlie and Lewis work on *Switching* unimpeded by Bob, who is too busy steering his project. Charlie One's insights help with all of this.

Charlie takes the lead in developing the arc of the plot for *Switching*: the opening tension between father and son, the resentment the son feels over his father's power and control, the father's veiled fear of losing his youth. Charlie makes the father recently divorced, with Mom a somewhat irresponsible fading beauty, once a model, now playing the field in the new, hip fern bars. A light dusting of jokes about short skirts and varicose veins helps. Dad is more responsible—Charlie makes him the owner of a medium-size company, like his own father. Charlie realizes that he isn't just ripping off the commercial movies that he saw in his past life, he is rewriting his parents' marriage. This lets him address some of his feelings about his parents, especially the anomalies that have developed from his coming back to them in time, and his concern about their marriage. He hammers at the keyboard. Dialogue comes fast and sure. Startled at how well this works in the script, he sees finally that using his own life is going to be key from now on. He has material others do not.

Lewis has a better feeling for the kid in the movie, Ted. At first this bothers Charlie, but then he realizes that his own mind is in its worn fifties, far from the frustrations of a normal teenager. Lewis is pleased by Charlie's willingness to let him shape Ted's character.

Charlie plays to the notion that he is about thirty, and so is wiser, a few years older than Lewis's twenty-eight.

There are interesting twists in the screenplay, driven by Charlie. When Ted takes over his dad's body, he starts treating his ex-wife/ mother with greater compassion, even an energetic friendliness. In the same spirit as *Back to the Future*, the screenplay mechanics have to play on the humor of the Oedipal situation, without a tragic con- summation of the mother-son relationship. Edgy scenes of marital ardor are avoided. Lots of hints, no real stuff—a new, hip brand of humor. Everybody's read *Oedipus*, after all—or at least the critics have, and all the humanities majors will follow them. In the end, after Dad loosens up as Ted in high school—the screenplay has the backseat stuff that Charlie knows so well—Ted subtly brings some fun back into his father's relationship with his mother, and the divorced par- ents are reconciled after the switch is undone. A happy Hollywood ending. Freud would have lapped it up.

Rog Ebert has said he knows that Philip K. Dick has moved to Orange County, which gives Charlie an opportunity to explore the mystery of his life, in the guise of a Hollywood person trolling for material. Phil Dick has washed up in an apartment complex in Santa Ana, his life in the Bay Area having shipwrecked. "Try the novels!" Rog urges.

Not only does Charlie appreciate that film versions of Dick's works will be good box office, he also finds the man's askew writing strangely sympathetic. When reading Dick, Charlie is able to touch upon his background unease about living his life again, and the tremulous fear that his world might again flicker and dissolve.

So down the 5 he goes, past the endless light industrial sprawl, down to Orange County. Getting off in Santa Ana exposes Charlie to street scenes he never knew in his first life. Commercial signs are in Spanish, and darker men in cowboy hats, shades, and thick mustaches loiter on corners. Momentarily he recalls something from a dream he had at Elspeth's, but the image doesn't quite solidify. Yet the emotional terror of that dream starts to seep into the edges of his perception of this barrio. Driving himself through the ethnically jumbled streets of Santa Ana cements Charlie's unease, but his Thomas Bros. map gets him to Dick's modern condo building. Parking is easy. He rolls the windows closed and keeps his wallet with him.

When he approaches the door of Dick's small condo, he hears something like a cheap motorbike banging. Charlie starts a bit, then takes a deep breath to settle his nerves before knocking on the door.

Dick jerks open the door and peers out into the sunlit day like a bear from a cave. After some words and a handshake, Charlie says, "I could hear you hammering on that Olympia"—a nod to a typewriter surrounded by stacks of manuscript paper—"like a woodpecker on meth."

Dick's eyes twinkle. "With one letter change, I am indeed a wordpecker on meth."

"Really?"

"I did it back in the sixties, not anymore." A shrug. "Gone semi-straight."

"Wow," Charlie manages, looking around the one-bedroom setup.

He has just reread *The Man in the High Castle* and expected a rather dour sort. But soon enough Phil is clowning around, tossing off funny lines. Charlie savors the ironies of the man who will be known for words he never wrote, like "attack ships on fire off the shoulder of Orion" in *Blade Runner*, a movie he will never see.

But Dick is not burdened with Charlie's double knowledge. He insists on showing off his stereo with glinting, mischievous eyes. He starts Wagner's *Tannhäuser* prelude and after a few moments asks, "Can you hear the nuances from the left speaker?"

Charlie nods.

"Good, good. I can't. I went to a doctor to check and found that I'm losing my hearing in the left ear. Good news. I was afraid it was my speakers!"

A woman abruptly comes in the front door in a hurry and without looking at them strides into the bedroom. Charlie stares in her direction when she barges out carrying two suitcases.

Phil just shrugs. "Girlfriend moving out."

Charlie murmurs some commiseration, knowing the vagaries of women only too well.

Phil says, "You'd guess that a guy who won the Hugo for best SF novel would do better with women."

Charlie thinks it doubtful and changes the subject. "Do you ever think about the meaning of scripture, transcendental matters?"

"Uh, some." Dick's eyes widen a bit.

"Believe in an afterlife?"

Dick looks down and away from Charlie.

But Charlie won't stop. "Let's say the church I currently don't attend is Episcopal."

"Ah! I'm a friend of the Bishop Pike brand of Christianity," Dick says with evident relief. Then he speaks of hearing a voice from the cosmic sky but allows that what he heard from on high tended to vary often.

Spending time with someone else who has gone to strange places is comforting for Charlie. And there could be some film possibilities, if the timing works out.

Once people are ready. Once I'm ready, Charlie muses as he drives back.

Charlie keeps looking for new approaches, angles, leverage. He has already scored once, but he can't just sit on that. A puff piece in the back pages of the *New York Times* reminds him about a book that's getting buzz at Putnam's, by a nobody named Puzo. He moves in early and nabs an option on the film rights to Mario Puzo's *The Godfather*. Book rights in hand, he reaches up the studio hierarchy with Merrill's help to get the chance to pitch the story to the studio's head honchos directly, as a producer.

Charlie flash-reads the book manuscript to prepare for his pitch and finds that it's nearly all narrative, essentially stories Puzo has heard, laced together in a family saga. That's how Charlie recalls the movie—a tight-knit immigrant tale as the kid Michael Corleone rises. The later films are about loyalty breaking down as Michael sacrifices his brothers to his own survival and widening power. In the end the three-film series is a tragedy, but there's no way to sell all that to the studio.

So he pitches from his memory of the first film, not from the book. At first the reception is stiff, phlegmatic. At the studio meetings his enthusiasm is intense, because he knows the movie that can be made of *The Godfather*.

His verve shapes it up as a big deal indeed, and he finds himself quoting lines like "Women and children can be careless, but not men." He knows instinctively that will work with the male studio elite, and it does, especially with the help of his new ally, Merrill.

He frames scenes with his hands, telling the story of the movie, not the book. The studio's first read of the book draft was so-so. The project started out as a knockoff movie called *Mafia*, a minor picture because everybody thought that crime movies were dead—but Charlie changes all that.

He fights to get another new seventies guy, Francis Ford Coppola, as director. Coppola is Italian and gets the family unity subtext immediately. They kibitz on the script, and when they get the green light, Coppola helps with the casting and Charlie arrows in on the right candidates—easily done, since he recalls by heart the talent that made it a classic in Charlie One's world.

He could just let the *Godfather* casting go the usual studio route, which will pick out Redford or McQueen or some other pretty boy. That would be smart, safe. But to make it what it can be, he decides to force through the same choices that Francis Coppola and Bob Evans did in that other, Old Charlie world. He has to get Brando.

Al Pacino will come on board if Brando does, Charlie learns—in fact, the whole rest of the cast will. In the Charlie One world, the drama pivots around Brando. But Brando is in decline, Hollywood's gossip says. Still, his name carries immense weight with studios and distributors. Brando has changed agents yet again and now has Sue Mentis representing him. Trying for a comeback, rumor says.

The day arrives when Charlie has lunch with her at Chasen's, where the waiters have learned to get over his long hair, even when he shows up without Greenway. His heavy tips haven't hurt.

He wastes no time and proceeds to pitch *Godfather* to the well-attired, fortyish Mentis before their plates arrive. Sue's sardonic smile tells him she is not just used to saying no, she likes it. She says, "Charlie, you know I love you—"

"I thought we played on different teams."

"—but we've got another big deal going."

"We can make it worth a lot, Sue."

"Brando is already worth a lot. More than you got."

"Then we go with McQueen."

"Good choice."

So it's to be hardball, Charlie realizes. "It's not the dinero, then."

"It's not just the money." She lifts two eyebrows, acknowledging that this violates the faith they all share.

She sighs theatrically. "Marlon wants to do this other thing."

There is no other thing, not that Charlie can recall. The next big role for Brando is in Coppola's *Apocalypse Now*, and that has to come after the Vietnam War, which is only now really starting to grow warts. Brando's role in that was sour, too, not a big career lifter. So crafty Sue is bluffing. But he senses that he should let it go for now, let it simmer in her mind. They talk of other things over lunch, particularly the latest shake-up at Action Pictures. Gossip is Hollywood's grease.

But the game continues. Charlie starts up a rumor that McQueen is going to get the don casting, even though he knows McQueen is all wrong for the part. It's easy, just some clipped remarks and eye rolls amid the sushi and Sauvignon Blanc at some parties in the Hills. That circulates, and sure enough, Sue calls him. He picks up the phone and her voice says only, "Dinero."

"Half a mil up front—"

The phone slams down hard and he thinks through the dial tone. He waits for her to call again. Of course, Sue knows he is waiting and so doesn't call, lets a day go by. But he is the buyer, she the seller, so he lets the hours play out.

Two days later he picks up the ringing phone at home and her voice says, "You know they're all crazy, Charlie. Brando won't hear a number that doesn't have seven figures."

"Tell him I'm doing this for him, Sue. This is gonna be a great flick and it will put him back on top."

"He's already on top."

Charlie allows himself a sardonic smile. "Top of the scales?" Hardball time. Everybody knows Brando is gaining weight. The papers have started printing pictures of Brando getting out of swimming pools, a sack of guts.

"He can get back in shape in a weekend. Women love his body, you know that."

"I meant it about putting him on top again."

Sue has got to be worrying about that but doesn't dare acknowledge it. Brando has been moping around in his mansion on the hill for years—no movies, no press, no money for Sue.

She huffs into the phone. "Got to be better than a mil."

A break in the armor. He allows himself to grind it in. Dealers like to deal, so they are disappointed when the deal goes too easily. "We're looking at a big cast here. Not a lot of camera time for Marlon. And I have McQueen and De Niro ready to go."

Dial tone again. Charlie smiles, enjoying the game.

He doesn't have a lot of cards, but he knows this should work. *Godfather* appealed to him last time and still does. It's mythic, goddamn it. In this new Charlie Two world, he has to make it go.

Sue knows he is waiting for her, just like last time, and he can sense the clock ticking in her head a few miles away. He is at home sipping a Cabernet, watching the phone—and it rings. "We'll take it at one point five mil."

"It could be too late. You should have come back at me sooner. I'll have to dial fast to stop the McQueen deal."

"He won't want the work." But her voice has slid a note higher, tighter.

"McQueen can do it." He doesn't even get all the four words out before she slams the phone down.

He makes sure he can't be reached that night or even before the midmorning. When Sue comes on, he cuts off her greeting—itself a telling sign, melodious—in midwarble and says, "I had a tough night with Coppola. He's scared that Brando will be too headstrong for a young guy like him to handle."

"Marlon is a craftsman, a pro."

"Come on, he's a moody method actor and that train's leaving the station."

"If you can't—"

"I can get some more cash. Not a lot. I got a mil out of the studio for the part."

"Not enough."

"That's a deal breaker."

"Damn." For the first time she sounds deflated.

He lets the feeling of having missed this boat play through her. Negotiations are all about the pauses. Then, mildly: "You're a manager, not an agent. You get the full fifteen percent, not a mere agent's ten."

She has to laugh at that. "Charlie, goddamn you, it's a deal."

"I'm grinning over here. It'll make him king again, I'm not kidding."

"Charlie . . ." A sly slide in the voice. "There was no other big picture."

He holds the phone until she runs out of air. "Sue?"

"What?"

"No McQueen, either."

This time the phone bangs even louder, but he holds it away from his ear. And grins.

Putting together movies for shoots is like watching dandruff grow, so Charlie has time to think. Just before shooting begins, he recalls Spielberg and brings the kid in as a subshooter, doing the outlying, establishing shots that Coppola is too busy to handle. That lowers the cost, too. Charlie is tempted to use some of his own savings to buy some profit points, but after an afternoon with his accountant he realizes that he doesn't have enough. While he's been busy playing New Prince of Hollywood, his expenses have shot up.

But he still makes time to see Michelle. Her UCLA roommates take him for a fellow student with his long hair and facial fur. Charlie makes a point of pulling his hair back in a ponytail as he walks into her dorm, letting Michelle's friends see his unlined forehead and eyes. Around them he says that he is in his twenties and interested in film school.

Michelle doesn't approve of this deception, any more than she likes his endless Hollywood parties without her. But she is very pointedly "a liberated woman of the 1970s," a phrase that she trots out frequently. Charlie has to suppress laughter whenever she wields it. Not that Charlie doesn't appreciate it. No, he basks in Michelle's questioning mind, her eager curiosity about the world, her intellectual sparks.

16 Postproduction on *Godfather*. All the elements come together—raw film, sound, dialogue, music, effects. The soup that comes out of blending them is a frame-by-frame fix. The elements fight one another unless you get the taste just right; that is the art and science of postproduction. You see it in the dailies. The director picks out his frames, and the editor stitches them together, and if he's good, the dailies send euphoria through the small crowd that sees them. It runs like that while you're shooting, and then you go back in and string the dailies together. You look at them, happy at first. Then the floor falls out from under you and you're on your ass. It is a long parade of crap, with great bits in between, smothered by wrong scenes and bad camera angles and chopped-up sequences.

Charlie learns a lot from the endless screenings and interminable editing and persistent arguments with Coppola. The first time Coppola sees the death march of scenes, the big, broody man fears that it will all fail, fears that he simply isn't up to the job.

But the work is only beginning. Charlie learns that dailies are like brides on their wedding day. All beautiful, no matter what they look like. Then comes the buyer's remorse.

Bob is surprisingly calm. "The sooner you get behind schedule, the more time you have to make it up," he says airily over a canteen lunch. They have just watched five different cuts of the restaurant shooting scene, and everybody around the table wonders if it will work at all.

Charlie says, "That's why we keep the earlier scene, where Michael gets instructed to get rid of the gun as soon as he's shot the two of them. He comes out the restaurant entrance, looks for the getaway car, I guarantee you the audience will be yelling, 'Drop the gun! Drop the gun!' Dead certain."

They blink, consider. Charlie knows this will be true because it happened the first time he saw the picture.

It goes on forever. *Dick* was easy, with few sets and standard shots. On the dark days when studio execs come by for a look and leave stony faced, everybody upstairs wants to make out that this is Charlie's baby. Bob's way of conveying this is to say, offhand, "If you can't figure out who's going to be the scapegoat when things go south, it's going to be you."

At first he doesn't like this, waiting for a vice president to come take off his head, but then he sees that it plays to his hand. He knows what they cannot. So he makes impassioned speeches about sticking to the vision, and it gets them through to a final cut.

Charlie learns from it all. He has never bought into the auteur theory, that everybody is there to "serve the director's vision." Not that the screenwriters are king either. After exposure to the reality of Hollywood, he sees that producers call many of the shots and make most of the money. Being below the public radar has advantages. You can live well as a producer without being famous to the larger public, without having people turn green or livid at the mention of your name. Plus, no autographs.

At the *Godfather* opening, the Action Pictures gang clusters around Charlie at the postviewing party. Bob is now a trusted lieutenant, but he's visibly unsure whether the film is going to pay off.

He eyes the crowd around them at the rented room in the Beverly Wilshire and nervously whispers to Charlie, "You ready to do this?"

No, thinks Charlie.

"Yes," he says.

Godfather opens to good reviews, but nobody else sees what is coming. Except Rog Ebert, who calls it a classic. Charlie takes him out to dinner next time he's in town, tells him lots of insider stories about making the film. Swears him to secrecy, which is the sure way of getting the story spread. The crowds outside the theaters grow fast. The wave of '70s American cinema is growing, and Charlie is among the first out there to greet it, riding his second-life surfboard.

He circulates, adds to the backstreet buzz. Always, Charlie One rides in the back of his mind. He knows that his dual lives give him a telling advantage. Everyone in Hollywood talks too much, as if they're trying to convince one another that they're really the hottest thing in town. He cultivates affectations just ahead of the style that will come, and so helps define it. He wears baseball caps in meetings before Spielberg does, shows up at parties in big-kahuna Maui sunglasses, plays soulful Edith Piaf softly for background office music, sports an authentic beat-up leather bomber jacket when everybody else is still big on antiwar bumper stickers.

As the first wave of 1970s films breaks, he acquires a reputation for being a quick study through endless pitch sessions, script reviews, and on-set revisions. Sixteen-hour days too, of course. He can glance through a script, then go into a meeting and command the room with insights into the backstory, subtext, foreshadowing, carry-through, the whole three-act litany. This comes from sheer experience with life, from Charlie One's knowing how people saw the world through narratives, and of course from Charlie Two's voracious pursuit of his new life. Working with a new brain, too. He thinks about mind versus brain—experienced software imposed on a young, sharp operating system. That helps a lot. He can feel it—quick, sure jumps of intuition and logic, like running hard, sweat stinging his eyes, and seeing a creek ahead, and then just gliding over the frothing churn below.

Everybody attributes his expertise to talent. But he knows that experience is a lot more reliable. Still, it is gratifying when a cameraman tells him a saying going around: "If Moment gets in a revolving door behind you, when you exit, he'll be ahead of you." He laughs and takes the cameraman to lunch. That's rare enough in itself to make the story take off.

He carefully mines his last-life memories of the final thirty years of the twentieth century, and from those sepia images he fashions his strategy. Bet on the smart horses. Charlie One was a stone-cold movie fan and Charlie Two remembers a lot, but it's not like he can quote dialogue and reproduce the plot moves in the films he saw. No, he has to find the real talents and attach them to himself. Sometimes he'll suddenly recall a sharp scene, a camera move, and get it done—but Charlie knows his limitations.

He picks up on gossip about a Spielberg TV movie, quick and deadly and done on a fingernail budget—and of course it is *Duel*. A mere TV knockoff from some unknown, a Paramount flak tells him, but weeks later he catches it a few minutes into a rerun, and it is very tight, exciting.

The *Godfather* shoot got Spielberg some good word of mouth, but then Charlie became busy and lost track of him. Now the kid is back on the track he will follow. Charlie makes plans to snap him up.

Charlie wangles an invitation to a party put on by some backers, after he finds out that Spielberg will be there, looking for start-up money to do real movies. The party is in one of the big houses up in the Hills. Charlie arrives early, gets the meet and greet done, nods all around. Then he spies his target and moves in. He ropes Spielberg in with a movie idea he has, invoking the day when they met in Laguna

Beach. Charlie uses ocean memories, outlines a plot. He can see Spielberg's eyes light up, then get canny. The film is going to be an adaptation of the Benchley novel that's been making the rounds for months without success. The book is only in bound galley, awaiting hardcover success, but Charlie takes up its cause. It has a good title, but the conventional wisdom is that the crowds don't turn out to see animal movies. Charlie knows better; the title is *Jaws*.

One morning in Michelle's bed, before her first class but after her roommates have left, Charlie confesses. Lying naked on his side, his long hair flung back and his eyes soft, he says, "I love you, Michelle."

She doesn't look at him, staring up at the ceiling, her hands on her naked abdomen, just above her untamed pubic hair. "I guess I love you also."

Charlie is stung. He gets up on his hands, a four-legged beast peering into her eyes. "What does 'also' mean?"

Michelle hesitates. "So . . . what would we do? I don't want to get married."

Charlie knows that line full well, with its left-off ". . . right now." What should he say next?

Michelle has an agenda and Charlie's silence gives her the opportunity. "Charlie, I have some questions about . . . you know, your life. Screenwriting—all that. There are some things about you that don't really add up. You say your mother is, like, forty-two—"

"She's forty-four."

"—so how can you be twenty-eight?"

Charlie frowns. He has been sloppy with his offhand self-history, yes. He could invent a story about his mother getting pregnant in high school, but it just wouldn't fit with his overall narrative about life in Chicago, his father running a car-parts business, his sister. . . .

"How can I trust you if your life doesn't make any sense to me?"

Charlie sits on the edge of the bed and hangs his head, his long hair touching his thighs. He feels tired of it all, tired of bearing the burden of two lives on his own, sharing none of it.

"Okay, okay. I'm really twenty-one. My mother had me when she was twenty-three, after she married my dad."

"No way! No way you're twenty-one." Michelle gets out of the bed and walks around to confront him, her small breasts bouncing as she thrusts her finger at him. "I know twenty-one. I know the frat boys here at UCLA. They're twenty-one. You're not."

"I'm not a frat boy."

"All right, all right! I know freaks and hippies, too. I know guys who worship Frank Zappa and Jack Kerouac, and they still seem like callow kids to me. Why do you think I'm not fucking them?"

Charlie begs her to stop with his eyes. How to explain . . . ?

But she shows him no mercy. "And furthermore, how does a kid with no college know so much—so much about everything? You have comments about all my classes, you've read all my goddamn assigned books, for Chrissake!"

"Not true. I hadn't read Eliot's *Four Quartets* until you showed it to me." Charlie feels a small sense of pedantic victory. He didn't like T. S. Eliot in his past life, only coming to appreciate him after being . . . reborn, as he has come to think of it.

"Eliot, Eliot! Who gives a fuck about one English—"

"American, really."

"There you go again. You even know that."

Michelle kneels down in front of him and their heads bend down together, touching at the hairline. Charlie tries not to see the irresistible curves of her long torso before him. Then he realizes that she is crying, and lust flies from his mind.

"I'm sorry, baby. I'm so very sorry."

"Talk to me, Charlie." Her sob tears at him. "Tell me what it is. Why can't I make sense of you?"

"If I told you something really crazy, something absolutely insane, would you stay with me? Could we make a life together? Could we be open and honest with each other from then on?"

Michelle smiles at Charlie like sunshine between rain clouds, tears still on her face. "Of course, honey." Her glowing face takes Charlie's breath away. "You are the only man I have ever truly loved."

"Okay, then." Charlie takes a breath from far below his lungs and starts to talk quickly, dispassionately. "I was born in 1952. I grew up in Chicago. I went to the University of Chicago for a bachelor's, then to the University of Minnesota for graduate studies. When I received my doctorate, I took a temporary faculty job in Massachusetts, before I went to GWU in DC. I got tenure there. I've been married twice."

"None of this makes any sense, Charlie." Michelle's mouth is tight, unreadable.

"I died in 2000, when a truck ran over my Volvo." He shrugs, trying to lighten the impact. "I woke up in 1968. In my head I'm in my fifties."

Michelle gets up and walks over to her chest of drawers, her long, beautiful back turned to him. "So this is how you explain knowing everything."

"Uh-huh."

Michelle quickly turns to face him, her long, straight hair swirling like a honeyed liquid. "So! I have my choice. Either you are the world's greatest liar, or you're insane." A high laugh.

Charlie stands up slowly, like he's about to be shot.

Michelle's face darkens with flitting anger, desperation, confusion. Despite her youth and beauty, Charlie finds it the most terrifying countenance he has ever seen. Michelle starts to back away slowly, facing him. "Charlie Moment, if that's even your real name, I'm going to go into the bathroom and lock the door. I'm going to stay there until you leave. If you are still here when I come out, I'm going to call the police. Do you understand me?"

"Michelle, I can prove it all to you." He will make some predictions, she'll see them come true. . . . Torment tears at his chest. He cannot breathe.

"I don't want your proof. I don't want any of this, do you understand?"

Michelle reaches the bathroom door, her mouth knotted up in a frenzy, and then in a blur of motion slams and locks the door with a sharp snap.

Charlie crumples back onto the bed, staring at the ceiling. The room around him begins to flicker. He hears a roaring sound. The light above the bed becomes two. Then the room splits, doubles, and spins. Rumbles. Bangs. He hears Elspeth's harsh laughter, a gunshot. Then the truck runs over him again. Trudy's lips smile down on him.

Not even dressing, he runs out of the building down the two flights to the street, and out into the blinding sunlight of Westwood. Within an hour he is in police custody.

Part III

A Bifurcating Cusp

17 The last seven years have worn hard on Charlie, hard but profitable. While not every film has been a success, he has been by far the most successful writer-producer, now just producer, in the pantheon of Action Pictures. Merrill, now CEO, clings to him like a sailor on the raft of the *Medusa*. While the other producers have had some success, they have also come up with too many duds. Charlie is the undisputed king of family entertainment at Action, so much so that Disney, Buena Vista in particular, has started to sniff around him for head of filmmaking. He is famous for his unerring nose, thanks to his dimming memory of what worked in the world of Charlie One. But Charlie has no interest in taking up the family values banner of the Disney operation.

Time. More time . . . and drugs.

In his case it was epilepsy drugs supplied by Dr. Habib that really changed his life. After the police picked him up that day he ran through Westwood skyclad, he was taken to Cedars-Sinai and placed on a hold.

That time there was no warning. After the Haldol and benzos had stabilized him, he spent some grim days in a locked ward going over his symptoms with the burly Lebanese physician. The man was smart enough to realize that schizophrenia and mania weren't the problem.

What Charlie and the shrink agreed on was a diagnosis of temporal lobe epilepsy. Charlie was given a prescription of valproate, a series of blood serum tests, and eventually a discharge. Naturally, Merrill had to pay off several Hollywood gossip reporters to prevent the news from leaking out. It was just a normal cost of business for the studio.

Charlie was pleasantly surprised to find that the flickering stopped completely once he went on medication. His past life became faint to him, though he could still retrieve the outlines of the movies of that life well. After years of psychotherapy he put Charlie One into cold storage. The story that Charlie developed in therapy with Habib was that his teenage self had developed a delusional past life in order to make sense of his epileptic moments. Even his young life in Chicago became a distant thing. Southern California plus medication made it easy to live in a state of oblivion.

But there was fallout from chronic medication. He found that he couldn't write well anymore. On the positive side, Charlie had more patience for movie production machinations. As he had already started working as a producer, dropping screenwriting from his brief was no difficult progression. People expected you to move up the pyramid.

As usual, Bob is the first to arrive to the evening's party. The studio keeps him as a vice president in charge of project development. Charlie looks at Bob's scripts from time to time, when Merrill wants a break from swatting down Bob. Finally quitting smoking hasn't done much for Greenway—drawn, wrinkled, and pale in the neck, he looks even thinner.

"Welcome, my man," says Charlie. Bob looks confused.

"My old friend," amends Charlie. Bob seems content with that.

"So how's the boy wonder?"

"Fine. Haven't changed since our eleven o'clock meeting."

"Right." Bob nods knowingly, his eyes somehow filmy, those of an old snake now harmless without its fangs.

Charlie knows the word is that he and Robert Evans are Hollywood wunderkinder, one pretty and the other just intuitive. But Evans is the real thing, of course. . . . Sighing, he asks, "What'll you have?"

"Any pineapple juice? All my stomach can manage these days." Bob's eyes darken with distracted worry.

"Heartburn?" asks Charlie politely.

"Something like that." Bob takes the juice and walks over to the picture window's sharp, broad view. Bob is slow and a bit shaky. Charlie suspects some type of cancer, perhaps with chemotherapy, but he knows better than to ask.

Bob has an undercurrent of anger toward Charlie, or perhaps just Charlie's success, or Charlie's success combined with his youth. Charlie has occasionally set Bob off and regrets the tirades that have followed. In years of experience Charlie is older than Bob, which only makes Charlie feel more residual unease about having used Bob to get to Hollywood, to become a mogul by the time he turned thirty, even though the rest of the world thinks he is now about forty. The swollen face, slower movement, and weight gain from his medication have helped solidify that impression. Only Bob knows that Charlie is still a comparatively young man. Except for Michelle—if she can be counted. If she ever believed him.

He feels now that he can see through the authorized version of whatever's passing by in the daily news. He can reliably affect an elegant unsurprise at the grossest crimes and follies, especially those of the world's anointed. He can put on parties like this one with a distracted air, something the medication only helps.

Merrill also arrives fairly early, trailing his wife, Debbie. Merrill obviously doesn't worry about Debbie getting fed up with their life together. Not a pretty woman in middle age, but strong and reliable, more than strong enough to weather the babe eruptions that come with her husband's exalted position. Merrill is only a man, after all, and Hollywood is the succubus. Experience has taught Charlie that every marriage is a secret known to at most two people, sometimes only one, or no one at all.

The room fills up quickly now with noisy displays of joy unfelt. The glittering women, the men in thousand-dollar jackets that artfully hide their middle-aged spread, the catering people in waistcoats and dress shirts, all milling together in an odd dance. Charlie is playing the Vangelis soundtrack from *Chariots of Fire*, one of his recent successes for Action Pictures. "You've got to know how to choose the right people" is his latest saying when people praise him. The music soothes him, helping him enough to work the room better, even though medication has dulled the energy that his physical youth should provide.

The party fills with the clammy odor of people working hard at having fun. Charlie is drinking scotch, the sharp slug of it burning, and yet it hardly has any effect on him. He retires to the fun room, where he is pleased to find Sid, a former actor who now lives on the fringes of Hollywood, his main commerce being to supply the elite with pure cocaine. Sid has the sleek gray look of a retired greyhound—too thin and ineffably nervous, flicks of tongue around the lips, the nose slightly runny. Sid leaves the upper buttons of his shirt open to show an abundance of chest hair that he thinks attracts the ladies, when all he needs is the vials of white powder that he is known for.

A nod from Charlie is all it takes.

They go into a bathroom together, where Sid efficiently produces a small mirror and lines up the white powder. Charlie takes the coke up his nose with a rolled-up twenty. First his nose burns, prickly and brimming hot, and then the familiar rush sweeps over him, soothing and elevating at the same time. Charlie thanks Sid, proffering the twenty. Sid shakes his head. They both know he will do well from his invitation to Charlie's party. Charlie's fix is a gentlemanly commission, appropriate to the occasion and the comfortable contempt that they have for each other. The odd camaraderie of knowing the world differently through each other.

Maybe there is even an idea for a movie in that. A buddy pic. Two guys in a druggie shoot-out at the Hollywood Corral? Charlie likes these bolts of inspiration, coming when he is at a peak from the simmering coke joy. They remind him of his days before valproate. He takes out his notebook and jots down the idea.

Charlie wanders back to the high ceilings of the living room, beaming a smile at all of his guests. Most of them know that he's high now.

The minutes flow by effortlessly, and he even manages to be friendly toward an East Coast investor, a very bald man with a weight problem and a scotch who rarely comes west, but this time has managed to arrive without his wife. Charlie flicks his head at Chantel, a black semipro whom he casts in his pictures for occasions like this one. Mr. Gruberman will be well taken care of this night, and Chantel should raise excellent money for his latest picture. Pleased with having done everyone a good turn, the definition of momentary sainthood in Hollywood, Charlie slips through the sliding doors to the pool.

A few of the younger couples are softly stroking each other with talk about their upcoming films. Against the water's pale-blue shimmer, they are dark cutout figures, highlighted by the deep red of the sun that will disappear in a few minutes.

18

On a blurry Sunday morning, his father's call wakes him.

"Charlie, your mother and I are going to try a separation. To see if we can't get our heads together for another try at life."

"Uh . . . another try?"

"I just don't know, Charlie." A tired sigh, though it's morning. "Your mother—well, your mother hasn't really been herself lately."

Charlie has already heard from his mother. He recommended that she seek out a psychiatrist for some antidepressants. He has gotten to know the practice of psychiatry well, perhaps too well. But he doesn't mention this to his father.

"You and Mom aren't . . . getting along?"

"You know, Charlie, she doesn't seem to be doing that well."

More bland phrases trickle by. Somehow Charlie's father has quit smoking, with Charlie's enthusiastic support, and has recovered some of the youthful spring that he was never able to regain in Charlie's previous life. This has filled Charlie with hope that his father won't die so soon, but for some reason it has left his mother estranged, gray and cool. Charlie suspects that his father is having an affair, though his father hasn't given him any reason to think so.

He speaks with warm concern. "What are you going to do, Dad?"

"I'll be getting an apartment closer to the factory. Won't have to drive as much. That way maybe I'll have more time to think. Your mother will have the house to herself, now that Cathy's settled in Wisconsin."

Thoughts of the strong young woman that Catherine has become fill Charlie with pride. They no longer fight, but they still have yet to become friends as adults. He senses that she suspects that something is odd about him, which makes him wary about disclosing too much in front of her. *Or maybe it's just the usual sort of sibling distance*, he thinks.

"Catherine is going to join a pretty big law firm," Ned Moment says.

"What, Rendum and Devour?"

"Who?"

"Forget it, Dad."

"Well, James's mother called to let me know that he is doing better at the VA hospital. He wants to see you. I guess they've lowered his dose of tranquilizers. His mother says you're the first person he's asked for by name."

The flight into Chicago is a welcome relief from Charlie's work week. The dinosaur picture isn't going well. The mock-ups of the dinosaur heads keep looking wrong, moving awkwardly, and the computer-generated images aren't working out. Charlie wonders if he hasn't tried for something too early. Maybe he should have waited for Apple to develop the new animation software that will dominate the industry in the nineties—or did, in his past life. Not even hiring Spielberg has helped that much. *Maybe I should have pulled Crichton in*, Charlie thinks. But he can't stand the guy.

His limo driver picks him up at O'Hare and whisks him to the VA hospital.

When they get there, the lawns are patchy, brown, with crabgrass and scrawny trees. His breath blows thick fog as he walks toward the hospital, each step heavy.

Inside the foyer are three black men in wheelchairs, one of them slumped over. *Is he dead?* Charlie wonders. *Probably just sleeping*, he reassures himself.

He asks for the long-term psych ward. In the elevator there is an old white man on a gurney, no attendant. The man talks to himself with eyes closed, incoherent muttering, troubled but without panic. There are restraints at the man's wrists and ankles. *Why no attendant?* Charlie asks himself. The elevator door opens on Charlie's floor, and he leaves the man on the gurney to go on riding up and down, alone, babbling.

Back down . . . back up and down in time, maybe. Or maybe that's just a delusion, going back in time. Big unknowns he has ceased to entertain for more than such glancing moments.

He has to sign in with a fat security guard sitting in front of a steel mesh gate. Charlie's hand trembles with the cheap pen.

"Name of patient?"

"James Weston."

The guard stands up with no display of interest, unlocking the gate in slow motion. Once Charlie is through, the guard snaps the locks shut. Charlie wonders what the man would do if Charlie got into trouble. He pushes the thought away and goes through an open area with a loud television. Dazed men in bathrobes watch a game show. One has a trickle of drool running off his chin. Charlie nods but none of them look in his direction.

Down a hallway smelling of feces, looking in the doorways at beds occupied by unrecognizable lumps, he comes to a bedroom where an older pale man sits at a desk and James gets up to greet him. Charlie straightens his back. James looks twice his years, his blond hair now a white fringe around his pate, skin like parchment.

"Charlie!" James's smile animates the wrinkles around his eyes, a spider's web over dark hollows.

Charlie almost tears up, but controls himself and offers James his hand.

"So Mom contacted your father?"

Charlie nods, his throat choked. He is back in his past life, when his father told him that James had killed himself.

But James seems happy now. "Great of you to visit. I don't see many people. Sit down! Take my chair—I'll sit on the bed."

Charlie hesitantly sits down on the unsteady chair, while James swings easily onto the bed. "How'd you get here?" James asks, and Charlie avoids mentioning the corporate jet. "How is Hollywood?"

Charlie clears his throat and croaks, "Great."

"Good. Good." James becomes pensive, his smile fading. "Have you told anyone else?"

"About . . ."

Suddenly Charlie sees they both know what they are talking about, but Charlie can't say it.

"About your reincarnation."

So James has put together Charlie's huge success, straight from high school, with that one moment when he revealed himself. He hoped the dope would fog that all away.

He plays it straight, stiff lipped. "No. Well, sort of. I tried once, with a girl. But she just thought I was crazy. Then the shrinks figured that I have epilepsy."

"Just a bit crazy, like they see me."

"But you had shell shock after Nam."

"That just opened my eyes, Charlie. I began to see what it was all about, see? You coming back in time to see me." James sits up, pale eyes peering at Charlie. "The messages in your movies. Don't think I haven't seen them, because I have, boyo. Don't miss a single one."

"I'm just making movies."

"No, you are the Messenger." Charlie can hear the capital.

"Maybe I was confused about what was happening to me in high school. Even between seizures, you aren't necessarily normal with my type of epilepsy."

James shakes his head, exasperated. He jerks up onto his feet, lips pressed white, and looks out the bedroom's tiny window, through a soldered metal grille. He's in a prison. "No, you have a mission. You have come back in time to warn us."

"Hey, please."

"No, I should have seen it when we went in for our induction physicals. Everything you said to the recruiting sergeant. About the future, about Vietnam, about Nixon."

"Don't forget. I was wrong about Nixon getting that war-waging bill passed. He never had to take over the country the way I said he would. None of that happened."

James turns, fists clenched. "But only because you did that movie. So people started to love the guy. He didn't turn out so bad after all. You know—the country really rallied, man. We beat the commies because of you."

A long pause. "I . . . I never wanted any of that to happen."

"But it did." James steps toward him, hands grasping the air.

"My psychiatrist says it was all a delusion, all that past-life stuff." Charlie feels dark bile flowing up into his throat, all the questions he has suppressed for years in the neon Hollywood glare, with the helpful cloak of medication, with therapy persuading him that he could have had delusions. "Maybe you're the only one who still believes it? Maybe I don't, anymore." Charlie reaches out to James, but James flinches. He still doesn't like to be touched.

James retreats to the rumpled, stale-smelling bed. "I'd believe you, maybe"—a sudden rush of words and flashing eye-energy—"if it wasn't for that movie you did about going back in time to the fifties, man. Where the guy could have been a crooner but decided to sell appliances for his father? And there were all those babes that he didn't do the first time, but he gets around to the second time."

Damn, was he that transparent? "Yeah. *Back to the Five-and-Dime.*"

It made far more cash than the one Charlie One knew, mostly

because he had the balls to give a lead to Barbra Strident, as she was known in Hollywood. She added zip to the whole thing, demanding script changes and adding funny lines, too.

"That wasn't just a movie, man. That was real. That was you, you coming back and fucking Trudy, like you never did before."

"Well, actually, I did before, James."

"But not like that. Man, you owned her pussy."

Charlie reddens, which surprises him. He looks down at the stained linoleum floor. Some of the stains look like dried blood.

James twists his lips in earnest agony. "You were telling me in your movies that it was all true. You were telling me that it was all right, that what I was going to go through would mean something." James is winding up, muscles straining, thick cords bulging from his neck. "Like the whole thing with my platoon getting blown down, burned meat, the smell—it would all mean something, Charlie. My life would . . . mean something."

Charlie edges toward the door. "Where's the washroom, James?"

James's eyes fill with tears. "Down the hall, off the playroom."

Charlie hurries off to find the guard, running away from his double life, from the force of his friend's paranoid disintegration, from the corrosive pressure of time past, time present, and time future.

19

"Hello?"

It's Charlie's father, and it isn't good news. Charlie stands rooted, face frozen.

James has died. The funeral will be in three days. Charlie doesn't need to ask how it happened, and his father doesn't elaborate. They say goodbye with tenderness, their voices resonant with things best unsaid. Maybe because they both know that it could have been Charlie awaiting burial, if Charlie had caught any of James's bad luck.

Charlie's father greets him at O'Hare with a hug. The two men share small talk. Charlie's father remarks that his son seems younger, but Charlie doesn't comment. There are some things that straight men still don't share, like grooming tips.

Illinois doesn't do them any favors, the sky gray and the grass dying around them, the leaves gone from the skeleton trees. *Like a Bergman setup shot*, Charlie thinks automatically. "Is Mom coming?"

His father hesitates. "She phoned to tell me she is."

His father's voice sounds brighter, and he's no longer smoking. Could his father have a new woman in his life? Charlie wonders if that might be the thing that is pulling his father out of the downward spiral that killed him the last time. If so, he will embrace it. *Survival is more important than marriage.*

"I understand, Dad."

"Catherine will be there. The two of you can catch up with each other."

The group around the grave site is painfully small. Charlie is grateful to his sister for coming, though he recalls that she didn't know James that well. Few did. Catherine probably came to check up on the suddenly rocky family she's in.

There is a familiar overweight woman there with three children and a barrel-chested, bearded husband. Charlie dimly remembers James dating her a few times, though not her name, and idly wonders if James was able to overcome his aversion to touch.

James's adoptive mother is grim, in a black wool overcoat obviously purchased for the occasion. She and her sister, who never liked Charlie, send beams of heavy-lidded coldness his way, making him wonder how much James said to them. *Perhaps they blame me*, Charlie thinks, *for James's eventual insanity. They don't know that it happened to him anyway, in another life, even without the visitor from the future.* Charlie's head spins with thoughts of his two pasts, and the two lives that James had, both so unfortunate. Briefly he fears a flickering episode and freezes. But it doesn't happen, so he relaxes a bit. *Maybe I have grown past all that*, he wonders, *even without the medication.*

The others are faces dimly recalled from his high school yearbook. The intoning Episcopalian minister hurries through the burial service. Charlie stands in front of his parents, his sister beside him. In the middle of the burial incantation, Catherine puts her gloved hand in his, her first solid gesture of affection in two decades. Charlie's eyes tear, the burial scene becoming a blur of blacks and fading green.

Catherine corners Charlie at the reception in the house that James grew up in. Catherine's eyes search his, strangely friendly and predatory at the same time. He can smell vodka on her breath. She could never hold the stuff.

"James told me about you."

"About what?"

"Coming back from the future."

He attempts a shrug, despite a tremor in his chest. "You didn't believe him, surely?"

"Not when he first told me." Her flat, factual words send a shock up his spine, a snaking of fear. Forcefully she whispers, "Now maybe I do."

She glares. "How *else* can I understand how my geek of a brother could become, like, one of the most successful people in Hollywood?" Catherine's hands cut the air as she makes her case. "Then you just turned around and became, like, this totally creative guy. Where do all those ideas come from, Charlie? Don't tell me there's anything normal about you, okay, 'cause I sure won't believe you."

"I—I—it's not what—I . . ." Charlie realizes he is babbling and that he has to get his sister away from the rest of the party. He grabs her arm and leads her, almost shoves her, out the front door of the house.

Without their coats, the November air bites, but they barely notice.

Catherine turns on him, eyes wild. "So James wasn't crazy. You *were* telling him all that weird stuff. You were! Then he would phone me up and practically sob into the mouthpiece about you."

A wave of remorse sweeps over him and his face crumples up. Yes, with that one conversation he drove James toward oblivion, even if Vietnam finished the job. Now the tears run down and he tastes their sorrow.

"I'm so sorry, Catherine. I had no idea."

"Well, isn't it about time that you tell me about it?"

Catherine stands firm, challenging him with every line on her face, the crook of her elbows, the angle of her bare knees.

Charlie takes a deep breath of cold air and launches into an explanation. How he already lived a complete life, until middle age at least, then died in a car accident only to wake up on his birthday in 1968, knowing all about the next thirty-two years. Only it hasn't turned out quite how he expected. He made the film about Nixon, which changed the man, changed the way people saw him, anyway, and then there was no martial law, no circling of wagons with the Cold War Democrats, no hardening of democracy into something resembling imperial Rome, Democrats and Republicans joyfully throttling the world together—the Pax Americanum, they would call it, once the Soviet Union had disintegrated under Chernenko and China had collapsed from starvation and disease.

"You mean, none of your movies are actually original? You *stole* all those ideas?"

He gives her a wrecked smile, thin and ironic. "Well, I had to write them out again, really. I couldn't remember all the details, so Bob Greenway and I invented a lot of stuff as we went along."

"Is there anything about you that I can trust?"

"Do you believe me, about this life?"

"No. I don't believe it." Her mouth works, sags. "And I do believe it, some damn how. It's the only way to make sense of you going off to Hollywood just out of high school and succeeding, when you were such a dork."

"Thanks, sis." Charlie smiles ruefully, but with some relief.

"I'm not sure I can forgive you keeping this secret from me for all these years. Whether it's true or not."

Her crisp anger makes him look at her down the long corridor of years he has journeyed. He smiles, to save it in memory.

20

Charlie turns to Dr. Habib again and gets an increase in his valproate dose along with some benzos. The pain of his two lives clashing has become overwhelming. But once again the drugs help him dull everything.

It doesn't take Merrill long to realize that Charlie will be of no use to him until he recovers. Merrill tells Charlie to spend the winter at his cliffside house in Laguna Beach, where the press won't pay attention. Laguna is an exotic far-off island as far as Hollywood is concerned.

A 405 traffic jam makes Charlie take the Pacific Coast Highway from Long Beach, driving through the barren naval proving grounds, through Huntington Beach, then Newport Beach, until finally the terrain opens up and he zooms alongside the ocean in his Mercedes. Once he's past the beach houses, it's up the hill and around the bend to the bohos, artists, and gays of Laguna Beach.

Merrill's beach house turns out to be a white modernist structure barely clinging to a cliff, eight bedrooms and enough bathrooms that Charlie finds a new one each day his first week there. The Pacific view is breathtaking, and Charlie can see Catalina Island lazing like a promise on the western horizon when the morning mist clears. It doesn't take Charlie long to find the cliff walk north of Main Beach. The flowers exhaling scent by the cliff walk make him feel like he has been given a day pass to heaven. But after a few times walking alone, he feels more like he is in purgatory.

In time he can return, maybe with a little pizzazz, as a prodigal mogul. In time. He has also lost his bag of pills in the move and finds energy returning. For the first few days, he fears a return of the flickering. But it doesn't come. And now his body is starting to feel resurgent, even without white coke. And Charlie One has come back, with a strange clarity that valproate forestalled for years.

As he watches the sun set over Catalina Island from his balcony, the clouds meeting the mist in a thick rhapsody of simmering reds and hot oranges, Charlie decides to solve the riddle of his second life. He will find its meaning, or he will make one—something more than making money. He needs to understand what has happened to him. It has become a hunger.

A new birthday, he thinks.

The memory of his visit to a library in Chicago comes back to Charlie as the fog of medication lifts, his venture into the mysteries of physics. There was one person who piqued his interest, the alternate-worlds guy, Hugh Everett.

Now Charlie wants to know more. His researcher from Action Pictures finds a library listing that reveals that in August of 1964, Everett started Lambda Corporation, to apply military modeling solutions to various civilian problems. "Responsible for research in mathematical techniques and models; selection; programming," the report said.

Charlie has his studio staff make an appointment, and after a train ride from New York, where he has a financials meeting with a team of bland suits, to Washington, DC, a cab takes him to the small suite of Lambda offices on the fifteenth floor of a glass and concrete box. The reception room has an excellent view: the Lincoln

Memorial two miles away, the Washington Monument about a mile farther, and the Capitol dome some two miles beyond that. *Power on display*, Lambda seems to announce.

Everett looks smart—intense, pudgy, with side-whiskers and a professorial goatee, topped by a high, shining forehead. Charlie introduces himself using the Hollywood producer credential his staff played to get him this appointment. He brings up the many-worlds model, and Everett says, "One night in 1954, after a slosh or two of sherry, me and my Princeton classmate Charles Misner were making jokes about the ridiculous implications of quantum mechanics."

Everett's face lights up. "That's when I had the basic idea behind my theory. So I began developing it into a dissertation."

Everett launches himself toward a bookshelf, then plops down a dog-eared manuscript. Charlie notes the big, bold letters—"Thesis submitted to Princeton University, March 1, 1957, in partial fulfillment of the requirements for the PhD degree"—with signatures by physicists below.

Everett talks fast, voice flat and clipped. "When I was twelve, I wrote letters to Albert Einstein raising the question of whether it was something random or unifying that held the universe together. I mean at the basic theory level. Einstein was kind enough to answer."

He thrusts a photocopy at Charlie, who reads the letter dated June 11, 1943:

> Dear Hugh:
> There is no such thing like an irresistible force and immovable body. But there seems to be a very stubborn boy who has forced his way victoriously through strange difficulties created by himself for this purpose.
> Sincerely yours,
> A. Einstein

Charlie has to admit he's impressed. "Wow, he answered kids?"

"Yeah, and I met him once. Pretty old then. He couldn't follow my theory at all. I told him there was a substantive parallel between my relative state and Einstein's relativity. See, quantum mechanics had this observer who supposedly collapses a wave function, chooses one outcome. Nonsense! There's no theory of collapse, none at all. See, the external observer comes in just the way that Einstein had to defeat, when he showed there was no privileged inertial frame."

Charlie doesn't know relativity and this is getting way above him. He manages, "Einstein couldn't see that?"

Everett smirks, lights a Camel with a steel lighter. "Bohr couldn't either."

"But what does it mean in, say, our lives? If—"

"Look, physicists themselves are obliged to be their own epistemologists. *Die Welt ist bizarr,* as the Germans say."

"But we can't prove your theory, right?"

"My view is falsifiable, sure—if quantum mechanics proves wrong."

I wonder what he'd say if I told him about my life, Charlie thinks, and decides not to. It would mean a quick rejection. Everett must have met others who—ah.

"Have you met anyone who claimed to come from some alternate time track?"

"Huh? No, but I get plenty of objections from people who think I've made the universe—get this!—too big." He laughs, shakes his head.

Charlie smiles, nods, leading him on. "That must freak people out."

"You bet." Everett grins. "They feel tiny and insignificant and think that nothing matters in this world. Look, that makes no more sense than getting depressed when you find out that cows are bigger than you. What's the goddamn big deal about bigness? A cow is much bigger than you, but it is a ridiculous animal and you are a valuable person. You know it's a cow. It doesn't know anything. It just stands there eating grass and mooing. And if it were bigger, that would only make it more ridiculous. Then we eat it."

"I guess no one has any idea how to reach these other universes of yours?"

"Nope, nothing in the theory about that. People in all branches of the wave function were equally real."

"So there are more of you? And me?"

A shrug, as if all of this is obvious. "Gotta be. The number of branches of the universal wave function—it's an *uncountable* infinity." Everett sucks in smoke and expels a plume with relish.

"Does human consciousness play a role in all this?"

Everett smiles, shakes his head. "Nope, to think we humans have any say in the particular quantum world we're in would require an idea Einstein hated—'spooky action at a distance,' entanglement."

"Couldn't these worlds get entangled through the human mind?" Charlie is desperate to connect Everett's ideas to his double life.

Everett waves this away. "Look, why care? I'm guaranteed immortality already! My consciousness is bound at each branching, after all. My other selves will follow whatever path does not lead to death—and so on ad infinitum."

"So you don't care about this world?"

Everett laughs, belly shaking, and pounds the table. "Love me, love my wave function!"

A digital alarm clock plays a short synthesized tune. "Hey, time's up. At eleven thirty every morning, everybody here has to drop whatever they're doing and eat. Beats the lunch crowd." Everett stands and waves a hand at Charlie. "It's fun to get back to my old ideas." Then he adds ruefully, "Seems most physicists have turned against them."

21

Sid has arranged for the private investigator to come down to Laguna Beach. A rainy November Tuesday, and the man is more than an hour late.

When Charlie answers the door, he faces a middle-aged man with little hair, a damp plaid suit, and a studiedly bland expression hanging like a shawl over his face. "Mr. Moment?" A flat voice, too. Jack Webb objectivity. Charlie nods. Rain patters down into the silence. A beat passes as they eye each other in the gray light.

"Frank Flangetti. Mr. Field said you would be expecting me."

"Nice to meet you."

They shake hands formally, Flangetti withdrawing his hand quickly, guiltily. "Sorry I was so late."

Charlie lures the man into his living room by backing away from him. Flangetti moves forward, guardedly examining his environment. It is like a status dance. "Nice place you have here."

Charlie thinks that Flangetti has ex-cop written all over him—modest background, deference to wealth but inside a suspicion of it, almost a resentment. Or maybe Charlie has made too many cop movies.

"Me and the boys, at least my guys when I was still with the OC

Sheriff's Department, we really liked that film you did with the bomber."

"*Speed.*"

"Yeah, that's the one. A bomb in a bus. That bad guy was so realistic."

"Did you mind that he was an ex-cop?"

A shrug. "I've known some bad ones, in my time."

Charlie has Flangetti sit down but remains standing himself. Silent.

"You want me to find someone, Mr. Moment?"

"Yes, in a way, I do."

Flangetti takes out a small spiral notebook and a pencil. "Name? Last known location?" He looks up expectantly.

"I'm afraid a name will be hard."

"Can you describe her?"

Charlie frowns. "It's not one person. It's a group of people."

"An organization?"

"Maybe."

A shadow of exasperation darkens Flangetti's face. "Do you have any leads to share with me?"

"Yes." Charlie finally sits down and looks up at the ceiling, scratching at his beard with his left hand. "I am after people who know about certain things."

"Is this a blackmail case?" There is a note of pleasure in Flangetti's voice.

Charlie laughs grimly, almost with derision. "No, not at all, Frank. This is a case unlike any you've had before."

"Okay." Flangetti's forehead is a field of curving furrows.

"I can't tell you what my goal is, but I can supply you with a lot of leads."

"All right. I've had some tough projects before. You don't work in vice for eleven years without seeing more than your fair share."

Charlie has no more time for prevarication. He stands up and begins pacing, barking instructions at Flangetti. "Here are your leads. Time travel. Monica Lewinsky. Reincarnation. *Twelve Monkeys.* Yahoo.com—"

"Yoo-hoo come?"

"I'll spell it."

Over the next half hour, Charlie spells out miscellaneous names and details from the late 1990s, anything that no one could know after Ford's second successful presidential campaign. He ignores the expressions that pass over Flangetti's face. He doesn't even look at the man. He directs him to small ads near the backs of magazines, personal messages in the classifieds, short ads on radio stations. Then he ushers Flangetti out without further explanation. *Go.*

Despite the morning's foggy rain, the afternoon clears. Sunlight sparkles off the high waves booming below Charlie's cliff house. He flips through an overwritten script sent by messenger from the studio and snorts. More and more, Hollywood's basic rule is the law of thermodramatics. To get more audience, turn up the heat. Go back to the pulps, use a touch of wit, do the Lucas-Spielberg scrub, and presto! The land of megabucks. He scrawls *REWRITE!* across it. Muttering, he tosses the script into a corner and tries to forget it.

Then it occurs: rewrite is exactly what he's doing to his life. This is a chance to rewrite a previous draft of Opus Charlie. And who in humanity wouldn't want that?

He is listening to "Time Out of Mind" from Steely Dan's *Gaucho* LP when the thought occurs to him that he doesn't need to act older anymore, setting off on a new life within a new life, with the swelling from the abandoned medication coming down. He can be himself—whoever that might be. Charlie Rewrite.

He goes to the bathroom and ransacks the cupboards for a shaver. His beard is too thick to be cut with a small blade. With scissors from the kitchen, he hacks away at the beard. A few cuts and a lot of shaving cream later, his bare face stares back at him, a face he hardly knows. It strikes him as juvenile at first. But after a few theatrical frowns and smiles, mugging at himself in the mirror, he makes a connection between the young face and himself. New Charlie. Not even Charlie Two anymore. Just New.

His suntanned nose and forehead look odd, framed by virginal white skin around his mouth and below his cheekbones. He puts some lotion on the tanned areas, and the contrasting colors of his skin look a bit less severe. Charlie decides to tan the rest of his face before going out during the day, so that he won't look like some freak staggering up from the town beach.

Lying out on his capacious sunlit balcony, Charlie lets the warmth of the sun bake some of the tension out of his body. He needs to stop being a slob. The medication made his belly soft again. A wheeze to his breath, a heaviness in muscle and bone. Not as bad as forty-eight-year-old Charlie One after his slack, joyless decades back east. But not good.

He can get that fit body back. He will unravel the riddle of his existence. He will enjoy life more. He will let go.

The ersatz French restaurant on the Pacific Coast Highway amuses Charlie, the vintage junk masquerading as antiques, the colorized black-and-white photos in the john pretending to be hand-colored photogravure from the nineteenth century.

The gay waiter is very nice to him, nicer than Charlie is used to in brittle Hollywood. He's not a celeb here, either. Then he realizes that he must look a lot cuter without the beard, less manly. He still feels self-conscious about the stylish short haircut, even with the mousse and gel washed out a few hours after he left the salon. The little spikes made Charlie feel like an absolute idiot, leaving aside the creepy sensation of the goo against his scalp. Charlie One never tried anything of the sort. But maybe the waiter's interest is some kind of positive review of his new appearance.

Feeling much better about himself, he pays his bill in cash and wanders out onto the evening street. Looking both ways, he decides to cross over to the sidewalk closer to the beach.

He looks into the windows of the shops as he walks by. The lit-up storefronts of the Laguna Beach antique shops impress him with their window displays of genuine medieval furniture, dark carved wood almost shimmering with age. The past is always with us. In his case, he is in a past avenue veering far from that of his first life. But little details of the past of Charlie One do not match this time. That Nixon and the Republicans would actually get some love along with respect amazes him, and he still wonders if his *Dick* film was the cause. And he has never found any trace of Bob Greenway in his memories of the last life.

22

Phil Dick leans forward, eyes piercing. "See, damn near all my work starts with the basic assumption that there cannot be one single, objective reality. *Cannot*."

Charlie leans back and nods, putting on his pondering face, as he has learned to do with Phil. The man is wearing baggy trousers and a worn shirt, a Berkeley bohemian with wrinkled clothes, stringy gray hair, dirty fingernails, an apparent indifference to shaving. Not Hollywood, no.

Charlie can see the throat muscles straining as Phil's reedy voice squeezes out, "So y'see, I really want a last scene, toward the end. When we've overthrown the Nazis, and their leaders—including Adolf!—get tried for their war crimes. The führer's last words are *Deutsche, hier steh' ich*—which means, 'Germans, here I stand.' Damn powerful stuff."

"That takes the movie pretty far afield—" Charlie begins.

"Look, one major theme of my stories asks the question, What constitutes the authentic human being? So this movie, the universe where the Axis won, it's only shadows in our universe."

"Uh, yeah . . ."

"I want to have Hitler *not* get hanged, but fade away, kinda evaporate, to suggest that it's not necessarily real. See?"

"Isn't that something like ending it with 'it was all a dream'?"

Phil stands, pumped with energy, scowling. "Hell no! That's not what I mean at all."

Charlie stares at Phil. Getting through the script phase is always tough, with lots of notes and bright, new dumb ideas from the usual suspects. But Phil keeps showing up *here*, at his home, waving a copy of the latest revision. It is 6:00 p.m. on a Friday, usually Charlie's time to take a dive into the Laguna Beach scene—bars with ocean curlers crashing white nearby, overpriced beers, cocky Ray-Bans, carefully tuned tans, perfect hair. But he didn't want to turn Phil out and risk pushing the man into some lurching act-out scene at the studio. No, better to let him spout his steam here. *Writers!* he thinks. *I'm one, but sure as hell not like this.*

With careful calm he says, "I'll take this new slant up with the studio guys. Kick it around a little. New idea for an ending."

"Those pikers don't know an ending from their own ass!"

"Um, well, y'know, Phil, I have to work within the studio system—"

"That's your mistake. You should be an independent. Monumental Pictures—get it? Your name, Moment, is sort of in the name."

Going independent will be a fine idea a decade or so up ahead, Charlie knows, but not now. Especially when he's wrapped up in his rocky personal life, which is leading . . . where? He realizes suddenly that he has no idea. . . .

To cover his sudden confusion, he begins, "Phil . . . I . . . really—"

Phil waves this away and says, "Look, what I'm getting at is kinda like something where I live, just a few miles from Disneyland. For years they had the Lincoln simulacrum running there. Like Lincoln himself, pretty good robot. So that Lincoln was only a temporary form, which matter and energy take"—he spread his arms wide—"and then lose."

Charlie wonders if Phil is onto something or just daft.

"See, the same is true of each of us, like it or not. Fake realities will create fake humans. Or fake humans will generate fake realities and then sell them to other humans—turning them, eventually, into forgeries of themselves. So we wind up with fake humans inventing fake realities and then peddling them to other fake humans. It is just a very large version of Disneyland, see? You can have the pirate ride or the Lincoln simulacrum or Mr. Toad's Wild Ride—you can have all of them, but none is *true*. But a movie can be! See?"

Phil has succumbed to the American faith that if a novel is good enough, important enough, it will be made into a movie, and so become immortal.

"Ahhhh . . . ," he begins, pauses. Charlie knows now that Phil has an odd tap into the reality Charlie sees all too well. But how to now get the man off this tirade, not let it disturb the movie script they are trying to hatch?

Phil says, "Y'know, people think we science fiction writers predict the future. I remember that the US Department of the Interior made a thorough prediction of trends in 1937, and they missed atomic energy, computers, radar, antibiotics, and World War Two. Yet they all kept on with this simpleminded, linear extrapolation that was merely a new way to be stupid in an expensive fashion."

"Uh, so—"

"See, I want to write about people I love, and put them into a fictional world spun out of my own mind, not the world we actually have, because the world we actually have does not meet my standards. I can see now that the universe is information and we are stationary in it, not three-dimensional and not in space or time. We're something like computers, really, compiling our reality as we go. Charlie, I am a fictionalizing philosopher, not a novelist."

"I think *High Castle* will make that clear to the public," Charlie says to mollify the man, and get him to move on.

Phil shrugs off the idea and sits, his face knotting. "See, I've been having . . . visits. Visions."

"Like?"

"Like I've lived other lives. I'm sure of it now. Like I'm remembering something that was real, solid—recalling it at last."

"You remember being where?"

"The visions continue to get more real, specific, recovered memories. Scenes of ancient Rome—jammed streets beneath those temples, torches, riots. All superimposed over my boring Santa Ana neighborhood. I'll look at a local playground and see a Roman prison. Behind a chain-link fence I saw iron bars peeking through. Children playing, laughing—but I saw overlaid on them Christian martyrs, sobbing, about to be fed to lions or the gladiators. People on the street, they had Roman military uniforms or tunics. Stone walls, brass doors, right beside Trader Joe's."

Could this be some error in Phil's transition from an earlier life? Static blocking his memories, until now, in his fifties?

"I didn't go back in time, see, but in a sense Rome came forward. To me. My past self was getting through by insidious and sly degrees, under new names, hidden by the flak talk and phony obscurations, at last into our world again."

Charlie thinks, *A clue?*

"Suppose that time stopped in A.D. seventy, the year the temple of Jerusalem was destroyed by a Roman siege. Everything that happened afterward was an illusion, see? So our world is still under Rome's dominion."

Definitely woo-woo. But Charlie lets the man ramble on, hoping for some nugget of truth. Could Phil be some scrambled, reincarnated self?

"I believe the Roman Empire is active, not just images I can see. It was embodied in the tyrannical Nixon administration, for sure. They're responsible for the assassination of Martin Luther King Jr. I—"

"What's your role in this, then, Phil?"

"I'm an undercover Christian revolutionary, fighting to overthrow the empire. That's why I react so much when I see a passing pretty blonde wearing the fish emblem, the Christian sign."

"What's all this mean?"

Phil leans back and peers at the ceiling, eyes veiled, breath shallow and fast. "Here I'm going to call on your faith in me. I'm telling truth here. I got this through revelations that start with a portal of pink light. These memories, they always start with that pink. It's a spiritual force that unlocks my consciousness. It's divine, see? It grants me access to esoteric knowledge. So I've fictionalized these experiences in a novel, *VALIS*. Stands for 'Vast Active Living Intelligence System'—which is what's telling me this. It's a transcendental, mystical mind, see?"

Charlie doesn't know what to say, but Phil is on a roll anyway. The man leans forward and words fly from his mouth at machine-gun pace, a hoarse fusillade.

"I'm forming up a trilogy, all constellating around a basic theme. In the novel a guy I named Horselover Fat—who's really me, my name translated from Greek and German—comes across a perfect description of the Black Iron Prison, which we all live in, but set in the far future. If you superimpose the past—say, ancient Rome, where I lived and rebelled—over the present California in the twentieth century, then superimpose the far future world. In the future, y'see, drug use is widespread, and the age of consent has been lowered to fifteen—more fun for all, I guess. So you got the empire, as the supra- or trans-temporal constant. Everyone who has ever lived is literally surrounded by the iron walls of the prison; they are all inside it and none of them know it. Except those of us who can see the past, lived there."

Charlie doesn't know how to respond. Phil throws out his arms as if to an audience, and bursts into rasping song.

> *"Flow, my tears, fall from your springs!*
> *Exiled for ever, let me mourn;*

Where night's black bird her sad infamy sings,
There let me live forlorn."

Phil sits down, grinning. "That's from the sixteenth century. I learned it as a boy—in that century."

"You mean you can recall yourself in multiple past lives?"

"Yes! I doubt my previous selves ever knew their past, but now I do. God pointed it out to me with the pink light." He leans back and sighs, contented. "Y'know, the technical term for this is 'theophany'—self-disclosure by the divine."

Charlie recalls that when he first woke up as Charlie Two, he toyed with the idea that he was being divinely reincarnated. That phase lasted maybe a month. Then he started looking into physics.

"Why does it have to be from God?"

Phil seems startled by this. He considers, face furrowed with passing emotions, and then says abruptly, "Okay, take a science fiction approach, then. I'll put it this way. We appear to be memory coils—that is, DNA carriers capable of experience—in a big, computer-like thinking system. See? So all of humanity, through time, has correctly recorded and stored thousands of years of experiential information—lives lived, stored. We're in this system now, see? And each of us possesses somewhat different deposits from all the other life-forms, data stacked up. Sometimes, like my past in ancient Rome, there's a malfunction—a failure—of storage. Some info comes right into our experience. We feel it, see it, again."

"How much of the life do you recall?" *Nearly all of it, like me? But then, I was a historian, not a pulp writer on speed.*

Phil waves this away. "Snatches, mostly fights. Plus boring manual labor—we have no idea how easy we have it today!"

"So is this VALIS thing useful?" *Like telling you what movies will be hits?*

Phil brightens. "Yeah, once when I was with VALIS, I got an

insight. The system, VALIS, it told me my infant son was in danger of perishing from some unnamed malady. So I take him to the doc, who does routine a checkup—no trouble or illness, the doc says. But I insisted that he run thorough tests, paid extra for 'em. The doc fussed and argued, but I stood firm and he eventually complied, though there were no apparent symptoms. They discovered a hernia! It would've *killed* my boy if I'd let it go. An operation made him survive. I attribute that to the intervention of VALIS, the network."

Charlie sits back and thinks while Phil relates another event. He had an incident of "xenoglossy"—which Phil says was the sudden ability to speak Koine, a common Greek dialect during the high point of the civilization. His wife transcribed some, and a linguist identified it. "I had it for days, then gone. But it came back when I took Sandoz."

"Sandoz?"

"LSD-25. I took it to test if I was mentally ill. I passed."

"Speaking Greek on LSD."

"Yeah, what else? Look, I know my kinda divine madness sounds like somethin' mental, but it wasn't. Sharp, clear memories—from two thousand years ago."

Charlie wonders if these were psychotic breaks or a religious experience, and how would one tell the difference? And if not psychosis, is Dick's mental universe rooted in the same weirdness as his own?

Once he started actively working with Dick after coming back from Illinois, he noticed that Dick still used amphetamines to write fast, even now, with movie money coming in. His refrigerator was stuffed with bottles of amphetamine pills jammed in next to premade milk shakes. Phil gulped the pills by the handful and washed them down with the milk shakes, calling them his "happiness pills" and "nightmare tabs."

Phil seems to read Charlie's mind. "I know, I know—I admit it, I'm a flipped-out freak—"

"Have you ever had, uh, anything happen to you that was . . . uh, like reliving history? Your own personal history?"

Phil looks suspiciously at him. "Maybe . . ."

Ding-ding goes his doorbell. With relief he holds up a hand to stop Phil and bounds across his living room to answer it himself.

"Ah!" Charlie cries in relief as he takes a script from a studio messenger. "Sorry, Phil, I promised I'd read this—it's in an auction, last day."

Phil fidgets, eyes dancing, and in a burst of energy says, "Hey, good idea, go to those script guys, but get that new Hitler ending in the script, right?"

Charlie can but nod. Phil does not know that screenwriters regard original authors as pests.

Within a moment Phil goes out the door like a man fleeing devils, slamming it. But then, that is his style, yes, the whole massive bulk of fearful demons half seen.

Could poor Phil be a degenerated example of multiple rebirths? Or reincarnations, maybe a better term? Has Phil ratcheted down through millennia, somehow passing through different bodies? Then others who claim to have past lives are plausible candidates. Could weird double lives be muddled in the minds of people farther down the pipeline of time?

23

On a dusky corner Charlie comes across a bar he hasn't noticed before, the Sandpiper Lounge on South Coast Highway. A departing drunken beach couple throw open the bar's door, and ringing reggae crossed with Jimi Hendrix floods out, tight Caribbean offbeat *thump-thump* accents married to long, distorted notes from a warpo guitar. *Was there music like this the first time around?* he wonders. *Worth a closer inspection*, he says to himself, and goes inside.

An attractive young black girl with shiny dreadlocks and Rastafarian rag clothes sings sulky notes into a microphone. The music is slow, methodical, but she bounces through it all, springing off the balls of her feet, rocking her shoulders backward and forward. Her verve captivates Charlie, standing just a few yards away from the bandstand.

Her lyrics are about time, magical time, precious time, just enough long liquid time to be with a lover. *Time*, Charlie thinks, *the mystery in my life. Am I a time traveler, or is this all a complicated illusion? Is life nothing more than an illusion, a distraction impairing our awareness, our spiritual evolution? Can't hire a detective to find that out . . .*

Charlie notices an improbably pallid guitarist throttling the neck of a Stratocaster. The melodic line is laced with feedback, both mechanical and alive, so striking that the singer stops bouncing to look at the guitarist creating the wash of sound.

With a twinge of guilt Charlie realizes that the blond guitarist reminds him of James. Charlie gropes for a stool to sit on.

The music is so good, complete and enveloping, Charlie loses all sense of time and place. At least, he does until a taciturn beach blonde wearing a tight pink body shirt drops a cocktail napkin on the stained wood of his table.

"What'll it be?" she yells at him, barely audible over the music.

"Scotch. Double."

The band finishes its song with an abrupt crashing chord. They confer briefly, then leave the small stage. It looks like a break, because they leave their instruments behind. Charlie's eyes follow the blond guitarist with a morbid curiosity.

"Good, huh?"

Charlie looks around to find a slightly plump girl with curly brown hair sitting next to him, in clothes far too good for the beach bar.

"Sorry, I didn't notice you."

She pushes his arm slightly. "You sure know how to hurt a girl's feelings." Her smile is warm but her jaw is set at an angle.

Charlie smiles back at her tentatively.

"You look familiar," she says.

"You might have seen me before."

"In here? I don't come to the Sandpiper that often."

"It's my first time."

"How do you like the Rebel Rockers?"

"Amazing!"

Her eyes flicker, appraising him. "You down here from LA?"

"That easy to tell?" He must have a city hardness now.

"Just a feeling." A bold, assessing gaze. "Going through a divorce?"

So this woman has him in her sights. And something about her attracts him.

"I'll admit it."

"Good. I hate guys who act like they're single, even if they have two kids and a wife back home in Irvine."

Ouch, thinks Charlie.

"You look pretty young to be going through a divorce." Her eyes are saucers of curiosity.

"I got married when I was twenty-one."

"Wow, that was dumb."

Charlie smiles to himself. *But then, you have no idea what I've been through, do you, so young and self-confident?*

"How old are you?" he asks.

"Don't you think that's kind of a personal question?" She tosses her head back, somehow moving closer to him at the same time, lowers her eyes, and turns her shoulders toward him.

"I guess."

"Twenty-nine. Think I'm too old for you?"

"Could be."

"You're what, thirty?"

"Close enough."

"Are you an attorney?"

Charlie laughs out loud and shakes his head. "I don't stoop that low."

"Okay—doctor? Just out of your residency?"

He has to smile. "Not even close."

"Yeah, I guess you are a little too alive to be an MD." She pushes an attractive silk scarf to one side, creamy white décolletage coming into Charlie's view. He notices that her perfume must be expensive because it is subtle, but he doesn't recognize it.

"No, I work for Action Pictures."

"Do you know Steven Spielberg?"

"A bit."

"Wow." A dazzled-fan expression flits across her face, and she quickly replaces it with a hip smile. "I love his movies. Such great ideas."

"Thank you." Charlie thinks Spielberg isn't so much an idea type as a genius at choosing the right shot and cadence, but that's too much to convey in a bar.

A grin spreads across her face. "Are you one of his assistant directors or photographers, like that?"

"No. I'm more of a management guy."

"Oh. You seemed more like a creative person."

"Sometimes I am."

When Charlie wakes up, a seagull is tapping on his floor-height bedroom window with a yellow beak, its head cocked to one side. Charlie opens an eye, wincing from the sunlight, catching the tang of the salty air, and gets an appraising look from the dusty gray seagull. The gray-and-white bird wobbles alongside the window, marching on the balcony like it owns the place.

Charlie grows tired of ornithology and sits up in bed. The girl from the night before is snoring slightly, her light-olive flesh oddly striking against the white sheets. Charlie searches his mind for her name, draws a blank. She was all agog at his movie creds, a cheap shot on his part, though he kept them vague. He even used some stale insider jokes ("What's your movie about?" "It's about to make me rich") and she laughed merrily. The sex was mechanical, and her chuckling, crooning pleasure felt like an audition.

He goes to the bathroom to pee, and when he gets back, the woman is slowly shaking the night out of her brown curls.

"Nice place"—she yawns—"oooof! . . . you have here."

"Belongs to a friend of mine."

"Some friend. It's not Steven Spielberg, is it?" A glow rises in her voice.

"No. My CEO."

"Cool." She lifts her knees up, hugging herself. "What's it like in Hollywood?"

"Pretty much the same as everywhere else. Envy, jealousy, greed, vanity—"

"Thank you. I was in a sorority—I don't need life lessons."

"USC?"

"Yeah."

"I figured."

"Humph. And you?"

"I didn't go to college." He enjoys the lie, partly because the woman would never understand the truth.

"You talk like you went. You know, in sentences."

"I've done some screenwriting. It helps."

"Any movies I might have seen?"

"*Dick. Godfather. Jaws. Indiana Jones. Dinosaurs Lost in Time.*"

"Bullshit." She makes a scornful face.

"No, really."

"Then you must be—"

The phone rings, cutting her off.

24

Flangetti contacts Charlie in the spring about meeting to share his findings. The day is hot, with horsetail clouds skittering across an azure sky. Charlie is wearing his gym clothes, planning to go to the beach afterward for some pickup basketball. He's already had his run and push-ups and weights. Going off the valproate is giving his body back his youth.

The private dick is wearing the same plaid suit. Bad taste is eternal. Flangetti has found a miscellany of things for Charlie to look at. Something about a minor actress called Mona Lewinsky. A mail-order service called Yoo-Hoo, which sells customized greeting cards. Flangetti has brought science fiction, plenty of it. A novel called *Replay*. A book by Jack Finney, *Time and Again*. *Timescape*, by James Benford.

"You might find *Timescape* interesting. The guy who wrote it teaches at the University of California. Chemistry, something like that."

"Berkeley? UCLA?"

"Nope. UC Irvine, just up MacArthur from PCH. You haven't seen it?"

"No reason to." Except for working with Phil Dick on the *High Castle* screenplay, Charlie has become the Hermit of Laguna Beach, reading scripts sent down by messengers, working the phone. Even meditating.

"You might enjoy the novel. I couldn't get past the third chapter—all those English people, kinda boring. But it's about 1962 connecting with 1998. It was like some of the things you say."

"Boneford?"

"Benford."

Charlie reads the novel all the rest of the day and on into the night. He finishes by noon the next day, his hair matted with sweat, bread crumbs on his rumpled shirt. He lies propped up on the white cushions of his Bauhaus sofa, cans of Coke lined up on the glass coffee table next to him. Too much to take in . . . He closes his eyes and falls asleep instantly.

The phone rings: James. He wants to know when Charlie is going to join him. Charlie tries to think of an excuse, but he can't find one. He stammers as he tries to beg off, but James keeps insisting that Charlie join him.

The phone rings again. Charlie wakes with a start, sour mouthed.

James? It was a dream. The goddamn novel has screwed up his reality. *Much more of this and I'll be talking to the walls. And they'll answer.*

James Benford's office is packed with books and papers, a few astronomical paintings of planets and galaxies on the walls. He seems to organize by the fossil method, with oldest paper on the bottom of teetering stacks. The man himself has a full ruddy-brown beard and thick plastic glasses, and is moderately tall and fit.

"Now, what can I do for you, Mr. Moment?"

"Charlie."

"Call me Jim. I've seen several of your movies. I was surprised by *Dick*, I'll admit."

"I was too."

Benford's frown says he isn't sure what to make of this remark. He clears a chair for Charlie to sit in. They get comfortable, Benford rocking slightly from side to side and wringing his right wrist in an odd way, as if he is trying to stay limber.

"I just finished reading *Timescape*."

Benford's chest visibly swells. "Did you like it?"

Writers are always praise hungry. "It's the most important book I've ever read."

Benford pauses. He must get crank visitors, who usually open with outrageous admiration. Charlie knows that he wonders if this beardless young man in gym clothes could really be Charles Moment of Action Pictures. Benford remarks that he has heard about him from his friends in the B-movie business, but the face doesn't fit his mental image of the man.

"I've recently shaved my beard off, if you're wondering." Charlie finds Benford almost perfectly transparent. He likes that about the man.

"No, no. I'm just not used to people from the film community having such a high opinion of my work."

"Yes, I know what you mean. I do have an interest in optioning the novel for a movie." Charlie can see the cash registers lighting up in Benford's eyes. *No harm in that*, Charlie thinks.

"Well. Really."

"But today I would like to talk with you about the ideas in the book."

"Really?" Benford's eyebrows ascend almost to his hairline.

"Yes. In your book you have the physicists in 1998 send a signal to the physicists in 1962, altering history. Using those faster-than-light particles, tachyons."

"Yep. It's an alternate-universe plot, really."

"So you think there are multiple alternate universes?"

"Um, maybe."

"Like that episode of *Star Trek* with the bad Kirk and the bad Spock?"

Benford laughs. "Sort of."

"And time can flow both ways?"

"I got a fan letter with a joke about that. A barman says: 'We don't serve faster-than-light particles here.' Then a tachyon enters the bar."

Charlie doesn't laugh and neither does Benford, who shrugs. "Physics jokes are tough. So, yes—paradoxes arise with time travel. The Grandfather Gotcha, I call it. Though I don't think that we could actually send your body back to 1962, for example."

"What about my mind?"

"That depends on what you mean by 'mind.' Why do you ask, anyway?"

Charlie thinks about what to say to Benford. Should he just tell him the truth? *No. I need to get what I can from him as a scientist. I don't want him backing away from me as a lunatic.*

"I have a screenplay device in mind."

Benford scowls skeptically. Maybe he's already been burned in Hollywood's labyrinths. To deflect him, Charlie asks, "What do you think of Everett's multiverse idea?"

Benford blinks. "Fun to think about, logically defensible. Nobody really believes it—but I found it handy. Writers are magpies."

Charlie keeps his voice flat and factual. "*Timescape* was economical, supposing that the Everett interpretation didn't really apply to *every* event. That it only worked when there was a causal paradox."

Just as Charlie has often seen many Hollywood writers brighten when a studio figure likes their ideas, Benford nods eagerly. "Then the universe splits into as many versions as it takes to cover all the possibilities. No more than that. So you could send some grandfather-killing message and Grandfather would die. But not in the universe you are doomed to inhabit. Instead, another universe appears, unknown to you. The new universe is entangled with the first, while the paradox is created. Then they part ways. In the new one, dear old Grandfather dies and you never happen at all. No paradox, since the tachyon signal that killed Gramps came from your universe, where you're still stuck."

Charlie nods. "Nifty. Any evidence for that?"

Benford shrugs. "I've got a plasma lab to run and grants to write. Those are the real science fiction—the fantasy is the budget section."

"But how does the time travel part work in your theory?"

"In *Timescape* I tried to finesse the paradoxes by combining special relativity, those tachyons, with quantum mechanics." Benford yawns. "Right now people like Tipler are advertising making a time machine using a rotating black hole with the mass of a small galaxy. If you don't have tachyons, time travel seems to require vast projects."

Charlie sees Benford is losing interest. A knock at the door diverts the man's attention further—a student's head appears. "Come back during office hours," Benford says curtly.

Charlie counters quickly, "So what would a time travel theory look like?"

"You'd have to go with the full-bore Everett interpretation. See, in quantum cosmology there is no single history of space-time. Instead, all possible histories happen simultaneously. For the vast preponderance of cases, no problem"—he grins—"that ontological bloat of an infinitude of worlds has no observable consequences. It's just a way of talking about quantum mechanics."

"You mean they don't exist?"

"Not in any way you can measure. Think of unending sheets stacked on end and next to one another, like the pages in a magazine. Time lines flow up them. A causal loop snakes through these sheets, so the parallel universes become one. If the grandson goes back in time, he crosses to another time-sheet. There he shoots Granddad and lives thereafter in that universe. His granddad lived as before and had grandchildren, one of whom disappears, period. Game over."

"So time travel occurs because of . . . what?"

"Y'see, quantum mechanics always furnishes as many linked

universes as there would be conflicting outcomes—it's quite economical. All those universes form part of a larger object. According
to quantum theory, that big library of sheets is the real arena where
things happen." Benford gazes out one of the windows of his office at
the hills of the UCI campus and sighs. "Cosmic stuff indeed."

Charlie ventures, "What could cause, say, transfer of—well, maybe
identity?"

"Huh?"

"Minds, I mean. Transfer of minds, information? The whole quantum thing, that kind of connection entails—what did you call it?
Entangled?"

"Two things that share the same quantum mechanical description.
We call it the state function."

"So two things that are twins—"

Benford laughs. "Not exactly. Hell, I'm a twin."

Charlie blinks. "Fraternal or identical?"

"Fraternals are just womb mates. We are the closest form of identi-
cals, mirror twins. Very close in interests, too. Greg is doing research
at Physics International."

"A physicist as well? I guess genetics count. So are you two—"

"Quantum entangled? Nope—takes a lot more for that! We're big,
classical objects, not wispy quantum stuff like information." He
laughs merrily. "Look, let's go to lunch."

Charlie can see Benford is getting restless, not a man for endless
talk. Glancing at the man's itchy hands, Charlie is uncomfortably
aware that real science is done by people with dirt under their fingernails.

Benford turns out to be an agreeable fellow, from Alabama by way
of his father's military postings in Japan and Germany. Just a bit
southern. Talking with animation as he and Charlie walk through
the UC Irvine arboretum on their way to lunch, he seems far more

interesting than the social scientists Charlie One had to work with. *Or have those colorless figures just faded in his recollection?* At least this physicist uses little jargon and cheerfully acknowledges that there's plenty nobody knows.

Benford takes him to a hamburger place at the student union, improbably called Bogart's. The menu items are named according to Bogart movies: Maltese Falcon, Key Largo, High Sierra, African Queen. But the food is good and cheap, though they sit at a plastic table with their food on trays. *Not quite Beverly Hills*, thinks Charlie. *But not gloomy George Washington University, either.*

For the first time in this life, Charlie relaxes and talks with Benford, using his full vocabulary and insight. He doesn't have to pull punches the way he has to at the studio, even with Bob Greenway. Charlie feels a wave of gratitude to Benford, as if the physics professor wrote *Timescape* expressly for him.

But Benford is talking, and Charlie knows he shouldn't behave too oddly, not if he is to get Benford's help. ". . . Paul Davies's book on time asymmetry was really the first step in this direction. What I did was make it something real, something that would engage the reader's imagination."

"Without the usual Jules Verne style of magical science."

"Or H. G. Wells, a more appropriate point of reference."

"Indeed."

Benford pauses to take a giant swig of his Coke and bite into his burger with gusto, a little relish falling unnoticed onto his short-sleeved shirt. For a man who has written a novel about time, he seems not to have enough of it. Charlie takes advantage of the pause. "I was wondering about making some changes to the plot, to see if you could find a way to justify them in terms of physics."

Benford makes a wordless murmur of assent while chewing, though he looks skeptical of Hollywood plot contrivances.

"Let's say we think about sending signals back in time without changing the physical makeup of anything in the past. Suppose we don't even use any equipment. Just the mind."

Benford swallows. "Like the time travel in Finney's *Time and Again* or Grimmond's *Replay?*"

"Exactly." It was Grimwood, actually, but never mind.

Benford is quick. "Or *Peggy Sue* . . ." Charlie feels a tremor of fear and stops himself. "Or my *Back to the Five-and-Dime.*"

"The film where the guy goes back to the fifties and has a career as a singer?"

"Exactly." Charlie is relieved that Benford didn't catch the slip. Although why should he be worried about a movie that has not been made in this world, Charlie thinks, that Benford couldn't have seen? *Perhaps I have the illusion that Benford is a time traveler too? Could he be another one? I'll have to watch for that.*

Carefully, Charlie returns to the crucial issue. "How could we explain that in the screenplay? What sort of physical principle might justify the plot device?"

"Why do you want to go there? We can use tachyons, faster-than-light particles, if we have machines sending signals through time."

"I think the movie audience would find the machines and the tachyons a turnoff. Too complicated."

"So you want to film my novel without the hard-SF trappings?"

"Sort of."

Benford bristles. "Then what would be left?"

Charlie drives back to Laguna Beach disappointed by the way the meeting turned out, especially after the rapport that he felt he established at first with Benford. Maybe it was Benford's fear that Action Pictures would rape his book, Charlie thinks. A reasonable enough dread.

In any case, the physics professor said good-bye without providing a theoretical scenario for Charlie's form of time travel, though he said he would think about it. Charlie has hopes for Benford, but also a sense of unease. It was tense keeping up his facade around someone who might pick up on the slightest anachronism or counterfactual error. But as he drives along PCH, the gentle waves and salty air of the Pacific calm Moment, sea breezes filling his lungs as he swoops along the curve above a crescent beach at the edge of town. Balmy, beautiful, time stands still.

But as Laguna Beach itself slides by, his mood darkens. Benford's talk of twins and quantum entanglements has set his mind buzzing, fretful. He hasn't thought of his second life as a swap. Charlie One asleep on his sixteenth birthday—what happened to that fresh young mind? He has it riding in him now, but is it somehow copied . . . elsewhere?

Now the horror of it descends, all the darker as the bright California sunshine around tries to cheer him up. Do Benford's off-the-cuff remarks mean that Charlie Two woke up as that truck smashed into the Volvo in the year 2000? Then the swap killed Charlie One and let Charlie Two be reborn, in some balancing quantum justice?

He tries to put those thoughts aside and concentrate on driving up the hill to Merrill's house. But his mind will not quiet.

It's not as if this life didn't have a darker side before. There was the flickering, and the dreams, nightdreams and daymares where he seemed to inhabit other people and other bodies. Even after he was placed under Habib's care, the weirdness laced through his Hollywood years, even as the medication pushed the flickering and the dreams away—his previous life submerged. Even while medication and therapy built up his defenses against his dual life, he felt displaced from other people. He has come to view the endless lines of people, tramping on stirring dust, from the outside. For them, life is a long march, an endless column of souls moving forward through surrounding dark. In that crowd nobody knows where they're going, but there is plenty of talk, and the fools, some called philosophers, pretend to understand more than they're saying. There is merry laughter, too, and somebody is always passing a bottle around. But now and then somebody stumbles, doesn't catch himself right, and falls back a ways. Or just lurches aside and is gone, left behind. The dead. For them, the march stops at that moment. Maybe they have a while longer, lying back there on the hard ground, already wreathed in fog—time to watch the parade dwindle away, carrying its lights and music and loud, fearful jokes.

For us, the dropouts are back there somewhere, he thinks, *fixed in a murky timescape I kept busy forgetting. That I have seen more than once.*

That's all for them now. It came for Charlie One. And what of his second life?

Once home in the cliff house, Charlie flips open *Timescape* and tracks down the idea that resonated in his thinking: "When a loop was set up, the universe split into two new universes. . . . The grandson reappeared in a second universe, having traveled back in time, where he shot his grandfather and lived out his life, passing through the years which were forever altered by his act. No one in either universe thought the world was paradoxical."

But what does the wave think? The connecting currents? The wave stores information, just as a mind does, and can link brains in separate universes through the information, the mind. Charlie looks out at the foaming sea muttering at the foot of the town and thinks of waves overlapping, summing up into white, salty combers that burst over the heads of unlucky swimmers. Waves of quantum whatever, rebounding from the hard rocks of wholly different universes, carrying their surging energy and information from one hammered shoreline and then out to another, a vast, teeming ocean—or rather, a timescape—forever in ferment.

He stares out at the tossing froth a long time before he notices that the answering machine is beeping. Interruptions! But he hits the button and listens. Flangetti's voice startles him out of his concentration. "Look in the Classifieds section of the latest *Harper's Magazine*" is the message.

Charlie races back out to his garage and guns his Mercedes down the hill, zooming through traffic—to the newsstand by Main Beach. He slams to a stop in a handicapped parking place and runs to the magazine display. In the latest *Harper's* he flips to the classifieds. There it is.

> Seen the footage of Monica with the president?
> Do you drive a Sienna? Colin Powell as secretary
> of state? Call 201-555-6666.

"This isn't a library, mister!"

He has been staring at the page, openmouthed. Charlie throws a twenty-dollar bill at the vendor and jumps back into his Mercedes.

After running back into the house, he grabs the phone from the front hallway and dials the number.

The speaker counts out five rings. Then a buzz. A deep, slow voice with a slight English accent follows. "Manhattan. Forty-two West Twentieth Street. Sunday, two p.m. This message will not repeat." There is a squeal and a click, then the dial tone comes back.

Charlie is stunned. What should he do? What should he do?

He dashes to the kitchen, gets a paper towel and a pen, runs back to the phone, and redials. The message is the same, only this time he has the presence of mind to scribble the address down.

This is late Friday afternoon. Making sure he has his credit cards with him, Charlie goes back out to find a travel agent.

Part IV

The Bridge of Sighs

Time is the greatest teacher, but in the end
it kills all its students.
—Hector Berlioz

25

The rental car doesn't handle very well, and Charlie isn't accustomed to the tight side streets of Manhattan, with all their illegally parked cars and pedestrian traffic. *Damn*, he thinks, *why didn't I get a limousine?* But he doesn't want anyone to know what he is doing in New York City.

The flight was not optimal. He recalled that long-vanished era, when Kennedy was Idlewild and the MetLife Building atop Grand Central was the Pan Am Building, and winging across a continent felt like a marvel. He got to LAX late and so inched past seats filled with squalling babies, muscled guys in Stallone-style T-shirts, girls in flamingo-pink tank tops, obese armrest hoggers, divorce lawyers jabbering, women in owlish spectacles burrowing into their reading.

He prowls the jammed streets, punching the car's radio. It begins playing:

> *He's gonna recommend you*
> *To the spirit in the sky.*

He snaps it off.

Yes—there is the address, a large "42" in black iron on one of the two gray pillars flanking an imposing entrance. Amid the packed streets a parking place is empty only a block away—a New York miracle. It's 1:46 p.m. *Will they mind if I'm early?*

He decides to wait it out in the car. The voice on the tape sounded exact, severe. His mind churns feverishly with memories, the car accident, coming back in 1968, reading *Timescape*, having Trudy for the first time all over again, the vortex of turbulent time. He checks his watch again: 1:51 p.m.; time is crawling. He has to get out of this car. He straightens his tie and picks up his jacket. Locking the car, pulse hammering, getting onto the sidewalk, and putting on his jacket take a few more seconds. He makes his way down Twentieth Street, absorbing the tang and bustle of the city. This is an older section, and everyone rushes by in a hurry with New York tightness constricting their faces. A lot of mice in this concrete cage. Haughty ladies parade past in their let-them-eat-cake creations, hand-stitched with gilt embroidery and trimmed with guiltless fur. Some are ornately wrapped stick girls straight out of *Vogue*. Within yards of these are hippies in their sacred squalor. Some are blank faced. They all carefully do not notice one another. Islands in a sea of graffiti, litter, menace, loitering, vandalism, boom boxes, sidelong glances.

He likes the contrast. He walks half a block and comes upon some more remnants of the 1960s, crouched figures murmuring some Hare Krishna chant. Charlie wonders if Hindu reincarnation might intersect with his weirdness. Is the point of life to attain nirvana and vanish from the endless round of lives? In the Hindu faith no one recalls their past lives, but Charlie can. If someone becomes enlightened, then, do they vanish from Charlie's rewritten lives? Or are they replaced by some dead thing without the crucial soul, a robot who plays the part but cares nothing for the outcome? A chilling thought. He moves on.

Charlie kills a little time by stepping into the alcove of a head shop to look at the display window. Some of the gear will be illegal in a few years as Nixon's War on Drugs takes tighter hold, maybe the Dark President's worst legacy. He lets himself wallow a bit in nostalgia. He has been so concentrated on his career and troubles, the era has been slipping by him unnoticed. Grinning, he crouches down to look at a lava lamp bloom a dollop of luminous red goo—

The street explodes behind him. The blast slams his face into the glass. He rolls sideways, stunned.

Shaking his deafened head as he stands, Charlie sees a car that has exploded only yards away. It burns furiously as the smell of gasoline curls up into his nostrils. A sharp, stabbing pain comes from his shoulder. He reaches for it and finds his shirt torn away, blood seeping.

The smoke thickens, chokes him. He steps out onto the street and sees that by standing in the alcove, he narrowly avoided most of the blast. Some bodies lie crumpled, probably hit by shards.

Is this a political act? Terror, the Weathermen—didn't they blow up a house in Manhattan around this time? No, that was 1970 . . .

He starts toward the fallen bodies, which look like bundles of rags. Maybe they're dead. Then he stops, his head swirling. The bodies on the pavement bring him back to his visions of the parade of death. Hardly reasoning, he staggers onward to number 42 and up the steps to the hooded entrance, breathing hard.

The large gray door has a small brass plaque: THE SOCIETY. *The Society of what?* Charlie asks himself. Fire rages only half a block away, and his adrenaline is out of control.

No call button, no knocker.

He looks at his watch and its display comes into focus, showing exactly 2:00 p.m. The door opens on its own, without a sound. Charlie recoils slightly, his skin alive with thousands of erect hair follicles, while his ears ring.

A white-haired head pokes sideways around the door.

"Ah, Mr. Moment! Please come in, sir." Charlie realizes that he can hear again.

Charlie starts to panic. Why would they know his name?

The old man swings the door open with only a glance at the chaos and sirens in the street beyond. He is dressed in the drab blue uniform of an English college porter and moves slowly, but his eyes have a sparkle that belies his deadpan mouth. Eerily, he keeps his eyes on Charlie and, except for a slight sniff at the sour stink of smoke, does not seem to register the shouts and clanging fire alarms.

"Please come in, sir." The porter's repeated intonation is now more of a command. It is clear that he doesn't like to hold the door open for too long, his left shoulder straining against an impulse to swing the heavy wood shut.

"Sorry." Charlie slips across the threshold, still dazed, entering a high-vaulted reception area smelling of linseed and berry bread. The light level is low, in tasteful pools.

"Not at all, sir. You are often like this."

Charlie stops, blinks, not following what the porter is saying. He leads Charlie by example toward a large dark-mahogany check-in desk. Suddenly moving quickly, he slips under a leaf of wood, raising it momentarily as he ducks his head, then turns to face Moment from the other side of the counter.

"May I . . ." Charlie's voice chokes up on him, but he recovers after coughing slightly. "May I ask your name?"

"Phelps, sir." There is something cloaked about the porter but not unkindly.

"There was an explosion out there. People are hurt. Maybe we should call—"

Sirens wail in the distance. Phelps smiles and shakes his head. "I am sure the authorities are taking charge, sir. But—ah!—I see you are wounded. Let me assist."

Phelps takes a few minutes to clean and dress Charlie's wounds. He barely noticed three gouges to his back and legs. Quick and deft, Phelps applies the compresses expertly and even tapes over the tears in the shirt and pants. He has the medical supplies close at hand. Charlie feels himself trembling but says nothing. Faint cries and sirens echo in the vaulted hallway, as if the events outside are distant, minor. The uncanny, cool calm soothes Charlie, and some focus returns.

Charlie has no idea how to continue their conversation, but Phelps comes to his rescue. "The chevalier will be coming downstairs momentarily, sir."

"Chevalier?"

"De Seingalt."

"And do I know Chevalier de Sein—de Sein—"

"Chevalier de Seingalt, sir."

"Yes."

The porter's eyes twinkle. "All Europe knows the chevalier, and much of America, too, sir. You probably know him better as the gentleman Casanova."

"Who? Isn't that, like, a myth, or an expression?" Charlie is relieved to be talking about a name, instead of the circumstances of this encounter, where he is at such a disadvantage.

A booming man's voice cuts sideways across the large hallway, a voice round, self-confident, almost sardonic. "Ah! Charles!"

Charlie Moment turns and sees a nondescript middle-aged man wearing a dressing gown richly embroidered in bourbon and gold lacing, with matching cap and slippers, advancing toward him with a broad but supercilious smile. His cheeks are a bit pouchy and pale, but there is a powerful sense of presence to him. Something about the canny eyes.

"How I look forward to these meetings of ours!" The voice drips with scented oil. They shake hands. The chevalier ignores the porter, who gets out a large ledger and busies himself. "Though I gather there has been a disturbance on the street again."

"This kind of thing happens a lot?" Charlie manages.

"Only on this day." A shrug.

Charlie's head spins, trying to understand. He sucks in a breath of cool air, tinged with a dry ceramic odor and a strong perfume.

"This way, dear boy!" The chevalier leads Charlie into a den off the hall. This room also has tall ceilings, but the pattern of the chintz-covered furniture and matching wallpaper is so strong that the den has an intimate quality. The chevalier directs Charlie to a well-stuffed chair close to the one he drops himself into.

"How do you like the Morris?"

"Um, what?"

"The pattern, dear boy. The other residents quite like it, but frankly, I still prefer good baroque ornamentation. A bit of a girl dancing nakedly over the fireplace, something with some fun in it, not this rather Persian sort of thing, abstract flowers. No life to it."

Charlie is struggling to keep his mind focused. *Persian, Morris, baroque? Who is this man, and how does he know me? From magazine interviews?*

Charlie becomes aware that the chevalier is looking at him analytically, like a painting or a piece of sculpture.

"Do I know you? I mean, have we met, um, Chevalier?"

"Call me Giacomo. We have too much in common to stand on title or ceremony." The chevalier leans forward and slaps Charlie on the thigh. "Though I see you have that to learn."

Charlie shifts his body slightly away from the man but leans forward from the waist, so that the distance between their eyes remains the same. "And what is it that we have in common?"

The chevalier's eyes widen and he spreads his hands outward in a comic display of amused confusion.

"Reincarnation. Cycling. I don't know what you would call it?

Perhaps time travel. That seems to be fashionable right now. Didn't you put it in your movie *Peggy Sue Got Married?*"

Charlie clears his throat. "I'm sorry, but I haven't heard of that film. . . ." His voice trails off.

"That's it! Coppola did *Peggy Sue*, didn't he? We didn't like the way Coppola presented the Society, not at all. You should have seen Albert! He was beside himself."

"Albert?"

"Einstein."

Charlie is stunned. "Einstein?"

"He's quite a fellow. You will love meeting him." The chevalier raises a hand above Charlie's thigh, but Charlie crosses his legs in time to escape another slap. The chevalier's twinkling eyes reassure Charlie that he isn't offended by Charlie's demurral.

"I know this must be a bit confusing for you, Charlie. But you think on your feet, a quick study."

The chevalier breaks off to stare intently at Charlie, his smile growing even larger. "It's so good to have you back! Let's have a little dinner, shall we?"

Back? wonders Charlie.

The dining room has still more traditional decor, muted red wallpaper and a white linen tablecloth covering solemn mahogany. The shiny service on the sideboard is enormous and silver, Louis XV perhaps, or Georgian. Charlie isn't sure. The cultural history of the 1700s is vague to him.

The chevalier picks up a floral china plate and takes it over to the buffet. "Let's see what Phelps has spirited forth. He is so ingenious about getting food from the local places. Please, my boy, help yourself."

Charlie contemplates the lunchtime fare, a greasy parade of Italian sausage, fried eggs, thick bacon, toast, marmalade, and a gelatinous chutney that looks like a botanical experiment gone very wrong.

"Any fresh fruit?" he asks.

The chevalier laughs. "Fresh fruit! Charles, you are so charming. Haven't you realized yet that we don't need to worry about those slow, lingering deaths, the pollution of the arteries, the teeny-tiny vessels in the brain?" He clutches his midsection, practically winded. "That's for others to worry about. We just exit, you know, when we choose."

"When we choose?" Charlie is dumbfounded. How much does the chevalier really know about reincarnation, or time travel, whatever it is? Could this be a ruse?

The chevalier seats himself at the head of the table and gestures toward the ornate place setting on his right. He removes the embroidered cap from his head, exposing a shiny pate.

As Charlie seats himself, the chevalier makes a theatrical face, showing disgust. "Not a very good appearance, is it? You know, we can't be too choosy about the body we get when we're no longer cycling through our own lives."

Charlie's face now shows the confusion that runs through his mind. He has virtually ceased thinking coherently. *Just take it in*, he realizes. *Understand later.* The patter of the chevalier, mixed up with so many hints, has seized his nervous system from his suddenly icy feet to his prickling scalp, like a jittery vertigo. He also worries about the flickering coming back.

The chevalier dramatically pauses, examines Charlie's face closely, and then reaches over to pat his hand. This time Charlie doesn't even flinch.

"I have quite forgotten myself. I'm sorry, Charles. But when reincarnates enter the Society building, it's like"—the chevalier uses his hands in a flourish that Charlie has never seen a man use—"well, it's like resuming a love affair. We have so much to offer each other, so alone in our predicament. Charles, can you forgive me?"

Charlie nods mutely, not knowing why.

"There." The chevalier takes a large handkerchief out of his pocket and dabs at his eyes. "Yes, that's right. You don't know my story, and I can't expect you to understand your own fortunate situation until you know that of another reincarnate."

"Reincarnate?"

"Yes, dear companion. We are the few who consciously cycle through time, bodies, and universes. But it doesn't make sense just to say it like that."

"Okay, then," says Charlie.

26

The chevalier tells Charlie his story for the rest of the afternoon, how he first died in prison in Venice and then came back to life only to be arrested again. And then died again trying to escape from the prison. And again, until finally he found a way out.

Charlie rises from his chair, dizzy, breathing shallowly. His legs are weak. *How long have we been sitting here?* he wonders. His watch shows 7:15 p.m. An age has passed.

Yet he gets the point of this long story. Casanova's case shows what a price can come with what seems to be a simple boon—new life. So Charlie's simple second draft of his little life is just a first gesture, really. A first rewrite. Casanova did not say so; he simply showed. That was this lesson. Charlie's first. There will be more, he is certain.

"I . . . I have to go."

The chevalier rises, reaching toward Charlie with one hand but not touching him. "Very well. But I expect you for dinner tomorrow night."

"Who would be at dinner?"

"I have a small affair in mind—perhaps just the two of us and Albert."

"Albert."

"Yes. I have already mentioned him to you."

"Albert . . . Einstein?"

"At least, most of him. I'm afraid his present body isn't quite that intelligent. But he is still an excellent companion at the supper table."

Casanova smiles wryly, an eyebrow arched. "Say, seven p.m.?"

Charlie nods slowly, numbed by it all. Yet he knows that Casanova is telling him the truth. There is no other way to make sense of his second life.

"Perhaps Albert can illuminate for you the awkward situation that you and I share," Casanova says grandly as he ushers Charlie to the door and opens it. Not thinking, Charlie steps out into noise and stench.

Charlie blinks, startled by the chaos outside. He nearly forgot it. The ruined car sits off to his left and he stares at it. Cleanup crews push debris off the street with hoses and brooms. The bodies are gone. Police are everywhere, and a burly one scowls as Charlie starts down the sidewalk. "Hey, whatcha doin'?" another growls.

"Uh, I was visiting there, number forty-two. What happened?"

"A car blew up. You see anything?"

"Uh, no." *Don't get involved.* "Gas tank?"

"No, a goddamn bomb. Geddouttaere."

The cop waves him off and Charlie walks away from the still-smoldering car. The stink is ebbing away, but more cops guard the end of the block. Crowds mill beyond the yellow-taped scene perimeter. He slips into the mob to avoid attention and has to work his way around several blocks to get back to his rental car. It's untouched. He drives slowly away, mind blank. Overload.

The drive seems to take forever. Traffic crawls and his mind wanders. *"The world is too much with us." What poet said that? Wordsworth, yes.*

His hotel's reception area is eerily empty. Still uneasy, he goes up to the clerk behind the registration counter, a string bean with glasses, and asks for any messages.

"Yes, indeed, sir. I have one that I took myself. Here you are, sir." The man hands over the message. "It was a young woman, sir." His voice trills with tenor amusement.

"Thank you," answers Charlie indifferently.

He opens the small envelope as he walks toward the elevators. The acrid smoke smell is still on his clothes. *Dinner at top of hotel. 8:30 p.m.* He wonders if it is a predatory starlet, trying to get cast in a movie. But then he shakes his head. He could use a drink anyway. *At least it would be a familiar distraction*, he says to himself. *Something to calm me down.* The car bomb, Casanova . . . lots to process. Let the unconscious work on it while the body gets distracted.

He has a long, strange moment in his room as he changes shirts and pants, gets a bit fresh. He sinks onto the bed, eyes the ceiling. Casanova told him a lot through indirection. The tossed-off lines, lightning-quick humor—all diversions from the dark, horrid tale. Casanova has been through many lives by now and knows things he will reveal in time. But his first lesson was about the pain. Most of it not physical.

The restaurant swims in warm shadows, pricked by glowing ivory lights of the taller buildings nearby. Small candles flicker on round tables set in elegant linen. The big room's quiet comes from draperies, muffling talk from the cloistered tables. The air is cool with a hint of pine. Time slides by in a slow calm. As Charlie approaches the maître d's station, a woman by the window waves at him. He doesn't recognize her, but he nods anyway and lets the maître d' lead him to her table.

She stands as he approaches. He feels somehow older from this gesture. Her lithe body in a conventional little black evening dress leads his eyes upward to her intense, exquisite face, framed by a black bob.

"Gabriela." She offers her hand delicately.

"Charlie Moment." Her grip feels firm, warm, pleasant.

They sit down with perfect concordance. To his surprise, Charlie is relaxed, in his element. He has dealt with women like this many times before. They always want something, but who doesn't?

"Thank you for meeting me for dinner. I know we haven't been properly introduced." Gabriela's face is composed, direct but not challenging.

"Not at all. I'm traveling by myself, so the company is welcome." Charlie tries one of the more charming smiles in his repertoire, as if sharing an implied joke. But Gabriela does not reciprocate. He notices a cast to her eyes that he finds odd, an analytical appraising look, almost cold. A lawyer? He is instantly on guard.

"I know that you met the chevalier today."

Charlie's heart hammers like a snare drum, hard and rattling. Nothing to do with Hollywood. For an instant he feels his life veering out of control, but he reins himself in. Cautious.

"You know . . . you know Casanova, then?"

"Intimately."

Charlie's first thought is that she might be one of Casanova's current lovers. Then he realizes that Casanova probably wouldn't be so indiscreet with this woman about meeting with Charlie today, so a possible carnal relationship wouldn't be enough to explain her knowledge. He ventures, "So then. You're a reincarnate."

"Of course, Chharlee." She pulls her hair back on one side, revealing a platinum ring on her marriage finger. No diamond, though. Charlie feels a heady, dark mixture of desire and aversion, head-spinning—this flood of allure and alarm somehow remind him of something that he can't place. She smiles dryly and says deliberately, slowly, "This is your first time back, isn't it?"

"Ah . . . yes." Charlie looks up to catch the attention of a waiter passing by. The bald, paunchy man glides back toward them at speed.

"Cocktail, sir?"

"Glenlivet. A little water, please." To steady himself. And gain time. *"The world is too much with us."*

"And does madam need something more?"

A glance from Gabriela's eyes chills Charlie. "No, thank you, Frankleen. The martini is excellent, as always."

The waiter looks somewhat flustered, but he bows slightly and turns with a flourish to get Charlie his drink.

"Do you enjoy it, Chharlee?"

"Reincarnation? Sometimes. Sometimes I do. Sometimes I don't. But I'm new to it." He pauses, looking first at his fingers, then at her fingers, then in her eyes. "How many times has it been for you?"

"I may have lost count." Gabriela's smile is dazzling, her teeth gleaming like pearls caught between her lips—lips wide and thick with red and sardonic mirth. Charlie feels dizzy again. He looks away from her—from the eyes that echo with lives led, Charlie knows, at the edges of the human condition. Down long corridors he cannot guess.

When confused, go literary. He learned that trick in Hollywood. "Are we devils, fallen angels, ghosts perhaps, or demons?" he asks.

Gabriela chuckles, a strangely deep musical sound. "Maybe all of those things. I am not one for definitions."

His scotch arrives. He brings it toward his mouth with relief. "Cheers!"

Gabriela slowly raises her almost-empty martini glass to the level of their faces, then abruptly taps his glass with hers. "To eternity."

Charlie smiles, making an effort to wrest some sympathy from Gabriela, so young looking but reeking with the lilies of many funerals.

"Let's go to your room, Chharlee." Direct, unblinking.

He considers, then sees that they do not want to discuss this in public. At the back of his mind plays the memory of the car bomb slamming him into the glass.

As they enter his suite, she slides by him swiftly in the narrow vestibule, her rich breasts rubbing against his arm in succession. She stands beside the bed and puts her arms over her shoulders to reach the back of her dress. It comes off in a swirl of black fabric and tan flesh, ending up on a chair nearby. The rest of her attire is well prepared—silky black lace, stockings, and spiked mules. Classic. Timeless. Perfect for an immortal.

Charlie feels the old familiar surge. But it does not leach away his apprehension. His temples pound with alarm.

She raises her arms to her sides, presenting herself. "I know you're afraid of me, Chharlee. But that's only because I am the first woman who really knows what you are. You will find that my knowledge is a good thing."

"I hope so." Charlie takes off his jacket and begins to unknot his tie, looking out at the Manhattan skyline, away from Gabriela.

She comes toward him, her hands meeting his back and then sliding around to his chest. He can feel the nails of her fingers raking him like surgical instruments. Her hands expertly undo his belt, unzip him, then pull down his underwear and everything else with them.

She spins his body toward her, laughing. The playground of the immortals . . . at the sport made to carry life forward. Taking him into her mouth, she artfully shows centuries of practice. Time sweeps him up, twirls him about, and Charlie finds himself on the bed, straddled, ridden, spun, teased. Then in swift hurricane bliss there comes sweat on her skin, his face knotted, his thighs pumping, her knees gripping his thighs, sweet long oblivion—until a wave of pleasure drowns all thought.

Gabriela pulls him down to lay his head between her breasts. "There, there, Chharlee boy. See, you don't have to fear me. I want only good things for you. Many, many good things."

"Mmm. Did you come?" Charlie is barely thinking. And thankful to be so.

"Not yet, honey. But don't worry. I will."

The nightmare comes back. Or is Charlie awake? He finds himself sitting on his side of the bed, clutching the edge of the mattress with both hands. Panic. Raw, searing horror.

He is staggering up a hill, hard rock and hot sand, the heat of his body rising up inside, darkness floating all around him, even as the sun burns his scalp.

He turns and finds Gabriela lying on her side, facing him, her eyes luminous. Gabriela, or Elspeth. They are the same. The feeling of their tight, strong bodies riding him—colliding memories fret and tingle. Their faces so hard, eyes glowering as they come, slapping his thighs rhythmically, sometimes his feet.

Charlie lurches up, groaning with fear. He staggers to the washroom, and there he finds a strange man's face in the mirror—dusky, worn, a full bristly mustache. Panic seizes him. He slaps his face hard, fast. His cheek blooms red. He remembers turning sixteen a second time, standing next to his father in the garage, the cool Chicago morning, a new Dodge Dart. Then his mother's face—slack and despairing in the hospital in 1996; brimming with contented joy at the dining room table in 1968; lips pursed, eyes agog, reading his manuscript. Squealing brakes. The truck runs over him again. A red-pain pressure sweeps him into dark unconsciousness.

Gabriela shakes Charlie. "*Tocayo?*" she asks.

"Yes, I hear you, Gabriela." So tired. So tired. "I . . . just . . . don't feel like opening my eyes."

She sighs slowly, coldly. Her hands let go of him. "*Chingado.* I guess not."

Tired of time.

27

In the morning Gabriela is gone. She must have been quiet and quick not to have woken Charlie. He is bleary and hungover from his claustrophobic dreams, from the hammering waves of lust and fear that consumed him through the night.

He doesn't have the energy to think about where she might be now. Somehow, trickling up from his unconscious, he has the feeling that reincarnates—Casanova's word— must go in and out of one another's lives in ways quite different from the normals. This allows him to turn his mind away from the mysteries of Gabriela, crawling back away from the edge of the precipice he seems to have found in his sleep. For the first time he regrets no longer being on valproate.

Carelessness and inattention, rely on them, he says to himself.

Where did I hear that, he asks, *or did I read it? This life, or the last? Does it matter? Will the flickering come back?* It was worse than the dreams.

He rises slowly from the bed, grunting with the effort, every muscle complaining. Shakily he works through washing and shaving. Dressing takes careful attention as he struggles with the previous day's injuries, aggravated by the rut with Gabriela.

Thinking of her again brings a pulsing anxiety that has no focus but skitters across his mind. After a while he recalls Casanova's expressive face, centuries of watching life's triumphs and tragedies. Seeing Casanova will help, he thinks. He only has to make it back to the Society building, to the chevalier's calm recitations of reincarnation as a practical matter. But Charlie's problem is getting through the day.

The cover of the hotel magazine catches his eye. It's the Met's new exhibit, something about turn-of-the-century interior decoration in New York City. The article talks about the designs of William Morris, and Charlie remembers the chintz of the den at the Society. The chevalier doesn't like Morris, Charlie recalls with a tincture of amusement. He decides that it will be the perfect distraction, wallowing in the past at the Metropolitan Museum, especially a past he hasn't had to live through, not even once.

Certainly not twice. Distraction beats abstraction, every time. Let the unconscious deal with it.

First: a New York deli breakfast. He can find fatty refuge in a fragrant pastrami omelet.

His cobwebs, nightmares, and inertia get dispelled by the shadowy end of an afternoon at the Met. Charlie feels better as he again walks toward 42. The explosion lives on only in acrid burns marring the pavement and stinging his nose. Brown soot still clings to the corners of the head shop. He abstractly notices that the glass is shattered farther along from where he hit his head. It was a damn near thing. The car carcass is completely gone.

He wonders if the explosion had something to do with the Society as he starts up the steps to the door.

Somehow he is eerily calm, ready to face the mysteries of being a reincarnate. Whatever his newfound understanding will yield, he is ready to embrace it. What has he got to lose? Not life, not anymore.

Life will surely be more complex now, he realizes. But he has the example of Casanova's resilience, his serene embrace of the life reincarnate, to guide him.

* * *

A second meal with the chevalier must be a matter of course at the Society. The new initiate's return, each one shaken or transformed in his or her own way, and so needing some deft touch of ritual. Charlie wonders briefly about all the people Phelps must have seen in the entrance hall. And how old is this address, number 42, anyway? When was the Manhattan grid, with the numbered streets, set up? Nineteenth century, certainly, but . . . Charlie fails to place the decade in his memories of American history.

Phelps is clearly not in a chatty mood as he leads Charlie back to the dining room. At the table Charlie sees the chevalier seated next to a nondescript man of perhaps fifty, jowly and deep eyed, dressed in a ratty sweater. The chevalier talks animatedly, but his companion is paying less attention, so the sad eyes catch sight of Charlie first. The man purses his lips enigmatically and his eyelids lower, owlish and intense.

Something about that face . . .

The chevalier turns to find Charlie and rises quickly with a hand curl. "Charlie, dear boy!" He extends his arm toward his companion with a courtly flourish. "This is Herr Doktor Professor Einstein!"

Rising slowly, Einstein seems slightly distracted. "More correctly, I was Einstein, for a while. But I am now just Al, please."

Al? Al Einstein?! Charlie looks from one man to the other, but this is not a joke. Not even the Al part.

Einstein has a little remaining hair, now graying a bit. His clothes are simple, informal, and rumpled. But above those ride twinkling eyes, a tilted smile. Yes, this could be the great man. Something matches.

Charlie shakes Albert's hand awkwardly, then sits at the head of the table, where his place is set. Dinner with Einstein. What do you say?

Einstein leans forward and pats Charlie's hand. "I am a thorough American now, unlike before, when I merely lived here." And indeed, he has nearly lost the heavy German accent. He is even wearing loafers. "So is why I chose to go by Al. The American habit of short-ening everything, you see."

Charlie tries to make conversation and somehow gets through it, knowing he is not doing a good job of it. What should he say? *Hey, what's up with that relativity thing of yours, Al?*

Oblivious to the unease of his companions, the chevalier is delighted with his dinner of lamb chops and aromatic mushrooms, signaling Phelps to bring out something to imbibe. The porter rolls in an elaborate wine trolley with several freshly uncorked bottles, their corks standing at attention beside the bottles for the obligatory sniff of the connoisseur. Phelps pours them a robust Zinfandel. Casanova speaks calmly, left eyebrow rising slightly: "I must warn you that the explosion that greeted you on your last visit may imply bad news."

Charlie stops a glass of aromatic wine halfway to his lips. "How do you know?"

"I have agents here and there—even among the police, my tradi-tional enemies. They found a radio relay in the car ruins. Someone was waiting for you and triggered the bomb. Their timing was a bit off, I suspect."

"Why would anyone want to kill me?"

"I have suspicions, but there are too many possibilities." Casanova waves his hand in dismissal. "It depends on what others suspect you may do."

Einstein shakes his head. "These people, they would profit from thinking before they act."

Casanova smiles wanly. "You were always averse to violent solu-tions, as am I. Loving your enemy is always more, as the Americans say, fun. But we reincarnates suffer from a certain amount of, so to speak, fratricide." His smile turns rueful.

Einstein nods. "In the 1930s I spoke out in favor of conscientious objectors to war and said that if even two percent of the men refused service, governments could not make war at all. People wore lapel buttons with '2%' on them." He laughs. "Then many thought it was a campaign for two-percent beer! So much for idealism."

Charlie laughs dryly and pushes the conversation backward. "So that bomb, it's about the Society."

"Alas, yes. They lay in wait for you. I shall take measures to insure your safety here, have no worry."

Charlie hesitates, realizing that there is a lot more here that he should know. Why didn't the mysterious "they" try to kill him today as well? "How so?"

"Some wish to prevent you from altering their, well, their world. Once you understand the Society, you may use your knowledge of the present future to change time past and thus that future." Casanova shrugs wryly, gesturing toward Albert. "It is all very complicated and must be learned, as I did, from experience. Even a genius"—a nod toward Einstein—"cannot convey in a learned lecture the lessons of multiple lives."

"Hey, this is my life they're . . ." Charlie stops, realizing that this is not just about him.

"I am afraid you will find us of less help than you might hope, Mr. Moment." Albert smiles as if he is frowning.

"But you're the smartest guy who ever lived! And call me Charlie, uh, Al."

"I have had to adjust my preconceptions, Charlie." Einstein pronounces the name delicately, as if it is in a foreign language, and of course it is. Charlie isn't sure what Albert, the former Einstein, is talking about. The man's eyes hold a deep quality like sorrow, but the mouth smiles easily and there is an air of submerged mirth.

As if to confirm this, Einstein tells a joke. "An infinite number of mathematicians walk into a bar. The bartender says: 'What'll it be, boys?' The first mathematician: 'I'll have one half of a beer.' Second mathematician: 'I'll have one quarter of a beer. Third mathematician: 'I'll have one eighth of a beer.' Fourth mathematician: 'I'll have one sixteenth of a—' The bartender interrupts, 'Know your limits, boys,' as he pours out a single beer."

Charlie does not follow it but laughs anyway. To Charlie's surprise, the chevalier seems to get the joke.

Relax, ease off. Don't press these learned gentlemen from out of time. He listens dutifully as Einstein just jumps into conversation, ignoring niceties, telling more obscure jokes about physicists, as if everybody knows them on a first-name basis. Charlie already understands Casanova well enough to realize that he prefers things lively and convivial. And maybe with his guests a bit off balance? To add to the metaphysical fun? Charlie resolves to try to be engaging for the sake of the chevalier.

Albert smiles again, perhaps more amicable, certainly less cryptic. "I am not as intelligent in this incarnation, and I wasn't so bright in my first life either."

"But you were Einstein, good fellow!" The chevalier frowns. "Surely all modesty is false, for otherwise it would not be modesty."

Albert allows himself a thin smile. "I still seek the truth, even about myself."

"I am not one for word games," Casanova says.

"The original Albert Einstein had an extremely fine brain," Einstein says. "Quick, intuitive, infinitely curious. As a boy, he stared at objects to figure them out, until his parents thought he was abnormal. Of course, he was. I am afraid I could only make a little use of that mind."

Casanova frowns again. "But that Albert was one of the creators of our world, dear man. Or at least he was while in your hands."

Albert spreads his palms far apart in a gesture that combines supplication with apology. "I will only take credit for realizing what a fine opportunity he was for me, as a reincarnate."

Casanova waves this away irritably. "But all that work you did, taking the natural philosophy—as they say now, the physics—of this century from 1905 onward, and as well finding a way to communicate it to the world."

Charlie is dizzy. *What was that about 1905?* He tries to recall what he read about Everett's work, and what the man said to him. Then there were Benford's ideas. He is struggling.

"It is not that I'm so smart; it's just that I stay with problems longer. You know very well, Giacomo, that I leaned heavily on everyone around me. On my wife, on Marcel Grossmann, that good man, and upon my former professors. The mathematics were very hard for me. I completely missed the entire idea of space-time as a fundamental, and left it to Minkowski—one of my own professors, during my faltering graduate student years!—to point it out, years after the 1905 paper on relativity. What a blunder."

Casanova turns to Moment with affected pique. "Well! This is the man, Charlie. This is the man who is getting a grasp on how this strange universe brought us back to our times. He may finally unravel our cycles of time. He was the one who explained to me what I was, why what I had gone through mattered."

Einstein's expression is patient, almost beatific. "No, not really, Giacomo. I have made only a crude fumbling at the whole problem of how we are reincarnated. The why of it eludes me."

Charlie frowns and then speaks. "So it . . . it's got something to do with Everett's multiverse?"

"Worse, it lies deep in the swamp of quantum mechanics."

Another street sign. "And that relates to your relativity . . . how?"

Einstein stares into space as if someone else has entered the room, but the three of them are alone together. His voice comes out as a whisper, echoing down a long corridor of reflection. *"Raffiniert ist der Herrgott, aber boshaft ist er nicht."*

Charlie just stares at him.

Einstein comes out of it and says, embarrassed, "Subtle the Lord God is, but malicious he is not."

As he says this in English, Charlie catches a slip into a thicker, solemn German accent, as if using the language again brought back muscle memory.

"Uh, is this some sort of . . . transcendental thing?"

Einstein blinks. "I have problems with this word, 'transcendence'—it lies only a few doors down the street from 'incoherence,' and it's easy to get the wrong address."

Casanova laughs, and Charlie wonders if he can keep up with these two. Einstein smiles at his confusion and launches into a line of patter, eyes dancing. "On my seventy-fifth birthday, that of Albert, I should say, out of the blue I got a pet parrot delivered to my doorstep on Mercer Street."

Casanova chuckles, knowing what is coming.

"The parrot, it was fretful. I tried to cheer the parrot up with jokes." Einstein takes on an American wise-guy voice. "How do I order beer in a bar? I say, '*Ein Stein* for Einstein.' Then I ask the parrot, 'What's the difference between a wild boar and Niels Bohr?'

"Answer: When I say that God doesn't play dice, a wild boar doesn't tell me to stop telling God what to do." Al shrugs.

The two older men laugh heartily, and Einstein spews out the next lines. "I hated the one who developed the exclusion principle—Wolfgang Pauli, he was. I wanted to exclude him! The guy who thought I was wrong about quantum mechanics? So I taught the parrot to say, 'Pauli want a cracker?'"

They laugh again and Charlie sort of gets it. "Al—uh, Albert . . ." He can't call this man Al, so Albert will have to do. He begins uncertainly, "You said, about relativity—"

Einstein talks right over him. "I had a dream where I made love to Rita Hayworth for an hour. Well, for her it was an hour. For me, thirty-five seconds. That's relativity."

Charlie finally actually laughs. Einstein surges on. "You know the history of science. Newton is standing on the shoulders of a giant.

The giant says, 'How much can you see from up there? Can you see this guy I keep hearing about, this Einstein?'"

Einstein thinks this uproarious. He sits back, gleeful, satisfied, and Charlie senses a despair behind the jokes, a fatigue that comes from vast, lived time.

"I was there at the beginning," Einstein says suddenly. "Let me explain some things to you, Mr. Moment."

"Call me Charlie, please."

"Ah yes, I recall—as you wish." His eyes regard him across an abyss Charlie can sense but not define.

28 Albert's story in some ways is like a class, in some ways like a confession.

His tale grew out of a lonely Jewish art student's remorse, his infinite lingering regret over the Jewish Holocaust of the twentieth century. He had been born into the twenty-second century. When the man who would eventually become Einstein was young, Casanova's discovery, or rediscovery, of reincarnation was well known. It was, or would be, one of the foundations of twenty-second-century psychology as well as physics—that time loops in multiple cycles of recurrence. Mortals knew only linear time, the *temporal ordinaire* that they experienced as they proceeded over the four-dimensional manifold that was all of known reality before the twenty-first century. They lived and, more importantly, died with a worldview that included only three dimensions of space and one of time.

Albert tells Charlie that in his time, his first life in the twenty-second century, they already understood quite well the labyrinths of time. We live our lives in cycles of reincarnation, he explains, but in most people the cycles are unconscious. For most of us, we only experience these cycles in déjà vu moments, at times when we seem to know vastly more than we could possibly have learned from our terribly finite lives. Sometimes our dreams will betray our more tangled journeys through time, but even then most people are in no position to make sense of such visions, of the full complexity of the universe. They had the firm feel of reality. Charlie thinks of his dreams of the previous night and has to agree.

Albert apologizes for the vagueness of his explanations. "You see, Charlie, this body is not very bright. It used to belong to the son of Einstein's gardener, a boy that I made a great impression on so that I could enter his mind around the time Einstein's body died."

Charlie feels uncomfortable upon hearing this. He looks back and forth at Albert and the chevalier. "So both of you reincarnate in other people's bodies?"

Casanova chuckles. "Of course, dear boy! How else could we be here? My original body never made it to the nineteenth century, and Albert here was born after 2100."

"So how does that work?" If you're in a dumber brain, how does that feel? And are you really *you* any longer? He knows that these are people who understand him, but he is not sure that he wants to understand them, to understand what he has become . . . or what farther reaches of temporal perversity will come next.

The chevalier leans forward and puts his hand on Charlie's upper arm, patting it. "It was only with the greatest difficulty that I escaped my cycling through my original body, the original Casanova."

Albert speaks warmly: "Better to think of it as a time-loop, Mr. Moment."

"Charlie."

"Ja Charlie."

"So this quantum thing—"

"Ah, that is question, yes. Quantum mechanics in the time of the original Albert was always talking about 'reducing the wave function' and other hand-waving exercises. There was no theory of what that phrase meant. None! Bohr—remember my boar joke?—said that the mind, making a measurement, reduced the many possible worlds that could be, down to the one that is. To me, that was magic."

It sounds that way to Charlie, too, so he nods.

Einstein gazes wistfully into the distance. "Nature wants the simplest conceivable mathematical ideas. But God knows more mathematics than we do, and always will . . . perhaps he does not even need it."

Charlie was still lost. "But Everett's ideas sounded pretty complicated to me. In a multiverse 'quantum' means . . . what? That lots of things could happen, but . . ."

"God might like to play dice, as people like Bohr and Pauli the Parrot thought. God might like complexities, as Everett does. I have very nearly given up on this God."

"God?"

"For some, miracles serve to prove God's existence. For me, the absence of miracles proves the same thing. All we need is that the cosmos is comprehensible. That it follows laws. That itself deserves our awe."

"So God reveals himself in some kind of harmony of all that exists?"

"Yes."

Charlie drills on. "Even if we can change it? Alter our lives, over and over?"

Einstein looks irked, then shrugs. "This is what I struggle with. Every day."

"And reincarnation makes it harder to understand anything!" Charlie says forcefully. He hears the strain in his own voice, thin and beseeching. "I mean, you seem to be hinting—"

"I am sorry to be so vague. I do not know the answers and am unsure of even the questions." He laughs, a rueful bark. "When I was a professor, my lectures were disorganized. Until I became famous, of course—then my every stumble became a charming anecdote."

Charlie gives a dry chuckle, but for once Einstein was not trying to be amusing. The deep eyes crinkle. "Finally I saw that rather than be 'the sage on the stage,' it was better to be 'the guide on the side'— for that is how we may understand this perversely strange universe."

"Strange, sure, but . . . perversely?"

"Why . . . ," Einstein says cautiously, "why does this quantum mechanical universe want to let us few hold on to our awareness as we cycle?"

The chevalier shifts irritably, distracted. "Every time I died, Albert, I would go back to that moment when I was arrested in Venice, pissing myself, to be put into the Leads prison, travel across the Bridge of Sighs. Over and over I had to escape from that pestilential hole in the roof. Sometimes I would miscalculate and end up in the flooded dungeons. So: the universe wants to torture me?"

The chevalier shudders slightly, while Albert's face softens as he looks at his friend. Charlie sees that they are brothers in their predicaments of time, and he has a dim apprehension that he is being drawn into their fraternity. If God runs the world, why is there so much evil in it?

"But let us not even talk about that." Casanova sweeps a hand through the air. "I decided that if I could reenter my own earlier self, then it should be possible to enter into other selves—to slide sideways, as it were."

Albert nods slowly, almost smiling. "The dimensionality of this is quite complex, Charlie, but to explain it properly requires knowledge of quantum computation."

"Not to mind, not to mind, dear friend. Far beyond us, I am sure. Best to see this as a skill, eh?" Casanova beams, and Charlie sees again how the man can suddenly focus his charisma at will. No wonder women toppled. "I made a study of my life, developed my skill. Where could I reenter again, in my next life? I studied Kabbalah, Taoist writings, the entire literature of reincarnation."

Albert says mildly, "Suggestive, perhaps. Quantum—"

"Not again, please!" Casanova waves this quibble away. "I took a position as a librarian at Dux, to research, to accumulate books. I told powerful friends my plan to master reincarnation. Many of them thought me a fool, but some still had a burning hope in their eyes— the passion to escape death. A common affliction among their accustomed company—those who compete to see who can be the least devout." The chevalier laughs with both derision and merriment, eyes bright. "When of course I only wanted to escape my own life."

Albert speaks softly. "What a life it was, Giacomo. A life any man would envy."

The chevalier turns to Albert and puts his hand on the man's shoulder. "All pleasures of the flesh, even of the heart, become tiresome through repetition. When I died, my last words were, 'I have lived as a philosopher, and I die as a Christian.' For I knew I was at my end. *Wrong!* My sensual exploits came as naturally as slurping oysters from the bodice of a nun in a Venetian casino. No, my goal was freedom. Even as I was a prisoner in the dire prison of Leads, yearning to escape, I grew to understand that each of us is trapped in our own eternal cycle, whether we are aware of it or not, endlessly repeating our lives. God laughs at us as we flail about in his damnable creation!"

Al says dryly, "When you emptied fools' purses, it was to cure them of their folly by opening their eyes, no doubt? You could win over old popes as well as young girls."

An eager nod. "When I did so, they enjoyed it. I swindled hordes of nobility, met Benjamin Franklin, Bonnie Prince Charlie, Frederick the Great, Catherine the Great, Pope Clement the Thirteenth, Rousseau, Voltaire, and Mozart."

Casanova smiled fondly. "Madame d'Urfé was my first effort. France's richest woman, an occultist fruitcake of the first water. She became convinced that my skills could procure her eternal life, by enabling her to give birth to an immortal child to which her own soul would be transferred. I tried again and again to assemble the circumstances, to prepare her for my entry into her mind."

"Even though she was a woman," says Charlie.

"Dear boy, it didn't take me long to realize that women were my only hope. I was never close to other men. My own brother I fought with over and over again—we never got along, and through so many cycles I became utterly weary with him. Immortality's truest enemy is boredom."

"Ah yes," Albert says with a sigh.

The chevalier speeds on. "The older men who were my protectors or sponsors—I never saw myself in them. The younger men with whom I shared my fascination with the pleasures of the flesh, they were mere objects to me, assistants in intrigue and at times paltry accessories to my carnal passions. I had grown tired of them, as I was tired of myself.

"I recall my resonance with a woman named Leonilda, who I finally realized was my daughter by one Lucrezia Castelli. Dear Leonilda was married, alas, to an impotent old marquess and badly wanted both a lover and a child." A lingering, whispery sigh. "So . . . I obligingly impregnated her, more or less with her mother's approval. Two decades later I encountered a young marquess in Prague who was probably the product of this union, and thus both my son and my grandson. You see, life can be complex—even before you relive it!"

Charlie watches carefully as this man from another era whirls through innumerable pasts, eyes dancing with memories. He recalls the Hollywood cliché for time passing, a whir of calendar pages. But this—a man of vast age, experiencing it all with flickering eyelids. Then the chevalier's face turns from purple overcast to bright as his memory returns to his evident passion. "And of course, love itself saved me. That there was someone who would welcome me into her brain, give herself over, out of love, sympathy, consilience—union."

Charlie feels almost embarrassed to listen to the man discuss what for Charlie seems like a transcendental sex change, but Charlie says nothing. He is aware, though, that Albert is looking at him quizzically yet with sympathy in the large brown eyes.

The chevalier's palm smacks the table, startling Charlie. "Henriette! It was her. Don't you see, Charlie? Love is the solution, to truly love and be loved."

The man's hand is on his arm, but Charlie is entirely under Casanova's control now, unable to turn away.

"I had lived it so many times in my mind, though it had come before my arrest and imprisonment. But the vision of Henriette had never left my mind." Casanova's voice lilts with passion. "And that day! That magical day when I saw her under the covers in the count's room, imagining those thighs shifting beneath the sheets. She was my destiny."

Albert breaks in. "So his mind-loop intersected with hers as he was dying, and he found himself in her body, looking out from under the sheets to see his younger self."

Casanova nods vigorously. "And it was love, dear boy! I loved her so much, and she me, that we could give ourselves to each other. I became my own lover, and Henriette's lifestream joined mine."

Charlie takes a big breath, as though he is in danger of drowning in all of this. He has heard too much. "Chevalier, are you telling me that you willed yourself to reincarnate into the body of one of your lovers from before your imprisonment?"

The chevalier holds a handkerchief up to his moist eyes. "Yes, dear boy! We were now truly as one, and I was free."

"So . . ." Charlie hesitates. "What happened to her?"

"I was the dominant mind within our spiritual union, but her presence, her soul, had joined with me. I became delightfully binary."

"The two cycle-lines were merged," interjects Albert. "It can happen, though it is difficult."

Charlie whispers, peering at Casanova, "So she's . . . in there?"

Casanova's face tightens. "She is now still with me, as are the traces of the others I have traveled through over the centuries since."

Charlie's head swims. "Did you tell your younger self what had happened?"

"Ah, dear boy, there you have me. There is something in me that cannot confront the unconscious—those people unconscious of our cycles of reincarnation—with the flat fact of the eternal cycles."

Charlie turns to Albert. "You too?"

"I have not had as many times or opportunities."

Charlie struggles to right his emotions and tries to change the subject. Albert is his refuge. "So are you a . . . a physicist now?"

"I drive a taxi in the Bronx. It soothes me during the day. Maybe when there is little business, I do some calculations. I publish under a pseudonym. At night I come back to the Society and talk with the chevalier, think through some science."

29

In his hotel room, Charlie throws his clothes at the chair next to the bed, stretches, and goes to the bathroom wearing just his underwear. He stares at his face in the mirror, overcome with the sense of being himself, and himself alone.

The conversation could have gone on all night, but he couldn't handle it. The two stately gentlemen led him out of the Society building through a gray, cold underground tunnel that reeked of age and dusty stone. For safety's sake, they said. Some paintings set into the walls seemed to honor members, their faces stiff in the style he recalled from eighteenth-century portraits. A few he recognized but could not place. They let him out through an anonymous wooden door, onto a street two blocks away. He hailed a cab and got back to his hotel, edgy and watching for potential assassins.

Now he has to process what he heard. To figure out if he is in too much danger to pursue this any longer.

He thinks feverishly. *Could I move laterally, invade other people's heads? Will I grow tired of my own life? Could I even manage to leave it?* He shakes his head.

He hears a click from outside the bathroom and freezes. *I don't even have a weapon.* He stands in a crouch, hands out. The door opens. . . .

Gabriela slinks into the bathroom. She is in more silky black clothes, perfect for her tan flesh, red lips, and glossy hair. She comes up to him and with a sultry smile murmurs, "Learn much?" as she slides her hand in his boxers, kissing his shoulder.

Soon she is on her knees on the bathroom floor, and then within minutes Charlie rolls off her, breathing hard. This turns out to be the preliminary.

Gabriela wastes no time. "How was it, meeting Albert?"

He blinks. She truly knows every goddamn thing. "Interesting. Interesting and sad."

"Sad?"

He sighs to gain time, to think.

"Chharlee?"

His head swirls still, but he feigns sexual stupor. She will take that as a compliment. He speaks slowly, as if half-awake. "Albert has a sad quality below his joking. He wanted our time to turn out differently. He went to a great deal of trouble to find his way into Einstein's brain, and then it didn't work out."

"Few things do, even when you get second chances."

Charlie is silent, running his hand through her hair. So easily they slide into ordinary talk about such wildness. He wonders what he would have done, had he been born in Albert's time, with Albert's talent for lateral reincarnation. And what conceivable quantum whatsit could cause that.

Charlie shrugs. He doesn't dare think of what Casanova's many centuries might have been like. Maybe it's a miracle the man still seems human.

Gabriela rolls onto her stomach, her eyes brightly questioning. He can see her with a useful distance now, depending on her sensual vortex as a snare. "So, how was my friend the chevalier?"

"I imagine he's always the same—extravagant, full of himself." Charlie is growing inclined not to express too much sympathy around Gabriela. She interprets it as weakness.

"The old bastard. You know, he wanted to do me."

"Well, who wouldn't?"

"I can't believe it doesn't bother you."

Charlie pauses. "Hey, I'm from Hollywood."

She laughs. He knows he should be cagey around her, but he needs to talk to someone about all of this. Hollywood has trained him to think out loud, because that's how movies get worked through. Block it out in talk, then leave it to the writer. "It's hard for me to know just how to react to the Society. I'm not even sure about you."

A cloud passes across the brightness of Gabriela's face, but she shakes her head to banish it.

The next day Charlie and Gabriela go to the Metropolitan Museum. Charlie wants to see the ancient Egypt exhibit again, to get the feel of what a culture based on an early idea of reincarnation looked like. The heavy stone offers him little clarity or inspiration. So many, many hieroglyphics, signifiers that he knows he will never take the time to decipher. Gabriela struts about in a short skirt and strappy thin heels, her quick steps rap-rap-rapping out her impatience as he tries to find some connection with the long-dead culture. Dispirited, Charlie gives up. They go to the museum lunchroom, Gabriela in the lead. Her fast walking irritates him. As they settle down to their thin sandwiches, Gabriela spears Charlie with a curt declamation. "You could make a difference, you know."

"Sure. Like how?" Charlie has learned to ask questions of Gabriela, rather than give answers. Questions are safer, so long as they aren't too personal.

"Wasn't it a shame the way the sixties turned out? All the promise, and then Nixon coming in and shutting down the revolution."

"Such as it was. It wasn't really going to be a revolution."

"Oh, there you're wrong."

He raises his eyebrows. "Really."

"What if Nixon had been shot in 1969?"

"We would have got Spiro Agnew."

"Who couldn't have been reelected. Such a slimeball."

"So?"

"If Nixon hadn't ridden in like he was some kind of peacemaker, endorsed by the Kennedys and even Johnson . . . Think about it, Chharlee."

Something sparks a quiver of apprehension in Charlie, but the momentum of Gabriela's words overcomes the prickling apprehension. He seizes on her plan like a raft in an ocean. *Could I . . . ?* "But it's already happened. There's nothing we can do about it now."

"No, no, Chharlee. You have already seen how your film *Dick* changed the Nixon administration. Such a small thing—but it altered the seventies for the better."

"Fewer died, anyway."

"Ah yes, but—since then the world has rested comfortably under the yoke of the Establishment. Too comfortably! Fine for your movie career, that people just stopped caring about politics."

He grimaces, ego wounded. "I'd like to think I did more—"

"But think, *mi amor*. What if they went on caring? What if all that idealism from the sixties didn't die? If the goddamn national unity movement hadn't papered over our civil rights?"

Gabriela's nails dig into his bicep.

Huskily she whispers in his ear, "We might have let Vietnam be for the Vietnamese. We never would have taken over Cambodia. Think, Chharlee!"

She imagines she has won him over, but the leaden weight in Charlie's belly tells him she has not. He will not kill. She, plainly, will. She has. And she wants accomplices. Now he knows what she is. And what he is not. He is going to get away from her, despite the allure she can unleash with a single lowered eyebrow, a sullen glance.

30

"Albert," Charlie says, "I'm really glad you decided to come out."

The deep eyes crinkle with mirth. "I am more of an American now, my friend. How could I resist a trip to Hollywood? And possibly to change history in a good way."

They are riding in the back of a limousine, edging off the freeway to Studio City. Albert peers skeptically at the humming, flashing metal river of cars rushing by them. Food is placed before them on a low table with indentations for glasses.

"Glad you feel that way. Look, I brought you here straight from the airport for a reason. I got the heads-up on this pitch session just this morning, too late to change my schedule."

"I have my work to keep me occupied." Al shows a lined pad with equations on it in a big, sprawling hand, black ink. "I have had some new ideas. You stimulated me to renew my quest."

"You do math in ink?"

"To keep me honest. If I am wrong, I go back and cannot erase. I must do it all over."

Charlie blinks; he stimulated Einstein? He hunches forward earnestly and peers into Albert's eyes. "Here's the trick. I want you in on this pitch. So I've got to go in there and sell these guys on my idea, see? The one I asked for help on? I was going to show you around, but—"

"Movies are decided on in this way?"

Charlie laughs. It is a pleasure to puzzle Einstein.

It occurs to Charlie that Einstein's "spooky action" occurs in the past, rather than "at a distance." This is the only thought that seems original, or at least frames an interesting misunderstanding of his.

"So why is it that we die and go into the past? Not the future?" Charlie asks, cutting into a veal sausage. The velvety texture is bliss, chased down by a Sancerre.

"The past has been created," Einstein says. "The future, not yet. That is all the choice the great Quantum Mechanic in the sky"—his eyebrows shoot upward comically—"has on his holy quantum menu."

"Look, I don't know a differential equation from a differential gear shift. What's this guy Everett—who seems to get some respect, whom I met—got to do with what's happened to us?"

Einstein smacks his lips at the sausage, dabs it with mustard. Maybe Casanova has made him more of a sensualist? "This Everett fellow was a mensch to point out—with some scorn, I gather—that the collapse of the quantum wave function into one outcome had no physics behind it. None! Zilch! Bohr, that likable fraud, treated it as magic—a wave of the hands. Or else an observing mind, I suppose Bohr's, forced the quantum choices to implode down to one. But does that mean that all these ensuing branches of the universe are equally real? If so, then they are uncountably infinite."

"You're not a fan of infinities."

Einstein sniffs, raises the eyebrows with a sly wink. "Not appealing, *nein*. I prefer some constraint on multiplying infinities. God cannot have such a budget, I once said! Infinities, they are a sure sign of wrong physics—as with these black holes, I once thought. I always opposed the idea of them. So I was wrong there. But not about Everett, eh?" A trick of glinting mirth in the eyes.

Charlie shrugs. "When I met the guy, he was damn sure he would last forever, in some parallel world."

Albert raps the limo's side table with a knuckle, knocking over the mustard. "Everett's error was to think the wave functions would go on splitting forever, amassing endless variations. The universe's system cannot go on acquiring more information, exfoliating space-times like shedding leaves. That violates thermodynamics—no getting something for nothing! The entire universe, all particles in it, everything, will erase the earlier of these leaves, to conserve memory space."

"So other space-times get edited away?"

"They must. So their world lines terminate."

"And the people on them?"

"We all die eventually." Einstein chuckles merrily. "As we always suspected. This solves the problem of the bloated ontology this Everett imagines."

Charlie doesn't know where to go with this. Snuffed-out universes? "Everett, people after him—they have plenty of equations—"

Al has lost his patience. "You *und ich*, we know the experience, yes? We are doing the experiment. These equations . . ." He bursts out in exasperation, "*Das ist nicht Mathematik. Das ist Theologie.*"

Yes, Charlie thinks. *Not dry mathematics. Theology. But . . . what god of quantum mechanics should be worshipped?*

An hour later, after some coffee and quick coaching by Charlie, he and Al are on the studio lot. It has taken just two weeks to shape up Charlie's ideas for the new movie and skate them across the Hollywood landscape. He used agents, mouthpieces in the *LA Times* (WHAT'S MOMENT WORKING ON? the headline read), and the always available gossip network. He's been gone a while and that works for him too. Plus, Action has had an expensive flop, and that always makes a studio desperate.

Albert looks wonderingly around at the midfifties beach bungalow on the Action Pictures production lot. Casual rattan furniture slouches beneath movie posters of the studio's past triumphs. Showbiz magazines are lit by sunlight that cuts like a blade across the reception room. There's even a surfboard leaning against the wall. Albert is still puzzled. "You . . . audition . . . the concept? Like a sort of seminar?"

"Uh, yes." Charlie eyes the new receptionist, a statuesque blonde artfully considering her fingernails. She presents a half profile to the reception room, in case somebody important is there. "These investment guys get a dozen ideas a day, choose maybe a few a year. It's a numbers game."

"You . . . pitch . . . then . . ."

"There's an old Hollywood saying, like in baseball. The guy who can pitch usually can't hit. But I've got a reputation around here for spotting good movie ideas early, then developing them." For fun, he raises his voice to startle the receptionist. "Stars can make a movie finally happen, but I can make it start."

Einstein nods, still a bit dazzled by this small island of surfer decor among the mammoth stage sets and fake big-city streets of the studio wonderland. The receptionist looks up and gives them a plastic smile. "Mr. Spielberg will see you now."

Showtime. Charlie leads Albert in and they go through the ritual handshakes. Spielberg studies Albert, trying to place the face, and Charlie hastily explains that this is a new assistant. Big in the European film community. Instantly all interest in Albert fades. Status is always in play, the only real Hollywood currency. You're only as good as your last picture, Charlie reminds himself. But he steadies himself with the knowledge that he is off his medication and in better shape than he has been in years.

The crowded long table has a mixture of middle-aged investment pool guys together with younger producers in their midthirties.

Charlie knows enough of the perpetual pursuit of fashion to recognize that the younger men are Los Feliz/Silver Lake hipsters this season, jeans and black shirts, carefully maintained two-day stubble giving their smooth skin a certain rugged authenticity. Only five years ago they probably had two roommates and toward the end of the month ate cereal for dinner. They had started hustling scripts when they were buying jug red wine, driving beat-up Toyotas, and hanging out in Sunset bars to "network" and incidentally case the tribes of aspiring actresses who were their natural prey. Most come from backgrounds in film studies or journalism, and few are women, still. Now they hide behind dark glasses, style victims of hipitude. Despite their lounging back on sofas, some wearing the baseball caps and jeans Steven Spielberg has made into a uniform, this is Hollywood red in tooth and claw.

After the ritual offering of coffee, Charlie starts his pitch. It helps that he is outlining a movie he can now recall well from the world of Charlie One, then a 1985 science fiction–comedy film directed by Robert Zemeckis and produced by Steven Spielberg. Thanks to Charlie, Action now has Spielberg in its stable of directors, and he is peering intently at Charlie.

With quick images and plot turns, Charlie holds them firmly for ten minutes. Outlining the story. Highlighting the nostalgia for a simple, better America. Delivering crisp one-sentence summaries of the characters. "I call it something," he finishes, "that gives the audience the idea right away: *Back to the Future*."

Sid Sheinberg, a savvy Spielberg adviser, has been lounging at the end of the rattan table, eyes lowered. Now he jerks up. "This Professor Brown guy," he says, "I want that changed to Doc Brown, makes it more folksy."

Charlie readily agrees, suddenly recalling that that was how the Charlie One universe had it. This guy must have made the call then. His head swirls a little, wondering at the convergence of ideas. Sheinberg goes on, "Second, the title should be changed to something like

Space Zombies from Pluto. That'll tie in with the Marty McFly–as–alien jokes, see?"

Spielberg looks askance and Sheinberg goes on. "So then Marty, who's gotta convince his father to take Marty's mother to the prom, does this shtick dressing up as Darth Vader from the planet Pluto. Sight gag, see? The audience gets it but Marty's mother doesn't."

Charlie knows this is dead wrong, but Spielberg takes care of this, shaking his head. "Sid, Sid," Spielberg says, "I'm as fond of those old fifties crap movies as you are, but . . ." Spielberg raises his eyebrows and tilts his head, sign enough.

A long moment passes, or maybe it's just Charlie's heart pumping faster. Nobody speaks. Edgy eyes behind the dark glasses.

Then Sid smiles. "Okay, maybe I'm being a little down-market, just joking around some." Obviously Sid is too proud to admit he was serious, so he nods, lets the title stand.

The investors sitting along the outside rim, in chairs, not couches, have been watching this byplay intently. Now they come chiming in, eagerly endorsing the idea. Charlie knows he is years ahead of the coming nostalgia, but Spielberg gets it. He has a gift for being ahead of the curve.

That's what Charlie is counting on. The Spielberg momentum. Then the session turns into a free-for-all, with the assistant-this and associate-that types earnestly getting in their ideas.

As momentum builds, the room gets into character logic—who is this McFly kid, anyway?—and people chip in revealing moments that could illuminate character while driving the plot forward. The kid's father has to be a loser, starting out, check. Charlie puts in the idea that the father could be a science fiction writer who can't get published. "Since after all, this is a science fiction film."

That stops the assistants. One says, "This is all about high school. The audience thinks science fiction is about outer space, rockets, monsters. . . ."

The idea dribbles away. They all look to Spielberg.

"Time to domesticate science fiction, then," Spielberg says. "Make it part of life." And the juniors go back to tossing in ideas.

Some of these Charlie recognizes from the original movie, so he chimes in, giving those ideas some momentum in the room. But in a few minutes these fade and people start trying to top one another.

They do riffs on the Doc Brown character. Everybody nods. If you must use scientists as characters, make them odd, nerdy, obsessed, self-important, or, even better, quite mad. The law always overwhelms the niceties that real people—businessmen, scientists, cops—would like in movie depictions of themselves, especially those niggling details, logic or truth. Charlie learned that long ago.

He and Albert watch as everybody in the room maneuvers for position in the new film, a project that is now obviously going to get made. It's the feeding stage; each gets his turn at the fresh prey. In Charlie One's academic world, the rule was, Everybody has a right to their own opinion, but they don't have a right to their own facts. In Hollywood, he has learned, the part after the comma does not apply.

With a nod from Charlie, Albert speaks up, as Charlie coached him. "Let's be clear on character logic," Albert says. "As revealed by action, of course."

Quickly he runs through some clever plot turns Charlie recalled from the original film in the Charlie One universe—the fight with Biff outside the senior prom that's seen from two different points of view. The heart of the movie. Albert peals this out crisply, well rehearsed. It works. Charlie can see the expression of surprise and then delight on Spielberg's face. So do all the lessers.

"Those are my thoughts," Albert concludes modestly.

Spielberg nods, purses his lips. "You're a . . ."

"Screenwriter," Charlie puts in. "European. He works with me."

Spielberg glances at Sid Sheinberg, who is now cowed and just nods. "You'll do the first take on the script, then," Spielberg says. It is the cusp moment.

The meeting breaks up, though everyone is pumped. Even Albert. Charlie reminds him that this is a collaborative biz. "Even though the whole thing gets started by a writer having an idea"—or just stealing one, he reminds himself—"writers aren't primary."

"Never?" Albert seems bemused, eyebrows rising.

"Never."

"I remember," Albert says, "from that comic strip *Peanuts*, one in which Snoopy wears a T-shirt saying 'What I really want to do is direct.'"

"Right, that's where I stand—between the directors, actors, and writers. Mr. Middleman." He shrugs. "Wanting to be a screenwriter is like wanting to be a copilot."

He fills Albert in as they walk out of the studio-lot streets, avoiding the crews shooting background takes for various films. In the '90s, Charlie explains, the biz evolved until style became content. "Any schmuck with a viewfinder was an auteur—or will be, in the Hollywood of the 1990s. I still get tangled up with tenses in this reincarnation thing."

"I too."

Charlie nods, somehow happy that even the inventor of relativity has problems with all of this. They reach the end of the phony street-scene block, and there is the limo and driver, ready to whisk them from wonderland to gritty LA reality. Albert is impressed with the ease and opulence of Hollywood. He stops and looks around, as if searching for something profound.

Charlie gently ushers Albert into the Lincoln, the ferocious air-conditioning fluffing Albert's hair. He is starting to have an idea.

"See, Albert"—he slams the door and reaches into the limo refrigerator for a bottle of gin and another of tonic, to celebrate—"only a few directors got final cut back in the sixties. In the 1970s they got some artistic autonomy, sure. The auteur theory, they called it. But fewer got that than you'd think. The young-buck guys like me got into the early creative track, lots of meetings, and then by actually writing the script. Or maybe just an outline—good dialogue is hard."

Albert shakes his head. "In physics, is much easier. You write the paper, send it in. But in films, has no writer ever had what you call this final draft?"

"Not often. There was a time—say, for *Butch Cassidy and the Sundance Kid*—when they just shot the script written by one guy. That was in the late sixties, when Hollywood broke open. I was there! Not now. Not unless the director writes the script—which by the 1990s was common. It's all about the quest for power."

"That explains much," Albert says.

"Making good, big movies depends often on one strong, creative person big enough to defy the grinding media locomotive that wants to run on old, familiar rails." Charlie shrugs; this is ancient news to him, and he sees now how little the audience—which Einstein the outsider represents—knows about how the biz works. "That strong guy may be a star, a director, or even a producer. But it's for damn sure never a writer."

Albert rolls down the window of the limo and leans out to enjoy the wind in his face. His glad grin strikes Charlie hard, a ghost of a memory of his childhood dog catching the breeze out the window of a Chevy. Charlie's mind reels with the sheer dizzying whirl of the timescape he now traverses. Time slides back and forth, logic seems like a mere memory. Life is a crazy mirror in which he lives with reflections.

Charlie offers Albert a gin and tonic from the shaker he has just rattled. "We'll do this together. And we're not going to use many special effects in *Back to the Future*. I don't like them. They're often just ways to cover script problems, by distracting the audience with spectacle."

Albert nods. "Yeats I think called this—I read him while I was learning English, as Einstein—'asking the will to do the work of the imagination.' I liked that; it occurs in physics, too." Suddenly Albert laughs. "But then, Yeats never got a script into production, eh?"

Charlie feels the twists of time back away now, easing up. Albert has it right; they have a movie to make.

Albert leans forward as if he understands Charlie's mood. *"Auf Deutsch*—I mean, in German—there is an old saying: You can teach technique, but you can't teach talent."

"Damn right." *I'm no Einstein, but—we know that we have talents.* He takes a long pull of the gin and tonic, mostly gin. "Hey, this is Hollywood, remember. Logic and facts don't matter if you can keep the viewer's eyes moving. That Law of Thermodramatics. Plot momentum trumps all other suits."

Albert gazes at him steadily. "You have an idea."

"May be wrong, of course . . ."

"My calculations, I must work on them. About how universes, linked by quantum phenomena, can slip minds across, at the cusp moments in a life. It is about entangled states, I see that—though the mathematics is thick, clogged. Not logical." Al leans back, sighs. "Logic will get you from A to B. Imagination will take you everywhere."

Charlie laughs, nods, takes a breath.

"We're drawing flies to honey with *Back to the Future*, right? It's another way of going at this splitting-time thing, combing the world for ideas. Drawing the reincarnates out. Trying to understand. Laying open the whole, well, the whole goddamn space-time of it." Charlie realizes that the gin has hit him hard.

"All physics is metaphor," Albert says, smiling.

31

Bonny Doon Road turns out to be a labyrinth that feels less like a street than an adventure in navigation. Below a sky the color of washed-out jeans, Charlie and Albert maneuver the curves north of Santa Cruz.

"You truly think bringing in this man is necessary?"

Charlie shrugs at Albert's question, because he has entertained it often enough. "He's written a lot about alternate lives in several novels—*Job, The Door into Summer,* some others that involve enough hints of cross leaping through timescapes to maybe be useful. He knows how to plot. I can use his name for clout in Hollywood on this next movie. And we can learn from him."

He doesn't say Heinlein might be a reincarnate himself, but he suspects that Albert sees that.

The Robert Heinlein circular house is already something of a legend, a property built by the man himself, with a redwood cathedral shrouding it. The tawny land itself is clear because redwood litter is highly acidic, shutting out all but other redwoods. As he and Albert cruise by, they see rings of smaller trees rising up where a giant redwood recently stood.

There is a fence and gate. Charlie presses an audio button, and a dry, flat voice asks, "Yes?" Charlie gives his name and refers to the letter and phone call they've had. "Ah, yes, sir."

The gate clicks open and they drive in, then park just short of the front and porte cochere of a circular house. A dahlia perfumes the front entranceway. Charlie notes a pump house between the frontage and the steep part of the hill leading to the house. Heinlein was an engineer and likes to do things for himself, so it fits that he has his own water on the property.

"That's the Commie Shed, gentlemen," the midwestern voice says behind them. Heinlein is a dapper man in gray slacks and a crisp white shirt, smiling as he beckons them into the house. Charlie can hear the tall corn in his voice.

"When we bought the property, the agent said that shed was used during the 1950s to conduct surveillance on a communist cell nearby." Heinlein chuckles. "We use it for garden tools."

Charlie introduces himself and "Albert, my screenwriter," though of course Heinlein knows perfectly well who Charles Moment from Action Pictures is, from their earlier correspondence. As they go through the wide entrance, Charlie feels a draft coming out, ruffling his hair. Responding to his puzzled look, Heinlein says, "We keep the house overpressured. Keeps down dust and helps the sinuses."

"Like an air lock," Charlie says as Albert stares at their host. Heinlein nods, pleased. "I built this place to be practical, tight as a ship— and as a spaceship."

A Swedish fireplace dominates the room, and along the curved outer wall and broad window is a built-in banquette. Above it is a shelf of books by many authors, and atop the books, dust jacket face out, is *The Number of the Beast*. Exactly the novel that made Charlie suspect its author might be a reincarnate, and here it is. In the book's universe, people can travel to instantly accessible universes from the present one, using hand-waving physics. Its dense structure puzzled Charlie One, and his Charlie Two layered memory was vague. But the book snagged Charlie's attention.

"Wow," Charlie says, turning to a wall that displays a painting of a man near a network of Martian canals, eyes covered because he is blind. "This is the illustration Fred Ludekens did for 'The Green Hills of Earth' in 1947, yes?"

"You, sir, are a gentleman and a scholar." Heinlein beams.

Charlie has decided to treat this meeting as a pitch session and so has done his homework. It helps that Heinlein's early novels nailed themselves in his teenage imagination. His work is best approached when young, Charlie now sees with hindsight, because it asks the basic young man's question: How should you live, growing up into a culture you didn't make? Maybe Heinlein can help Charlie regardless. The movie project he has in mind is right down Heinlein's alley.

Everything in the house is built in and trim, efficient. A work table before the banquette holds a working globe of the earth and a brass cannon that figures in Heinlein's best novel, *The Moon Is a Harsh Mistress*, Charlie recalls.

Heinlein notices Charlie's gaze and says, "That was the original working title for my *Harsh Mistress* novel—a symbol of freedom, *The Brass Cannon*."

Albert asks what the cannon means and Heinlein chuckles. "Once there was a man who held a political make-work job, shining brass cannons around a courthouse. He did this for years but noticed he was not getting ahead in the world. So one day he quit his job, drew out his savings, bought a brass cannon—and went into business for himself." Albert smiles.

Charlie takes it all in: a Mars globe and autographed pictures of astronauts. Charlie recalls that during the first moon landing Heinlein shocked Walter Cronkite on national television by saying that inevitably women would become astronauts. He was always far ahead of his time. This guy has the future in his bones. Beside these artifacts of a real working writer—and not just a script technician like Charlie—is a woman's nude photo. As Charlie studies it, Heinlein says, with a sweeping hand, "Gentlemen, my wife."

Charlie turns. She is as compact as her husband, a head shorter, with graying hair and an impish grin. She catches Charlie eyeing the nude photo and says, "Nope, not me. Wish it was!" She waves aside his apology with a hand holding a hardcover novel, *Job*. He read it while Charlie One, a jaunt among alternate realities—perfect for their emerging project. *This past keeps surprising me, somehow.* Albert says, "I have just finished this. Your heaven is ruled by snotty angels, and in hell everyone has a fine time. I wonder if you have lived such lives."

"In the 1940s," Heinlein says, "I belonged to photo clubs in Los Angeles. We hired models, and this was my favorite, Sunrise Lee. She could not fall into an ungraceful pose. But I, of course, fell for this lady." Another broad pivot to his wife.

"Your photo?" asks Charlie.

"Indeed—the only one of my photos that I hang in my home. Don't want to provoke Ginny, y'know."

"I wouldn't be provoked—only envious," Ginny says.

With a wink Heinlein says, "Whenever you realize you're winning an argument with your wife, apologize immediately." Turning to her, he says, "I apologize for dragging business into the house. This is movie stuff."

They file past Ginny's piano and along built-in bookcases to Heinlein's working room. Charlie stands beside an electric typewriter that Heinlein offhandedly calls the "coffin." He bought it from a funeral home, he says. "They didn't want their typing up bills to disturb the mourners or the dead. For my part, I didn't want to keep Ginny awake when I'm on one of my marathon writing sessions. But now"—he waves at a Zenith computer on another table—"I use one of those, too."

"You came here to not be a target, yes?" Albert asks quietly.

Heinlein nods. "Yes sir. I originally chose to build a house in

Colorado, away from nuclear targets and out of the fallout drift patterns." He slaps his knee ruefully. "So then, in 1957, the North American Air Defense Command followed my same reasoning. They set up headquarters there to correlate data from the Distant Early Warning Line. Then the US Air Force Academy set up shop nearby! To grind my face in it, NORAD built the biggest possible target, their operations center, into Cheyenne Mountain—my backyard! Colorado Springs was the biggest nuclear target in the US."

Albert laughs along with Heinlein. Charlie has noticed that Albert often finds a way to work nuclear issues into his conversation. Perhaps the burden of beginning the US nuclear weapons program with a letter to President Roosevelt weighs on him, down through his lives.

"So I took my revenge," Heinlein says. "I hammered Cheyenne Mountain flat in *The Moon Is a Harsh Mistress*, bombarded from an attack platform the Air Force hasn't thought of—the moon."

"Then let me bombard you with our idea, Mr. Heinlein," Charlie says. Charlie decides it would be a good idea to follow the man's formal, military manner. They are all still standing, Heinlein ramrod straight. With a courtly gesture he tells them to sit on a long couch. They do. Then, so fast Charlie sees it only as a flicker of motion, there is a small silver automatic pistol in his hand.

"Welcome to reality, gentlemen," Heinlein says casually. "Mr. Moment, you hesitated just long enough when looking at my relevant books to suggest that you are one of the reincarnates."

Charlie freezes, realizing they have been overconfident.

Albert says slowly, "Quite right. We are here to ask your assistance in a project to gather others, using Hollywood."

Heinlein nods but the gun never wavers. "We are of you, but we do not play games with history." Ginny nods too.

"Good," Charlie manages, recovering his self-possession. "Neither do we. I apologize for not announcing ourselves properly."

"Then I am certain you will not mind standing again, turning, leaning forward onto the back of that couch."

They do so, and Ginny frisks them expertly, patting them down, running hands down their pant legs. "Nice and safe," she announces. "Robert, be seated. I'll hold the gun at a distance." Crisply, as though rehearsed, they take their positions.

Charlie is startled at their casual certainty. They must have done this before. He says slowly, "We want to make your novel *The Door into Summer* as a feature film." Charlie's hopes that this line will have impact dwindle away. Heinlein looks unsurprised. "Um. But change it around a lot."

"To make the time paradoxes work out somewhat better, yes, we think so," Albert offers.

Charlie speaks carefully. "The idea is to pull together reincarnates, to make us a constructive force in the world. Our film could be a kind of rallying call." A sigh. "Some aspects of your novel are unfilmable— for example, the extensive work on robots. But we'll keep the basic idea, your ideas, of a man going back in time to change events."

Heinlein nods. "You know my work?"

"I grew up on it," Charlie says truthfully.

Heinlein peers at them intently. "So how do you want to do the leaps through time?"

"A time machine."

"No cryonics for going forward?"

"I think it makes the movie too complicated. 'One miracle at a time,' H. G. Wells said. I have the money to buy the rights, if you are amenable," Charlie says, to buy time.

Heinlein seems restless and abruptly stands up. "You've passed muster, gentlemen. Ginny, let me put that on safety."

He drops the pistol into his pant pocket. "Maybe there is some common purpose that could be developed among reincarnates. Let me mull this a bit."

"Do you oppose those reincarnates who play the changing game?" Albert asks. Charlie realizes he is holding his breath. He did not see this coming.

"Casanova sent you, didn't he?"

"No," Charlie says, "he doesn't know about us coming here to see you."

Heinlein looks irked and also nervous, almost afraid. He leans across the dining table and his eyes flash. "Why a movie?"

"Let's say it's a way of getting the whole suite of ideas on the table," Charlie says. "To draw some others in."

"I don't want to be mixed in with some of those others," Heinlein says, his steady gaze moving between the two men. "They have"— his eyes narrow—"their own ways of changing the future."

"That's true," Albert remarks casually. "But men and women of goodwill should stand together against a mutual threat. That is independent of politics, I would think."

"You don't get milk by shooting a cow," Heinlein says quickly. "Destruction is a bad game. I prefer to make the future with ideas, books, work."

"And so do I," Charlie says. "Help us get these ideas into the mainstream, that's a start. You've written plenty about this—short stories, novels—and you have a feel for how we can spin this movie the right way."

Heinlein visibly considers this, glancing back at the kitchen, where his wife is scraping leftovers off the plates. Charlie wonders how much she knows.

"Why now?" Heinlein asks.

"The game's afoot," Einstein says flatly.

Heinlein studies them both, considering. "I have a lot of questions I'd like answered myself."

Albert spreads his palms. "Perhaps we can help. I do know about some matters you have treated in your novels, dealing with relativity and time. I know this from a past life."

Heinlein's eyes widen. He gets it. "You . . . are Albert—Einstein." A broad grin spreads across his face and he seizes Al's hand, shaking it vigorously.

Albert nods and continues on, unperturbed, gently drawing his hand back. "We all wish to know more. We started in different places, me in a land far away. It was inevitable that I end up here, and that these dramas play out here."

"You're from that Casanova guy?" Heinlein asks again. "I went there once, had some drinks. Not my type. Old-style grand."

Charlie says mildly, "We know him. This is our show, though. We want to bring together other reincarnates using this movie. It will make their ears perk up."

"Why now? Why the USA?"

Charlie has an answer to this, the small realization that gave him the idea, back in New York City with Gabriela. "Reincarnates have a lot of questions. The USA is the place where you can find the freedom to raise them. Can you think of any other country that has a national anthem that's packed with questions?"

Heinlein frowns. "I wrote some stories, novels . . . and I get some odd letters, sure. But a movie . . . Do you think this could really work?"

Charlie doesn't dare answer. He doesn't know, of course. Life is uncertainty. So is history. If the guy who saw so much of the future doesn't know, well . . .

Heinlein says abruptly, "I don't much like creation by committee, but maybe I can help with the dialogue. Now the big questions." Raised eyebrows. "What are you planning to do about the black hats among us reincarnates?"

Charlie shrugs. "I think we have to deal with the bad-actors as they come at us. And the movie is to help us find the nonplayers, the reincarnates who just want to get on with their lives—their many lives. But don't want to let history mess with them."

Charlie feels some relief at getting the core of their argument out in the open.

Einstein beams, saying, "If we knew what it was we were doing, it would not be called research, would it?"

32

Charlie knows enough to let Spielberg run the show whenever he turns up. With his posse in tow, Spielberg goes straight to Robert Zemeckis—who has taken over shooting the movie, since Spielberg is overbooked. "I'm just here to kibitz, Bob." Spielberg's gaze is concentrated. "I also want to meet with that writer, Al, who gave us that great twist."

Charlie steps forward. "Steve, Al's down working with the set crew on the DeLorean. He wants it to look a little more spiffy."

Spielberg nods. "The way Al has it in this new rewrite"—Spielberg waves a sheaf of paper—"we anchor the scene here." Spielberg sweeps his arms around the Universal town-square set, the courthouse with big clock overhanging like a metaphor, dominating an actual functional street that has appeared in thousands of movies for the last half century. Hometown America, suspended in time. "So now Marty meets Doc in the parking lot of Twin Pines Mall. They come here, town square, time looms over them with the clock image. Doc shows him the DeLorean, modified into a time machine. It needs gigawatts—let's have him pronounce it 'jigowatt,' okay? Sounds trippier—power from a plutonium-powered nuclear reactor."

Albert appears, coming up from the set crew, talking to Heinlein. Their eyes are bright, and Heinlein marches beside Albert's casual gait. Spielberg goes over to Albert, nodding to Heinlein. "Just got these new pages, Al," Spielberg says. "Love them. Cutting from drama to humor. Where'd you learn that?"

"Much of it is from my friend Mr. Heinlein." A nod. "And of course Charlie."

Spielberg nods, fast and sure, seeming to find the three of them a team of mysterious originality, the trio he goes to when he needs something more.

The whole set moves faster now. Wiry and intense, Spielberg moves around the shoot as the last light fades from the western horizon. They are working hard to finish on budget, so they do only one take of Doc programming the DeLorean time machine. They watch as Doc enters November 5, 1955, as the target date.

Watching a film getting made is like waiting for grass to grow. Charlie tires of it and ambles over to Albert and Heinlein, whom he now has the privilege of calling Robert.

"As soon as this is done, we'll move to 1955," Charlie tells them.

Heinlein's eyes dance with anticipation. "I'm glad Spielberg liked that material I wrote. It's close to my heart."

Charlie likes it too. He didn't put in all the intricate, funny plot twists when he pitched it with Albert. The whole motif—Marty's finding that his father in 1955 is a nerdy teenager, and his mother a goo-goo-eyed schoolgirl—leads into great jokes. And the paradoxes work. Marty, not his father, gets hit by a car, so his own mother gets turned on to him. But Marty realizes that he won't exist at all unless his parents fall in love. The Oedipal stuff fits right in with Heinlein's own obsessions, and he has written some great dialogue.

Albert nods. He did not want to name Doc Brown's dog Einstein, but admitted that Heinlein's idea played well in the scene already shot. "Ideas, they change. When I died as Albert, a pathologist made off with my brain. Nobody knew this until a pupil in a fifth-grade class mentioned that, as he put it, 'My dad's got Einstein's brain.' So they discovered that one area of my brain, part of the parietal cortex, was swollen with neurons."

Heinlein frowns. "So that . . . what? . . . That explained . . ."

Albert shrugs. "Was that the cause of intelligence, or the effect of decades I spent exercising the brain?"

Heinlein nods. "So I guess the question is how your mind worked, not your brain?"

"I had no special brain, no special talent. I was only passionately curious. As I still am."

As Doc Brown does a retake, Heinlein asks diffidently, "Do you think as hard now?"

Albert eyes the crowd. There are always onlookers who turn up on a set, but he seems to be seeking someone. "I think upon the time-loop problem—our problem, my friends. I wait for a revelation. Truth comes as a sudden illumination for me, a rapture. Nature likes simplicity. But in this repeating of worlds, of time—I do not know what nature has in mind."

Charlie says, "If it has a mind."

Albert laughs. "I wonder if we do, even. Back when I first came to America, as the Great Man, this fellow Edison—already quite old—sent around a pop quiz. He thought scientists were too abstract. Especially me, he said. There were a hundred fifty questions. What country drinks the most tea? How do you tan leather? What is the speed of sound? So the reporters asked me if I knew these things. I said I could look those things up. The hard part was thinking!"

The film gets done, with the usual stack of hassles. Charlie is kept busy with the last cuts, fitting it into a neat, short package. It has just enough newness to tickle the noses of the public.

With the final cut done, Charlie feels like a serious drink. He takes Albert and Robert to Musso and Frank's, a Hollywood institution decades old, dispenser of millions of martinis to movie minions and majesties alike. Ancient waiters in red half coats glide through the gossip-thick air. In the back room the long bar shields bartenders who could be the fathers of the white-haired waiters from the yammering crowds.

Their service is slow, so Charlie eases through to the bar. "Three vodka martinis, olive, a bit dirty." By the time he's back, Heinlein is quizzing Albert on physics.

"Better to use the German, *Verschränkung*, which is a kind of intimate entanglement," Albert says. "I called it *spukhafte Fernwirkung*, or 'spooky action at a distance,' when I was the smart, famous Albert."

"If that means there's faster-than-light travel—"

"It doesn't," Albert says. "I know you want to go to the stars, but alas . . ."

"That's a shame."

Albert sips his martini, smiles, and says quietly, "Everyone complains about the laws of physics, but no one does anything about them. I have been working on a theory, though. It shows that it is also possible to create entanglement between quantum systems that never directly interact, through the use of entanglement swapping."

"Which means?" Heinlein ignores his martini.

"We set up conditions with our minds. They are the predicates here."

"Just thinking?" Heinlein looks affronted. "Not doing anything?"

"Both, actually. We make certain events occur, and if our minds are entangled with the opening between two emergent quantum systems—that is, this present universe and a fresh one forced into being by our actions—then our minds will dictate the nature of that new universe, its time line."

Heinlein blinks, takes a sip, smiles. "Just so I get to do something."

A gang of their film people come by their booth, gushing about finishing the shoot on the movie. Bright eyes and flashing white

teeth tell Charlie the scuttlebutt is running in their favor. He sits
back and lets Albert and Robert bask in the envy-glow for a while,
using a thin smile to distance himself. The studio crowd will think
him either drunk or above it all, doesn't matter much which, and
he likes to let ambiguity keep them guessing; it helps maintain the
Moment aura.

Albert has put a packet of papers on the seat between them. There
is the usual shooting script in its binder and on top a different sort of
typescript. Albert and Heinlein keep talking while Charlie sneaks a
look at what turns out to be the abstract of a scientific paper.

> In a quantum universe theory, because of com-
> plementarity relations, it is not possible to give
> numerical values to all field operators through-
> out a specified physical motion. In fact, the state
> of motion is specified by giving numerical values
> on only one spacelike surface. Entanglement
> proceeds from this state. The simplest case is an
> entangled EPR pair of two qubits. Extension to
> N-state particles (i.e., particles whose states lie
> in the N dimensional Hilbert space) is straight-
> forward. The future of the state of motion can-
> not then be determined from the field equations,
> which are in general second-order differential
> equations. Therefore the action principle, which
> was enough for the classical theory, is no longer
> enough. The actual quantum state of the density
> matrix—for our purposes, the mental state of
> one or several minds—must be cohered with the
> action. Motion and thought must occur on the
> same time surface. This retains the sense of indi-
> vidual identity and continuity. Of course, a single

> mind is the easiest case. Here we analyze this in
> a new way, using a state vector matrix notation
> for clarity.

As if this were not bad enough, he cannot even understand the title above it. Or recognize the name. He flips through the manuscript—equations, thickets of notation in Greek.

The bright eyes from the studio eventually drift away with waves and "Let's have lunches," and Charlie whispers, "Uh, Albert, is this yours?"

Albert smiles as though caught in a minor sin. "Yes, I am polishing it for *Physical Review*. I use a pseudonym, in a way—my current name."

"These phrases—'quantum state of the density matrix,' 'must be cohered with the action'—mean . . . what?"

"The quantum of information—physicists who have no ear for music call it a qubit—is like a particle of meaning. One can regard our universe as a sum of all its qubits. Your mind is many, many qubits. A swarm of particles, in a way. When coherently engaged, it can be teleported to anywhere else in space-time. The group wave functions—though I do not like that term—are overlapped. The most welcoming portal for such is a complex mind very much like yours—if there is one. So if a separate universe exists—through quantum splitting, but I will skip over that—with someone like you in it, your mind can go there." Albert takes another sip and looks at the noisy crowd around them the way an eagle looks down on lands below.

Heinlein gulps. "What makes that happen?"

"Trauma, it seems. Like an organizing shock wave. That forces quick attention, and thus coherence, on the mind's many internal connections."

Heinlein nods. "Nothing focuses the mind like the prospect of a hanging, as somebody said."

Charlie says, "What's special about minds?"

"Mathematically, they have the density matrices with the greatest cross correlations. Minds hold the highest information density of all things. Through entanglement they can grasp across the abyss between quantum universes. Like throwing a rope over a raging river, then hand over hand across it." Albert smiles, as though he has just thought of this metaphor.

His eyes wander in the direction of the starlets nearby. Charlie can see his mind is elsewhere, so he asks, "Minds can span universes, find fresh lives—especially at crunch points, big emotional events?"

"True, not simply trauma. A profound emotional shock, a triumph— those could work also. It would seem, from studies done in my last time line, that minds have their greatest correlations when threatened. Evolution selected for that—engage the entire organism at moments that menace its existence."

"I thought evolution was about enhancing reproduction, leaving lots of offspring. . . ."

Albert smiles, winks. "And when you do that, do you not feel whole, intact?"

"Orgasms are—"

"Many qubits flying!" Merrily Einstein clinks his martini glass against theirs in turn. "Pleasure is evolution's way of saying, 'Do that again!' my friends."

"So our minds have a kind of immortality that plants, say, don't?"

"Even perhaps animals."

"So there is an afterlife for people with 'density matrices with the greatest cross correlations,' eh?" Heinlein says skeptically. He, too, is distractedly watching the starlets flounce about.

"This I do not know. At first I thought intelligent people had the greatest probability of making the transition. But I have met stupid reincarnates aplenty."

Charlie looks back at the scientific manuscript. "What's 'EPR' mean?"

Albert waves this away. "An old paper."

"And *E* stands for you, right?"

Albert purses his lips. "An early attempt. Yes, me, also Podolsky and Rosen, who worked with me at Princeton in the 1930s."

"So these ideas go way back," Heinlein says.

"And far forward. Physicists in this area are getting ideas now for experiments. In a decade or two they will, if this time line works out as did my initial one, propagate entangled particles hundreds of kilometers. Then whole containers of gases will be so entangled."

Heinlein brightens. "Step by step, building up to more complicated things."

"Done with machinery, so far," Einstein says ruefully. "For minds, difficult to do experiments. But we know, gentlemen, that minds can entangle to other universes if their coherence is enough."

"So you're on the trail of a theory about what happened to us. Bravo!" Heinlein finishes his martini, signals for another round. "Then maybe we can learn to use it. Make a technology."

It is as though the gossip-gabble around them has ceased to exist, Charlie notices.

"I'm a practical guy," Heinlein says, "but I know this: there's nothing more useful than a sound theory."

Charlie studies them, such different types who, surprisingly, get along well. Albert is the key. He is mainly interested in being left alone, to live his own kind of life, have his affairs and entanglements, and pursue his lifelong search for truth—a search that began and now continues outside the academic establishment, indeed never fit comfortably within it. Not that Hollywood is any better.

Still, Charlie feels his skin tingle. They are getting closer to a truth they may never reach, but the journey is satisfying in itself. They are not mere motes tossed around by some unseen God; there is mechanism, and so maybe control. That is good enough, yes. For now.

* * *

Back to the Future, at its Westwood Cinema premiere, is appreciated by the jaded Hollywood crowd, who even laugh at the more Oedipal scenes from 1955. There are still some Freudians around, a lot of them screenwriters who have been through analysis. Rog Ebert laps it up, and he and Charlie exchange insider jokes with sly grins during the after-party. But Charlie is more interested in whom the film will flush out from under cover, which reincarnates will come his way, and what they might do together.

Not engaged in a conversation, he lets his eyes wander for a moment and finds himself fixed in the sights of—Gabriela. There she is, the ravening mocha body in another wraparound little black dress. *She knows how to find me.* Charlie quickly infers that she has finagled a date with the Action Pictures executive near her who is talking to an assistant director.

It is only a matter of moments before Gabriela takes him off to the side. "So, señor, you have put us up on the screen for anyone to see!"

"You know I haven't done that, Gabriela." Her eyes flash. "But yes, I want to meet other reincarnates. This is kind of my calling card."

"And to what effect, I think?"

"Well, we'll have to see. Won't we?" He uses a straight stare, challenging her. He has written scenes like this before.

She turns and stomps off as heavily as her sharp heels allow. Then he shakes his head and takes a few steps back. Gabriela is too much for him right now.

But the night will have another surprise. Driving up to his Wilshire high-rise condo, he sees a woman waiting at a polite distance behind the valet.

Once he has surrendered his car, he looks briefly at the woman, finding her familiar but unplaceable.

She smiles back at him. "Michelle. Don't you remember?"

He looks again. The frizzed-up '80s hair has led him astray. Underneath a layer of sophisticated makeup and thirtysomething fattening, it is the face of the woman he fell for hardest.

"Michelle, of course!" His Hollywood manners allow Charlie to recover impeccably. He offers her his hand.

She takes it but moves toward him, alcoholic vapor and perfume breaking over Charlie. His chest squeezes brutally. It's as if the years since their last morning never happened. He looks directly into her eyes, almost faltering, as her pupils bear into him.

"I know about you, Charlie."

He takes a step backward, but she won't let go of his hand.

"Um, Michelle, would you like to come up for a drink?"

In the elevator she wraps her arms around him and pushes her body against his. For Charlie it is awkward, confusing. A cadence of emotions pounds at him—fear, longing, hurt, none of them unmixed, all of them bewildered, strays from a life that he feels is slipping away from him at the end of a long evening. Why does he mean so much to people, he wonders, when he is just passing through their world, a migrant through his second incarnation, with so many up ahead?

Inside his condo Michelle pulls away from him and smooths the shiny blue fabric of her dress. The mixture of girl and woman that he fell for is long gone, along with the shimmering long blond hair. Her jawline is firmer, eyes shrewd. The creature before him is harder, yet perhaps more desperate than the morning she rejected him.

He wanders toward the bar, avoiding her stare.

"You werrren't lyyying to me, werrre you?" Her consonants are slurred.

Charlie is measured. "No, not at the end."

"I read about your movie. In the magazines. It's all there. I know."

"What are you having?"

She tosses her head, just as she did long before, a gloriously free movement of neck and hair, like a flag of independence. It brings Charlie's first quivering of desire. "Vodka tonic."

"Oh . . . kay.

"You son of a bitch, I should have listened to you." She takes an unsteady step toward him.

"How could you have believed me?"

"It would have been so much better if I had."

Charlie allots himself one rueful smile, no more.

"I know you're thinking . . . you're thinking that I want the money, the fame, all that kinda stuff."

"No. Of course not."

"Fuck yourself, Charlie Moment. You can fuck yourself." She abruptly puts the drink down and throws her arms around him, leaning heavily against him.

"It's okay, baby."

She makes an indistinct sound, and Charlie wonders if it is a whimper. "Just hold me. I need you tonight."

In the morning Charlie wakes up first. He listens to Michelle's quiet snoring and watches the white sheets move around her body almost imperceptibly. *What the hell am I doing?* he thinks. He didn't need to be told to realize that Michelle's life has not turned out well. But then his hasn't either.

So there they are. Just two souls floating through time, his bobbing in the waves of Albert's four dimensions—or was it eight, that string theory thing he mentioned?—a bit longer than hers. But still incorporeal flotsam. No more.

Charlie gets up slowly and quietly, almost afraid of what Michelle will say when she wakes up.

It doesn't take him long to assemble his keys and wallet, put on some clothes, and flee. Albert will help him through this, Charlie is certain. He has to be with someone who will understand.

33

Charlie drives the Santa Monica Freeway steadily, staying in the slow lane so he can keep up with Albert's ideas. Traffic isn't bad after 10:00 p.m., but he feels uneasy. The night of the premiere has left him uncertain about the rest of this particular life.

"I think we will learn nothing profound from our fellow reincarnates," Albert says suddenly, peering out at the dim parade of cars. It's as if the man can read Charlie's thoughts.

"Well, we've had twelve turn up so far." Charlie is particularly unwilling to accept Einstein's intuition, since it matches his own. He glances over at the face as worn as old leather. Charlie went back through Einstein biographies and studied the original face's evolution from a steady, certain gaze to the wise grandfather of glimmering eyes, the smile a tantalizing blend of mirth and sadness. This man beside him is not that one anymore. This Al shows a seasoned sagacity beyond that of anyone he has ever known. Centuries can do that to you.

Al stretches in the car's confines, as if grasping upward toward something. "Twelve, yes, nearly all actors or authors, yes, men and women of a certain caste. Or should I say, uncertain? They saw through our film to the truth. That does check your idea of drawing them out, ja. But they are actors who have the fundamental insecurity of the trade. Fueled, I suspect, by the enormous uncertainty that comes with being reincarnated."

Charlie bears down, his executive can-do-it manner extending even into this shadowy subject. "We can research the patterns common to their life experiences. Learn from that."

A *tsk-tsk* wag of the untidy head. "I like this term. Research is searching, yes—often with eyes closed. Blind truth. And the 're-' means that you have to do it again and again. Most people cannot take the tension of always not knowing."

Charlie allows himself a sardonic chuckle. "You'd think knowing you would live again—maybe even goddamn forever!—would make you carefree. But our fellow reincarnates aren't the happiest folks I've ever seen, by a long shot."

"Wisdom and melancholy are old, close friends."

"Even Casanova wore out his libertine self, seems like." Charlie has a sudden flash idea—*Reincarnates! Zombies, kinda! Wonder if those old 1930s flicks could use a Spielberg-style comeback?* But he turns away from that Charlie Two ferret-self and focuses on Al beside him.

It is Al's turn to chuckle. "Our friend seeks to fathom what all this means. I too. But when you *do* understand . . . ah, that is a sensation unlike anything in life. Seeing into God's mind. Better than passion, sex, women, fine wine."

"And fame, for you."

"The best thing about fame is that if you bore people, they think it's their fault."

Charlie laughs. Traffic ahead stalls and he switches on the radio.

"Beethoven!" Albert cries. "Too personal, almost naked." He clicks it off.

"Y'know, if your analysis works, you'll have proved that parallel universes exist, that maybe we make them with our minds. Lots of people will hate that idea."

"One of science's tasks is to open eyes and make people uncomfortable about what they see."

Charlie has long wanted to ask one particular question, and he finally braves it. "Do you think all this has a point?"

"I do not know what nature has in mind." A pause. "Or if it has a mind."

By now Charlie knows Albert's style—long thought, then these compact conclusions. "It makes me feel more secure, not less," Charlie says. "I don't fear death anymore."

"A mathematical series can be long but still not infinite."

It takes a moment for this to register as Charlie angles them between lanes, headed to Santa Monica. "So we don't get to just cycle forever?"

"Three of those actors were in their third and fourth incarnations. I liked the one named Niven. He was dapper, assured. But Casanova in all his incarnations has not met anyone with more than a few dozen lives. He has met over a thousand reincarnates, and none of them have gone around as many times as he has."

"Good point." *And no thanks*, Charlie thinks. *I'd rather stay blissfully confident.*

"This fact makes those who play the history game more understandable, you see. They use extreme methods because they will not have an infinite number of chances."

Charlie feels a rush of unease tighten his chest. They have taken risks, exposing their interest through *Back to the Future*. Now Albert has suddenly shifted the odds. "How are you feeling about history now?"

"When we were in the middle of a divorce—*ach!*—I came home to find my wife burning all my love letters to her. Already I had agreed that when I won the Nobel Prize—we were both so sure this would happen!—as a divorce payment she could have all that money. This was after I had published the general theory of relativity. So thinking of that, I said, 'Don't burn them.' 'Think of history,' I said. And she looked at me and said, 'I am, Albert, I am.' I see her point now."

"But you changed history anyway."

Albert turns to him with a patient smile. "It was a temptation and I succumbed. Now I am on T-shirts! I read still complimentary articles about Einstein and I wish my parents could read them." A sigh.

"I sometimes think of the greatest lesson we reincarnates have learned," Albert muses. "Those who ignore the mistakes of the future are bound to make them."

"So," Charlie ventures, "what is your . . . theory of us?"

"I have thoughts, calculations, but the key idea eludes me. I wish to know how to manage our own reincarnations."

"Our rewrites, I call them."

Einstein makes a polite chuckle sound. "You see life as screenplays? When I judge a theory, I think, 'If I were God, would I have arranged things this way?'"

"Seems reasonable."

"So for quantum mechanics, I had to ask—could the good Lord have created beautiful and subtle rules that determined most of what happened, but left some things completely to chance? That was bad enough! But to make us revisit what happened! What kind of Lord is that?"

"A no-rules-at-all Lord?"

Albert shakes his head, ignoring Charlie's question. "Yet such work is the only thing that gives meaning to life. My life, at least."

A sleek black car zooms by Charlie's left window. Then it is gone, speeding forward into the Santa Monica night.

He rolls down his window to get the cool night air in his face and focuses on their route. Heinlein likes to live near the ocean, and he called, saying he wanted to discuss strategy with them, whatever that means.

Albert doesn't notice Charlie's distraction. "So now I struggle with your time's new physics, adding what I know that your physicists don't. When I was young, we lived in a simple world. Energy makes physical systems do things. Fine."

He makes an exasperated *pffffft!* sound. "But now comes this quantum computation view, the latest version of how the universe works. People read their world in terms of what they know, the latest model. That started with the ancient creator gods, whose couplings gave birth to the cosmos. Then Newton's clockwork sky. Then the nineteenth century's vision of invisible force fields. All these led to the latest, that the universe is a vast computer. So now, with computers on our desks, we imagine that God works similarly. Information tells the universe what to do."

Charlie is confused by all of this and has to concentrate on traffic. A metallic taste fills his mouth.

Albert continues. "Already, in this time, there are experiments about sending information backward in time. Just tiny instants, yah, but the principle is important here, not the magnitude. Some backward time movement can be. Soon enough smart experimenters will send entangled particles and photons distances of hundreds of kilometers. So quantum effects can move in space and time."

"What makes that happen, the backward time leaps?" They are crossing the 405 freeway and traffic brakes. Los Angeles never sleeps, but it does slow down a lot.

"Events can become twisted together, if they share information. Like rubber bands threaded through each other, they are—an entangled state. So you touch a particle here, and far away a particle that was once related to the first, it too moves. Instantly! I regret calling them 'spooky action at a distance.' But I was criticizing the idea. It is ugly!"

Charlie glances over at Albert, who is now agitated, rolling down the window to get some air. "But you were right, Albert! Maybe the reincarnate loopers—"

"Being right brings not always joy. This I know. Many said my relativity principle was to blame for abstract painting, atonal music, formless literature, sexual freedom. I would allow the last, since I enjoyed only that—though often." His composure returns as the night air plays with his hair.

Charlie starts a new question, leading with "So this quantum information—"

"The path is poorly lit by consciousness, Charlie. That is our problem." A note of both awe and despair slides into Einstein's voice. "I wanted theories that kept us, we mere humans, out of the action. But somehow we are in it. For physicists of my time, the distinction between past, present, and future is only a stubborn illusion. Much more, the illusion of subjective humans. But we few know that there is another, deeper truth."

The tinge of salt in the air brings flavor into the car as they approach the coast. Charlie decides to give up. Enough metaphysics—if that's what it is—for the evening. They have Heinlein to deal with soon, and the guy is a bit of a drill sergeant.

"So . . ." Charlie hesitates, liking the sea breeze and wanting to hold the moment. "So why not play the history game?"

Albert sighs. "It is the obvious game but, *ich denke*, maybe not the right one. Politics fades, physics lasts."

"So your theory—"

"If we understand this—and I remind you that I came back from the twenty-second century to bring such work to light now, so perhaps in my way I am already playing the history game in my own fashion—then we will truly change the long tragedy of humanity, for the better."

"That twenty-second century—what was it like?"

"I was an experimenter." Albert shouts joyously, "Me! But"—he leans out the window, face to the wind—"I was the test subject, really."

"Huh?"

"These matters, of time and life, are of great interest nearly a hundred fifty years from now. Science knows of the reincarnates—though not much. They did experiments, like the quantum entanglements our era here is attempting badly."

Questions don't make Charlie feel so dumb. "So they used you to . . . ?"

"As a lab animal. I could cycle backward in time without dying, so they thought—I do not know what they thought. There was strange, silent machinery that aided my mind in casting back. Perhaps contours in my frontal lobe—they do allow faster synaptic correlations over a larger volume, we did discover that. So I tried and tried, every day. Sometimes I could go back a few minutes. Usually not. During one long day I . . . ended up here, your century. In . . . a body." These last words come as whispers.

A hard motor roar comes up on the right side of the car. Charlie thinks it is probably some kid in a hot rod making for the beach. He moves a lane to the left.

Traffic is heavy and they are going maybe forty. But the roar keeps up, and when he glances to the right, past Albert's gleaming profile, he sees the same black car that passed them before. As the black car comes steaming past, Charlie sees the rear window rolled down and a hand, a hand holding a . . . gun.

A sharp bark. Another. Another. Drops spatter his right cheek.

Charlie wrenches to the left again, head down, angling toward the fast lane. He swerves around the tail of a pickup truck and floors it. The car fishtails a moment and then gets straight with howling tires. He slams the pedal to the floor and the engine bellows as he guns it. He glances right. No black car.

But Albert is pitched forward and there is blood everywhere. The smell of it swarms up into his nostrils.

34

Heinlein jerks the door open. "You're late."

Charlie steps into the condo, blood on his shirt.

Heinlein wrinkles his nose. "Where's Al?"

Charlie realizes that he must smell of fear and blood. "He's dead."

Heinlein keeps his rock-solid posture, hands in the pockets of his smoking jacket. Only a twitch of his mouth shows any reaction. "You need a drink."

"I need more than that." Charlie tells him in short spurts about trying to save Albert. The brain sprayed across the car.

Heinlein finally blinks. "Damn, I was afraid that other reincarnates would come after us."

"I didn't think that way. . . ." Charlie abruptly sits on a white leather sofa. "And I was wrong."

Heinlein allows disgust to crease his pale features. His real self is coming out from behind the stiff officer carapace. "It is no pleasure to be proved right."

"How many lives have you had?" Charlie asks.

"Fourteen. Sometimes it's hard to even count them. It took me this long to understand."

"Understand . . . ?"

"How dangerous living multiple lives really is."

"Ironic, isn't it?" Charlie looks up into the man's sober face. There is rigidity there too, and something else.

"Maybe the single-lifers have it easy."

Charlie tells him more about how Albert died.

Heinlein nods and then says, "Usually they like to tangle up their opponents. Deflect them, maybe frame them for crimes, so they don't kill them all. The police will be after you."

Charlie then recalls hearing something like a bee buzzing by his head as he swerved the car. It must have been a bullet cruising close by his ear. "Cops, yes . . . I parked the car four blocks away."

"We should move it. That will buy time."

"Okay, I'll move it. You don't take risks, do you?"

"Not foolish ones."

"So you can stay alive in this time, influence the future with your books."

"We're just entering what I call in my future history series the 'crazy years'—for a reason. It's going to get crazy up there, just a few decades ahead. Right-wing frenzy, depletion of resources, wars. Stuff you wouldn't believe unless you lived through it all. Everything had to change."

"I still don't *get* it." Charlie rises impulsively and starts toward the balcony. He needs fresh air.

But Heinlein blocks him. "Don't go out there."

"Why?"

"This may not be over."

"It's . . . immoral. Albert . . . poor Albert."

Heinlein mutters, "Glad I had Ginny stay home. Knew it might come to something bad, but this . . ."

"I can see it makes sense," Charlie ruefully admits. "Deliberately staying under the radar of other reincarnates. Smart. They must be there, yes. And some of them will be dangerous."

A faint buzz comes from somewhere in the room. Heinlein stands up and goes to an end table by the sofa, fetches forth a pistol. It is dull gray and he handles it with ease. Charlie opens his mouth to ask something, and Heinlein puts a finger to his lips, shakes his head. The pistol is long, and as Heinlein checks it, tightening the barrel, Charlie realizes that it has a silencer. The buzzer must have been an alarm set to detect intruders.

Heinlein pads softly to the stairs and disappears. Charlie knows he is not to follow. Seconds tick by. A loud pop barks out. Charlie flinches, startled. Right behind it a soft coughing comes—once, twice, a pause—then another.

Standing, Charlie sees Heinlein's balding head rise back up the stairs. "Done," Heinlein says, face somber, but a vein visibly pulses in his temple. He holds the gun at the ready, eyes alert. "Let's police the area. Secure perimeter."

Heinlein systematically fetches plastic bags and finds his ejected brass shells. Until that is done, the man ignores the two bodies lying side by side on the wood floor of a dim downstairs bedroom. Charlie thinks about turning on the light but realizes that is a bad idea; it would light up the scene, as seen from the beach. He helps Heinlein stuff the bodies into garbage bags, folding them to fit. Both have automatic pistols they never had a chance to fire. Charlie's respect for Heinlein grows. "How'd you do it?"

"I rigged a distraction. A spark-ignited firecracker I triggered with a switch from the corridor outside. They both turned toward the sound, side-on to me. I shot them both through the chest, edge on. Best way to keep the round in the body, let it bang into some bones, make it hard to trace back to my gun. One was still moving, so I used another. They never got a shot in." This comes in a flat, deadpan voice as Heinlein seals the bags with tape, Charlie holding them together, trembling slightly.

Charlie realizes that Heinlein must have done something like this before. He thinks this through as he and Heinlein carefully go out onto the nearly deserted streets to move Charlie's car.

For once they get a break; no one is lingering, no one has noticed the gunshot, the hole in the windshield, and the slumped body of Albert. Heinlein hesitates over the body, murmurs something, and then gets in the backseat.

Charlie drives. Despite his dazed condition, he recalls that the car is in fact Albert's, officially. Studio perks dictated a car, so Charlie just put it through, though Albert barely drove at all. So by parking it on a meaningless street, they deflect attention from Charlie and Heinlein. With this in mind, they decide to leave the car angled onto a sidewalk several more blocks away from Heinlein's condo. They agree that their story will be that Albert dropped Charlie off at Heinlein's for some planning work on publicity for *Back to the Future*, then left to drive home. That would make it look like a street crime.

"What about the bodies, though?" Charlie asks.

"Know how to swim in the ocean?"

Heinlein remarks that he used the same trick in a past life, Heinlein-3, as he calls it. From his navy days in his present life, he has provisioned himself with a tough shore raft. They wait until 2:00 a.m. and haul the bodies out in plastic trash cans with wheels. They roll these down to the beach and then go two blocks south, where there is only a feeble city glow.

Heinlein inflates the raft with an air bottle and they throw the bodies onto the raft. Charlie takes the trash cans back to another house after washing them in seawater, so they will be missing in the morning and untraceable. When he returns to the raft, Heinlein has weighted the bodies with cabling and construction bricks he "happened" to acquire when he rented his condo.

The ride out is simple. Heinlein has a compact electrical motor, brought down at the bottom of another trash can; the battery was in the other can. The engine starts without noise and purrs them out through light chop. The sloshing rhythm rocks Charlie as he watches the shore glimmer dim behind a gathering sea fog. He sucks in moist air and feels nauseous from the metallic smell of blood that clings to him.

Heinlein angles farther south where he knows an old oil rig lies thirty feet down. He went diving out there one weekend for fun, in this same raft. They heave the bodies over and hope they become tangled up with the old piping down there. *If not, should be seen as a gangland killing,* Charlie thinks, watching the bodies disappear into waves that lap like black oil.

On the way back Heinlein sits up straight, face into the wind, officer of the deck. He runs the raft in on a wave, surfing it right onto the shore. Hauling the gear up and back to the condo is harder without the trash bins. Charlie finds his adrenaline gone and fatigue setting in.

They review the events, Heinlein calling it a "postaction assessment." He sits at the dining room table and cleans the pistol, oiling it well. The three brass bullet casings went into the ocean. After the review, with Heinlein doing nearly all the talking, Charlie says, "We just might get away with it."

"The law has trouble if they have no body. Also, we have no motive anyone would believe. So with our story—here talking over publicity and drinking—we're covered. Get your facts straight first. Then you can distort them any way you want."

He wonders how to get home, and Heinlein says, "Stay here. We need to talk."

Charlie peers at this man, who is still energized, and realizes that something inside himself has changed as well. "What's the plan?"

"Best to play the game subtly, Charlie. Because it's clear we—or at least you—have to play."

"Maybe so. In . . . in these lives before, you never disclosed to anyone you distrusted?"

"Seldom. Revealing myself to you and Al"—he spreads his hands, eyebrows arched—"sure, a gamble, but I decided to take it."

"You've done this before."

Heinlein bows his head, sighs, eyes distant. "And now it's happened again. Those bastards are still around. Best we can do is send them to the back of the line."

"I see . . . How many are they?"

"Just a few. A woman runs it now, as nearly as I can tell."

"And her name?"

"Gabriela, I think. She changes it sometimes. Quite the sexy bitch."

"I think I know her."

"You're in a complicated fix here, then. You're known to the Society. This Gabriela, a real shrew—she's picked up on you."

"Sure did. The same old way, too." Charlie gives Heinlein a thin smile.

Heinlein nods. "Yep, me too. At least she used good bait." They both laugh—a strained, rattle coming from Heinlein. "She's sure as hell a different kind of creature."

Charlie feels something surge in him and spits out, "We've got to stop her."

"Then you've got to elevate your game."

"What?"

"The history game. But be subtle. That's the hard part."

Charlie wonders if Heinlein is trying to put steel into his spine. "Maybe Albert will emerge again in another life," Heinlein muses. "It could even be on this time line—he has some gift and was trying to understand it. I'd like to see him again. He had some great ideas about what this whole giant puzzle might mean. Maybe . . ."

"I'd sure like that," Charlie says slowly, feeling fear in his bones now.

Heinlein says, "We're in far over our heads here." A strange grin, jaw set, eyes steady and narrow.

Charlie sees that he has to stop playing the fool in this goddamn game. He knows that he is done with this life. It is time to move on, to try again. Something quite different.

Part V
Discrete Recursions

Our years pile up like old magazines
We will not read again,
As though their seasons, though long,
could never end.
—"Yesterdays" by Clyde Fixmer

35 Einstein has the capacity to surprise and unsettle Charlie, even in death. The affable sage always met them in restaurants, so Charlie never went to his apartment building, which has a hardpan parking lot as centerpiece for the crumbling plaster construction. In a side yard framed with cinder-block walls, two Latino women are hanging clothes on a rusty whirligig. They are both in smocks that show pregnant bellies, while two small children in saggy diapers and smeared T-shirts play nearby. A rooster and two bedraggled chickens in a coop cluck at a scrawny dog that is either resting or dead. Albert in his famous life often said he could have been just as happy as a plumber, so perhaps his reincarnation had some fondness for the simple life. *This is a bit beyond simple, though,* Charlie thinks.

He got the address from Albert's ID last night and came here first thing this morning. As he mounts the rickety iron stairs, he surveys the neighborhood, a little barrio south of the 10 freeway, far from the

Hollywood Hills he can see shimmering in the sunrise. The front door of the apartment is easy to open by sliding a credit card into the latch. He finds little in the apartment, neat and clean and bare, with lots of books he couldn't possibly follow—until the notebooks. They are in a worn leather suitcase in the back of a closet. Many are in German. But some are more recent, and he finds the beginning of a paper in English, written in a swirling nineteenth-century hand with a fountain pen. Its title is "A General Theory of Quantum Teleportation of Minds" and the introduction begins:

> Most physicists view time travel as being problematic, if not downright repugnant. Gravity is well described by classical general relativity, condensed matter physics by quantum physics. So semiclassical quantum gravity (curved-space quantum field theory with the general field equations, coupled to the expectation value of the stress-energy) is a more than adequate model over a wide range of situations. This leaves the puzzling phenomena of mind transfers from what seem to be other, parallel worlds. Surely, quantum effects must cause this.
>
> Stephen Hawking's "chronology protection conjecture" asks, "Why does nature abhor a time machine?" I shall discuss a few examples of multiverse space-times containing "time machines" (closed causal curves). Predictable peculiarities arise, as expected. As Stephen puts it:
>
>> It seems that there is a Chronology Protection Agency which prevents the appearance of closed timelike curves and so makes the universe safe for historians.

> This theorem can be circumvented by minds, as I
> shall show here. A qubit distribution of appropriate
> density can avoid the usual decoherence problems.

"So he *was* working on a theory," Heinlein says when Charlie shows the notebook passage to him. "Good, but I doubt it'll be much use to us. Al wasn't a practical sort."

"So a theory exists, fine," Charlie agrees. "Probably those behind his killing wanted this theory to never see the light of day. Or any evidence that reincarnates exist."

Heinlein spreads his hands over the dining room table of his beachfront apartment, where all of Albert's papers are stacked. "Then why didn't they go to his apartment and take all this?"

"Maybe they haven't had enough time. Getting us came first. But, okay, maybe you're right. They killed Albert and tried for me because we're casting about, trying to find others like us. They don't want that. I doubt they like the idea of more players in their history game either." Charlie pauses, thinking, and Heinlein lets him. "They don't know the two gunmen are dead. Yet."

"When they find out . . ." Heinlein lets the thought hang there.

"We don't know how many of them there are. They may come after us—or we can go after them."

Heinlein's mouth works as he thinks, his eyes uneasily sliding to his front door. "I can't risk conflicts with such people. Ginny would never forgive me."

"You're that . . ." Charlie stops before he insults this proud man.

Heinlein lets the words out slowly. "Ginny . . . we've never talked about her, have we?"

"Since she's a reincarnate too." Charlie sees how this fits together.

Heinlein nods. "We have spent lives trying to find each other. You have no idea how the search down time lines can rob you of everything. . . ."

"How long?"

"I gave up counting for a while. It just depressed me."

Charlie makes a guess, based only on the man's face. "This is the first one since—"

"Since we fell in love, yes. In our first lives. She died before me. Okay, the number: I took thirteen time lines to find her again. We hadn't agreed on any rendezvous!" He slams his fist on one of Albert's leather-bound notebooks. "She made me promise, before I came down here—no risks."

"Living is a risk."

A bemused grimace. "So it is. We have no guarantee that we'll know we're resurrected. I'm on my ump-teenth life here, so it's looking probable I'll keep on doing this, but . . ."

"You can't leave her."

Heinlein looks plaintively at him. "I promised."

A change of tack, then. "You did damn well last night."

A flicker of a smile. "First time for me. To kill anybody, I mean. Except in combat, which with my philosophy I don't count as voluntary. Yeah, it did feel right. . . ." Again the wistful gaze.

Heinlein had no choice last night; he had to fight. But he is a man with a firm, hard-edged idea of honor, and he will never violate his oath to Ginny. Never risk leaving her alone.

So be it, Charlie decides. *I respect that. So . . . I'm alone in this. . . . And I've cut my ties to nearly everyone in this time line too.*

Charlie approaches the secret entrance to Casanova's lair, his eyes darting along the ordinary Manhattan street. Some kids are listening to a tinny transistor radio. The Beatles sing "Revolution" and long-haired heads weave to its wisdom. Somehow the '60s culture remains the touchstone for street types, more than a decade later. Some homeless men—scraggly, shirtless, cigarette-smoking, white—cluster under tree shade. Sunburned bikers wearing German helmets throttle their Harleys. Dumpees from cut-back psychiatric facilities lounge in doorways, slack jawed, their eyes wandering.

The day is cloudy and Charlie feels scruffy and tired from his red-eye flight. Forty-two West Twentieth Street, NYC, lies on the edge of the Flatiron District between Sixth and Fifth. Casanova has made himself central, perhaps as a safety measure, but . . .

Is anybody watching him? Even the acrid tar smell of warming blacktop seems ominous. He recalls the car that exploded on his first visit. That seems so long ago. He uses the code at the small punch pad beside the door.

There's a hard thump on the door and splinters spit into his face.

He flings the door aside and dives forward, hitting the floor.

He hears a sharp crack. On the floor he crawls to his right, getting shelter from the doorframe.

A smack to the far wall digs a hole. The door rebounds a bit, creaking.

Charlie twists, hooking his right foot onto the door. He pushes hard and slams it. The auto lock clicks.

He crawls quickly around a corner, then gets up and runs the hundred feet down the narrow corridor to the next security door. It opens just as he huffs his way toward it.

Phelps pulls the door aside before Charlie gets there. He keeps going, into a storage room with crates lining the walls. He stops, panting. "Fastest dash I've ever done."

"Commendable, sir. I saw the incident on our television system, and we have dealt with the problem outside."

"How?"

"One of our other cameras spotted the third-story window whence came the shots. The master has dispatched two of our defenders."

"I didn't know you had any."

"Always, sir."

"I want to see the chevalier immediately."

*   *   *

Casanova speaks from his comfortable love seat: "'But at my back I always hear / Time's winged chariot hurrying near,' my Charles. You seem to have avoided the chariot. Forgive me, I seize every chance to quote Marvell."

"Who was it?"

"We shall have a report shortly. Come sit, will you?"

Charlie finds a suitably deep leather chair beside the flickering yellow fire. "Sure. It's been months, sorry. I—"

"Do not regret growing older. It is a privilege denied to many."

"I came to tell you that Albert is dead."

"I know."

"Already? How?"

"*Res ipsa loquitur*, 'the thing speaks for itself.'"

"You have a network—"

"Allies, friends, some reincarnates who wish to forever remain unknown to others of us."

Charlie sits back. Phelps appears at his elbow with a glass of amaretto, takes another to Casanova. "It's morning!"

"You look as though you need it." Casanova hoists his bowl glass. "Whereas instruction does not always delight, delight always instructs."

"Who tried to kill me?"

Casanova beckons to Phelps. Charlie sips the amaretto, and its sweet, burning scent prickles his nose, its taste lancing through his airline-dried mouth and sinuses. It is just the right thing.

Into the room step two large men in shirts and ties, wool pants, and level hard looks. Casanova salutes them and raises his eyebrows.

"We know that shoot site, sir. They've used it before," the taller one says in a formal baritone. "Got away, left the rifle. Had a silencer on it, not a good one."

"I heard the shot," Charlie says.

"Yes, sir, you were in the cone that kind of silencer can't suppress, right out of the muzzle."

"They missed by maybe an inch."

"Yes, sir, our apologies. That apartment rented out three months back; we saw no activity beyond normal. They cleared out fast."

"How long ago did they use it last to shoot at your goddamn secret entrance?"

"Twelve years, as I recall," Casanova says. "I purchased the building, but—"

"Our error, sir," the taller says. "They looked like ordinary, upscale—"

"What happened twelve years ago?" Charlie shoots back.

"They killed Luther Burbank," Casanova says flatly. "A brilliant scientist."

"That's why you don't leave here very much," Charlie says.

"Alas, yes. Fortunately, much comes to me."

The tall man says, "I think I know how to track them, sir."

"Do it." Casanova dismisses them with a wave. "Repay in kind."

The men's faces harden as though they have heard this order before. They leave. As they go, Charlie can see they are muscular and graceful, lithe lions in an urban jungle.

"Why does this go on?" Charlie sits up in his chair, fists balled.

"To expect the world to treat you fairly because you're a good person, my friend, is like expecting a bull not to charge you because you are a vegetarian."

Charlie sits back, blinking. Adrenaline ebbs from him, confusion rising like a muddy flood. "Non sequitur," is all he can get out.

"Your work with Albert and that Heinlein fellow—not to my taste. How could you not expect to catch attention from those who play the history game?"

"Albert and I, we wanted to understand all this."

"All credit to you, my friend. Most of us are buffeted by our many lives, small boats in the frothing rapids."

"We can't do it if these murderers come after us in every life."

Casanova considers this, signaling Phelps to fill his glass. "Then you must secure a time line where you can work unimpeded."

"What? Kill myself?"

Casanova waves this away. "You are new to this. It is natural to indulge in solipsistic whining. Do not be embarrassed by it."

"Hadn't realized I was." Charlie feels insulted, but he has to stay on the favored side of this man who seems to know so much but care so little.

"Among our kind, dear Charles, the mind is not a vessel to be filled, but a fire to be ignited. I applaud your ambition—and in merely your second life as well!"

"Don't brush me off with an epigram, please."

"But I am not!" Casanova's expression shifts to his waspish story-telling cast. "Long ago I was walking with Samuel Beckett in Paris on a perfect spring morning. I said to him, 'Doesn't a day like this make you glad to be alive?' to which Beckett answered, 'I wouldn't go as far as that.' Luckily for him, he did not reincarnate. It would simply have depressed him more."

"Point is?"

"You have a gift for living. I could see it in your films."

"I'm surprised you caught them."

"Recall, I have lived through times much like these without your work—and with the works you so, shall we say, profited from."

Charlie feels his face redden. So Casanova sees his entire pattern of pirating movies. Casanova's pale eyes still regard Charlie with fondness, and a certain wry tilt of his mouth implies he could say much more.

"So how do I proceed?" asks Charlie.

"Why, when I told you, I recall you said a moment ago, 'What? Kill myself?'"

"How do I know I'll be reincarnated?"

"Aye, the puzzle. Yet my long, somewhat tortured experience tells me you will. I have observed those who reincarnate only once or twice, and they do not have your cast."

Charlie's forehead wrinkles with disbelief, so Casanova leans forward earnestly. "Most people are dull, unimportant cogs in an unimportant machine called society. They lack a certain spirit."

"Albert said it was about correlations in the brain. They make minds able to link, to quantum transport, to nearby space-times. Where those come from, I dunno." Charlie realizes he desperately wants Casanova to be right. But that also makes him cautious, a lesson Albert's death has taught him.

"My poorly educated mind observes that those who are on their last cycle have let joie de vivre give way to gaze de navel."

Charlie wonders if he is like that. "I don't feel any different than I did as Charlie One, and he didn't think he would live again."

"You lost your virginity, in a way—as did I, when first I died. Rest assured, the happily ignorant don't see the problem. Albert's correlated minds discover it soon enough. He termed us 'chemical scum that dream of distant quasars,' as I recall. Come, let us scum dine."

They move to the opulent dining room, now with a snowy dining cloth and a centerpiece with a delicate rose in a fluted vase. Charlie uses the time to frame his questions. Over a fluffy omelet with a Sancerre wine Casanova toasts, "I urge patience to us both."

Charlie shoots back irritably, "Why is patience a virtue and 'hurry the fuck up' isn't?"

Casanova chuckles. "At least you have the energy to be rude. Young Charles, patience because we have all the time in this world—and in the next ones."

"Ever hear of a guy named Delgado?"

A quick dash of concern flits across the ancient face. "I may have, just. In my many paths through these 'universes,' as Albert calls them,

I have seen your nemesis gang, those I term the history game players, use agents who are, alas, not of the reincarnated. Delgado I do recall."

"Why do I dream of an older Mexican guy?"

A sigh, raised eyebrows, and he finishes his glass of Sancerre, staring at the ceiling with an expression of regret. "Another phenomenon Albert attributes to these correlations. You can 'pick up,' as you Americans say, the lateral fragments of other minds."

Phelps steps forward to fetch Casanova's plate while Charlie ruminates on this. "I haven't met him, Delgado, so—"

"Then it is a forward event you dream of. You have not yet, but you will."

"What's Delgado's role?"

"They use him, those darker players in the history game, Gabriela's gang."

"You've known her a long time." A wave of loathing breaks over Charlie. Why, he's not sure.

Casanova ignores Charlie's bitter tone. "Delgado they used in the Kennedy shooting, I recall. He was conveniently located near Kennedy's peak, when he won an election or primary or something, so Delgado—"

"Robert Kennedy. Their work?" He does not let the shock slow him.

"Indeed, in one or two of the universes they perverted. Probably did in this one as well.

"I try not to recall too much about such matters." Casanova signals for more wine, then takes some almonds from a dish. "One reason I remain here, and seldom go out—except to see your films, of course. They are worth the risk."

Charlie shrugs off the compliment. "Where did this Delgado live? I dream of him in some desert, poverty stricken."

"They remove him from that, set him up nearer the site. He is an illegal immigrant and cannot move about without risk. They put him on the coast in California. Some town with that name."

"Coast?" Charlie envisions a map of Southern California, runs his attention down it. "Costa Mesa?"

"I believe something like that. I am not one for sordid details. There have been so many in my life now." A self-pitying gaze into infinity.

"What else can you tell me about them?"

"Little that I want to recall."

"You have to."

Casanova sits up and gives Charlie a stern glare. "I do not have to do anything."

"Sorry." He has to hold himself in check here. A conviction is blossoming in him.

"Alas, I'll never be free of them, those evil laterals. I am a lateral, but it seems being so has gone to their heads. They make worlds they wish to live in, birthed out of some demented political ideas. They are evil in flight. They remind me of the despicable events in Paris during my time of origin. Utopia was to come from a guillotine."

"How can we stop them?"

"We? I will never. I am not that sort. Not political."

Charlie now knows that he is that sort. "Do you want Albert back?" he says slowly.

"Of course. He is my favorite of all of you. . . ." Casanova brightens. "And yours, too, I'll wager."

"I'll wager too," says Charlie, realizing with a shock that he might just wager everything.

36 Charlie gets out of the limo, looking Hollywood in his shades, suit, and open collar.

The air carries the ocean's salt tang and soothes his skin. He walks along the beach and sees Heinlein strolling in a tight swimsuit with a belt and pouch, studying the waves as though he wants to go in. Empty sands stretch away on a weekday afternoon, and a wind whispers in Charlie's ears as he approaches Heinlein from behind. Since Heinlein's didn't answer his phone, he guessed the man would be here, getting exercise. Ten meters away, Heinlein suddenly turns, hand on his waist pouch, fetching forth a snub-nosed revolver. Says nothing.

"Have they tried again?"

"No, and I'm not giving them the chance. I'm going home."

"They can find you there."

"Ginny and I have a better perimeter there."

"So you do. Plus, you can improve it with tricky defenses."

Heinlein nods.

"I understand—Ginny's number one and there's no number two."

"Damn right."

"No desire to alter history along another time line, live there?" Charlie keeps his tone casual, as though this is not the crucial question.

A flinty flicker in the eyes. "Nope."

"What were you going to do with the pistol when you went swimming?"

"It's special manufacture, waterproof."

Charlie laughs and after a moment Heinlein does too.

There are sturdy cartons already filled and sealed inside Heinlein's living room, Charlie notes, all neat and ready to go. "Have the police come by?"

"No, but it's just been days. Nothing at all in the papers. I'll be gone in another day—you can tell the studio to cancel my contract."

"I wonder who those guys were?"

Heinlein mixes two gin and tonics. "No clues on the bodies." He sits down and scowls, shaking his head. "I'm guessing you're thinking of killing yourself, just to set things right in your next incarnation?"

"Mulling it over."

"Not my game." Heinlein's eyes narrow. "You don't have anyone to hold you here?"

"No. I've made a lot of movies and money . . . but I can do all that again."

"No special person, a woman you might miss?"

"In your terms, I'm a failure." *Maybe mine, too.* "They didn't really take. Well, maybe one." Images of the young Michelle fill his mind, so beautiful and fine.

"What happened?" Heinlein asks.

"It didn't turn out well."

A sad, slow nod, Heinlein's head bowing. "Me too. First wife. But I found the right one, finally." His head rises abruptly. "You're not afraid of dying?"

"Not really." Casanova said Charlie seemed like a recurring reincarnate. Charlie believes a man who has centuries of experience on his side.

"A man who is fearless cannot be courageous. He is also a fool."

Charlie decides not to take this personally. It's part of Heinlein's crusty persona. "Let's say I'm confident. Casanova thinks it's a spiritual thing, something in the character."

Heinlein chuckles. "Sounds like he is making stuff up."

"Look, we have the fantastic luxury of multiple lives—great, but we're still flotsam tossing on a random sea we don't understand. Or control."

Heinlein laughs. "My hat's off to you, sir. I'm headin' home."

Charlie's estate planner finishes the will and he signs. It's essential to straighten out matters with the studio, tie up deals and secure gains that occurred while he was away. Everyone assumes he is back to restart his career, but he ignores all questions, preferring to be enigmatic.

As the movie production work he knows so well goes forward, he says good-bye to it. He writes a legacy document disguised as a proposal memo, outlining ideas with titles: *Total Recall* (some help for Phil Dick), *Starship Troopers* (a departing gift for Heinlein), *The Shawshank Redemption*. (Stephen King doesn't need the money, but Charlie writes a set of production notes straight from memory in half an hour because it is such a good story.) Maybe they won't be great movies, but they will help two people who helped him.

He feels a strangely nostalgic loyalty to his Charlie One unhappiness, a sense that his sad life in that distant world of A.D. 2000 was where he really belonged. He earned that sadness by his own actions. Should he now again live out a life of small decisions? He could have an easy Hollywood career, just let life flow and forget Albert . . . starlets and spotlights succeeding each other emptily.

Or . . . go for chances, grab at them—make a better world. Could he make a time line where his life helped?

The best part of nostalgia, he sees, is that it is about what lies in the past and can't be changed, only relished in retrospect and then put aside. *I'll let them be, those future years that would wrap me in comforts.* But nothing has been as important as his time with Albert and Robert.

The reincarnates who play the game might be surprised. He will keep punching in the clinch.

Now I can make my own timescape, a history I want to happen.

So the time has come to die.

Charlie holds a Saturday night special, the snub-nosed Victory .38, favorite of cheap crooks. His clenched fingers tremble slightly as they caress black metal, the weapon like a cobra that has to be captured by a firm grip behind the neck. He feels trapped in time's cycles, an insect in amber.

He thinks back to the last time he died. Even now, fear grips him. His heart hammers, sweat chills his skin.

Can I be sure this works every time? All that talk from Casanova and Albert, I never got any hard numbers about how often the whole reincarnation thing works, or when it starts to fail. Does it always work for a new reincarnate?

And again . . . is this what Casanova meant about what I would decide to do? Do reincarnates try to set their worlds straight?

Maybe he is different. He doesn't want to live through all that bland future up ahead in the 1990s, with Pax Americanum holding sway over a zombie culture. This is about his future, too. Somebody is trying to kill him anyway, right? So why not steal their moves? *Do it myself. Stay in control.*

But he steels himself, thinking about the first time he died. Thinking about coming back to 1968, doing more with his life than running around Hollywood.

Charlie squeezes the trigger but stops short. He sees a hardening smile on Elspeth's face, and then Michelle's face, a mask of troubles.

He changes his mind. No .38 for him.

*   *   *

Charlie turns to a recreation that guarantees the greatest adrenaline surge without human distractions. Something with zest in it. A sport just starting. Skydiving.

He enrolls in a course offered at a small airport out by Banning, with a good view of the San Jacinto Mountains. The other people in his class are sober, careful, asking pointed questions. One woman, a bit overweight from middle age, gets so nervous she drops out. For many of the students, the class seems to be a deliberate challenge, a way perhaps of mastering themselves.

But for Charlie it is completely different; he is lighthearted, grinning and joking, quite unlike his classmates. They seem to be a mixture of control freaks and adrenaline junkies.

His heart pounds, though, on the first practice dive. With all the safeguards in place—an instructor floating on a tether nearby to pull the rip cord just in case, and a backup chute, too—he still must overcome his innate fear of throwing himself out an airplane door into the abyss. But he does. Knowing he may be immortal helps. How others manage it, he will never know.

Luscious green lands spread out below him. Even through his helmet visor, the view is stunning. He quells the momentary panic of sudden weightlessness, makes himself relax—and finds he is enjoying the accelerating plunge. A howling wind whips around him as his legs and arms splay out into the onrushing gale. His body tingles with pleasurable alarm. It's great fun, the sensation of rushing toward a goal, risking all—then the team leader pops his chute. Weight returns brutally. He sways and bobs, savoring the river below that snakes like the convolutions of time. Or at least his time.

He lands well, banging a knee into the ground but nothing more. The jump team has an after-jump celebration at lunch in a studiously dingy, dark, heavily curtained wannabe dive. Now the class chatters and laughs and swills beer in an orgy of release. Free of gravity! Like birds! A few say they wanted to do it to prove they could, but they'll never do it again.

Charlie takes a second dive the same day, not tethered to the instructor this time, falling by himself with a safety chute. Just for fun. There are five others in this jump, some quite experienced. Again he loves the view, the pressure of the atmosphere rippling his clothes, the rush.

Halfway down the staircase of the sky, he has a feeling of completion—a resolution to the paradoxes of his reincarnate existence. He will find a way to make a world he wants. As he pops his chute and blood rushes down to his feet, he feels that he again owns his life, the self-time that he inhabits through the cycles of reincarnation. He even lands without falling to his knees.

All five of the other skydivers land well too and then head off for dinner together with Charlie. Skydivers spend days training and seconds falling, so there is shared emotion, almost an afterglow, as the intoxication of flight fades. Instant camaraderie, thanks to the rush and the danger, like the bond of combat in wartime. It is a boisterous evening, aided with rituals of salutation that always involve alcohol. Hungry for a repetition of the release, the easy oblivion, Charlie goes back up the very next day.

Falling, the ground looming toward him, Charlie has a burst of insight. The plan arrives as one bright arc in his head, intact. The way forward is clear, blade sharp, certain to work. He is ready to loop through the timescape again. He can defeat the ugly history of 1968.

So he doesn't pull the cord on his chute.

37

Charlie's body jerks backward against his mattress. He gasps. His arms and legs snap inward to clasp his gut. Even though his heartbeat hammers hard, the panic doesn't come this time. He feels a great sadness instead, an ache.

Then he realizes: *It worked!* He feels a rush. Master of time itself. As he lies there, his mind works furiously, his body again a torrent of young energy.

Charlie resolves to put all doubt out of his mind. On Monday he will contact Owen, to get hooked up with the radical group. They will be the best prospect for help with his mission, and he has to move fast. Not that he can actually explain to them what he is doing or what his motives are. But he will tell them that it will be "a revolutionary act," and that should be enough to get their help. So long as he doesn't have to listen to them babbling interminably in Marxist jargon.

But on his birthday he first has to put in an appearance, be the teenager. He can then wait till Monday morning to go to school, just like last time. *Sixteen again*, he thinks, with a sad smile. Now his Hollywood experience might help. He will be an actor.

He wonders how many more times he will revisit his birthday.

Do an infinity of them stretch ahead? It is pleasant to return to this young body, full of energy.

Will I have to kill Delgado? A grim question. *After all, I've killed myself for this cause. . . .*

He reaches for the dim outline of his lamp and finds its switch with practiced fingers. This time the room amuses him, and he appreciates the distraction. The posters of Jimi Hendrix, Cream—he notices a smaller one of Pete Townshend, in black-and-white, doing a windmill bar chord on a Rickenbacker guitar, captioned THE WHO. MAXIMUM R&B. *Was that there before?*

He faces himself in the mirror—and there he is, young again. Long, greasy hair, dark eyes, hairless chest. A bit buff, yes. His image reassures him, almost soothes the strange echoing hurt of coming back.

He looks for the book by Greenway on his bookshelf. It isn't there. But the calendar still has the girl on the motorcycle, and the days are still crossed out before January 14. That reassures him too. *Death and rebirth are starting to feel normal,* he thinks.

When dawn comes, Charlie is dressed in his red T-shirt and jeans, just as before. He waits for the knock that he knows has to come.

And there it is, firm but not insistent. "Charles, can I come in?"

"Sure, Dad."

His father is wearing his dressing gown over pajamas. He holds out his hand, with its slightly yellowed fingers. "Congratulations on sixteen years, son."

Charlie looks directly into his father's face, knowing that he is going to hurt the fine man on this loop around, wanting to reconnect with his father before he unravels the man's world. He struggles to keep all these thoughts out of his face. He beams, eyes bright. *Acting, yes. A lot of this is going to have to be acting. But I can recall the script in this rewrite.*

"A big day, I know, Charlie." His father's smile is heedless. "I wanted to get you up before everybody else, but I see you're already awake."

Charlie nods and stands up. Mute, struggling to stay in his character, his younger self. The world is sharp and clear, bright reality.

"Come on, son. I want to show you something."

To the garage, through the kitchen. His father points at the Dodge Dart with a flourish.

"It's yours, son. I signed the papers on a Cadillac yesterday. Pass your driver's test, and you're a grown man."

This time Charlie just sighs, hoping that his father will take it as appreciation rather than resignation.

His father puts his arm on Charlie's shoulders and the warmth spreads through. "I know it's a shock, son, but you've been a good boy—mostly, I guess. It's time you got a little freedom."

Charlie looks straight ahead at the Dodge Dart. The stacks of years behind him come swarming up in him and he has to make himself say, "Thank you, Dad."

On the ride to the tennis club, Charlie avoids looking at Catherine, staring out the window beside him instead. The world seems steady, concrete, and only he knows that it is a soft thing, molded by those who can voyage through time and lives. The loops through time are stunning him yet again. Will he ever know what time truly is?

This time he dreads meeting Trudy. *How can he cope with young spirits again?* he wonders. *What does Casanova feel when he makes love to a woman for her first time, yet again?*

This time Catherine just ignores him, preoccupied with a quick kiss at a middle-school party the night before.

They sit down for lunch at the club. Before long his father goes off to play squash and his sister departs for her lesson, leaving Charlie alone with his mother. "I called Trudy yesterday," his mother says. "She will be here after she comes back from church."

Charlie nods quietly, hoping that his mother won't talk to him about Trudy.

"I know you like her, Charlie. Don't act cool with me." She takes his hand. "I know I have to give you up, Charlie. But not just yet, okay?"

Charlie knows that she only has days, if not hours, before her worst fears will be realized.

"It's a hard time for you, Charlie. You are becoming a man, but I know that you're really still mostly boy."

But her words are wasted. Charlie's mind has slipped into the future just a few seconds away—and then it arrives.

"Charlie!" Trudy's voice and the touch of her hand hit him at almost the same instant. She kisses the side of his head and plops down onto his sister's chair, all white, dimples, and blue eyes. "I thought we might get a squash game in, Charlie!"

As they turn the corner toward the locker rooms, Trudy stops him. "What about your squash racket?"

"It doesn't matter, Trudy."

"Charlie Moment! What's got into you?"

But this cycle he has no time for her, no desire. His mission has left his chest an echoing barrel.

Charlie turns from Trudy and walks away, unheeding, her protests echoing down the hall—around the corner, out the doors, fast fast, into the winter landscape. The cold will be his friend, he thinks. Snap him back into this new reality of what must be.

The walk to school on Monday is again eight blocks of winter memories, barely relieved by Charlie's plan not to do it again on Tuesday. He has a new name for this time, the Land of Ago. It reeks with memory, old fragrances, unfiltered car exhaust aromas, and an oddly slanted regret. Charlie Two had nostalgia, walking through all this savory churn. Now Charlie Three has nostalgia for his nostalgia.

Woodrow Wilson High is a gateway into the future that he has resolved to build, a future better than either of the two he has already lived through. Here, Eugene McCarthy is the great hope of the white kids afraid of the draft, as Charlie One was. Now that can change, the calamity looming just months away dissolved.

As he takes the steps two at a time into the redbrick building the day after his third sixteenth birthday, Charlie knows he has no time for high school boisterousness. The banging metal doors, clicking heels, and cacophony of teenage voices mean nothing to him. He has to get moving, change this world. Pretty soon the last days of the Johnson administration will start shaping up the "unity government," consolidating federal power and lowering a gray gloom over the decades to follow.

He has to act, and soon. But he's a teenager with no money, no real mobility, nothing. *Remember, you're just a kid.* But he will pull together some resources, use what he knows of this era, starting with Delgado—

"Hey, Charlie, you fuckhead." Robert Woodson punches Charlie right in the middle of his chest. But Charlie holds on to his books. He fixes Robert with a quiet stare that freezes Robert's grin.

"Sixteen and still a virgin, loser." But the challenge has no effect. Charlie has made it a stare-down, a screenwriter's trick—let the actors do the work, no dialogue. Robert shakes his head and stalks off to class, chastened.

Charlie goes straight to locker 555, where once again James is standing, face working with interior torments he cannot quite hide. Charlie can see them now, wonders why he could not before.

"Hi, Charlie. Sorry, but I didn't get you anything for your birthday."

Moment speaks softly. "That's all right, James."

"Just kidding." James reaches into his locker and pulls out a plastic-wrapped LP of Cream's *Disraeli Gears*, the huge cover a jumble of orange and red psychedelic images.

"Thank you, James."

"Sure, I guess." James is obviously confused to be treated with simple politeness.

A lanky boy with thick glasses yells at them as he walks by, "Ready for the test?"

Charlie just looks at him blankly. The boy grins sheepishly and scurries away.

"What's with the cool treatment, Charlie? Like, I'm your best friend since sixth grade, you jerk." James gathers his books together and locks up.

"Sorry, James. I didn't sleep well this weekend."

"I know. I'm getting a lot of headaches—can't sleep worth shit myself." He looks pointedly at Charlie's open locker. "Don't you think you should go to the test too?"

The history exam covers the American Revolution and the Constitutional Convention. Charlie breezes through the short-answer questions and the assigned essay. It means nothing to him anymore.

As expected, Mr. Owen is looking at him with soft eyes. *Must be gay*, Charlie decides. By now he has plenty of experience with gays in Hollywood; there are small signs he can't miss now. Nothing else fits. His teacher is wearing his threadbare black suit with its high polish, a white shirt, and skinny black tie. Standard costume for a down-market mortician, if Charlie were casting a movie.

Charlie returns to his essay with quiet resolve, deciding to do a professional job with it, if only to take his mind off what lies ahead.

He hands the exam paper in to Mr. Owen, leaning forward to arrange a meeting later, after Owen's classes. Owen's eyes narrow.

In the hallway after school, some distance down from the teachers' lounge, Charlie meets with Owen. *Might as well do it fast*, he thinks. "I have a revolutionary plan of action, Mr. Owen." Charlie keeps his voice neutral, factual. "I mean business. I will contact you again outside the warehouse where your cell meets. Eleven p.m. Bring someone who can be of use."

Owen's eyes bulge slightly and he nods quickly. A glow dances in his eyes, with a tinge of fear to his excitement.

As he approaches the old brick building in the Dodge Dart, Charlie sees Owen's skinny frame topped with that absurd beret, standing next to a slight woman wearing an army surplus jacket. *Elspeth*, thinks Charlie. *My eternal succubus.*

She moves quickly toward the car. He rolls the window down, and she speaks quickly and anxiously: "What is your plan, comrade?"

His voice rasps. "There is someone we need to liquidate, a counter-revolutionary of extreme importance." This antique polit-jargon is laughable, but he keeps a straight face and sees that such clichés register with her.

A quick intake of breath, then, "Can you tell me more?" Elspeth is playing along with his script, like she is in on the plot.

"No. Information is on a need-only basis. I have my directives from higher up." More clichés that go over just fine. Then he recalls a detail that Charlie One learned only later in his time line. "I was told to tell you this is a code eleven."

Elspeth seems confused momentarily. The simple password tells her he has moved up the pyramid of conspiracy and can be trusted. That's how rewriting works. "Okay. I'll get you some money and counterfeit ID. Meet back here in three days. One a.m."

"Done. I need a thousand minimum. And the ID better be good."

Charlie drives away without looking back. It seems incredible that so simple a ruse can work. But of course he knows so much more now.

One a.m. and Charlie is back with a bag of clothes and essentials. As a precaution he has gone into his mom's cash stash for safety, $200. Charlie Moment, master criminal. He's staying in role: teenagers do crazy, stupid things.

He plans to drive to Costa Mesa once Elspeth has set him up. Delgado worked in Southern California before he set off on his mission to Indiana to shoot Kennedy, so Casanova's faint recollection is probably right.

He waits for twenty minutes, then thirty. He wonders if Elspeth got caught by the cops when she tried to get him the fake ID.

But at 1:45 a.m. she shows up, coming fast out of the shadows in sneakers, getting into his car breathlessly. Her eyes dance, nostrils wide, a sheen of sweat on her forehead.

"Drive," is all she says. He speeds away from the parking lot, past her Beetle parked around the corner. "One eighty-five Oak, off Main." It's her apartment. *Could this be a setup?* Charlie asks himself. But Elspeth's firm hand on his thigh tells him what her haste is for.

After she has fucked him for an hour, coming twice, Elspeth lets him go. At the door her hug takes his breath away. Her face is iridescent joy, as if sex and revolution are one and the same to her.

"Good luck, Char-lee."

Then she is back up the stairs and he is getting into his car. *What is it about women and men planning violence?* he wonders. *What is the turn-on?* A cliché in the movie world. It just leaves him empty.

38

Charlie gets a studio apartment in Costa Mesa, on the second story of a drab structure not far from Harbor Boulevard. The older white apartment manager responds well to the dead president in lieu of renter's documentation. Charlie tells him that he will be enrolling in Orange Coast College. He knows that he will have to lie low after he takes care of Delgado, and just staying put in Southern California is his preferred strategy. Merge with the millions. He knows enough about it from coming to LA last time-loop around, and he has the option of bolting for the streets of Hollywood if he has to.

California law makes getting the pistol easy. With an address, after a few days for checks, he has one from Grant's for Guns on Newport Boulevard. At their firing range he grimly enjoys plunking .38 rounds into targets, imagining them to be the heads of history's villains. The professor's revenge . . .

Charlie starts hanging around the streets of Orange County, looking for Delgado. His cursory research in the 1980s suggested that the Latino worked as a janitor in a small garment factory in Costa Mesa, but he wasn't able to get the address.

After a few weeks of hanging around in Latino bars and near

factory entrances, Charlie takes a different tack. Maybe Delgado doesn't drink, or maybe the factory story was bogus. He starts to loiter near taquerias in Santa Ana, figuring that most of the Latino community will eventually pass by one or the other of Santa Ana's many Mexican restaurants.

After twelve days using the restaurant search strategy, Charlie spots a man who looks like the photos he found. Short and broad, but his bronzed face beaming with hope for his new life, away from the troubles of Mexico. And equipped with a mysterious sponsor who, Charlie knows, has been making sure that Juan gets what he needs to find his way among the Yanquis.

Charlie eases after the man. Nobody notices Charlie because Juan is a bit of a social success at the taqueria off Fourth Street. He doesn't lack arms to clasp or hands to shake, women to give his flashing white smile. His mustache is a full black brush, his eyebrows not yet accented by parallel furrows in his forehead.

Delgado goes into a dark Mexican restaurant down the street from the taqueria. The place swims in warm shadows, tinny mariachi music rattles off the walls, and nobody cares if a gringo slinks in. Charlie feels the weight of the gun in his pocket, the bulge under his long sweater. Delgado is sitting on the other side of the restaurant with a Dos Equis.

As Charlie peers through the gloom, a Latino walks briskly up to Delgado's table and sits down. Delgado seems almost to crouch in submission. Charlie hears him say, "Hombre!"

There is something familiar about the man.

Charlie watches as the hombre with the power orders food for Delgado. Then Charlie is startled by a young Latino waiter.

"Excusing, señor." The waiter expertly slides chips, salsa, a menu, and some water before Charlie.

When Charlie looks at the hombre again, his heart freezes in the middle of a beat. He has seen the hombre before, in Chicago. At Elspeth's revolutionary cell meeting.

Panicked and confused, he leaves a dollar bill on his table and moves out of the restaurant, eyes checking everyone he sees.

Over the next few days Charlie swims in swarming confusion. *What is the relationship between Elspeth and the Hombre? And what does Elspeth know about the Hombre and Delgado? Is that why she was so scornful of Kennedy before, last time?*

Charlie decides to play his cards with greater care. Heinlein's warnings surface in his mind with authority. There are people out there, people who may know about Charlie, or may not.

Charlie's one point of comfort is that he has told no one, not even Heinlein, about what he is doing. And certainly Elspeth wouldn't know.

Charlie's opportunity with Delgado comes during a street fair. Delgado is strolling down First Street, relaxed, almost childlike, talking to the street vendors. He stops to talk to an attractive Latina standing behind a table of handmade belts.

Charlie casually walks up behind his prey. "Juan!" he calls insistently, just over the din.

Delgado's head snaps around to face him. "Señor?"

"The Hombre sent me."

Juan drops his smile and shows the girl that he has to go with a few downward looks, comic sad-sack mouth, eye rolling—then a grin. It is a friend of the Hombre, and he has no choice.

Charlie drives away in his Dodge with Delgado. He gets Delgado's address, a small apartment where Costa Mesa runs into Santa Ana. Charlie parks outside and takes the man in. Delgado is chattering in Spanish, sometimes trying fragments of English, but Charlie just grunts.

The door to the small place closed, Charlie backs away from Delgado and takes out his gun.

The Latino stands his ground bravely, but his eyes seem to tremble. "No, señor. I say Hombre that I do as he say."

"No problemo, Juan." Charlie's tone is cold. Having killed himself deliberately in pursuit of a new history, he knows that he can kill Delgado if he has to.

But not this time. He makes the man put his arms around a pipe in the wall. The handcuffs snap on easily; Charlie has been practicing doing it with one free hand.

Charlie steps away from the man, the gun still in his hand. Delgado breaks his silence with, "*Por favor, señor.* No keel. No keel."

"No, not this time, Delgado. And you won't either."

Charlie sets about planting the carefully bagged cocaine on the unsteady linoleum table near the hot plate.

It is the work of minutes to get to a pay phone to call the police. After what seems like hours waiting half a block away in his car, Charlie sees two black-and-whites pull up in front of Delgado's apartment building. The man is led out a few minutes later, this time handcuffed by the police. An African American officer is not gentle as he shoves Delgado into the back of his patrol car.

39

In the weeks that follow, Charlie stays in his apartment, savoring the '6os vibe for a third time. He watches his eleven-inch black-and-white tabletop TV, following the primitive coverage of the primaries. Kennedy's speeches are transfixing the nation. Not as warm as his brother Jack, but much more of a visionary, RFK is indeed everything that Charlie hoped for. Again. *Just let that bastard Nixon try to beat this guy,* Charlie tells himself over and over.

April 4, 1968, was the day when Delgado shot RFK, back in that lost Charlie One world. Charlie thinks of that fading memory as his home time, that Land of Ago. Then it seemed as if Bobby was the only force holding the country together, the only white man the black community respected. The last bridge standing to the Land of Reconciling. Eugene McCarthy was the great hope of the white kids afraid of the draft. RFK was too tainted for them, with his years working for Joe McCarthy and then his tough attorney general stint with his brother—all still casting a shadow, at least for the children of liberals who read the *New York Times*. But Charlie knows that McCarthy will not be able to defeat Nixon, even if Johnson pulls Humphrey out of the campaign—as the home-time Johnson did. McCarthy was just too inept.

But *this* time there is no one-eighty by Johnson. Humphrey stays in the race—though well out of the primaries, leaving Kennedy and McCarthy to fight it out against the native sons, the pallid hand-puppet senators and governors standing in for Humphrey. Daily, in fever-browed press coverage rendered in stark black-and-white, Kennedy and McCarthy's followers grow bitter. They are hammering away at each other in primary after primary. Wallace has come in on the right wing, playing the race card. Wallace is short and brassy and reeks of small-town redneck—and he weakens Nixon's polls. But having Wallace in the campaign lets the crafty Republican take the center.

To Charlie, 1968 the third time around is a complete mystery. For a historian—as he once was, he reminds himself—the idea that politics is so flexible, tangled, and weird is still dizzying. He recalls that as a student he liked the solidity of the past. The present got shredded daily, but events a few decades back emerged from the fog of opinion and false talk, shaping up like strong stone, rising from the swamp of passing opinion.

Now he has used his knowledge to make a world he wants. Shaped the swamp of movieland into the granite of holy Hollywood history. He wonders if he has done the right thing.

It all comes down to California. Its 1968 primary becomes the hinge for the whole election. McCarthy and Kennedy are everywhere. Charlie hardly has time to eat. He goes out early for breakfast each day, avoiding crowds, and usually has corned beef hash and eggs, and buys all the papers. He devours every word, every newsmagazine, watches all the local and national coverage on TV. Even the *Economist* has an opinion about the primary. All of Charlie's hopes, the thrust of his three lives—all now pivot on the returns from the California precincts in June.

He thinks of Albert dying the last time around. *Is he in this world now, alive again? Or has he not reincarnated here?* Do any of the ordinary people around Charlie sense how precarious all of this is? How the universe teeters on the edge of an abyss—always, with each passing second, shaving bits of stone off the twisted rock of time?

No, of course not. He can barely stand it himself, and he has lived in this era several times. Practice does not make perfect; it makes you suspect, fear, worry. So he buys some good Inglenook Cabernet Sauvignon and starts in on it quite early on primary day. In the afternoon he goes out for more.

The California polls close at 8:00 p.m., and CBS comes in first with a projected Kennedy victory. Charlie finishes his bottle. Luckily, he has planned ahead and has two more.

Then CBS returns to some idiotic situation comedy. He very nearly throws his empty bottle through his set.

Charlie switches to NBC, waiting for them to call it for Kennedy too. ABC is still too small a player to matter. He ignores the regular programming, reading the day's *LA Times* and *Orange County Register* for background, waiting for the news bulletins and the 11:00 p.m. news. There is a brief interview with Sander Vanocur, but it is becoming obvious to Charlie that NBC isn't going to feature RFK as much as Charlie wants.

He switches back to CBS and is rewarded with a Kennedy interview by Roger Mudd. "Are you saying, Senator, that if the Democratic Party nominates the vice president, it will be cutting its own throat in November?"

"Well, again," says Kennedy, "you use those expressions. I think that the Democratic Party would be making a very bad mistake to ignore the wishes of the people and ignore these primaries."

Damn right, thinks Charlie, dropping his newspapers unnoticed on the floor. His hand looks for a bottle of Coke, his fingers finding it from the damp cold of the glass. *Got to keep my energy up. Need some water. But isn't there water in wine? Must be.* The Coke tastes of lemon and joy as it rushes down his throat. His life will be worth something again now.

Maybe he will go back to Chicago, take law, and make a differ-ence in the world. Even though he hates lawyers. Maybe even look up Trudy? But no, he has to follow this trajectory, or lose his own self-respect.

Roger Mudd is trying to push Kennedy to open up about the future of his campaign for president. "Are some of the delegates listed as leaning or even committed to the vice president, are they squeezable? Are they solid?"

"Roger, your language! I don't like either of those expressions."

Mudd laughs. "Well, that—isn't that the way you talk about it?"

"No, I don't go that far, I don't, I don't." But Kennedy laughs too.

Charlie can tell that this is the turning point of the 1968 cam-paign, the fulcrum of the whole tumultuous decade. Watching alone yet with millions of others, he sees Kennedy reassembling America, a continent tumbling apart since his brother's assassination and the mess of Vietnam. Only this time the presidency will unite the coun-try around respect for civil rights, a just foreign policy, and an end to politics as usual.

Charlie swallows. *If it took my death to bring all this about, it was worth it.* He lets himself sink into the moment, dreamy and warm. *"And malt does more than Milton can / To justify God's ways to man. . . ."*

Is that it? Expressing his hopes through action on a stage no one has ever imagined? Never have to pay the price of dying? He decides, coolly and without pity, to let all those old ideas—the baggage of liv-ing one mortal life—slide away. Down they go, on the greased skids of time. He feels reborn truly, as he never has before. He had to make a world he could live in. A world set right. He is no genius like Ein-stein, no agent of some ideology like Elspeth. He is instead carrying out an experiment with time. He could slip through many histories, many choices, merely by dying.

All to make a life worth living. A future worth owning. Worth being in. Not a world weighed down by a stultified America. No world he has seen . . . yet. Not anything built up from ideas, either. Action makes worlds. Theories come on the battlefield only after all has been decided, and then the wounded are shot.

Charlie celebrates by adding rum to his Coke, and he feels better than he has in years. His whole life is ahead of him, and a new future for the country.

But he has the victory speech to look forward to. Around midnight Kennedy mounts the stage with his wife, Ethel, by his side. *She is great looking, for all those kids*, thinks Charlie, all tension gone from him.

Kennedy begins by congratulating Don Drysdale for pitching his sixth straight shutout, making the crowd laugh over the diversion. He thanks his campaign manager, Steve Smith. Then Cesar Chavez, Rosey Grier, and a slew of others. He thanks his dog, Freckles, and finally his wife, Ethel, though "not in order of importance." The crowd laughs some more.

Then Kennedy turns serious. He refers to the farmworkers who have supported him, not just in California, but in South Dakota, too, which is also counting its primary ballots.

And then to the meat of his campaign. "I think that we can end the divisions within the United States."

Charlie's heart surges. It is everything he wants to hear.

"We can start to work together. We are a great country, an unselfish country, and a compassionate country. I intend to make that my basis for running."

Kennedy offers change but also reconciliation. He congratulates McCarthy and his followers for their efforts. He makes sure that everyone in his campaign, and all his supporters, feel good about the night's victory. "My thanks to all of you, and on to Chicago."

He reaches out to the audience, which surges toward him. In the crush there are too many for him to exit through the ballroom itself. One of the hotel staff leads him out through the back of the stage.

Charlie watches the crowd and the jubilation, standing by himself in his apartment in his T-shirt and shorts, waving his rum-laced Coke. He turns on a radio for more commentary but finds it's playing "Good Vibrations" by the Beach Boys. He hasn't heard it in ages.

But from the TV comes an odd popping sound. The voice-over commentators are going on, but Charlie sees the crowd milling fearfully. He quickly turns off the radio. Something has happened. The camera jerks to sweaty, worried faces. Something is wrong, but no one knows what. The ballroom audience grows hushed. A bustle and shoving over by the side.

Steve Smith walks to the ballroom microphones. He quietly tells the crowd to disperse. Frowns, gaping mouths. The TV commentators begin stammering, voices tight and high, repeating rumors that someone has attacked Kennedy.

Charlie's chest seizes up with fear. They have succeeded. Again. He knows that Robert Kennedy is dead or dying.

40 Charlie spends the next three months drinking away the last of the money that Elspeth gave him. The Ripple bottles stack up in the garbage. The white-trash landlord finally evicts him, more in sorrow than anger. Charlie has made no secret of how he feels about Kennedy's assassination, and the landlord sympathizes. But he isn't the owner, and the pathetic, scraggly haired hippie has to vacate. As Charlie walks away, toting a bag of dirty belongings, his head spins. He needs a drink, bad.

Charlie ends up on the streets of Laguna Beach, facing an oncoming winter without enough cheap scotch to stay warm. He lies next to the boardwalk with a cap for spare change, begging only quietly, moving on whenever the police tell him.

One day, while sitting on one of the benches near the boardwalk, he falls into conversation with a grizzled Vietnam vet, Mike Clayman. Mike works as a bartender at the Sandpiper, down Pacific Coast Highway's surfer zone. Charlie has had a few passing conversations with him before.

In his alcoholic daze Charlie asks him about the reggae band he saw at the Sandpiper in 1988.

Mike laughs at him with good-natured ridicule. "Reggie band? What's reggie music?"

Dimly Charlie realizes that he is facing alcoholic dementia. Suddenly he feels a bit sober and very hungry.

"Nothing, man." It is hard for him to say what he wants, but he knows he has to. "Say, Mike, would you know if there would be any way I could earn some money around here, clean up a bit?"

"Charlie?" The burly man's voice is almost tender. "Are you ready to change?"

"Yes, sir. That I am, Mike, my friend."

"No more booze?"

"Nope."

"Like, I'll beat you up and throw you back in the gutter if you burn me on this, man."

"Absolooly."

Slowly Charlie puts himself back together. He works at the Sandpiper as their janitor for a time, living in a beach shack with Mike. The man is a dedicated Deadhead and doper, but he hates booze. He is the perfect bartender for the Sandpiper, where the staff are too relaxed, especially when LA rockers come south to slum and pick up easy chicks. Mike is the shepherd for the girls who wait the tables, and for Charlie.

After a while Mike lets Charlie tend bar when the going is slack, especially in the afternoons. He is impressed with how quickly Charlie learns how to mix drinks, from a hundred different martini recipes that Charlie seems to have in his head. At least some of his mental machinery survived, though it needs oiling. Like Mike, Charlie has become an enemy of the demon rum.

But Kennedy's death hasn't entirely left Charlie's mind. He avidly consumes books about the assassinations of the 1960s, taking detailed notes about Lee Harvey Oswald, Jack Ruby, and Sirhan Sirhan. He recalls Martin Luther King's assassination on April 4 and wonders if he should have intervened there. In his first life Charlie saw the steady decline of the black underclass, and now he wonders if by saving King, intercepting the assassin, he could have altered that. King's followers kept on with Ralph Abernathy and the other solid lieutenants, but then media tramps like Jesse Jackson and the comically incompetent Al Sharpton turned a once-lofty movement into a parody of what King had built.

Then caution descends on Charlie. He failed with Kennedy; best not to take on yet another task in the shifting landscapes of time. So he returns to Charlie One's habits: do your homework and maybe things will work out.

He keeps boxes of files under his bed in Mike's apartment. He looks for signs of conspiracy in each assassination case. Especially he seeks out the telltale signs of losers picked up for brainwashing or manipulation. Charlie is convinced that Sirhan Sirhan was a tool of the Hombre, with the parallels between Sirhan's odd behavior and the oddities of people suffering posthypnotic suggestion.

Many times Charlie considers going back to the Society building in New York, but he suspects that he might be killed if he visits again. That car bomb outside on his first visit—was that the same people who killed Albert? Clever, to try it before Charlie even met the man.

It makes Charlie's head whirl to think about his life, and his time, as pawns in a larger game. *Better to lie low. Play for . . . time. Do what Heinlein did. Maybe there is another way.*

Charlie does go to Orange Coast College, earning stellar grades taking courses part-time. But he enrolls under a different name so that no one will be able to find him, especially not the Hombre. Of course, he doesn't resume contact with his family back in Chicago. He starts to play the stock market, mostly emerging tech stocks. Then he buys gold just before the price takes off. All these moves he recalls from some economic history papers he wrote back in Charlie One's 1980s. Sometimes research pays off in unexpected ways. Eventually he has enough money to transfer to the University of California, Irvine, to get a bachelor's degree in history. He doesn't look up

Jim Benford there, since he's designing fusion devices at Livermore, yet to get the offer from UCI. All things in their time.

Time somehow accelerates for him. He learns to relax and enjoy life as it comes. There's always more coming, after all.

He is in graduate school at UCLA when the book on the Robert F. Kennedy assassination is published in 1978. He devours it in his graduate student cubicle, looking for signs of the Hombre.

He thinks he has him when he reads about a mysterious man who is supposed to have been with Sirhan Sirhan and a young woman at the Ambassador Hotel. But there is too little about the other man to be sure. He slogs on.

Then a detail jumps off the page. There are several descriptions of an unknown girl in a polka-dot dress, seen behaving oddly right after the assassination. At first he thinks it odd to wear eye-drawing polka dots, but then he realizes that people would look at the dress, not at the face of the person wearing it. So he delves into the raw material of transcripts, tediously scanning. A few people have fragmentary memories. The hair color, to some blond, to others brown. One says the girl had a "funny nose." Funny nose . . . with an odd point to it? Sort of blond.

Elspeth!

She isn't hard to track down in the UCLA library's archives. Already she has published four scholarly articles and a popular piece in *Ramparts* magazine, after getting her doctorate from Harvard. Now she is hiding out at the University of Toronto as an assistant professor of political science.

Charlie dips into the reserve of cash he has salted away and takes a plane to Toronto. He has some questions to ask a certain attractive young lady.

Charlie's mind churns on the flight. The taxi ride from the airport is endless. Even in the late 1970s, Toronto seems to go on long after it has made its point. Diesel fumes and jackhammers and vaguely French suits. Charlie's first stop is a hardware store called, for some reason, Canadian Tire. He has the taxi wait. Then it's off downtown for his little romantic get-together.

The University of Toronto campus is a sprawling urban monster, like some of the older American campuses, but with Canadian cleanliness and order. He is helped by a friendly middle-aged woman at a reception counter and soon finds himself outside Professor E. Halpern's door.

He knocks with as much dispassion as he can manage.

"Come in." Her voice has a descending tone, at once commanding and dismissive in its welcome. *She hasn't changed, then.*

He lets the door swing open wide before he enters and closes it.

Elspeth of course expects him. "Ah, Char-lee." Her smile is unreadable, but Charlie doesn't care. She rises to approach him but then thinks better of it and stands beside her desk chair.

"Why, Elspeth?"

"Why you, or why Kennedy?"

"I don't give a fuck about myself. Why Kennedy?"

She doesn't bother to answer him, just smiles, winding him up.

He converts his rage into an interrogation.

"That was your Beetle that Sirhan was in, wasn't it? It was you who called out, 'We killed him. We killed him.'" To this she still smiles. Doesn't move. "You put your hair up, didn't you? Bought a nice polka-dot dress, hypnotized the confused little bugger."

Elspeth's smile bespeaks triumph, the same expression he saw on Gabriela's face.

"You are, were, will be, Gabriela, aren't you?"

"Sort of, Char-lee."

"You have both been taking me for a loser, the dick you lead around."

A smirk. "It's a nice dick, Char-lee. Don't be ashamed of it."

Elspeth moves a bit closer to Charlie. He backs away slightly and fingers the hunting knife in his pocket. His mouth is dry and he can find no words. Air rasps in his throat.

"I just want to feel your body again."

Charlie feels stripped, humiliated in front of Elspeth, or Gabriela. Again. A feeling that familiarity does not improve.

"Who was the Mexican?"

"You mean Delgado? Nothing. Just a tool."

"No, the man who died in the desert, who killed himself with a gun, the Hombre, the one I have dreamed about."

"Ah." Elspeth's smile fades and she takes a step back to lean on her desk, the pretty curve of her pelvis pushing forward.

"That, of course, is Gabriel. Father to both Gabriela and myself. Father, lover, self. We are really one person, you know, Char-lee."

"You mean I have been fucking a Mexican guy?"

Elspeth looks cross. "Well, you've been fucking all of us. We're all here, you know." She gently strokes her forehead, an obscenely auto-erotic gesture that sends a surge of nausea through him, his breath shallow.

"And you wanted to add me to your menagerie?"

"You seem to enjoy fucking us, Char-lee. I think you would like becoming part of us. Think what we could do then. We are blessed, we reincarnates—and rare."

Charlie's guts are dropping out from underneath him; the room whirls. His throat clenches, refuses to let him speak. Her infernal smile returns, her eyes big and glistening. She is excited, nostrils flared just enough. He struggles, jaw clenched, and finally can relax. Control. *You're not really this kid.* Then he's back, his breathing calm.

"So why did you kill Kennedy?"

Her lip curls in scorn and he catches a smell from her, a smell of lust and anger. "We wanted to let Nixon destroy himself on his own with Watergate or whatever—he's such a paranoid, he had to fail.

Then that whole Cold Warrior establishment thing would unravel. America would get out of Vietnam. The eventual collapse of American world domination. But you haven't seen it all yet."

He knows to let her run on. She grimaces, teeth flashing, as if holding in a huge rage. "I know you want the same things, Charlee. You belong with us." Elspeth advances on him, puts her hands behind his head, and kisses his chin. Then her mouth moves down his neck toward his chest. Charlie's heart pounds with revulsion— not only for the monster that he finds Elspeth to be, but for his own attraction to her.

She unzips his leather jacket, her smile sliding into a leer of triumph. She unbuttons his shirt.

"You . . ." He struggles with himself, with confusion, fearing mental invasion. He has to play a role here, use what he learned a thousand years ago in Hollywood.

She blinks like a lizard, her seduction interrupted.

Fine. He puts a heavy earnestness into his youthful voice, using the skills he learned as a producer in Hollywood, where everybody was always your close friend. "You give me so much."

She blinks again, triumphant. "I am so happy with you, Char-lee. You have always been so smart."

He embraces her as his mind churns. Best to get away from here and think. Give her no clue that he is anything more than her pussy-whipped creature.

"You're wonderful," he murmurs.

41 The crisp black "42" sign is reassuring. Casanova remains as an anchor for reincarnates, the one stationary point for worlds in flux. Charlie looks around, but of course he is arriving here long before he did in the Charlie Two world. Maybe that matters.

Phelps again opens the door seconds after the knock. Of course; they have men watching their perimeter. This time there is nothing tentative about Charlie's entrance. "I want to see Albert and the chevalier immediately."

Phelps's bone-white skin creases with the patience of ageless time, a slightly raised eyebrow. "I fear that Professor Einstein is not available at this time; he would accomplish a much better explanation. The chevalier, however, is expecting you. He is waiting for you in the den, sir."

Phelps leads Charlie part of the way toward the den, returns to his reception desk. His eyes watch Charlie with resigned wisdom.

The chevalier rises as Charlie enters the chintz-stuffed room.

"Dear boy! You have come to us at a far earlier stage."

The beaming chevalier approaches Charlie with arms open, but the younger man backs away.

"I'm not sure I can trust you. Not anymore."

Casanova shrugs, spreads his hands in a gesture of sympathy. "Yes, I'm sure I have disappointed you." He sits down with a flourish and rests his head in his left hand.

Charlie's rage and confusion keep him upright, bristling. But at first he can't speak. His throat locks up. Tears of humiliation and anger sting his eyes.

"Why didn't you tell me about Gabriel, Gabriela, the whole fucking mess I am mixed up with?" His words rush out, ragged and breathless; his hands quiver.

"Gabriel and his crew? A nasty group, really."

"What is up with you people?"

The chevalier pointedly sighs with exasperation. "There is so much I have to explain to you." He offers a small glass of Amontillado, but Charlie dismisses it with a curt snort.

Some of the weight of centuries seeps into Casanova's face; he sighs. "When you first spoke with dear Albert, you must have realized that, for reincarnates, meddling with history is a perennial temptation."

The chevalier's smooth tone deflates Charlie's anger. Yes, he knew that; he had to. He had tried to do it himself. "So what have they been doing? And why?"

Casanova realizes that he has Charlie back under his spell. He pats the floral cushion next to him. "Quite an interesting case, dear boy."

Charlie eases himself to the edge of the upholstery. A bone-deep fatigue rushes up in him, and with it an insight. *Now this is the only real home I have.*

"Gabriel was a poor Mexican whose mission was to escape the— what do you call poor countries these days?—the second, no, third world hell that he grew up in. He was very poor. Very smart, though illiterate, but determined. He made his way out of Mexico, much as I made my way out of the Leads, by virtue of great resolve and grasping every opportunity. He died several times in the deserts of Arizona. He learned from defeat and death, as must we all."

Charlie whispers, "It all seems so futile."

Casanova nods, then brushes this away with a finger flick. "To continue, then. Finally Gabriel came here. He had followed clues."

"A goddamn newspaper ad?"

"I have forgotten. He may be brighter than his actions seem—certainly Albert feels that the brain 'correlations' required for reincarnation do not necessarily mean intelligence per se. We have many avenues for reincarnation, some quite subtle. Gabriel and I met, and he learned about lateral reincarnation, the fusion of minds across time."

Revulsion rises hot and bitter in Charlie's throat. "Do all reincarnates learn how to go laterally?"

"Ah, no, dear boy." The chevalier arches his eyebrows and a tender smile conveys resigned compassion.

"I'm not going to be able to go lateral, am I?"

"Perhaps not."

Better to cycle through his own body, Charlie thinks, *and no one else's.*

Casanova pats his hand. "Gabriel's great passion was to escape the limitations of his world, economically, intellectually, politically. He was so promising in those days—so full of hope that more education would make his life easier, would let him understand reincarnation. But every time he died, he would go back to Mexico, with nothing, and fight his way back here."

Like me, Charlie thinks. *Cycling, looping forever. Maybe this is hell and I don't know it. One made for those who keep trying to alter time. But they never learn. So they kill again. Only if you hope can those hopes be dashed again and again, throughout eternity. Even Dante had no idea this bad . . . .*

"Any interest in lunch, Charles?"

Charlie shakes his head emphatically. He can't think of food now.

"Pity. Well, I'm afraid, dear boy, that Gabriel has a lot of darkness lurking in his soul. Something to do with his mother, I fear. I had difficulties with my mother also. . . ."

Casanova glances sidewise, notices that Charlie has little time for Freudian theories, and hurries on with his explanation.

"So Gabriel was an angry soul from the start. Though he loved learning, he hated the bland rationalism of our time. He wanted to purge himself of his frustrations, and if that meant reaping a whirlwind of chaos for himself, and for this time, then he was happy to make it so."

Casanova sees that Charlie may finally be ready to speak reasonably, so he makes space for him in the flow of words. Charlie manages, "Gabriel was—or is—a kind of romantic nihilist? Like an anarchist?"

"You could say so, my boy. Gabriel hates some of the basic ideas that to me are of the essence of civilization. Understanding, openness, order, personal freedom. He lives for the drama of time, for the turbulence of unbridled authenticity—yes, I think that was his phrase."

"So, you know him pretty well."

"Quite intimately, I'm afraid."

"Gabriela?"

"Quite the little temptress, isn't she?" Casanova gives Charlie an arch look, a tilt of the head. Despite himself, Charlie feels a pang of brotherhood.

"Absolutely." Charlie releases a pent-up breath. "So, we understand each other."

Charlie still recoils from the thought of Casanova and Gabriel switching sexes, a grand gavotte among many partners, skin touching and blending, then Gabriel as Gabriela or Elspeth having sex with him. But the violence of his revulsion is fading.

"I know it's hard to understand, Charles, but for some of us, once we have been through many lives, the real difference is between rein-carnates and everyone else. The poor dear mortals, I call them, even though they cycle too, of course. They simply have no awareness that their lives loop back, go around, sometimes switch bodies. It's all so vague and unconscious for them, just fragments of dreams show them the truth about their plight."

Maybe they're lucky, Charlie thinks, *many lives but no memories.*

The chevalier's voice rises. "Whereas we, dear friend, know what is going on, as the complex flow of time sweeps us up and deposits us anew upon strange sands. Our understandings accumulate through time. We see so much, so we deepen." Charlie notices that the man's eyes are becoming moist.

Casanova stands, smoothing his clothes as he rises. "Now I really must insist, I haven't had a morsel." He takes Charlie by the arm. "Come, come, dear boy. You look terrible, I'm afraid to say."

The food and more soothing words help. Charlie waits until they are sitting quietly across the great mahogany table from each other, wineglasses in hand, before demanding, "What is my place in all this?"

Casanova hesitates, his mouth slanted with remorse. "Dear boy, I believe you are one of those reincarnates who will always be yourself."

"Thank God!"

"Yes, and you are happy with that, are you not?"

"You bet."

"I know that the gender blending, the passion slipping both ways, this bothers you, does it not?" The question is purely rhetorical, and Casanova smiles benignly to show that he understands Charlie full well.

"So, you are locked in your time, the late twentieth century. Not a bad time. Good dentists, the doctors aren't terrible. Well, they can't do much of anything to really increase our life spans, but for us that isn't an issue, now is it?"

"No."

"Regrettably, you have gotten rather mixed up in Gabriel's struggles. Even before your first reincarnation, they were hanging around you, weren't they?"

"Of course. I was *married* to Elspeth, for Chrissake."

"Indeed you were, weren't you?" Casanova blinks, purses his mouth with wry humor. "One forgets details. In any case, I'm afraid that Gabriel's bitterness has infected a number of lateral reincarnations. They work together over time, through time, spreading their 'authenticity' like a disease. You've seen something of that, I know."

"But what am I to *do*?" Charlie is anguished, pleading.

"Well. Well, well. I'm afraid that is rather up to you, my young friend. Gabriel's crew causes quite a bit of havoc in your time."

"I know he—they—must have been involved in several assassinations."

"I'm afraid so, dear boy. They do keep us busy. But it does become an ugly business, you see—discreetly removing our kindred when they cause trouble. There was another time in the last century, the nineteenth, when we had a bout of assassinations. It all got quite tangled. That is when I started to back away from getting too involved. I'm sure you understand."

"Yes. I know." He came close with Elspeth. But then he recalled, from a conversation right after Albert's death, that Heinlein had said something about sending them to the back of the line. That stopped him.

Casanova's face works with concern, and Charlie sees to his surprise that the man is getting flustered. Even immortals have worries. "Well, you are one of the stronger reincarnates. Your retention of memory through your reincarnations is excellent. Something to do with waves and coherence, Albert has told me—I can't follow the details. And of course you are rather intelligent, more than you at first suspected—even if sometimes, shall we say, overwrought."

"I'll admit to that. I must have seemed a good recruit to Elspeth. Easily duped."

"I fear so. They decided to intersect you early in life, to enlist your loyalties." Casanova shrugs, as if this is a common tactic he has often seen used.

"And they'll keep on, won't they?"

"Indeed, they want to have you to help them."

"And they don't know how I really feel, now that I know what's up."

"Yes, well, rather." Casanova leans forward with a weary sigh. "One has seen odd triumphs and laughable tragedies, bad booms and beautiful busts—I assure you I do not pun here—plus ragtag revolutions and obliterating wars, great achievements and deep ambiguities, too. One has seen grand theories rise, only to be toppled by stubborn facts. This is a fine time of leisure and freedom, this America of yours, freed from the factitious urgencies of earlier days. But not for long, as you know. In your several time lines you have seen it decline. Einstein saw much worse, up there in the twenty-second century, after the big regional wars of the twenty-first. I saw some especially ugly things in the nineteenth. Not that they reached forward into your time."

"He said they understand reincarnates somewhat in the twenty-second century."

"So they do. By the simplest of methods. Some reincarnate finally set up business as a prognosticator, telling everyone what would happen. Bets to make, minor political turns, stocks to buy. Nothing to alter the time line appreciably. That convinced scientists. But it was a wrecked age. Albert disliked it and turned to this era, working endlessly on his elaborate calculations. The comforts of mathematics! He has settled into our time now, these wondrous 1960s onward to the early twenty-first century, because he avoids the horrors that came from those World Wars." A sigh, as though these memories exhaust him.

Charlie sits back, feeling that he has now learned enough. "So can I prevent that dark American future?"

Casanova nods. "A fine idea. Worth attempting. Chaos is the law of nature; order is the dream of intelligence. I hope you can successfully, and often. For, as I'm sure you understand, I have had this conversation before. With you."

Charlie gets money from Casanova, who carelessly tosses banded stacks of crisp green bills at Charlie's open valise. Not since the mad days of Hollywood in the 1970s has he seen anyone so casually spendthrift. These rolls do not come with bags of cocaine, at least.

Charlie is coming to understand the ennui that drove Casanova through so many European cities, so many bedrooms. And he wonders if this understanding will lead him astray. Yet Charlie is not as amenable to the distractions of the flesh, not after his last encounter with Elspeth.

This time he will prepare better for his next reincarnation. He doesn't want to waste another life.

42 Sixteen yet again and pumped with that surging, zesty energy, Charlie drives his trusty Dodge Dart toward Memphis in search of a man who has a date with destiny, a date the man kept in Charlie's worlds before. This time Charlie is going to stop him.

These last months have remade Charlie. He can recall the plunge through the sky toward the thick forest. But not the impact. He can never recall the last moment, the final extremis, of any of his deaths. Probably it has something to do with the brain's ability to process experience into memory. Laying down the recording takes a while. A bullet crashing into a brain, or the ground slamming into it—none will allow the brain time to log in a real memory.

On the drive to Memphis he thinks hard. He is a player in the history game. But not the only one. *Somewhere out there Elspeth and Gabriel are at work. And Gabriela,* he thinks ruefully, *somewhere in the future, they will acquire her, too.* The entire grammar of reincarnate logic is tricky because mortal thinking is geared to sequential thought. Timescape loops demand a new tense, something other than time past, time future, or time present. Self-time is what really matters for reincarnates.

Leave that to the mortal academics of the future, Charlie thinks. He no longer sees himself as a scholar. Doing is the point, not learning.

He outlined his plans to the chevalier. Pleading, in a way. "I want to set things right, stop the King killing. Are they, or will they be, involved? Look into your own past lives. How probable does that look?"

Casanova shied away. "I really . . ."

"Think of this statistically."

So he pried the key information out of the Venetian. Now that he knows from the chevalier's many recollections which way Elspeth and Gabriel will intervene—from the time lines Casanova has passed through—he can intersect them upstream well before the Bobby Kennedy assassination. Even better, he is in time to stop the Martin Luther King killing. A whole new world beckons.

Casanova smiled skeptically. "Ah, you fresh cyclers. Your spirit brings back many memories."

Charlie realized that Casanova was never going to think systematically, much less scientifically, so he invoked the puzzles of self-time. "Can I just keep trying, maybe? See whether I end up in some place where they speak a language I can't understand? Where everything's changed beyond recognition?"

"Albert said something about how complexity grows from simple early time, a 'big bang' in the past." Casanova's eye-rolling expression was comic, perhaps unintentionally.

Only later does Charlie wonder what double-edged meaning might be hidden in the sentence "Your spirit brings back many memories." *How much change has Casanova seen?* But it is an imponderable he no longer has time for, since with Casanova's blessing and some thousands of dollars, he is now sure of what he can do—what he has to do.

He called his parents some days after his disappearance. Told them he had gone on the road, "hunting for his destiny." They were happy to hear from him at first, his father saying, "Doin' okay, then?" to which Charlie said, "Yep!" But then, as they talked on, his father got concerned and his mother started sobbing.

So Charlie hung up. His family's unhappiness is only a small hurtful thing, compared with what will happen if he doesn't act. What do events mean if they can be revised, rewritten by reincarnates? For all his knowledge of history, he has no answer. But he knows that he is going to do everything he can to undermine the plans of Gabriel, and there can be no qualms in dealing with reincarnates.

Aloud he says to the windshield, "I'll do better with my parents. Talk more. Be there. Help them through what I know they'll face, even in their marriage. Maybe give them stock tips. Money helps. They need me but they don't know it. I'll finally be *a good son."* The sudden ferocity in his voice tells him that this is a truth he must fulfill.

So he ponders as he drives the Dart to Memphis.

Charlie eases into the slow southern town, setting up in a cheap motel along the Mississippi that boasts COLOR TV, the big new thing. Memphis reeks of moist history. He recalls a joke his father once told about the South: It's dirty, hot, nasty, ugly—and that's just the people. The harshness of the joke was quite unlike Ned Moment otherwise, and it has stuck in Charlie's memory.

But as he strolls around Memphis, it is pleasant, the crowds earnestly having fun. Walking past a big house with a sweeping driveway, he is surprised to realize from the sign that this is Graceland, where Elvis lives. No crowds outside, no cops, just ordinary life with a pop star in the neighborhood. Elvis isn't an overhyped icon yet, and it will be decades before imitators stage events and drunks see the dead Elvis resurrected.

He hires a private detective the next day. Working from the memories of Charlie One's classes in American history, he gives a rough description of the man he seeks. The name alone is enough. The detective turns up James Earl Ray within hours. He even has an arrest-booking photograph. Ray is a career criminal, in and out of jail, and the police know where he is. Charlie doesn't question where the detective got his information, guessing that most detectives are ex-cops who have friends on the local force. Ray is staying in a seedy motel only two miles away, south along the muddy river. He's in town from his place, a used-up farm, farther south. He has some business in town, the detective guesses. Not much they can do about it, except circulate Ray's picture.

Charlie hangs out in roadside bars near Ray's motel, easing into the southern style. It's a nice neighborhood to have bad habits in. He is just a kid in khakis and a work shirt, his hair cut for respectability in a 1968 South that still associates long hair with drugs, raw sex, and Vietnam protests. His face is well hidden by a new shaggy beard and his full mustache, so nobody cards him when he orders drinks. Despite his disinterest, or perhaps because of it, a few women hit on him. He ignores them, even with their breasts braless in Technicolor shirts. He hangs back, trying to pick up the local accent, all rounded r's and chopped-off verbs. But nobody knows anything about Ray. Or won't talk.

The second night in town he is sitting in a big, down-home bar called the Left Hand. There are a variety of off-color jokes about the name. It's a white dive Ray might come to, jukebox blaring some good chord changes in otherwise lame-ass rock singles, with clicking balls on a pool table in the back, fried food tanging the air, sawdust floors that irritate Charlie's nose, and beer kegs behind the bar.

He strikes up a conversation with a young guy sporting a tiny goatee. Even in Hollywood years later, this is a look that maybe one guy in fifty pulls off well. And this isn't that guy. But he's useful for cover, because if Ray comes in, Charlie is less noticeable talking to someone. The goatee guy goes on and on, flaunting a burnished vocabulary, happy for an audience. Charlie tries asking questions to keep him going, but when he does, Mr. Goatee frowns, as though thinking is always going to be a bother to him. Fortunately, Mr. Goatee's mouth runs without fuel.

Then Ray comes in. Charlie recognizes him from the detective's pictures. Ray checks out the joint quickly, eyes skipping right past Charlie, and takes a step in. A burly guy greets him and Ray trades some friendly insults. Ray is of average height and somehow scrawny in his chinos and T-shirt. He probably thinks the T-shirt sets off his muscles, but mostly it advertises the swelling gut that laps over his thick black belt, like a lapsed promise after the swelling of his broad shoulders. James Earl Ray—*What kind of guy needs three names?* wonders Charlie—has a pinch-mouthed face and a compensatory arrogance that give him a loudmouth swagger, easy to spot. He steps back and gestures to somebody outside the doorway.

Charlie freezes. Into the bar stride Elspeth and Gabriel.

Charlie stops breathing. He never guessed this. Back in his Charlie One life, Elspeth always brushed aside the King assassination as a mere sideshow, not ideologically important. She lied, probably with considerable forethought. Now Charlie sees that they are behind it, too. His plans come crashing down.

They are oddly dressed, for them, in jeans and shirts and baseball caps. To fit in, he guesses. To leave no memories of a strange couple hanging around with Ray. Jeans and tennis shoes enhance Elspeth's casual sway, unmistakable as she walks to a booth. *Did she use that hypnotic talent to recruit James Earl Ray, now meeting them with studied casual glances, then strolling beside her, Gabriel behind both of them?* From Ray's peacock strut, Charlie reads the answer.

Elspeth turns to slide into a booth and her eyes sweep around the bar. He looks away just in time. He hopes his beard and mustache will make enough difference. His heart is thumping hard, in pace with the jukebox playing an old Bo Diddley number.

When he glances back in their direction a moment later, she is engrossed in talk. Their booth is toward the back, near the pool table's puddle of bright light. Smoke hazes the air and bites his sinuses. Charlie is out of their line of sight.

The goatee guy pauses in his disquisition, and Charlie fills the space between them with a vague phrase, "You got it right, man," and goatee goes right on, his motor mouth giving Charlie cover. Charlie manages to make his face look interested while he thinks furiously.

Amid the chatter and clink of the bar, a thin sliver of a plan opens up. His mind zooms ahead. Their team is now just repeating what they did before, stitching up the threads of time.

They're used to this. They loop through history, wreaking their intemperate havoc. As reincarnates, Elspeth and Gabriel can remake the world without cost, within their long spirals of self-time. Time and opportunity have little price for them, of course; they can just move on to another parallel world, try again. But the romantic collectivist chaos they want to create falls upon the mortals, who will never understand why they live through a history so ugly.

Delgado's shooting that crippled Robert Kennedy in Charlie's first two lives was a revolutionary's cat-among-the-pigeons pounce. Only it came from a desire to fit the world to the twisted psychic needs of their commingled minds. And then there was the actual assassination of Kennedy in Charlie's third life.

So . . .

Cut their loop. They can't return to a time line once they've left. Casanova was clear about that, at least.

Elspeth and Gabriel are old hands at this, have probably cycled through a dozen or more lives already. They have their own agenda, scooped him up when he was a naive Charlie. Fresh meat. And they saw him as a tool in their scheme to make a world Charlie does not want.

They carry memory into their next lives. They are well "tuned"—Casanova's word—to recall, just as Charlie is. Apparently, this is vastly unusual. Certainly, the vast bulk of humanity has no memory of its past lives, at least not when awake.

Listening to the goatee guy, Charlie fingers the Beretta in his jacket pocket. In the other pocket he carries a knife, just in case, a heavy-handled long blade.

They must have built up a labyrinth of payments, accomplices, all at the pivot points of their time. My time too, Charlie thinks. *They're toying with mortal lives for amusement. With certainty, for their own unending fantasies of power.* With certainty, he knows that he is gazing at a concentrated evil.

It is critical to stay away, beyond their view. Risky, but essential. In each cycling loop they know more. He is sure they have been busy little assassins indeed. *JFK? Did they do that, too?*

He can never reach back into 1963 to Dallas and check on JFK, Oswald, that whole sorry mess. He read a lot about it in high school, the memory still fresh in the national consciousness. Oswald was a loser who had no getaway plan. He dropped the rifle, paused to buy a Coke from a machine when a cop rushed into the School Book Depository, and then . . . took a bus back home. Picked up a pistol and a jacket. Walked aimlessly down the street. Stopped by a patrol officer who was searching for him. Oswald panicked and shot the officer dead. Then he rushed away and ducked into a movie theater, not even buying a ticket—so the ticket girl noticed him. More police following up on the dead patrol officer's radio call asked the ticket girl if she had seen anyone of Oswald's description, and of course she told them he was inside. They nabbed Oswald without firing a shot.

Not the actions of a man thinking ahead.

It seems implausible to Charlie that Gabriel would have tipped Oswald over the edge. Oswald was a crazy loser, period. Unlike Ray, who is just a lowlife gun for hire. Even if he did loyally take his secrets to the grave.

So here they are in a honky-tonk bar with Grand Ole Opry now belting from the juke in the back. Preparing to carry out the first big step in their strategy for ruining this world.

If he does nothing, that strategy will work surprisingly well. Ray will kill Martin Luther King with one shot that severs the spinal cord. In Charlie's previous worlds, Ray immediately fled from the rooming house where he had lain in wait. He got cleanly away from the FBI and eluded the whole national security net. He was over the border before a general alert went out.

Ray might have made it to some temporary obscurity, except he ran out of money. Elspeth and Gabriel must not have paid him all that much. Or maybe the man had just wasted it too fast.

In this time line too, presumably, it will run much the same way. She has thrown in a recruitment screw—he can tell from Ray's soft-faced look—and keeps Ray expecting more, to control him. Much as she did to Charlie, for far too long over two lives.

In those other times, Ray got to England and decided to hold up a bank. He had knocked over a few before, and nailed one in London. But his American accent narrowed the chase, and Scotland Yard grabbed him while he was waiting for a flight to South Africa at Heathrow. He explained that he had a plan, to get into a mercenary outfit there, help put down "the darkies," and ingratiate himself to the apartheid regime. Then the grateful South Africans wouldn't extradite a wholesome, fearless battler like him. Ray would be a famous man in a land that respected folks who did the right thing, and never mind the law.

Instead, in those parts of the timescape, Ray got a speedy conviction and a life sentence. There were mutterings about a conspiracy behind him, and some evidence of a shadowy gray eminence who paid Ray enough to run for a while. Ray himself hinted darkly that he had been hired, then clammed up whenever a reporter came fishing for a story. Conspiracy theorists long puzzled over clues to it all as late as the mid-1990s, amateur historians still tracking down details. The most popular notion was that Ray feared being killed in prison if he ratted out his funders. He never did, and died there, still hoping for a commuted sentence. Forlorn and neglected, he was tossed in the Dumpster of History.

Charlie is going to spare Ray all that torment. An anger boils up in him that clenches his teeth. Goatee catches this and wonders what's up. Charlie waves his query away, breathing deeply, trying to relax.

He peers intently at Gabriel to see if the man is armed. Charlie has been so intent on Elspeth, he has only glanced at the man, who now half turns toward Charlie. A shock runs through him.

The face. It is the lined, flinty-eyed scowl that haunted him in dreams. The mustache. Ever since he first screwed Elspeth as Charlie Two, that face has battered against his mind, seeking entrance. His dry-mouthed fevers were battles, not mere nightmares. He suffered those sweaty panics, thinking the next morning that the yawning jowls and looming faces were imaginary demons launched by some Freudian unconscious. But they were something far worse—a mind trying to slide across some dimension invisible to him, knifing into his humming mind, to possess him, rule him as a rider does a mere horse.

Elspeth-Gabriel-Gabriela. Parasites. Leeches sucking victims' lives into their vortex. Slavery of a stripe he never imagined.

He wishes he could get up and do something, maybe shoot some pool, just to ease his jumpy nerves. Ray is in his element, chugging down beers and regaling his audience of two with loud talk Charlie mercifully can't make out. Elspeth looks rapt, a great acting job. Gabriel's older face is distracted, eyebrows raised above glassy eyes, plainly just lasting out the evening. Gabriel is sacrificing for the cause, enduring even boredom. Ray acts the grinning fool in the steamy, thumping bar air. Charlie is staring into an abyss, bottomless, dark, cutting the world in two.

The goatee guy is a best friend by now, well into his fascinating life story. At least the winding tale of goatee's woes and triumphs, a saga only now getting past high school, has given Charlie a chance to decide what to do.

Finally the moment comes. Elspeth puts cash on their bill and waits for change, pretending to flirt with Ray, who ogles her from across the table.

Charlie chops off Goatee Guy in midsentence and slaps his cash on their table. "Gotta go. Later, man." He gets up and heads toward the exit. But he slows when he spots a wooden chair with a cushion seat. He has an idea and sweeps up the cushion. He gets out the swinging leather doors of the bar well ahead of Elspeth and Gabriel, the masters of time, and their hireling, James Earl Ray.

From a block away he watches the three come out of the bar. They head toward the river, over one block, and onto the poorly lit riverside path. The cool lapping of the water masks their voices as Charlie follows fifty yards behind, squinting in the dark to make out where they might turn. Birds chirp. No other figures loom in the gloom.

Ray's motel comes first, a cheap neon glow beyond the trees inland, behind a dockyard. A single figure peels off from their group. Charlie pins his plans on its being Ray. From the lurching steps, that seems right. Ray is headed back to his shabby motel.

The remaining two keep on in the moist air flavored with sultry river scents. They are headed downriver, along the high levee. Big hotels lie to the south in well-lit areas. Before that come two more blocks in quilted shadows. No craft on the river either. No moon, a stroke of luck.

Charlie moves forward fast, bringing out the Beretta from his jacket pocket. He needs to stay beyond their vision, and coming from behind gives him all the advantage. But they are hard to make out in the murk.

At about twenty yards' range he stops, holds the Beretta in the two-hand grip he practiced on Illinois shooting ranges, and chooses a target. The two are about the same height, and he wants to get Gabriel with the first shot. He steadies himself, thinking for the first time that he is shooting people in the back, against the movie cowboy code. Then he recalls the cushion, which he has stuffed under his belt. He whips it out, folds it over the muzzle—and pulls the trigger. In his mind he sees the king and queen from a chess game knocked off the board.

Even muffled, the crack is unbearably loud in the night silence. His target crumples, and he steps closer as the other figure turns to look. He fires through the cushion. That one too goes down. Feet pounding, breath sharp in his throat, he runs forward. In the pale glow from the distant city lights he sees Elspeth sprawled on the gravel pathway. Her eyes rove, blinking. He can't let her see his face. His finger jerks two more shots into her, the muffled noise startling him again. The queen has fallen off the board. She'll be back again—somewhere else, somewhen else, he knows.

There are a few rounds left in the clip, and he turns toward the shadowy shape of Gabriel, can't see it—and someone slams into him with a grunt. The impact knocks him over. He hits hard and a man drops on him. The weight whacks the wind from his chest. He gasps and brings the Beretta around. An arm pins Charlie's gun hand. A fist punches hard into his jaw. The world spins. He lets go of the cushion, which is shredded now anyway.

Charlie wrenches to the side. Another fist smacks his nose and he hears a snap as his cartilage gives way. The taste of blood bursts in his mouth.

He jerks his gun hand free and bashes the Beretta into the looming shadow over him. A grunt. He hammers the Beretta butt home again. Arms twist his left side and Charlie follows the momentum, rolling the man off him. Sticky fluid splatters on his cheeks, his eyes.

Faint light shows him the man's face. It is the face from Charlie's dreams, mouth agape. No eyes peer up at him. The face is covered in blood, the mustache soaked in a darkness that looks black but must be red, the skewed mouth wrenched with pain. Fists hammer punches into his chest. Charlie brings the Beretta around and pulls the trigger and nothing happens. A jam.

The face grits its teeth. *The dream, this is the dream. I've had this so many times—*

Howling agony erupts from the mouth. Fists pound into him. He answers with the Beretta. It slams down into the yawning mouth. Teeth shatter. He rams the butt into the mouth. Swings it high and brings it down on the bloody face, on the temples, hammering hard.

The body goes limp. Charlie staggers up. He fishes in his pockets and finds a round. Chambers it. Holds the Beretta. Points it at Gabriel's forehead and blows the brains out. The king has gone on to his next game.

See you again, bastard, thinks Charlie.

43

The next day he is lying on a dusty ridgeline, sighting down the scope of a hunting rifle. It was easy to buy and practice with, in the weeks before coming to Memphis, though the scope took more trouble, and sighting it in was a challenge. He gained new respect for hunters and certainly for soldiers; deer don't return fire. The sling is useful for field sighting, a frame to hold the sight steady while standing.

Still, he has never shot at someone who can shoot back. But he has to do it at this distance, maybe two hundred yards, or his strategy may not work. He trained with firearms, choosing his rifle by using a lot of gun shop advice from grizzled guys. Nobody likes to tell stories more than hunters, and he picked up useful lore. If he ever goes hunting for deer, the species better worry.

Humans are trickier prey. Following a gun manual, Charlie filed down the sharp points of his ammunition back at his motel, making them into dumdum rounds. A jacketed round with slight notches cut across the top makes the bullet deform on impact. He tested them on hardened targets and found the cut rounds broke into chunks along the crosscuts. They would gouge larger wounds, turning them into "man-stoppers," as one gun store clerk gleefully told him. But altering a bullet makes it less aerodynamic, less accurate at longer ranges. Life and death are all about trade-offs.

He has the Beretta automatic beside him as well, its rounds also slightly carved to enhance impact. All this preparation and training is new to Charlie. He understands now that, like most people, he thought a gun was just an appliance that conferred instant power. He recalls a great old Bogart line from *The Big Sleep*, some think a gat in the hand means the world by the tail.

That morning around 8:00 a.m., Ray went to a diner for breakfast. Charlie spotted him easily in the downtown, walking out to his car by the cheap motel and quite conspicuously loading a rifle in a sling case into his trunk. Nobody noticed. Guns were ordinary business in Memphis.

Charlie was jumpy after the two executions; or rather, he thought, "timescape relocations" would be a better term. *Go to the end of the line.*

Ray slouched out of the diner, not even looking around. He got into his beat-up Ford Fairlane with muddy whitewall tires and drove south, out of town. Charlie hung back in the light traffic, letting Ray get a hundred yards ahead. A pickup truck pulled between them and Charlie was happy with the cover. After ten miles going south, Ray turned off onto two-lane blacktop, driving fast. This is country enriched by the Mississippi's periodic floods, so crops and vegetation are rich. There are hills and even ridges, but mostly this is classic farmland, topsoil replenished by the grand ol' Mississippi. In a quarter mile Ray hung a left onto a dirt road headed away from the river. Charlie liked the deserted location and fell farther back, grateful for the pall of dust that blocked Ray's rear view. They passed an abandoned farm of worn gray wood and some cows, looking disappointed with the grass. From a rise Charlie saw that the road led into a narrow valley rimmed by an eroded ridgeline. In the distance he saw fields and then dense woods. *Time to bail out.*

He noticed a dirt track to the left that wound up along the ridge. Quickly he turned off, out of Ray's view through the dust. The Dart could barely creep along the track, bumping over the ruts. The dust stung his nose. Trees shaded the slender dirt trail and a gurgling brook broke across what was now barely a cow path. He followed the path along the ridgeline. Ray's car was not visible from above. In another half mile the path petered out, trees closed in, and Charlie stopped. He backed the Dart around so he could drive straight out. On foot, he took to the heights above the farm.

Now a silence descends as he scans the area in front of him. Below lies a hardscrabble farmhouse, some fences, a barn and sheds, the weathered ruins of a horse operation. It looks bleak and deserted in the grassland that once was cornfields. Ray's Ford is nosed into the farmhouse garage.

One more move to go. Take down Ray and the whole future changes. Charlie doesn't want to kill James Earl Ray, but he has resolved to do whatever is required to stop the man.

And here he comes.

Through the scope Charlie sees movement from the ramshackle farmhouse. He tightens his trigger finger and then wills himself to ease off. *Study the situation,* he tells himself. *All I have to do is injure him.* After shooting the two who were his certain enemies, he now feels a gut dislike of doing that again.

Ray does not go out on the warped wooden porch. He opens a side door under the overhang. He is barely visible to Charlie as he quickly steps out into the slight shade of midmorning. A dry wind blows up a dust cloud from the scrub fields beyond. Then Ray runs across a short space to get behind the side shed.

He knows I'm here.

Charlie has no time to fire. Ray moves fast. He is carrying a rifle that looks like a deer gun, a term Charlie did not know until a month ago. It has a magazine clip jutting below the breech and a short stock, curved at the end to a shoulder. A position shooter's gun, made for accuracy at range, with a long scope on top. Ray has realized that he is being watched, Charlie concludes. *Did Gabriel and Elspeth say something to him last night in that damned bar?*

Charlie's gun has a shorter barrel, and the breech feeds from rounds in the stock. Slimmer, lighter, made for maneuvering, not fixed-point shooting. That's why he has the tan canvas sling on it. He runs through this inventory in a quick second, making distinctions he did not even know weeks before. Ray would use his bigger, faster firepower. Plus accuracy. And experience.

Charlie sights through the scope. The rifle has about a hundred meters' good range and pretty good beyond. As he estimates the range at about that number, he is suddenly unsure. Charlie learned from the private detective that in Ray's scuzzball world he is not known as much of a gunman. Shooting King is undoubtedly the biggest assignment Ray has ever had. Before this Ray was a small-time grifter and occasional stickup artist, not a professional at much of anything beyond terrorizing 7-Eleven managers.

But Charlie has no illusions about his own abilities either. He is still a professor of history and some social science, commingled with a Hollywood producer and then an amateur conjurer of historical change. *A lot of swerves,* he thinks.

Charlie's only advantage was surprise. But he's blown that with his inept tailing job. So he waits.

Only seconds have passed. *Where could Ray have gone?*

He jerks his eyes away from the scope and sweeps to left and right. As he does this, Ray sprints from behind a shed, going right. Charlie jerks around to fire and gets off a shot, the sharp crack echoing back from the hills. Dust leaps up behind Ray and the man picks up speed, legs pumping. Charlie aims again using the scope, but Ray is now zigzagging. Charlie fires again and misses by even more. Ray vanishes from view in a wooded gully a hundred yards away.

Maybe I shouldn't have filed down those rounds, Charlie thinks ruefully. Lost accuracy.

Ray is circling around on him.

Ray will approach cautiously, so he has a few moments. *And what if Ray is a reincarnate too? The man is pretty simple, but Einstein said he had met such.*

The crucial element, yes. The reincarnates must die and never know who did it. That's why Charlie emptied the Beretta last night. Don't let them see who did it. They will not know to kill Charlie in another slice of the timescape. This will give him the advantage next time. Plus a whole new life he can lead without the gut-twisting fear of those evil people.

Charlie realizes that he is panicking, his breath coming fast. *Go slow*, he tells himself.

Reason returns. Ray can't be a reincarnate, because they would simply have enlisted him in their plan. Not just paid him.

Charlie gets up and carefully duckwalks along the narrow top of the ridgeline. The brush and rocks provide some cover, but he is acutely aware that Ray has a long history of gunplay. Mostly, Ray used pistols in stickups of mini-marts, with an occasional bank job, but there is no record of him even being suspected of a murder, the private detective said. Not very reassuring, with Ray scurrying about unseen on his flank. Ray knows more about this sort of thing. Probably western shoot-outs are a big part of Ray's fantasy life, whereas for Charlie they are the stuff of . . . well, movies.

He keeps remembering that King went down with one fatally placed shot. Maybe Ray is really good at shooting. If not at running from the police.

Charlie doesn't want to run. He wants to live in a time line where King and Kennedy live, a world that has a shot at being better than Charlie One's. And he sure as hell doesn't want to get sent back to his birthday right away. Nostalgia has played out, a limp dishrag of memories. He wants a decent future here, not an unending recursion where he always loses.

He holds his rifle at the ready and scans the jumble of trees and scrub ahead. A strong wind blows up from the plain. He cannot hope to hear Ray's approach.

Movement ahead.

Ray's head pokes up for an instant above a rocky flange maybe a hundred yards away. Then nothing, just the sigh of the breeze through sagebrush. Charlie squats down, afraid he's been located. Ray has moved fast. It's his territory.

A crack in the distance. A ricochet rings *pang* off a rock a few yards away. Another crack and a bullet clips through bushes nearby.

Ray has him bracketed.

Charlie clambers over to some brush that allows some view at an angle that should tell him which way Ray is moving. Nothing visible. Charlie is wearing a brown shirt and pants for camouflage. *Maybe that's good enough, but if not . . . the brush won't stop anything.* He duckwalks back behind some boulders and thinks. His odds don't look all that great.

He moves to his right and sprints across a short space, legs pumping, gets behind a big bush, darts his head over the edge. Ray is moving too. Charlie aims carefully at the shape just visible through a thin edge of a bush, and the man turns his rifle toward him just as Charlie pulls the trigger—

Charlie doesn't hear his round go off as suddenly a wham splits his head into a thousand pains.

He blinks and is on the ground, no memory of getting there. His view is cloudy and straight along the plain of pine needles extending far, far away. His right temple roars with roasting hurt. A throb fills his temple, makes his breath jerk. Charlie sees his right hand stuck out before him, lying on pine needles and dirt. It seems a long distance. His left arm tingles, but he cannot see it without turning his head. But even twitching his neck brings sharp, slanting agony.

He orders his right hand to come up to his face. The hand just lies there. He takes a big gulp of the moist air full of ticklish dust and thinks at the hand, *If you won't move, then wiggle.* The thumb and forefinger twitch. *Okay, now crawl over here.* The hand turns, but the weight of his arm is too much. Panting, he makes his shoulder move in a blunt shrug, and that rolls him up to a better view.

He peers into a beautiful blue sky an eternity away. Cotton clouds dot it, moving lazily, but he cannot focus on them well. His only feeling is a screeching pain he has ignored so far because of the hand problem. The skin on the right side of his skull is burning and wants to fly into the air. He turns his head to the right so he can command his right hand again, but that brings sharp pain sheeting over his brow and spreading across his forehead. His breath is ragged and someone is groaning somewhere. The long, low drone he heard is streaming out between his teeth.

His view of the eggshell-blue sky goes wrong as something sails over it. He blinks. The big, blocky thing hovering there is the rebel right hand. It has obediently come and now is completing its mission by diving down out of the beautiful sky he has really come to like. It slows as though someone else is in control and with a feather touch fetches up on his right temple. Sticky. Wet. And the sheeting pain shouts at him that he is doing something awful. He smells hot iron, and his fingers of the now-loyal hand twitch something there on his upper skull and the smell gets strong, cutting, sharp. He licks his lips and tastes sour dirt. An interesting phenomenon catches his gaze, which is still fixed on the lovely sky, where now he can see there are twice as many clouds. Each puffball has an identical twin companion near it, gliding as smoothly as before. *So the clouds are having babies in the sky.* Charlie struggles to comprehend this, how clouds can reproduce, and notices that a pine tree at the edge of his vision has learned the trick too. They seem fine looking indeed, two pine spires forking into that beautiful sky.

He turns his head to consider this and the world wobbles. His loyal hand is still feeling his scalp, where a long slit is pumping something liquid onto his fingers, a way of saying *Here I am* maybe. Charlie knows there is something important he has to do, so he puts aside the discovery of the doubling of things, though he will come back to it. The pain seems to better deserve his lazy attention. He feels his wound and knows that he has to bind it up. Blood is still trickling out of him. He has to do something and starts with a deep breath. *Whoosh.*

Then he blinks again and the world snaps into just one of everything, no twin pines. His hand explores the sliced and caked meat of his scalp. The oozing stuff is thickening and the iron smell is stronger. The crease runs from just right of his eyebrow and circles around the skull north of the ear. He knows the ear is still there because it scrapes his hand as it carries out its expedition. There is something very important he has to find out about this curious gash, so he lets the hand finger along until the channel gets shallow, and then it is no more, just as the hand starts to edge around to the back of his skull.

This is an important discovery. He files it with the double clouds and turns to the next problem, the low moan coming out of him. He forces his throat closed, finding a cut in his mouth that stings. Iron taste of blood. Now, without the moan, he can hear the breeze whispering through the pine trees. His breath is wheezing, as if he has run a long way. His head is much better, but the sharp pain wrapping his right temple is shouting at him now to do something. He knows abstractly that scalp wounds bleed a lot, but there is something else, something . . . *The problem of Ray, yes.*

He turns his attention to getting his left hand to work. He wobbles his head around, which at least does not hurt a lot more than holding it still, and there is the left hand, lying lazily on its own. He orders it to wiggle, but it is slow, sluggish. It also tingles and the fingers dance when he wants them to clench. This disloyal hand cannot support its own arm's weight and seems generally insubordinate to his tasks. It needs rest, so he turns to other jobs. He makes his eyes scan all around, even lifting his head a bit to give himself more view. *No sign of Ray.* He commands the left hand to get a grip on the sandy soil as his left elbow rises to give leverage. *Time to move.*

He dispatches his right hand to the job of getting himself upright. His vision lurches; the world spins awhile. Upright, he plots his next step. *One move at a time, take it easy.*

And indeed yes, it is surprisingly easy to tear the right arm off his cheap gray work shirt. The stitches come away with a yank. The sleeve is the right length, he figures, and so wraps it around his entire skull, hitching it into place over the crease. The sleeve snares on his right ear, shoots him a lance of pain. So he shifts it, gets it around all right. He ties an awkward big knot in the middle of his forehead. Cinching the sleeve helps tighten the knot further, and his temple sends sharp pains out to stop him. He pulls the sleeve tighter. He will have to stop the bleeding, and this hurts but is right. A quick glance down and to the right shows a brown bloodstain where dry dirt has been eagerly soaking it all up. The dark spot is about the size of a big dinner plate.

Oh yes, the problem of Ray.

He tries three times to get up. Each time the horizon tilts and he feels sick and with a thump he is on his back. Clumsy. *Where is Ray?* Charlie rolls onto his hands and crawls like an old dog across the dirt and needles. He heads for the pine tree he admired most. Its bark is like ash-gray scabs, so he can get his hands onto it. The first time he tries, the bark scabs come away, dumping him back on his ass. He works his feet under himself better. This time his hands spread wide of their own accord, knowing somehow what to do. He huffs with the labor of inching up, pulling himself, leaning forward on the tree and sniffing its pungent turpentine. His face presses into the tree, providing more support for his weight. Carefully he wraps his arms around the tree and inches up it. *Lovely tree.*

Once up to new heights, he feels better. He surveys the landscape. When he turns toward where Ray was, he sees no sign of him. The world weaves around some like a lazy carousel and he holds firm to the pine tree. The right side of his scalp still aches and throbs, with occasional shooting pains.

Take deep breath. Now for the next step—literally. He holds on to the tree and takes a step, wobbles, straightens. His rifle is lying a meter or two away. He steps toward it, lets go of the tree—and falls forward, smack down, his cheek thudding right next to the rifle butt.

He allows himself several inhalations of the pine needle scent and gets up once again to all fours. With one hand he pulls the rifle into a vertical position, butt down. Hand over hand he climbs up it, grabbing the sling for help. This vertical structure barely sustains him, with the sling strap as a countertorque to use for a shaky stability. His left hand is still tingling, but he can make it work, holding the strap.

Now he tries a fresh maneuver. He realizes he can use the rifle with the strap in his left hand, as a crutch. He looks around again, still no Ray—then down into the barrel. There is goddamn sand in the barrel. *Think, now.* Gingerly he reaches down and flicks on the safety. *Careful . . .* He manages to tilt the rifle and blow the dirt out with puffs of shallow, wheezing breath. *Done.*

Now for the expedition toward Ray. He checks, breech loaded, safety off. He takes a dozen steps, careful to keep his balance. Edging around near the bush where the man was when the shooting started is a delicate business, working upslope. No grunts, no wheeze. Crafty. He leans forward a bit for a better angle and sees up ahead the toes of a work boot. The toes point to the sky, beautiful sky. So Ray is on his back.

Dead? Charlie is maybe fifteen yards away from the boot. He takes

two more steps, brings up the rifle-crutch, checks the safety again—
and Ray's voice says shakily, "I hear ya, damn it."

Freeze. Silence.

"Okay . . . take it easy," Charlie counters. "You're hurt, right?"

A long pause. A slight breeze stirs the bushes. Charlie can see no
movement of the boot. "I . . . I was trying to just wing you."

Then, "Yeah? Well, you sure did."

Bad enough that Ray can't get to his feet, then. Probably bleeding
out. "I have no quarrel with you, Ray. We can just walk away from this."

A suspicious silence. "Why'd you shoot, then?"

Maybe Ray doesn't know Charlie is hit too. "I won't let King die."

At least that's true, though Charlie wonders where this is going.
He is fresh out of plans. His left and right arms are in agreement
again, and he doesn't need the rifle as a crutch anymore. His head
is a big beating bass drum, cymbals added, but he can live with that
because he has to.

"They, those two, they already paid me to do King."

"Keep the money. Hell, I can pay you some more to just leave."

"Sure, and you shoot me from up here when I get in the car."

Ray is right. Or would be, if Charlie were a better shot than he is.
But Charlie can't think of a way around Ray's assumption.

"I have no reason to, Ray." He has learned this in movie negotiations; get personal, use first names. "This is just about King."

"Y'know, I was gonna enjoy nailin' that coon."

Jesus! The venom in the voice is startling.

Charlie takes a long breath, fighting the urge to just shoot this
man. *But . . .*

"That's why I'll give you some money. To not do it." Charlie wishes
he could tell Ray what is going to happen to him if he does kill King—
but then he has a more important idea. "Hey, are you a reincarnate?"

"Huh?"

"Do you know about the Society? Casanova? Einstein?"

"You crazy? Reincarnation? A Hindu?"

"The two that you were working with were members of a secret organization. You know anything about that?"

"Never heard of it. Hey, whaddaya mean, they were members?"

"I shot them last night."

Silence.

"Forget them."

Charlie sees the boot withdraw, as if Ray is pulling himself farther behind the bush. Then, Ray's voice ragged, "Damn, they were gonna plant some cash for me to pick up, after." No concern in the voice for his departed collaborators.

"I'll give it to you. Just don't kill King."

Is Ray's voice getting closer? Charlie can't see the moves. As quickly as he can, he walks over to a large stand of brush, moving uphill a bit. He chooses a tree to lean against and brings the rifle up to what he knows from movieland is the port-arms position. Then he looks out. Nothing visible. Wind stirs the trees. His heart pounds. All the practice and study hasn't prepared him for this. Ray is wily street trash. Not an even match.

A hoarse call. "Hey! You! How do I get this money?"

The breeze hums through the trees and Charlie tries to see movement. Nothing.

Into the silence he calls, "We can work a deal on this. But you've got to stop trying to get closer."

The breeze dies away. Charlie feels another whirling round of blurred vision and sags against the pine tree. Turpentine cuts in his nose. He makes himself breathe deeply. Use the smell to keep him sharp.

Carefully he checks again but sees nothing. *Maybe Ray has flanked him?* But the direction of the voice has not seemed to change. With the wind it is hard to tell, though.

Ray's angry voice seems to come from directly ahead. "You're white! Why you workin' for those niggers?"

"I'm not. And you get any closer and . . ." *Damn it, you're a screen-writer! Make something up.* "I'll use my hand grenades."

The breeze blows dust into Charlie's nostrils and prickles his nose. He grabs his nose, presses to stop a sneeze. He strokes the cool stock of his rifle and eases his finger onto the trigger. He knows that he is outclassed here and wonders why he feels fear, since he is immortal. But this is about outcomes, and what Charlie fears most now is futil-ity. Of yet another life trapped and claustrophobic in a world like the last ones he knew.

"You sure ain't got hand grenades." Ray's tone from straight ahead is sly, sarcastic, oozing with a bully's contempt.

Charlie, flat and factual: "Try me. Come any closer, you get one."

Silence.

"In the gut this time."

Silence.

Ray's boot was pointed upward. Probably that means he has some upper-body wound and is lying down. So the man could be dragging himself around, trying for a good position to fire. Or finishing up binding his wound.

Charlie slides over just a bit, sees nothing. Crouches.

"What was that you said about money?"

Ah! Ray sounds closer, but he cannot judge how much.

The contempt is gone and there is something else, a canny, nasal tone of calculation.

"I've got five thousand right here. I'll leave it under a rock. I'm going to move back and head down the side of the ridge away from the house. Five grand, Ray. You get the money, count it. Then you go down the other way, to the farm. Drive out of here."

"You don't have no damn grenades. How'd you get them?"

"How did I find you three last night? You're good at what you do, I'm good at what I do."

Sunlight beats down. Charlie takes out a wad of fifty hundreds wrapped in a rubber band and slides it half under a stone. The greenbacks are clearly visible. A breeze flutters the bills and he tastes sour fear in his mouth. Ray will take it, he's sure. *Then what?*

Ray has been quiet too long. "You come within throwing range and you get to check the grenade idea. Don't underestimate me."

Without waiting for an answer, Charlie begins slowly limping to the ridge edge, keeping low and watching for movement where he last saw Ray.

His head throbs ominously. He pats the makeshift bandage and finds it is sopping under a crust of brown blood that has already dried.

"You sound like a kid." Ray's voice comes from somewhere behind Charlie.

Let him listen and wait. Charlie tries his legs and they are good now. He can walk. But his vision whirls when he moves too fast and his head is booming hard.

Ray calls, "You just be calm, now. Kid."

Charlie reaches the steep drop down the side of the ridge. He looks back. He can see flitting movement. Ray is on his feet about fifty meters away. Slow, moving forward in a low crouch, rifle at the ready in his right hand. Ray limps across an opening and Charlie can see Ray's shirt has a wide bloodstain on it, covering his left side. The man moves unsteadily, catching himself against trees as he passes them. Intently he edges closer to where Charlie was, off to Ray's right side. The head does not turn.

Charlie could shoot him from here.

Ray calls out in a harsh, demanding bark, "Stay right there. Don't move."

A pure bluff. *I have a kid's voice, but I'm smarter than you and vastly older, good ole boy Ray.*

Charlie brings his rifle around and wonders if he should shoot. It's close. He doesn't need the scope, just the sight.

"Where's the money?" Ray shouts. "Where? Bring it out with you."

Charlie lowers his rifle and slips over the edge. Let Ray waste time trying to intimidate the bushes. Charlie makes his way down the slope, sliding, keeping balanced, rifle held high. He goes around a long flange of tumbled-down debris from an old slide. *Easy now, don't fall.*

He feels good about not killing Ray. Distantly he hears a faint yammering voice from the ridge above. Ray must have found the money and not found his prey, and his tone is snarling, loudmouthed, angry.

But Ray is not so stupid that he will kill King anyway, now that he understands that someone has scoped out his mission. Charlie learned a lot about low-grade evil in Hollywood. It never rises above the venal because it doesn't understand anything bigger than that. He trusts Ray's lack of principles.

Charlie angles away, careful to keep out of the line of sight from the ridgetop.

His loyal Dodge Dart is waiting. He eases off the hand brake and lets it roll down the slight slope in neutral. This carries the car over bumps and through sandy furrows, down to the narrow dirt road.

He turns the key, pops the clutch, and starts the car with its own momentum. He peels out, spitting sand. Nothing in the rearview. The blacktop state road is deserted and he turns north. Home is a long drive away.

Another Beginning

Charlie pulls his car off the interstate and heads for his parents' house. He is bleary eyed from the cross-country drive. The Memphis shoot-out is a day behind him and seems like another life, far ago, behind a gray wall.

His head is a single swollen bulge. He stopped in southern Illinois for some medical supplies, brushing off a pharmacist's urgent pleas. Some aspirin, bandages, iodine, disinfectant—that is all he needs. He stopped then at a diner, got food, and slurped up coffee. In the men's room he studied his pupils, saw they were of the same size, so he has no concussion. The bullet from Ray's rifle hit him in the skull, all right, but it then deflected and ran around, under the skin, and blew out the back, on its way to its own destiny. As he is.

He has driven nonstop, listening all the way to AM radio rock, Buddy Holly to the Beatles, whiny choruses and beating bass notes, letting it all wind up into his mind like smoke through the nostrils. He has taken long, sure drafts of America, that endlessly varying aroma, and thought furiously through passing rainstorms while peering into lancing, white-hot truck headlights. Interstate wisdom has penetrated quick and sure through him.

Now he has made history. He knows that history—no, capitalize that, Mother History—is a yawning timescape stretching far away from easy simplicities. What he has seen and felt are part of something bigger than any mathematical wisdom can comprehend. The timescape.

He has stopped the killing of Martin Luther King, along this time line, and maybe saved Kennedy, too. That was the next decision.

So what next? Maybe some perfect liberal state will come about, and maybe not. But once again the rolling parade of history will sing its own song, and who knows what America will come of that?

The sunset casts luminous yellow glows onto fluffy clouds above his dear old hometown as darkness gathers. He drives the local streets slowly, legs leaden and breath ragged.

A blare from a large truck shatters his tired musing. He jerks fully awake. A gleaming chrome Ford truck grille bears down on him. Charlie's Dodge Dart has run a light. He swerves abruptly and his wheels squeal, skidding sideways, then just missing another car. He jams down on the gas and breaks free, surging down a street that opens from the gloom like a birth canal.

He breathes fast, his head hammering at him, but he has finer things to think about now. Accelerating to get away from the truck brings back his first death.

He glides to a stop on a quiet, tree-lined avenue.

The surge of near-collision adrenaline clears his mind. He looks around before driving again. Feral vigilance tightens his throat. By the time his heart stops thumping, he is smoothly moving down his home street. His Avenue of Repeating Lives.

He eases the Dodge Dart to the curb just across from his house, and with a twist the engine dies. He sits looking at the warm glow of the windows, sure and steady against the coming dark. He rolls down the car window, tired and aching. *A manual crank, not some fancy electric whisk. Good ol' analog truth.* A cool spring breeze wafts moist scents into the car, aromas that ease the stark memories.

He knows one thing now clear and sure: a human life is not just a means to produce outcomes; it is an end in itself. So what should Charlie want from his fourth life?

He has an answer to work with now: look for the place where your deep gladness and the world's deep hunger meet.

He looks across the dimming street at home. Mom and Dad. He will return yet again, perhaps many more times. On the manifold of his timescape, reincarnation might slice many ways.

He was stuck in the same world and times as Elspeth, and the Hombre. For now he is free of them. If an infinity of other loops spiral through the timescape, what do they matter? He is here. *What was that 1960s mantra? Be here now.*

Gabriel's crew seem barely human to him, pathetic in their sexual labyrinth, twisting like lusting snakes. Revulsion wells up yet again, his stomach clenching. Then he swallows, pauses, and sucks in the reassuring fragrances of the midwestern spring night. He has time to get over it, in this particular self-time, this fresh loop from which his enemies have been eliminated.

After all, he is again just a brimming sixteen years old. He will get ready for the next round, decades ahead in his future.

He can look forward now to finding Albert and Heinlein again, and trying to fathom all the looping weirdness with them. Casanova has hinted of other horizons. There are other reincarnates, great and small, at play in this world. Compared with Albert and Casanova, he is nothing. Better, he knows he's nothing and that being nothing is fine.

The past isn't over. It isn't even past. Who said that? He can't recall.

The only failure is to live a life without risks.

It is up to him to shape all of this, to make it finally matter.

He will have a life that means something.

He gets out of the Dodge Dart, pats its warm hood, takes a deep, luxurious breath, and walks decisively across the street into a life remade.

AFTERWORD

The plot of this novel is intentionally a puzzle that the reader needs to solve, proceeding through it. But here are some hints. When Charlie dies first, he does not come from our time line. Our own historical time line arises later in the book, in part thanks to Charlie's own actions. But Charlie's narrative does not remain in our own time line. Rather, he proceeds to create yet another time line. That is why many of the specifics of the different time lines vary.

At the conclusion, Charlie has produced a time line he believes will lead to a better world than he or we knew. Because he has eliminated the assassins responsible for the attempt on Martin Luther King's life, and they intended to carry out the Robert Kennedy attack too, neither assassination occurs. Kennedy then beats Nixon in 1968 and the Vietnam war ends in 1969—a consequence that is not in the novel.

Spring 1968 was perhaps the most consequential season in American politics since WWII, in my view. I wanted to underline this by writing both a meditation on the implications of quantum mechanics (an ongoing issue, still) and on the fragility of our republic's history.

This novel is a conceptual sequel to my earlier work *Timescape*. That novel I wrote within the confines of how physicists thought about time in the late 1970s. Much has changed. Indeed, all the events of that novel now lie in our past.

Timescape was based on a paper I published in *Physical Review D2* in July 1970 (p. 263) under the title "The Tachyonic Antitelephone"— see, even in dry old *Phys Rev* you can have fun with titles, if you try. Written with David Book and Bill Newcomb, it remains the only scientific paper of the over two hundred I have written that doesn't have a single equation in it; the argument is logical, not really technical. In the late 1970s we used several ideas then current to frame an answer to the famous grandfather paradox that backward-in-time travel or communication provokes. By traveling faster than light, tachyons (if they existed) could send backward signals. It's all there in Einstein's theory of special relativity.

Timescape concludes with a solution to the paradox, based on an interpretation of quantum mechanics that has now gathered a considerable following: Hugh Everett's Many-Worlds Interpretation. He said that all the possible outcomes predicted by the probability analysis of quantum mechanics are separately real. Envision separable worlds peeling off from every microscopic event. Every event generates great handfuls of other worlds—a cosmic plentitude of astronomical extravagance.

I trimmed Everett's idea: only a paradox-causing event generates a split-off universe. That seemed intellectually thrifty and, further, made for a bittersweet finish: You can change that past, but it's not going to occur in your world. You've improved the lot of others, but not your own. It seemed a good idea at the time. . . .

The novel appeared, won awards, and has sold over a million copies in many languages. I moved on to other physics, other novels.

Imagine my surprise when, while I was visiting Cambridge in November of 1992, Martin Rees pointed out a paper in *Physical Review D*, the same journal where our old tachyon paper had appeared. Martin thought it important. Titled somewhat forbiddingly "Quantum Mechanics Near Closed Timelike Lines," it constructs a theory for effects in highly curved space-time that contains causal loops—"closed timelike lines," in the jargon. It was written by David Deutsch, who has been studying these matters for a decade at Oxford (not Cambridge, the site of the experiments in *Timescape*). "Contrary to what has usually been assumed," Deutsch says, "there is no reason in what we know of fundamental physics why closed timelike lines should not exist." In twenty pages of quantum logic calculations, he shows that no obstacle to free will or even grandfather murder really exists.

It's all done with the Everett interpretation. In quantum cosmology there is no single history of space-time. Instead, all possible histories happen simultaneously. For the vast preponderance of cases, this doesn't matter—the bloat of an uncountable infinitude of worlds has no observable consequences. It's just a way of talking about quantum mechanics.

Not so for time machines. Then a quantum description requires a set of "classical" (ordinary) space-times that are similar to one another—except in the important history of the paradox loop. The causal loop links all the multiple histories. Think of unending sheets stacked on end and next to each other, like pages. Time lines flow up, piercing them. A causal loop snakes through these sheets, so the parallel universes become one. If the grandson goes back in time, he crosses to another time-sheet. There he shoots granddad and lives thereafter in that universe. His granddad lived as before and had grandchildren, one of whom disappears, period.

Quantum mechanics always furnishes as many linked universes as there would be conflicting outcomes; it's quite economical. In this view, as Deutsch says: "It is only ever an approximation to speak of things happening 'in a universe.' In reality the 'universes' form a part of a larger object . . . which, according to quantum theory, is the real arena in which things happen." No one in either universe thinks the world is paradoxical. Cosmic stuff indeed.

If you know this, then such a past-altering act is the ultimate altruism: you cannot then benefit in any way from usefully adjusting the past (or suffer, either). Someone exactly like you does benefit (yes, a twin; and I wonder how much my being an identical twin has led to my interest in these ideas)—but you will never see him and cannot know this except in theory. Most of all, I was struck in writing the closing pages of *Timescape* with that glimpse of vistas unknown, whole universes beyond our grasp, times untouched. To me, that is the essential science-fictional impulse.

Since that 1992 paper, quantum entanglement, which Einstein termed "spooky action at a distance," has entered the logic of quantum causal loops. This I sketch out in the present novel. It is a field of restless energy. Can entanglements leak between the multiverses? What would make that happen? Our own minds have the highest information density we know, so perhaps entangled minds can skate among the quantum layers of space-times we do not know.

I'll leave the logic that led me to my work on the present novel now, for ultimately, whether ideas work in fiction is up to the reader. I do want to reassure readers that the ideas that come up in the second half of the novel emerge from current speculative thinking.

This novel has characters based on real people I knew, now deceased. This brings in the many associations with the above ideas, as I have mined them for fictive uses. I intend no insult to them, and indeed mostly these are sketches of people I miss very much. My memories of them became part of the mix. Writers are magpies. (I also use this blending in my alternative history novel of the Manhattan Project, *The Berlin Project,* too. If there is a writers' adage even more important than *Show, don't tell* it's *Write what you know.*)

Then, too, there is the issue of the greats I did not know. William Shakespeare, whose imagination seemed limitless, who traveled freely to magical isles and enchanted forests, did not—could not—imagine different times. The past and present are all the same to Shakespeare: mechanical clocks strike the hour in Caesar's Rome, and Cleopatra plays billiards. So even our finest, most expansive writer from centuries past did not reflect, as we moderns do, on time as fluid.

As the Queen said to Alice, "It's a poor sort of memory that only works backwards."

"So in the future, the sister of the past," thinks young Stephen Dedalus in *Ulysses*, "I may see myself as I sit here now but by reflection from that which then I shall be."

So, too, with Casanova, a protomodern. It is widely agreed by those who have made a study of him that Giacomo was far kinder to his lovers than was the manipulative Don Giovanni, for whom a woman was no more than a notch on his belt. (The real Casanova is reported to have attended the Prague premiere of *Don Giovanni* in 1787 and, according to Michael Sturminger, had "a close friendship" with Da Ponte.) I tried to convey him as speaking in a plummy, variable accent that suggests someone who, though born on the Continent, attended English boarding schools. He also exudes that vague state of impassioned indolence, emerging into an impressionistic portrait of a libertine from the age of Enlightenment. Sex is the flip side of the coin, death the other.

Then, again, Heinlein, whom I did know for decades. I've tried to echo his voice, its cadences and ideas. He was fond of repeating George Bernard Shaw's saying "The reasonable man adapts himself to the world: the unreasonable one persists in trying to adapt the world to himself. Therefore all progress depends on the unreasonable man." I've tried to convey him, as I did Phil Dick. Phil actually said many of the lines of dialogue I've reproduced here. He was one of the oddest people I've ever known, in a life rich in odd people trying to get even.

And Einstein, yes. A visitor to Einstein's office in Prague noted that the window overlooked the grounds of an insane asylum. Einstein explained that these were the madmen who did not think about quantum mechanics. He was fond of a German saying of life: *Der*

Appetit kommt beim Essen. "The appetite develops as one eats." Quantum mechanics can be like this; look at the many variations it has inspired, like Deutsch's.

We moderns have all learned to visualize history as a time line, with the past stretching to the left, say, and the future to the right, perhaps because we have been conditioned Sapir-Whorf-style by a left-to-right written language. Our own life spans occupy a short space in the middle. Now—the infinitesimal slide of the present—is just the point where our puny consciousnesses happens to be.

This troubled Einstein. A lot. He recognized that the present is special; it is, after all, where we live. (In Ted Chiang's fine tale *Story of Your Life*, Louise says to her infant daughter: "NOW is the only moment you'll perceive; you'll live in the present tense. In many ways, it's an enviable state." The film of that story, *Arrival*, gets at this admirably well.) But Einstein felt that this was fundamentally a psychological matter; that the question of now need not, or could not, be addressed within physics. The specialness of the present moment doesn't show up in the equations; mathematically, all the moments look alike. Now seems to arise in our minds. It's a product of consciousness, inextricably bound up with sensation and memory. And it's a fleeting image, tumbling continually into the past.

Still, if the sense of the present is an illusion, it's awfully powerful for us humans. I don't know if it's possible to live as if the physicists' time-symmetric mathematical model is real, as if we never make choices, as if the very idea of purpose is imaginary. I haven't tried. We may be able to visualize the time before our birth and the time after our death as mathematically equivalent, though it's a stretch. Yet we can't help but fret more about what effects we might have on the future in which we will not exist, than about what might have happened in the past when we did not exist. Nor does it seem possible to tell a story or enjoy a narrative that is devoid of intention.

Choice and purpose—that's where the suspense comes from. What is your purpose on Earth? There's your story.

As Einstein said, "Space and time are modes by which we think, not conditions under which we live." I feel that these are not properties of the world we live in, but concepts we have invented to help us organize classical events. There are others, too. Yet to be discovered . . .

Physics is the belief that a simple and consistent description of nature is possible. Occam's razor slices sure.

We human beings, even those who have been studying quantum mechanics for a long time, still think in terms of classical concepts. We evolved to do that. It helps us live.

The real world simply is quantum mechanical from the start; it's not a quantization of some classical system. The universe is described by an element of Hilbert space, a mathematical region in which vectors and calculus can function in useful ways. Quantum mathematical concepts are easily done in such abstract spaces, which can have any number of dimensions. All of our usual classical notions should be derived from that conceptual regime, not the other way around—even space itself. We think of the real space through which we move as one of the most basic and irreducible constituents of the real world, the essential underpinning. It might better be thought of as a good approximation for primates who evolved on flat plains and threw spears in a simple gravitational field, so a parabola was a beautiful, useful curve. This works at large distances (meters) and low energies (ours)—where we smart primates live and die. But reality may be a far broader thing. Indeed, it must be.

Hard science fiction is about the beauty of a small "reasoning reed," in Pascal's phrase, that can see past its own mortality and wonder at the vistas beyond. Its essential drama lies in that huge leap of scale.

Michael Rose helped me start the novel, though of course I finished it. I thank for readings, suggestions, and corrections many people, especially Blanca Cervantes; Gregg Rickman; John Silbersack; Joe

Monti; Elisabeth Brown; David Truesdale; Sheila Finch; David Brin; Kathryn Cramer and her husband, the late, much missed David Hartwell; Martin Rees; David Deutsch; Gary Wolfe. Especially, thanks to my identical twin brother, James Benford, who agreed to stand in for me at UCI to show that the second Charlie time line is not ours, and for getting me interested in Einstein's twin paradox when we were ten years old.

Gregory Benford
February 2018